Sheikh's
CAPTURED
BRIDE

Lynne
GRAHAM

Kristi
GOLD

Kate
HEWITT

MILLS & BOON

Published in Great Britain 2017
By Mills & Boon, an imprint of HarperCollins*Publishers*
1 London Bridge Street, London, SE1 9GF

SHEIKH'S CAPTURED BRIDE © 2017 Harlequin Books S.A.

The Sheikh's Prize © 2013 Lynne Graham
The Sheikh's Son © 2014 Kristi Goldberg
Captured by the Sheikh © 2014 Kate Hewitt

ISBN: 978-0-263-93100-6

09-0517

Our policy is to use papers that are natural, renewable and recyclable products and made from wood grown in sustainable forests. The logging and manufacturing processes conform to the legal environmental regulations of the country of origin.

Printed and bound in Spain
by CPI, Barcelona

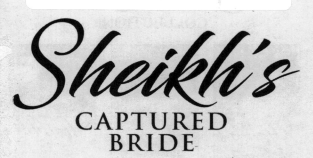

Sheikh's

CAPTURED
BRIDE

Sheikh's
COLLECTION

May 2017

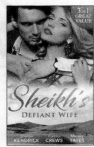

June 2017

July 2017

August 2017

September 2017

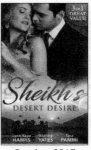

October 2017

THE SHEIKH'S PRIZE

LYNNE GRAHAM

Lynne Graham was born in Northern Ireland and has been a keen romance reader since her teens. She is very happily married, with an understanding husband who has learned to cook since she started to write! Her five children keep her on her toes. She has a very large dog, which knocks everything over, a very small terrier, which barks a lot, and two cats. When time allows, Lynne is a keen gardener.

CHAPTER ONE

ZAHIR RA'IF QUARISHI, hereditary king of the gulf state of Maraban, leapt up from behind his desk when his younger brother, Akram, literally burst into his office.

'What has happened?' Zahir demanded urgently, straightening to his full six feet three inches of height, his lean powerful body tensing like the army officer he had been into immediate battle readiness.

His face unusually flushed, Akram came to an abrupt halt to execute a jerky bow as he belatedly recalled the niceties of court etiquette.' My apologies for the interruption, Your Majesty—'

'I assume there's a good reason,' Zahir conceded, his rigidity easing as he read Akram's troubled expression and recognised that something of a more private and personal nature had precipitated his impulsive entry to one of the very few places in which Zahir could usually depend on receiving the peace he required to work.

Akram stiffened, embarrassment claiming his open good-natured face. 'I don't know how to tell you this—'

'Sit down and take a deep breath,' Zahir advised calmly, his innate natural assurance taking over as he settled his big frame down into an armchair in the corner of the room and rested his piercing dark-as-night eyes on the younger man while moving a graceful hand to urge him to sit down as well. 'There's nothing we can't discuss. I will never be as intimidating as our late father.'

At that reminder, Akram turned deadly pale, for their late and unlamented parent had been as much of a tyrant and a bully in the royal palace with his family as he was in his role as a ruler over what had once been one of the most backward countries in the Middle East. While Fareed the Magnificent, as he had insisted on being called, had been in power, Maraban's oil wealth had flowed only one way into the royal coffers while their people continued to live in the Dark Ages, denied education, modern technology and adequate medical support. It had been three years since Zahir took the throne and the changes he had immediately instigated still remained a massive undertaking. Angrily conscious that his brother worked just about every hour of the day in his determination to improve the lives of his subjects, Akram suddenly dreaded giving Zahir the news he had learned. Zahir never mentioned his first marriage. It was too controversial a topic, Akram acknowledged awkwardly. How could it not be? His brother had paid a high price for defying their late father and marrying a foreigner from a different culture. That he had done so for a woman clearly unworthy of his faith could only be an additional source of aggravation.

'Akram...?' Zahir prompted impatiently. 'I have a meeting in thirty minutes.'

'It's...*her!* That woman you married!' Akram recovered his tongue abruptly. 'She's out there in the streets of our capital city shaming you even as we speak!'

Zahir froze and frowned, his spectacular bone structure tightening beneath taut skin the colour of honey, his wide sensual mouth compressing hard. 'What the hell are you talking about?'

'Sapphire's here filming some television commercial for cosmetics!' Akram told him in fierce condemnation, resenting what he saw as an inexcusable insult to his elder brother.

Zahir's lean strong hands clenched into fists. 'Here?' he repeated in thunderous disbelief. 'Sapphire is filming *here* in Maraban?'

'Wakil told me,' his brother told him, referring to one of Zahir's former bodyguards. 'He couldn't believe his eyes when he recognised her! It's lucky that our father refused to announce your marriage to our people—I never thought we'd live to be grateful for that...'

Zahir was stunned at the idea that his ex-wife could have *dared* to set a single foot within the borders of his country. Rage and bitterness flamed through his taut powerful frame and he sprang restively upright again. He had tried not to be bitter, he had tried even harder to forget his failed marriage...only that was a little hard to do when your ex became an internationally famous supermodel, featuring in countless magazines and newspapers and even once in a giant advertising hoarding over Times Square. In truth a mere five years ago he had been a sitting duck of a target for a cunning schemer of Sapphire Marshall's ilk and that lowering awareness had left an indelible stain on his masculine ego. At twenty-five years of age he had, thanks to his father's oppression, still been a virgin, ignorant of the West and Western women, but although he hadn't had a clue he had at least *tried* to make his marriage work. His bride, on the other hand, had refused to make the smallest effort to sort out their problems. He had fought hard to keep a wife who didn't want to be his wife, indeed who couldn't even bear for him to touch her.

More fool him, he reflected with hard cynicism, for he was no longer an innocent when it came to women. The explanation for Sapphire's extraordinary behaviour had become clear as crystal to him once he shed his idealistic assumptions about his wife's honour: his bride had only married him because he was wealthy beyond avarice and a prince, *not* because she cared about him. Unpardonably, her goal in marrying him had simply been the rich pay-off that would follow their divorce. He had married a woman with all the heart of a cash register and she had, not only, ripped him off but also got away scot free while he had paid in spades. At that reflection, his even white teeth ground together, tiny gold flames igniting in his fierce eyes. If only he had been dealing with her in the present as a male who now knew the score, he would have known exactly how to handle her.

'I'm sorry, Zahir,' Akram muttered in the seething

silence, ill at ease with the rare dark fury that had flared in his brother's face. 'I thought you had a right to know that she'd had the cheek to come here.'

'It's five years since I divorced her,' Zahir pointed out harshly, his lean strong face impassive. 'Why should I care what she does?'

'Because she's an embarrassment!' Akram rushed to declare. 'Imagine how you would feel if the media found out that she was once your wife! She must be shameless and without conscience to come to Maraban to make her stupid commercial!'

'This is all very emotive stuff, Akram,' Zahir countered, reluctantly touched by his brother's concern on his behalf. 'I'm grateful you told me but what do you expect me to do?'

'Throw her and her film crew out of Maraban!' his brother told him instantly.

'You are still young and impetuous, my brother,' Zahir replied drily. 'The paparazzi follow my ex-wife everywhere she goes. Try to picture the likely consequences of deporting a world-famous celebrity. Why would I want to create headlines to alert the world's media to a past that is more wisely left buried?'

When Akram had finally departed, still incredulous that his brother had failed to express a desire for retribution, Zahir made several phone calls that would have astonished the younger man. It was a supreme irony but Zahir's coolly astute brain was perpetually at all-out war with the volatile passion of his temperament. While it made no logical sense whatsoever he wanted

the chance to see Sapphire in the flesh again. Did that
desire imply that he still had some lingering need for
closure where she was concerned? Or was it simple and
natural curiosity because he was currently facing the
prospect of having to take another wife? Once, in a desperate search for a solution to his seemingly incurable
problems with Sapphire, Zahir had read books about all
sorts of strange subjects before he finally accepted that
the simplest explanation of the apparently inexplicable
was usually the closest to the truth. Since then events in
his ex-wife's life had suggested that his sceptical convic-
tions about her true character were spot-on. He had wed
a gold-digging social climber with not an atom of true
feeling for him. After all, he was well aware that Sapphire was now cosily ensconced in a live-in relationship
with the award-winning Scottish wildlife photographer,
Cameron McDonald. Presumably she wasn't having
any difficulty bedding *him*… Zahir's dark eyes burned
afresh like golden flames at that incendiary thought.

Saffy dutifully angled her hot face into the flow of air
gushing from the wind machine so that her mane of
blonde hair wafted back in a cloud over her shoulders.
Not an atom of her growing irritation and discomfort
showed on her flawless features. Saffy was never less
than professional when she was working. But how many
times had her make-up already needed retouched in the
stifling heat? It was simply melting off her face. How
many times had the set security had to interrupt filming to make the crowd of over-excited spectators back

away to give her colleagues the space to work? Coming to Maraban to film the Desert Ice cosmetics commercial had been a foolish mistake. The support systems the film crew took for granted were non-existent.

'Give me *that* sexy look, Saffy...' Dylan, the photographer, urged pleadingly. 'What is wrong with you this week? You're not on form—'

And as if someone had zapped her with an electrified cattle prod, Saffy struggled to switch on the expression he wanted because she hated the fact that anyone should have noticed that anything was amiss with her mood. Inside her head, she fought to focus on the fantasy that never failed to ignite that much vaunted look of desire on her face. So ironic, she reflected momentarily, so very *cruelly* ironic that she should have to focus on what she had often dreamt of and never yet managed to experience in reality. But when she was working a shoot costing her clients thousands of pounds was not the time to allow all that old bad stuff to resurface. With the strong determination that was the backbone of her temperament, Saffy forced the distressing memories back down into her subconscious again and then mentally searched to extract the required familiar image: a man with jet-black hair down to his broad brown shoulders, a man who positively oozed raw animal magnetism from every pore with a lean powerfully naked body encased in warm gilded skin. In every image he would slowly turn his head to look at her, revealing fiercely stunning eyes of gold surrounded by black lashes so lush they acted like eye liner on a guy already so sav-

agely masculine and passionate that at one glance he
took her breath away. And all those wretched frustrating
responses swam back through her taut body in a wave,
her nipples beading below the scrap of silk she wore,
her entire body dampening with shocking awareness.

'That's it…that's exactly it!' Dylan crooned in enthusiasm, leaping around her posed figure to take photos from different angles as she shifted position with
languorous ease, that image inside her head like an indelible tattoo below her skin. 'Lower your lids a little more—we want to see that eye shadow…brilliant,
sweetheart, now *pout* that gorgeous mouth…'

A couple of minutes passed before with a tiny jerk
of displacement, Saffy returned to the present and was
suddenly plunged back into the heat, the noise and the
curious crowds, her huge bluer-than-blue eyes reflecting her discomfiture at the massive attention they were
attracting. But Dylan had got the shots he wanted and
he leapt around like a maniac punching the air with satisfaction. Her single-minded concentration on her role
gone now, she looked out above the crowds and saw a
vehicle parked at the height of a giant rolling ochre-col-
oured sand dune with a robed figure standing nearby
holding something in his hand that glinted in the sun.

Zahir had his high-definition binoculars trained on his
stunningly beautiful ex-wife. With her glorious mane
of golden hair blowing back from her face like a sheet
of gleaming silk and seated atop a pile of giant fake ice
cubes, she would have looked spectacularly eye-catch-

ing by any standards. But in the beauty stakes, Sapphire occupied a category all of her own and the sight of her took Zahir's hot-blooded temper to new and dangerous heights. He was outraged that she was appearing in public in Maraban clad in only a couple of scraps of azure silk that displayed the surprisingly bountiful mounds of her breasts, the smooth skin of her now bejewelled midriff and the incredible svelte stretch of her very long and perfect legs.

He watched the men involved in the shoot dart slavishly around Sapphire, offering her drinks and food and fussing with her hair and her face, and he wondered with vicious coarseness which of them had had the pleasure of her beautiful body. After all, she might live with Cameron McDonald, but the UK tabloids had, nonetheless, exposed the fact that she had had several affairs with other men. Clearly she was anything but a faithful lover. Of course, it was possible that Cameron and Sapphire enjoyed a civilly negotiated 'open' relationship, but Zahir was not impressed by that possibility or even by the concept of open relationships. He didn't sleep around, he had never slept around even when he finally had the freedom to make such choices. His ex-wife had to be a bit of a slut, he decided with dark brooding bitterness, his lean strong face set granite hard at the acknowledgement. He had married an embryo slut and, worst of all, she was a slut he *still* lusted after. At that final disturbing admission, Zahir ground his even white teeth while perspiration beaded his upper lip, his tall, powerful body furiously tense and aggressively aroused by his perusal of that perfect body and even more perfect face.

Sapphire, the one mistake he had ever made and the payback had been unforgettably brutal. He had endured indescribable punishment to keep her as his wife for even a year. She owed him, she definitely *owed* him for twelve months of unadulterated hell. Add in the millions she had received from him since the charade of their marriage finally ran aground in a divorce and he had every right to feel ill-done by, every right to still be aggrieved and hostile. She had used and abused him before walking away unharmed and considerably richer. Maybe it was finally payback time, Zahir reflected grimly, his adrenalin spiking at the idea. And bearing in mind that she and her film crew had chosen to come to Maraban and film without the permission of the relevant authority, she had put herself and her precious high-flying career in his power. And the very thought of Sapphire being in his power was the most seductive image that Zahir had indulged in for years. He lowered the binoculars, thinking fast, squashing the disconcerting logical objections already trying to assail him to persuade him to restrain his primal responses. It wouldn't be the same between them now, he reasoned angrily; he was not the same man. This time around he had the weapons to *make* her want him back.

That process of self-persuasion was incredibly seductive. Throughout his life Zahir had very rarely done what *he* wanted to do, for the necessity of always considering the needs of others had taken precedence. But why shouldn't he put his own desires first for once? He had already checked Sapphire's schedule and she was due to leave Maraban within hours, an awareness that merely made him all the more single-minded. Zahir made his plans there and then with ruthless cool and the same kind of fierce, almost suicidal resolution that had once persuaded him to take a foreign wife without first asking his despotic father's permission. As that reality and comparison briefly occurred to him he stubbornly suppressed the piercing shard of unease it awakened.

With a sense of merciful release from the strain of being on show, Saffy stepped into the site trailer to change. She shed the skimpy silk bandeau and slashed skirt and peeled off the fake navel jewel before donning white linen trousers and an aqua tee. In a couple of hours she would be on her way home and saying goodbye to the joys of Maraban couldn't come quickly enough as far as she was concerned. After all, it was the last place in the world she would have chosen to visit, but civil unrest in a neighbouring country had led to a last-minute change of location and nobody had been willing to listen to her necessarily vague objections. But then the fact that nobody had a clue about her past connection to Maraban or Zahir was a relief. Thankfully that period of her life before fame had claimed her remained a deep dark secret.

So, in spite of all he had once had to say on the score of corrupt hereditary rulerships, Zahir had still ended up taking the throne to become a king. But then, according to what she had read in the newspapers, the citizens of Maraban had not had a clue what to do with the offer of democracy and had instead rallied round their popular hero prince, who had rebelled with the army against his old horror of a father to protect the people. There were pictures of Zahir everywhere: she had noticed one in the hotel foyer with a vase of flowers set beneath it rather like a little sacred shrine. Her lush mouth twisted as she questioned the thread of bitterness powering her thoughts. He was honourable, a big fan of justice and was very probably an excellent king, she conceded grudgingly. It really wasn't fair to resent him for what he couldn't have helped. Their marriage had been a disaster and even now her thoughts slid away from the memories with alacrity. He had broken her heart and dumped her when she failed to deliver and she wasn't really sure that it was fair to hate him for that when by that stage she had been urging him to divorce her for months. Everyone made choices, everyone had to live with those choices and a happy ending wasn't always included.

But she had a good life, she reminded herself doggedly as the security team cleared a path for her through the crush of spectators to the waiting limo that would whisk her back to the airport. She now had three glorious days of freedom to look forward to, and a tired sigh escaped her as she touched an admiring fingertip to the silky petal of an impossibly perfect blossom in the beautiful bouquet displayed in a vase inside the limo, while only vaguely wondering where the flowers had

come from. When she got back to London, she would
first catch up with her sisters, one who was pregnant,
one who was desperate to conceive and one who was
still at school. Her eldest sister, Kat, was thirty-six and
considering fertility treatment while still being full of
the newly married joys of her life with her Russian billionaire. After a sticky interview with her tough brother-
in-law, Mikhail Saffy was a little less enamoured of
her sibling's blunt-spoken husband. Mikhail had demanded to know why Saffy hadn't offered to help Kat
when her sister had run into serious debt. Well, *hello,*
Saffy thought back angrily—Kat had never told Saffy
that she was in trouble and, even if she had, Saffy knew
she would have found it a challenge to come up with
that kind of cash at short notice. Having made a major
commitment early in her career to help support an Af-
rican school for AIDS orphans, Saffy lived comfortably
but not in luxury.

   Saffy's twin, Emmie, was pregnant and Saffy had
not been surprised to learn that Emmie didn't have a
supportive man by her side. Saffy was painfully aware
that her twin did not forgive those who hurt or offended
her and in all probability the father of Emmie's child
had made that mistake. Saffy knew better than anyone
how inflexible her sibling could be because the relationship between the twins had long been tense and troubled. Indeed Saffy could never suppress the surge of
the guilt that attacked her whenever she saw her sister.
As young children she and Emmie had been very close
but events during their troubled teen years had ripped

them apart and the two young women had never managed to repair that breach. Saffy would never forget the injuries that *her* reckless behaviour had inflicted on her twin sister or the many years of suffering that Emmie had endured as a result. Some things were just too bad to be forgiven, Saffy acknowledged sadly.

In any case, Mikhail and Kat would undoubtedly assist Emmie in her struggles as a single mum—certainly, Saffy knew better than to offer assistance that would be richly resented. But she could not understand why Emmie had chosen to make a big secret of her baby's paternity. Saffy winced at that thought. While it was true that Saffy had never told her sisters the humiliating truth about her own failed marriage, she felt that she had had good reasons for her silence, not the least of which was the embarrassing fact that she had totally ignored Kat's plea that Saffy get to know Zahir better and for longer *before* she married him. Just common sense really, Saffy conceded wryly. Getting married at eighteen to a guy you had only known a couple of months and had never lived with had been an act of insanity. As immature and idealistic as most teenagers with little experience of independent life, Saffy had struggled from the outset with the role of being a wife in a different culture. And while she had struggled, Zahir had steadily grown more and more distant, not to mention his penchant for disappearing for weeks at a time on army manoeuvres just when she needed him most. Yes, she had made mistakes…but then *so had he*.

Satisfied with that appraisal, which approportioned

equal blame for what had gone wrong in the past, Saffy emerged from her reverie and noticed in surprise that the limo was travelling down a wide empty road that strongly reminded her of an airport runway. As the route back to the airport entailed travelling through Maraban city, she frowned, gazing out in confusion at the emptiness of the desert surrounding her on all sides. Strewn with stones and occasional large volcanic rock formations, the bleak desert terrain was interrupted by little vegetation. And so pervasive was the march of the sand that it was steadily encroaching on the road, blurring its outlines.

Saffy had never warmed to Zahir's natural preference for a lot of sand in his vicinity, had never learned to adjust to the extremes of heat or to admire the austerity of such a landscape. Where on earth were they going? Could the driver be taking another route to avoid the city traffic, such as it was? Her smooth brow creasing, she leant forward to rap the glass partition to attract the driver's attention, but although she saw his eyes flicker in the rear-view mirror to glance in her direction he made no attempt to respond to her. While Saffy was annoyed at being ignored, his behaviour also awakened the first stirrings of genuine apprehension and Saffy rapped the glass harder and shouted for him to stop. What on earth was the stupid man playing at? She didn't want to miss her flight home and she didn't have time to waste.

As she withdrew her fingers from the glass her knuckle brushed against the flowers in the vase and for the first time she noticed the envelope attached to them. She snatched it up and ripped it open to extract a typed card.

It is with great pleasure that I invite you to enjoy my hospitality for the weekend.

What on earth? Saffy stared down at the unsigned card. Who was inviting her where and why? Was this why her uncommunicative driver was travelling in the wrong direction? Her even white teeth gritted in angry frustration. Had her lightly clad appearance at the shoot caught the eye of some local randy sheikh? Possibly even the guy in the sand dunes with the binoculars? What did he think she was? Dial-a-tart? No, no, *no!* Her blue eyes flashed like twin blue fires. No way was she sacrificing her one free weekend to pandering to the ego of yet another rich man, keen to assume that the very fact she made her living by her face and body meant that she was an easy lay available to the highest bidder! Desert Ice cosmetics was always willing to serve her up to VIPs as the face of its product and the some-what racy reputation bestowed on her by the tabloids encouraged the wrong expectations and made rejecting amorous men even more of a challenge.

No way on earth was she spending her weekend with some man she hadn't even met! She dug through her bag in search of her cell phone, intending to ring one of her colleagues for assistance, but she couldn't find her phone and only finally accepted that it wasn't there after she had tipped out the contents of her bag on the seat beside her. She had had her phone in her hand before she got changed, she recalled with a frown. She had set it down…and clearly she hadn't picked it up again! She ground her teeth together and just for the sake of it attempted to open the door beside her. She wasn't surprised to find it locked and it really didn't matter, she conceded ruefully, for she had no intention of risking serious injury by throwing herself out of a moving car.

Conscious of the anxious glances the driver was now giving her in the mirror, she lifted her head high, her brain working double time. She might feel as if she were being kidnapped, but that was a most unlikely interpretation of her situation in a country as old-fashioned and law-abiding as Maraban. In addition, no Arab host would want an unwilling guest in his home. Indeed making a guest uncomfortable was a big no-no in Marabani culture, so once she politely explained that she had a prior engagement and apologised for being unavailable, she would be free to leave again…only by that time she might well have missed her flight home. Her lush mouth took on a downward curve.

Only minutes later, the limo came to a halt by the side of the road and with a click the door beside her opened. Saffy's brow pleated as she climbed out and she thought about making a run for it. But a run for it to where? It was the hottest part of the day and she would burn to a crisp. In addition the road was still empty and they had travelled miles through unbroken desert. As she pondered the unavoidable fact that there was nowhere safe to run to, a large four-wheel-drive vehicle drew up at the other side of the road. The driver jumped out and opened the passenger door wide while regarding her expectantly. Clearly it was an arranged meeting for her to be transferred to another vehicle. Did she accept that? Or fight it...but fight it with what? She glanced back into the limo and studied the glass vase that held the flowers. It was the work of a moment to smash the vase against the built-in bar and retrieve a jagged piece of glass, which she cupped awkwardly in her hand because she didn't want to tighten her fingers and cut herself on it. Straightening her slim shoulders, she crossed the road and climbed into the four-wheel-drive. The door slammed instantly behind her.

Was she in any true danger, she asked herself irritably, or was she at even greater risk of being swept along by an over-confident belief that somehow she was still in control of events? As soon as they arrived at their destination she would make it very clear that she wished to return to the airport immediately and if anyone dared to lay a single finger on her she would slash that person with the glass. Now was not the time to wish she had taken self-defence classes.

The vehicle moved off and performed a U-turn to pass directly in front of the limo and drive down a stony track that ran straight out into the desert. That change in direction took Saffy very much by surprise and she looked out of the windows in dismay at the giant looming sand dunes coming closer to tower all around them as the rough track streaked doggedly ahead. It was very bumpy and very hot because there seemed to be no air-conditioning in the car. Perspiration beading her brow,

Saffy gripped the safety rail above her head and gritted her teeth, thinking that possibly she should have made a run for it while they were still on the highway. As the track inevitably vanished beneath the sand the powerful vehicle roared endlessly over the shallow mounds that had taken its place, forging a zigzagging path between the dunes. Finally, when every bone in her body felt as if it were rattling inside her skin, the vehicle began to climb up the steep side of a dune, the engine whining at the strain. At the top she peered out of the window and focused on the sole sign of civilisation within view: a stone fortress with tall walls and turrets that looked remarkably like an ancient crusader castle.

Oh, dear, she thought with a sinking heart, for it didn't look as though it would offer the comforts of a five-star hotel and where else could they possibly be heading? And who in their right mind would invite her to such a remote place? Aside of a herd of goats there was nothing moving in the castle's vicinity.

The car thundered down the slope towards the building and big black gates spread slowly open as they approached. Through the gates she glimpsed surprisingly lush greenery, a welcome sight to eyes strained by sand overload. The vehicle lurched to a halt and she breathed in slow and deep when she saw staff clustered round an arched entrance. Maybe it *was* a hotel; certainly it looked at least the equal of the one she had stayed at in the city. As Saffy stepped out heads bowed low and nobody looked directly at her and nobody spoke. Saffy was in no mood to speak anyway and she followed in the steps of the older man who shifted his hand to gain her attention. Her shoes clicked on a polished marble floor and the blessed coolness of air-conditioning chilled her hot damp skin but nothing could have prepared her for the awe-inspiring sight that met her eyes. The amazingly spectacular hall stretched into seeming infinity in front of her. Fashioned of gleaming white marble and studded with gilded pillars and ornate mirrors, it was as unexpected in its sheer opulence inside those ancient walls as snow in the desert. She blinked in bewilderment, gazing up to scan the heavily decorated ceiling far above, which rejoiced in a gloriously well executed mural of a sunny blue sky dotted with exotic flying birds. A few feet ahead her guide hovered to wait for her to move on again.

Her mouth tightening, Saffy walked on to descend a shallow flight of stone stairs and walk through tall gilded doors into a vast sunlit room, which, although draped in luxury fabrics, was traditionally furnished in Eastern style with low divans and beautiful rugs carefully arranged around a central fire pit where coffee could be made and served in the same way as it might have been in a tent. It was a statement that her prospective host respected the old ways from the far-off years when the Marabani had been nomadic tribesmen. She pushed the piece of glass into her bag.

'*Qu'est-ce que vous desirez, madame?*'

Startled, Saffy turned her head to see a youthful maid eager to do her bidding, and well did she recall that sinking sensation at the familiar sound of the French language, which was more commonly spoken in Maraban than English. For a girl who had dismally failed her GCSE French exam, communicating in French had been a major challenge five years earlier.

'*Apportez des refraîchissements*...bring refreshments,' another voice interposed in fluent accented French as smooth as honey warmed by the sun. 'And in future use English to speak to Miss Marshall,' he advised.

Tiny hairs prickling eerily at the base of her skull, her eyes huge and her slim body trembling, Saffy stared in disbelief at the man in the doorway. In the corner of her eye the maid bent her head, muttered something that sounded terribly servile and backed swiftly out of the room through another exit.

'*Zahir...?*' Saffy framed in shaken disbelief.

CHAPTER TWO

'WHO ELSE?' ZAHIR enquired silkily as she backed away small step by small step.

Saffy's heart was in her mouth and she was desperately short of breath because her every instinct for self-preservation was pumping full-blown panic through her tall, slender length. Zahir? Zahir, the King of Maraban. *He* was responsible for bringing her to the castle/fortress/palace, whatever it was? *He* was the host who wanted her to enjoy his hospitality for the weekend? What kind of sense did that make for a male who had divorced her five years ago and never once since alluded to their former relationship in public?

Yet he stood there, effortlessly self-assured in a black cotton shirt and jeans, a casual outfit that however emanated designer chic, for both garments fitted his very tall, well-built frame to perfection. He was one of the very few men Saffy had to look up to even in heels because he was several inches over six feet. Unhappily the sheer impact of his unexpected appearance shattered her renowned composure. For so long she had told herself that memory must have lied, that if she were to meet him again she would not be so impressed as she had been at the tender age of eighteen. And yet there he stood, defying her every ego-boosting excuse. Luxuriant hair with the blue-black shine of polished jet accentuated his absolutely gorgeous face, drawing her attention to the slash of his high exotic cheekbones, the proud arch of his nose, the stubborn jut of his strong jawline and the beautifully defined, wide, sensual fullness of his mouth. He had the lean powerfully athletic physique of a Greek god. And the fiercely stunning dark eyes of a jungle predator. He wasn't safe; she saw that now. Zahir was not a man who played safe or who gave his woman the freedom to do her own thing, not when he had come to earth convinced of the fact that he always knew best. She had been way too innocent at eighteen and yet already damaged, she conceded painfully, much more damaged than either of them could ever have guessed. In spite of the surge of disturbing memories, butterflies still leapt and fluttered in her tummy at the stirring sight of him: dear heaven, she acknowledged in even greater shock, he could *still* rock her world.

In defiance of that disturbing conviction, Saffy flung her head high, shining layers of wheaten blonde hair sliding like heavy silk back from her face and tumbling off her shoulders. '*You're* responsible for bringing me here?' she demanded shakily, her voice embarrassingly breathy and insubstantial from the level of incredulity still gripping her. 'Why on earth would you do that?'

Eyes of heavenly blue clung to Zahir's lean dark face. His astute dark eyes narrowed, hardened, kindled to burning gold as he allowed himself a slow steady appraisal of her lithe figure. Tall and slim she might be, but unlike many models Sapphire had womanly curves and the fine cotton T-shirt she wore could not hide the high pouting curve of her breasts or their beaded tips, any more than her white linen trousers concealed the long supple line of her thighs, the delicious peachy swell of highly feminine hips below her tiny waist or the dainty elegance of her narrow ankles. The pulse at his groin kicked up hell in response and he clenched his teeth together, willing down that threat to his self-possession. If he was honest he had expected to be a little disappointed with her when he saw her again face to face, but if he was equally honest she was even more staggeringly lovely now than she had been as a teenager. Shorn of a slight hint of adolescent chubbiness, her flawless bone structure had fined down.

Zahir surveyed her with smoulderingly bright eyes, instantly resenting her effect on him. 'Since we parted, you've cost me over five million pounds. Maybe I was curious to see what I was paying for. Maybe I even thought I might be due something in return…'

Angry resentment surged from the base of Saffy's insecurity and discomfiture. How dared he talk back to her as if he had done nothing wrong?

'Just you stop right there… Are you out of your mind?' she blazed back at him full tilt. 'What the heck gives you the right to bring me here when I don't want to be here?'

'I wanted to speak to you.'

'But we've got nothing to talk about!' Saffy scissored back without pausing to draw breathe. 'I never expected to see you again in this lifetime and I don't want to speak to you, not even to find out why you're talking about five million pounds that I certainly didn't receive!'

'You're a liar,' he retorted quietly, using that deadly quietness he had always had the power to deploy once he had got her to screaming point. It was impossible to deflect Zahir from his target.

'I have to ask—on the score of the five million pounds you mentioned—what planet are you living on? I haven't had a penny from you since I started working!' Saffy snapped out of all patience while desperately trying to recapture her cool and with it her wits.

'Denial won't cut it,' Zahir scissored back with cool contempt. 'I have paid you substantial alimony since the day you left Maraban—'

'No way!' Saffy sizzled back at him, enraged by his condemnation. After all, she was very proud of her independence and of the fact that she had never taken advantage of his great wealth, believing as she had that their short-lived and unsuccessful marriage gave her no right to expect his continuing support. 'That is a complete lie, Zahir. You gave me money when I first left and I needed to use that until I started earning. But I never wanted alimony from you…I told my solicitor that and he must have informed you.'

'No, since your departure the money has been paid every month into a trust fund and none of it has ever been returned,' Zahir informed her with infuriating certainty. 'But at this moment I should warn you that that may not be your most pressing problem.'

Saffy gritted her teeth. She was shaking with rage and shocked by the speed with which her usually easy temper had gone skyward. She had forgotten, oh, dear heaven, she had actually forgotten how easily Zahir could push her buttons. 'Why? What may be my most pressing problem?' she slung back scornfully, hot pink adorning both her cheeks.

'You and your colleagues shot your commercial without first lodging a request for permission to do so from the Ministry of the Interior.'

'I know nothing about that!' Saffy proclaimed in instant dismissal of the charge. 'I've got nothing to do with the legal requirements or arrangements for filming abroad—I'm just the model. I go where I'm told and you had better believe that Maraban was the last place on earth I wanted to come!'

Zahir tensed, an even brighter sliver of gold lightening his dark eyes. 'Why so? Maraban is a beautiful country.'

'Surely that view depends on your standards of beauty?' Saffy snapped back with lashings of scorn. 'Maraban is eighty per cent desert!'

The gold effect in his eyes heightened to flame level. 'Had you still been my wife I would have been ashamed of your narrow outlook!'

Saffy loosed a cutting laugh. 'Mercifully for me I'm no longer your wife!'

The insult made him tense even more, his big shoulders squaring, the wall of his strong abdominal muscles tightening visibly below his shirt. His eyes held her fast, held her as completely as if he had her pinioned to a wall, those extraordinarily beautiful eyes of his set below well-defined ebony brows, eyes rimmed with thick curling black lashes and stormily bright with aggression. 'Mercifully for us both,' he murmured levelly.

Inexplicably his agreement wounded her and she sucked in a sudden surge of air to fill her deflated lungs in the seething silence and decided to concentrate on basics. 'So the shoot took place without permission from some authority—what does that mean?'

'That the film was confiscated at the hotel where you and the crew were staying,' Zahir advanced grimly.

Saffy took a hasty step forward. '*Confiscated?*' she repeated in horror. 'You can't do that!'

'I can do anything I like when people break the law in Maraban,' Zahir responded levelly. 'Filming was not authorised.'

'But you have the power to overlook it. I'm sure the company just made a mistake if they didn't seek permission. The location was changed at the very last minute—there probably wasn't time!' she protested. 'Is that why you've brought me here? To tell me this?'

'No...I wanted to see you again,' Zahir confided with shocking cool.

And she remembered the shock of that honest streak of his, his ability to cut through all the rubbish people could spout and hit the bottom line without hesitation or embarrassment. 'Why would you want to see me again?' she prompted stiltedly.

'You only have to look in the mirror to know why,' he fielded without skipping a beat. 'I want you. Just once I want what should have been mine when I married you and what you have since given to other men...'

Shock engulfed Saffy in a tidal wave. She moved back from him again in dismay, disbelief and bewilderment. Her ex wanted her to have sex with him?

'Unless, of course,' Zahir murmured silkily, 'you truly *do* find me physically repulsive...'

Saffy backed away another step, thinking that there was surely not a woman alive who could find Zahir repulsive. She certainly didn't; never had, in fact. Was that the impression she had left him with? Guilt rippled through her, for she was agonisingly aware that he could not possibly have overcome her problems for her five years earlier. It had taken years of therapy for Saffy to find the solution and to come to terms with what she had learned about herself during the process.

'If you can convince me that you do, I will let you go,' Zahir purred, literally stalking her across the room with fluid steps.

Zahir wanted to sleep with her. So, tell me something new, a wry little voice said inside her head. It was like being plunged back into her marriage without warning, unable to give him what he wanted and needed. The most appalling sense of inadequacy gripped her afresh. She had failed him and not surprisingly he was bitter. But that was no excuse whatsoever for his current behaviour. 'You virtually kidnapped me!' she accused rawly.

'I sent you flowers and an air-conditioned limo. How many kidnappers do that?'

'You've got to be crazy... I mean, are you even thinking about what you're doing?' Saffy gasped, stepping back against a piece of furniture and sidling sideways to avoid it and to keep moving further out of his reach.

'I don't *think* around you,' Zahir muttered flatly. 'I never did.'

Saffy was more than willing to kick his brain back into gear. 'Zahir, you're a king...royalty doesn't do stuff like this!'

Zahir flung back his darkly handsome head and laughed with rich appreciation, even white teeth flashing against his bronzed skin. 'Sapphire...my father kept a harem of a hundred concubines in this palace. Until very recently indeed, royalty did indeed do things that were neither socially nor morally acceptable.'

'Your father? Had a *harem* here?' Saffy parroted in consternation, her heart beating so fast as he stalked closer that she was convinced it might burst right out of her chest. She refused even to think of that nasty old man, Fareed, having had a hundred unfortunate women locked up to fulfil his gruesome requirements. It wasn't a surprise though: her father-in-law had been an out-and-out lech.

'I have no harem...no wife,' Zahir pointed out.

'Those are the only positives you have to offer in your own favour?' Her voice was careening up and down as if she were on a vocal seesaw. She was locked into his eyes, those amazingly beautiful amber eyes, which had struck her like a thunderbolt at eighteen across a crowded department store. 'Stay back…'

'No, been there, done that, paid the price,' Zahir countered, running a forefinger slowly down over her cheekbone so that in some strange way it seemed perfectly normal to turn her cheek into his hand.

Saffy looked up, clashed with his eyes, experienced a light-headed sensation that did nothing to collect her wits, and swallowed painfully. How could he be so gorgeous that she couldn't breathe? Why was it as if the world had stopped turning and had flung her off into space? She was completely disorientated by his proximity, the very heat she could feel filtering from his lean powerful body towards hers even though their only connection was the hand resting against her face. 'Zahir?'

He lowered his proud dark head. He's going to kiss me, he's going to kiss me, a crazily excited voice chanted inside her head and both anticipation and denial warred inside her. And then he *did,* firm, sensual lips circling hers, the pressure steadily deepening even as a shriek alarm of shock shrilled through her trembling body. He parted her lips, let his tongue dart between and it felt like the most erotic caress she had ever experienced because the taste and the flicker of movement inside her mouth were indescribably sexy. Heat burned in her pelvis, her nipples swelling taut, abrading the cotton covering them. That intoxicating intense physical reaction was exactly what she had wanted to feel for a long time but he was the very last man on earth she wanted to feel it with.

And yet she couldn't will herself to break free while his tongue tangled with hers, touching, tasting, *savouring,* a low growl breaking from his throat while his fingertips stroked her neck where it met her shoulder. Unholy pleasure was ricocheting through her treacherous body as it awakened to sudden life, hot, damp sensation tingling at her feminine core while her breasts swelled and ached. Gathering every atom of her strength, she pushed her hand forcefully against a wide muscular shoulder and broke free. 'No...no, I don't want this!'

His gaze filled with sardonic amusement, Zahir studied her hectically flushed face with satisfaction. 'Liar,' he said thickly. 'You always liked my mouth on you.'

Saffy felt the rush of heat below her skin and momentarily closed her eyes while she blocked him out and fought for recovery. He was a demon kisser. That far, *they* had worked and the chemistry had misleadingly suggested a match made in heaven. In that instant, she loathed him for bringing the past alive again and reminding her of exactly what she yearned to find in another man's arms. Frustration filled her. Been there, done that, as he had said, although they hadn't actually *done it*. Did he feel cheated? Was that why he had brought her here? Why did he think that anything would have changed between them? It was not as if he knew what she had gone through in search of a cure. Crushing out that torrent of curious questions and musings, Saffy concentrated on the here and now.

'I want transport to the airport and the film that was confiscated,' she told him drily, straightening her slender shoulders to stand up to him.

Zahir viewed her from beneath the cloak of his lush black lashes, dark eyes bright as stars. 'It's not happening.'

'Then what would it take to make it happen?' Saffy prompted, determined to sort the situation out by taking the practical approach that generally served her well in difficult situations. 'That missing money you mentioned? I promise I'll look into that mystery and sort it out as soon as I get back to London.'

'Don't try to avoid the real issue here—I want *you*...'

Her mouth ran dry and her skin ran hotter than hot as he lounged back against the wall beside him and she noticed, really couldn't help noticing by the close fit of his jeans that he was aroused. She turned her head away, her tummy flipping even as she recognised the healthy discovery that the awareness of his arousal no longer made her feel threatened. 'But we can't always have what we want,' she pointed out tautly, hanging onto her cool with difficulty. 'And you know that bringing me here is crazy. Your people would be scandalised by this set-up.'

'I'm a single man and not a eunuch.'

'You're also intelligent and fair—at least you used to be,' Saffy countered with determination.

'Then you will understand that I seek justice.'

'Because you didn't get either the wedding night or the bride of your dreams you think you can magically turn the clock back?' Saffy lifted a fair brow. 'Good luck with that without a time machine.'

'You're *staying*,' Zahir declared with razor-sharp emphasis. 'And I don't want the girl you were five years ago. I want the woman you are now.'

'But the woman I am now is living with another man,' Saffy slotted in curtly, shooting the last bolt in her rejection routine, which she usually regarded as worth using only at the last ditch but his sheer persistence was ruffling more than her feathers

'And he shares you with whomever you choose to stray with,' Zahir retorted, unimpressed, his wide sensual mouth compressing with speaking derision.

Saffy stiffened as though he had slapped her in the face. Evidently he had come across the silly stories about her that the tabloids printed and believed them, actually believed that she slept around whenever she felt like it. But then she had only to be pictured emerging from a man's apartment for the press to assume she was engaged in an affair, but the truth was that she had some very good male friends, whom she visited, and had learned to treat the reports with amusement, for there was really nothing she could do to stop lies about her appearing in print. That, she had learnt, was the price of a life lived in the public eye.

'That is not true. Cameron and I are very close. He's my best friend,' Saffy admitted, throwing her head high, reluctant to lie to him about that relationship but happy to take advantage of his ignorance if it acted as another barrier between them.

'I don't want to be your best friend. I want to be your lover.'

Saffy's lovely face snapped tight and turned pale. 'And we both know how that panned out five years ago,' she reminded him flatly. 'Let me go, Zahir. Bringing me here is reckless and illogical.'

Zahir studied her with veiled eyes, a grimly amused smile tugging at the corners of his handsome male mouth. 'Perhaps that's why it feels so good.'

Saffy had shot her last reasonable bolt and she was stunned by his indifference. 'You don't know what you're saying.'

'I have never been so sure of anything,' he shot back in rebuttal.

The last string of restraint broke free inside Saffy. She had had a very long, hot and tiring day and now Zahir was plunging her into the nightmare of her better forgotten past. 'But you can't be serious...you can't *really* intend to keep me here against my will!'

'I will do nothing that causes you harm,' Zahir replied stubbornly.

'But keeping me here against my will is causing me harm! What gives you the idea that you can do this to me?' Saffy lashed back at him, her temper finally slipping its leash and her voice rising on a shrill note.

'The knowledge that I have achieved it. Your colleagues have been informed that you have accepted a private invitation to spend another few days in Maraban. Nobody will be looking for you or concerned that anything is amiss,' Zahir asserted with satisfaction.

'You *can't* do this to me!' Saffy erupted, infuriated by his self-assurance, his evident belief that he had covered all bases. 'And why? Nothing's going to happen between us. You're wasting your time!'

'No man looking at you could possibly believe that I was wasting my time in at least trying,' Zahir drawled with husky appreciation, his golden eyes resting on her delicate profile with possessive heat. 'It is a risk I take with pleasure.'

'But I *don't!*' Saffy slammed back at him in furious rebuttal. 'I didn't agree to this. Nobody tells me what to do or makes me stay somewhere I don't want to be and nothing on this earth is capable of persuading me to get into bed with you again, so you can forget that idea right now!'

'I will call Fadith to take you to your room...' Zahir pressed a button on the wall with a graceful brown hand, his bold profile set in uncompromising lines.

In outrage that he wasn't even taking heed of her objections, Saffy swept up a china vase on a stand and pitched it at him. It fell short and smashed against the edge of the fire pit to break into a hundred pieces.

Zahir enraged her by turning his handsome dark head and treating her to a slashing smile of very masculine amusement. 'Ah, that takes me back years. I had forgotten how you liked to throw things at me when you lost control of your temper. I will see you later when it is time to dine.'

And with that very cool and unruffled assurance, Zahir strolled out of the room and left her standing there in a tempestuous rage that she could do nothing more to vent with her target gone. Trembling from the force of her pent-up feelings, Saffy breathed in deep to find inner calm. He would pay; she would *make* him pay for this in spades!

CHAPTER THREE

FADITH REAPPEARED AND led the way down a corridor and up a flight of pale marble stairs. Shown into a room as traditionally furnished and comfortable as the room she had seen downstairs, Saffy breathed in deep. The furniture was ebony inlaid with gleaming mother-of-pearl and the bed was a fantasy four-poster hung in swirling silk that piled opulently on the floor at each corner. Saffy wandered into a bathroom with a sunken marble tub and every possible extra and suppressed a groan. As she returned to the bedroom Fadith was removing a tray from another maid's grasp to set it on a table.

'Thanks,' Saffy murmured, reluctantly lifting the mint drink she recalled from the year she had spent in Maraban. Maraban, the land that time forgot, she reflected grimly. She asked if there was any water and was shown a concealed refrigerator in a cupboard. She pulled out a chilled bottle and unscrewed the cap.

'Would you like a bath?' Fadith asked her then, clearly eager to be of service.

Saffy screened her mouth and faked a yawn before telling an outright lie to get rid of the younger woman.

'Perhaps later. I think I'll lie down and sleep for a while. It's very warm.'

Fadith pulled the blinds and scurried over to the bed to turn it down in readiness before departing. Playing safe, Saffy waited for a couple of minutes before heading off to explore. She had no intention of staying with Zahir and since there was no prospect of her being rescued she had to rescue herself. She walked across the vast landing on quiet feet, passing innumerable closed doors and peering out of windows into inner courtyards before finally heading downstairs. Ignoring the ground floor, she went down another flight into the basement, which she could see by the trolleys of cleaning equipment was clearly the servants' area. It was easy to identify the kitchens from the clatter of dishes and the buzz of voices and she gave it a wide berth. She stared out through a temptingly open rear door at the line of dusty vehicles parked outside while wondering what the chances were of any of them having keys left inside them. She wasn't stupid enough to think that she could walk out of the desert: she needed wheels to get back to the city. Without further hesitation she sped out into the heat and the first thing she saw was a four-wheel-drive full of soldiers at the far side of the courtyard. In dismay she dropped down into a crouch to hide behind a car. Of course there would be soldiers around to guard Zahir while he was in residence, she conceded ruefully. She inched up her head to peer into the car and then twisted to study its neighbour: there was no sign of keys left carelessly in the ignition. Meanwhile the soldiers trooped indoors. Saffy continued her seemingly fruitless search for a car to steal and dived behind a vehicle to avoid being seen when a couple of kitchen staff strolled out of the palace talking loudly.

One of them wished the other a good journey home in Arabic and she recognised the phrase as the young man threw his bag into the pickup and jumped into the driver's seat. He was going home? There was a good chance that he would be driving into the city. For a split second Saffy hesitated while she considered her options. The gates were guarded. It would be impossible for her to drive through them without being detected. Possibly stowing away in a vehicle being driven by a member of staff would be a cleverer move. Before she could lose her nerve, she scrambled over the tailgate and dived below the tarpaulin cover.

But the pickup didn't immediately move off as she had expected. In fact someone shouted to the driver and he got back out of the vehicle. She lay still, stiff with tension, listening to voices talking too fast for her to follow before the steps moved slowly away and she heard the driver moving back. Finally the door slammed again, the engine ignited and she expelled her breath in relief. Her original drive from the road down the track to the palace had been long and rough and lying on the rusty bed of the pickup, Saffy rolled about and wondered if the constant pitching gait of the vehicle would leave her covered with bruises. But she was willing to endure discomfort as the price of having escaped Zahir.

What on earth had come over her ex-husband? Their

marriage had been a train wreck and who in their right mind would want to revisit that?

And the answer came to her straight away. Failure of any kind was anathema to Zahir, whose callous old father had expected his son to excel in every field and who had punished him when he botched anything. Zahir was trying to rewrite the past. Why didn't he appreciate that that was impossible? People changed, people moved on…

Although she had not moved on very far, a tart little voice reminded Saffy, who was bitterly conscious that she was still a virgin. And time rolled back for her as she lay there and the pickup rattled and roared across the sands, threatening to shake her very teeth loose from her gums. Saffy had been eighteen and working at a department-store beauty counter when she first met Zahir. She hadn't wanted to go to university like her twin, had preferred to jump straight into work and start earning. Zahir had travelled to London with his sister, Hayat, who had been shopping for her wedding trousseau. Saffy still remembered seeing Zahir that very first time, her heart jumping inside her, her breath shortening as she collided with the most mesmerising dark golden eyes she had ever seen. Hayat had bought cosmetics while Saffy stared fixedly at Zahir and Zahir stared back equally transfixed at Saffy. She had never felt anything that powerful, either before then or since: an exhilarating and intrinsically terrifying instant attraction that swamped her like a fog, closing out the rest of the world and common sense.

'I will meet you after you finish work,' Zahir had told her in careful English.

He had told her that he was an army officer in Maraban. He hadn't told her that he was a prince or the son of the ruler of Maraban. She had had to look up Maraban online to find out where it was and her mother, Odette, with whom she had briefly lived at the time, had laughed at her and said, 'Why worry? He'll be gone in a few days and you'll never see him again.'

Initially Saffy had been desperately afraid of that forecast. After only a handful of dates, she had fallen for Zahir like a ton of bricks and she had been ecstatic when he told her he would be back the following month to attend a course at Sandhurst. She remembered little romantic snapshot moments from that period: sitting in a park below a cloud of cherry blossom with Zahir brushing a petal out of her hair with gentle fingers; lingering over coffee holding hands; laughing together at mime artists in the street. From the outset, Zahir had had the magic key to winning her trust, for, unlike previous boyfriends he didn't grab and grope and didn't expect her to leap straight into bed with him. At the same time, though, he was chary of the part-time modelling she was already doing, even when assured that she didn't do nude or underwear shots. She had recognised that he was old-fashioned in a way that had gone out of fashion in her country, but she had very much admired the seriousness of his quick clever mind and his unvarnished love for Maraban. Long before his course was over he asked her to marry him and he told her who he really was. And the news that he was a royal prince had merely added another intoxicating layer of sparkle to the fairy-tale fantasy she was already nourishing about their future together, Saffy conceded sadly.

Zahir had married her in a brief ceremony at the Marabani embassy without any of his family present and without his father's permission. With hindsight she knew how courageous he had been to wed her without his father's consent and she knew he had done it because he had known that his parent would never agree to him taking a foreign bride. Reality, unfortunately, hadn't entered their relationship until she landed in Maraban. Starting with the wedding night during which she panicked and threw up and ending with a daily life more like imprisonment than marriage, their relationship had hit the rocks fast. She hadn't been able to give him sex and neither of them had been able to handle the fallout from that giant elephant in the room. Any sense of intimacy had died fast, leading to backbiting conversations and even more of Zahir's constant absences.

The pickup came to a sudden jolting halt. A door slammed and a burst of voices met her straining ears. As the voices receded she began to snake out from below the tarpaulin, only then appreciating that it was almost dark. That was not a possibility she had factored into her plans and, climbing out of the truck, she soon recognised the second big drawback. It had not occurred to her that the driver might be rendezvousing with his family at a huge multi-roofed tent right out in the desert. Consternation swallowed Saffy whole as she stared round her at what she could see in the fast-fading light. There was no sign of a village, a road or anything else for her to focus on as a means of working out where she was. Biting her lip with vexation, she was pushing her bottle of water into the front pocket of her jeans when a tall pale shape clad in beige desert robes moved out of the tent.

'It's cold,' he said. 'Come inside.'

Disbelieving her ears, Saffy froze and gaped, her eyes straining to penetrate the growing darkness. '*Zahir?*' she exclaimed incredulously. 'What are you doing here?'

With one hand he tugged off the headdress bound with a gold and black circlet of cord and straightened, black hair ruffling back against his lean strong face in the slight breeze, his dark eyes bright as stars in the low light. 'I drove you here.'

'You...*what*?' Saffy gasped in disbelief.

'The security surveillance at the palace is the best money can buy,' Zahir drawled. 'I saw you climbing into the pickup on CCTV and I decided that if anyone was going to take you anywhere it should be me.'

'I've been under that tarpaulin for more than an hour!' Saffy launched at him in a rage of disbelief. 'I was so thrown about under it I'm not convinced my bones are still connected!'

Zahir shrugged without even a hint of sympathy. 'Well, it was your chosen mode of travel.'

'Don't you give me that!' Saffy flung at him through teeth that were starting to chatter because it was extraordinarily cold, but mercifully her temper was still rising like rocket fuel to power her. 'You knew I was in there!'

'Perhaps I thought a little shaking was a just reward for a woman stupid enough to climb into a car driven by a stranger when she didn't even know where the car was heading.'

Such a jolt of rage roared through Saffy that she was vaguely surprised that she didn't levitate into the air like a sorcerer. Her great blue eyes flashed. 'Don't you *dare* call me stupid!' she warned him in a hiss.

Zahir had never been the type to withdraw from a fight. He stood his ground, wide shoulders thrown back, stubborn jaw line set like granite. 'But it was *very* stupid to take such a risk with your personal safety.'

Saffy knotted her hands into fists and clenched her teeth together. 'My safety wouldn't be an issue if you hadn't kidnapped me!' she bit back.

'I kept you safe and I will continue to keep you safe and unharmed until you return to London because while you are here you are my responsibility,' Zahir countered in a tone of crushing finality. 'Now I suggest that you come inside so that you can wash and eat. I don't know about you…but I'm hungry.'

'Mr Practical…Mr Reasonable all of a sudden!' Saffy raged back at him, aggrieved by his unshakeable self-assurance in the face of her violent and perfectly reasonable resentment. 'How could you do this to me? I hate you! Get stuffed!'

Zahir expelled his breath in a slow sibilant hiss.

'When you are ready to be civil again, you may come inside and join me.'

And with that ultimate putdown, he was gone, striding soundlessly into the dimly lit tent and simply leaving her standing there. Saffy stamped her feet in the sand to express her fury and only just resisted an urge to slam her fists up against the metal side of the pickup. What a prune she felt—what a complete and utter idiot! Her bid for freedom had been seen and Zahir had stepped into the driver's seat to ruin her escape attempt. He had made a fool of her and not for the first time. It was many years since Saffy had been so angry, for in general she was the mildest personality around and quite laid back in temperament, but Zahir's dominant gene got to her every time. She gritted her teeth, stretched her aching back and legs and leant back against the pickup. Contrary to her every expectation of the desert, it was absolutely freezing and her tee was so thin she might as well have been naked. She couldn't stop shivering and she rubbed her chilled goose-fleshed arms in an effort to get her circulation going again. Seeing Zahir again seemed to have fried her brain cells.

When she couldn't stand the cold any longer she stalked into the tent, which was even larger than she had appreciated and even offered communicating doorways to other sections. Festooned in traditional kelims, it nonetheless offered sofas in place of the usual rugs round the fire pit. Zahir was being served coffee by a kneeling older man.

'What is this place?' Saffy asked abruptly. 'Where are we?'

'It's a semi-permanent camp where I meet with the tribal sheikhs on a regular basis. Although I know you would sooner be dead than sleep under canvas, it offers every comfort,' he murmured smoothly. 'The bathroom is through the second door.'

A wash of heated embarrassment engulfed Saffy's pale taut face. He was throwing her own words of five years ago back in her teeth, her less than tactful rejection of anything to do with tents and the nomadic lifestyle that had once been customary for his people.

'I suppose it's too much to hope that there's a shower in there?' Saffy breathed tautly.

'No, it is not. Go ahead and freshen up. A change of clothing has been laid out for you.'

Her gaze flickered uneasily off his darkly handsome features, her heart beating too fast for comfort or calm. Straight out of the frying pan right into the fire, she acknowledged uncomfortably as she brushed back the hanging that concealed a normal wooden door and stepped through it into a bathroom that contained every luxurious necessity. She stripped off in haste because even cold as she was she still felt sweaty and grubby, and her white linen trousers had not withstood the journey well. The powerful shower washed the grit from her skin and an impressive array of surprisingly familiar products greeted her on a shelf. Wrapped in a towel, she combed out her wet hair and made use of the hairdryer. Hot running water and electric in a tent?

Had he told her that that was a possibility she would have agreed to the desert trip he had tried to take her on soon after they were married. Or *would* she have? If she was honest, her fear of the intimacies of sharing a tent with him had lain behind her dogged refusal to consider such an excursion.

A silk kaftan lay over a chair with a pair of simple mules beside it. Leaving her underwear with her clothes, she slid into it, wondering what she would wear the following day and where he was planning for her to sleep. There were at least two more doorways leading out of the main tent for her to investigate.

'Are you ready to eat?' Zahir asked.

Eyes widening, she nodded affirmation and spun to look at him. He had shed the robes and got back into jeans. Damp black hair feathered round his lean bronzed features, accentuating those smouldering amber gold eyes surrounded by dense black lashes. Her pulses gave a jump. Butterflies flocked loose in her tummy and she swallowed hard, frantic to shed her desperate physical awareness of him. It seemed so schoolgirlish and immature to react that way after all the years they had been apart and the life she had since led. She was supposed to be calm, sophisticated…in control.

'No table and chairs, I'm afraid,' he warned her, settling down by the flickering fire with animal grace.

'That's OK,' she muttered as a servant emerged from one of the doorways bearing a tray, closely followed by another. 'So, you have a kitchen here.'

'A necessity when I'm entertaining.'

He had mentioned the tribal sheikhs he met up with but Saffy was already wondering how many other women he had brought out into the desert. She *knew* there had been other women. For a couple of years after the divorce and before the overthrow of his father, Zahir had made occasional appearances in glossy magazines with several different beautiful women on his arm. And those glimpses of the new and much more visible life he was leading abroad without her had cut deep like a knife and made her bleed internally. She had known that those women were sharing his bed, entangling his beautiful bronzed body with lissom limbs and giving him everything she had failed to give him. Divorce, she had learned the hard way, wasn't an immediate cut-off point for emotions, even emotions that she had no right to feel.

Zahir watched Sapphire curl up on the sofa opposite, looking all fresh faced and scrubbed clean just the way he remembered her, the way he liked her best, for with her stunning looks she required few enhancements. Her restive fingers toyed with a strand of golden blonde hair and instantly he recalled the silken feel of it sliding against his skin and got a hard-on. He crushed the recollection before it could stray into even more erotic areas and reminded himself that she was a beautiful shell with a cash-register heart. He was not at all surprised that she had dropped the subject of the five million pounds without any acknowledgement or adequate explanation. It might be pocket change to a member of his family, but it still mattered that she had taken so much and given nothing in return.

Perched with a plate on her lap, Saffy helped herself to portions of different dishes and dug in because she was starving. While she ate she studied Zahir from below her lashes, marvelling at the superb bone structure that gave his features such strength and masculinity. From every angle he was glorious. Sitting there, his attention on his plate and quite unaware of her scrutiny, he mesmerised her. Her breasts stirred beneath the silk, the tips growing tender and swollen. She dredged her eyes back to her food, her mouth dry, her heart hammering, images from the past bombarding her. Although consummating their marriage had proved impossible, she had learned how to give him pleasure in other ways. At that thought she shifted uneasily on her seat, moist heat pooling at the heart of her. He had never understood what was wrong with her. How could he have? But he had at least *tried,* assuring her of his patience while he did everything possible to set her fears to rest. Unfortunately her fears had been in her subconscious and not something she could control, fears from a hidden source that she had repressed many years before while she was still a child. All of a sudden she simply could not comprehend why he would bring her back into his life after a marriage that had turned into a hell on earth for both of them.

'Why on earth did you want to see me again?' Saffy demanded abruptly.

He lifted his dark head, stunning golden eyes locking to her. 'Few men forget their first love and you're the one who got away...'

Regret stabbed through her and she flinched, for they had begun with love in spite of the fact that during the year of marital strife that followed they had lost it again. The plates were cleared away and coffee and cakes served. She ate to fill the emptiness inside her, the hollow that never seemed to fill. She couldn't look at him, didn't dare look at him again, knew the temptation was a weakness to be suppressed at every opportunity.

'I wanted to see you again before I remarried,' Zahir heard himself admit in brusque addition, knowing that he would never have trusted himself to see her after that event had taken place.

Her golden head flew up, heavenly blue eyes wide with shock. 'You're getting married again?' she gasped, shattered at the idea although she couldn't have explained why.

Zahir raised a winged ebony brow. 'As yet there is no particular bride in view but there is considerable pressure on me to take a wife. Inevitably I will have to satisfy my people's expectations.'

Some of the tension eased from her taut shoulders and she lowered her head. Of course he would be expected to marry: it went with the territory of kingship. What did it matter to her? Why should the concept bother her? It was not as though she still thought of him as her husband. In fact she was being ridiculously oversensitive and it was time to grow up and don her big-girl pants. Exhaustion engulfed her in a debilitating wave then, reminding her that she had been up since five that morning. A yawn crept up on her and she stood up smothering a yawn. 'I'm incredibly tired...'

Zahir sprang upright and rested his hands on her shoulders to prevent her from moving away. Her mouth ran dry, her heart skipping a beat as she looked up at him, up over that full sensual mouth to the black-lashed golden eyes that wreaked havoc with her insides.

'Tonight you're tired.' His deep dark voice reverberated through her very bones, the husky nuances toying with her nerves like a secret caress. 'I won't touch you...'

Saffy shivered at just the thought of being in bed with him again. The image caught at her and not with the sense of threat that she believed she should have felt. A lazy brown forefinger grazed the length of her delicate collarbone, smoothed a passage up her slender throat while she struggled not to fall in a limp heap at his feet because her knees were threatening to buckle. She couldn't breathe, couldn't think while he touched her, and then he brought his mouth crashing down on hers with a hungry passion that should have frightened her out of her wits, but which instead stormed through her and set her on fire. There was a primitive sense of tightening and dampness between her legs, a sudden painful pulse throbbing through the peaks of her breasts. With every plunge of his tongue she trembled, lost in the hot, electrifying darkness of overwhelming physical sensation.

'Bed,' Zahir muttered raggedly, stooping to haul her up bodily in his strong arms, thrusting back a door with an impatient shoulder. 'I want you wide awake tomorrow.'

He laid her down on a big modern divan dressed in pristine white linen. When he had said, 'bed' in that deep thrilling tone her imagination had exploded into the stratosphere and when he released her again and moved back to the door, she frowned at him poised there in the dim light, black hair tousled by her fingers, the taste of him still on her lips, the sheer call of him to her senses overpowering. She rolled over and buried her hot face in a pillow. No, she didn't have a stupid bone in her body. She was looking for a man—had been for years—but he was not the one, although inconveniently he still seemed to be the *only* one she actually wanted, the only one she could even imagine becoming intimate with.

Angry tears of frustration stung her eyes. After the divorce had destroyed her faith in true love and happy endings, she had licked her wounds for years, terrified of getting into another serious relationship and meeting up with the same problems. But after therapy, she had longed to lose her virginity and have sex with a lover to prove that she was fully cured and had come to terms with her past. She had simply wanted to be *normal* as other women took for granted…how could that be wrong? Or selfish? Or immoral? And she did not need to compound her mistakes by being attracted to a man who had not only hurt her very badly once but who also had plans to marry another woman.

Zahir went for a shower—a very cold one. A great well of burning hunger was consuming him but it was cooled by disturbing memories of Sapphire shaking with unmistakeable fear when he had tried to make love to her during their marriage. Even with all the sexual experience he had painstakingly acquired since then, he was wary and seriously distrustful of the physically encouraging vibes she was putting out. He had been wrong before; why shouldn't he be wrong again? And while a faint sense of wonderment was stirring that he should actually have her in a bed again within reach, no sense of regret yet assailed him. In fact a merciless sense of all-male satisfaction was still driving him hard.

Saffy froze when she heard the door open again and rolled over, ridiculously conscious that her eyelids and her nose were probably pink from the overload of emotion and events that had brought overwrought tears to her eyes. She sat up in honest surprise to stare at Zahir, poised one step inside the door clad in only a pair of black silk boxers. Her throat closed over and she stopped breathing.

'There is only one bed…'

'It's not a problem,' Saffy responded as carelessly as she could contrive, rolling off the bed and yanking the bedspread off the mattress in almost the same movement. 'I'll sleep on the floor, although you *could* have taken one of the sofas.'

'I refuse to do so and you can't sleep on the floor.'

'I can do whatever I want to do,' Saffy told him, rolling herself into the spread and lying down beside the bed as well wrapped up as an Arctic explorer.

'Except when I'm around,' Zahir pronounced in direct challenge, snatching her up from the floor and planting her back on the divan with the strength that came so naturally to him.

'I'm not sharing that bed with you!' Saffy spat at him.

Zahir dealt her a derisive appraisal. 'Even when you already know that you can certainly trust me to hear the word no?' he queried in a very dry reminder.

Hot pink colour washed her lovely face and then receded to leave her pale and stricken. She was crushed by all that went unsaid within that aide-memoire, but equally suddenly she felt foolish making such a fuss about sharing a bed, and she squirmed out of the cloaking folds of the spread to slide below the sheet. 'This is all your fault—you should never have brought me here!'

Zahir almost laughed. She was shouting at him again, fighting with him, and he should have been furious at her lack of respect but he wasn't; he was too busy enjoying the novelty of being treated like an equal by a woman. Sapphire wouldn't bat her eyelashes at him, look down in submission and offer honeyed words of feminine flattery as the other women he met did. He climbed into the bed and lay back against the pillows. With Sapphire's mane of hair tossed all over the pillow beside his, the smell of the shampoo she used wafted into his nostrils, a familiar floral scent she had worn ever since he had known her, and that evocative aroma awakened too much that he would have preferred to forget. Slowly his lean brown hands clenched into fists, the tension in his lean powerful body extreme.

'Well, isn't this cosy?' Saffy mocked, determined not to show weakness again.

'Don't rock the boat...' Zahir purred softly in warning.

'Your English has improved so much,' Saffy remarked acidly, staring up at the boarded ceiling. 'Was that a by-product of your promiscuity with various Western women or did you actually have to study the language?'

His even white teeth gritted. The novelty of her backchat was fast dimming in appeal and he sat up to stare down at her. 'I was *not* promiscuous...'

Saffy stared stonily back at the lean bronzed beauty of his arresting face. 'None of my business.'

Eyes as dark a black and cold as she had ever seen them, he swivelled away from her and turned on his side and she caught a glimpse of his back, and anything else provocative that she might have said was forgotten instantly. Without thought she thrust down the sheet to get a better look. The once-brown silken sweep of his smooth, muscular back was marred with slashed and intersecting lines of scars. Before she could think better of it, she exclaimed, 'What on earth happened to your back?'

In an abrupt movement, Zahir flipped round to lie flat on his back again while colour crawled across his slashing cheekbones because he had forgotten to keep his shirt on. 'Not something I want to talk about.'

'But it looks like you were beaten...*whipped!*' Saffy burst out, unable to stifle her horror at the thought of anyone deliberately inflicting that amount of pain on him. His back must have been shredded to leave scars that deep and extensive.

In the nerve-racking silence, which only Zahir was capable of using like a weapon he switched out the light. She could recall so many times when he had shut her out like that five years earlier, keeping his own counsel, refusing to share his thoughts or even the details of what he did or where he went when he was away from her. He wasn't the confiding type, never had been, was very much made in the iron image of an army officer with the proverbial stiff upper lip. She compressed her lips on the questions tumbling on her tongue. Had he been caught, imprisoned and mistreated during the rebellion that had brought his father down? But surely his status as his father's heir should have protected him on either side of the fence?

Bewildered, even wondering why she should be so curious, Saffy closed her eyes and instead pictured him lounging in his boxers by the door and finally she smiled faintly in the darkness, the more disturbing images banished. He might have acquired a few scars but he was still a vision of bronzed masculine perfection, still her fantasy male from his perfect pecs to his six-pack abdomen and powerful hair-roughened thighs. He would either be highly amused or highly offended to learn that she pictured him when she tried to look sexy in a pose.

CHAPTER FOUR

SAFFY WOKE UP because she was too warm and then went rigid, for at some stage of the night she and Zahir had drifted across the great divide of mattress separating them in the huge bed and it was hardly surprising that she had overheated. Their bodies were welded together like two magnets and, compared to her, he put out the most extraordinary amount of heat. Even more disturbing, however, was the hard male arousal she could feel thrusting against her thigh.

He was always in that state in the morning: she had realised that while she was married to him. But the flush of awareness that shimmered through her was shockingly new, fresh and intensely energising and she shivered. Her fingers flexed against the male bicep they were resting on, colour flashing across her embarrassed face as a hunger to touch him flared deep inside her. It was a supreme irony that in the past, while she couldn't bear him to touch her, she had *loved* to touch him.

Black lashes dark as midnight and effective as silk fans swept up and she collided with stunning golden eyes and knew instantly what he was thinking. She

yanked her hand off his strong muscular bicep and
snaked back from him but she wasn't quick enough,
for Zahir had closed long brown fingers into her hair
to entrap her.

'Right at this minute,' he positively purred like a very
large predatory jungle cat on the prowl, 'I'm all yours.'

'I don't know what you're talking about!' she said in
desperation, a spasm of panic claiming her.

'Want me to tell you what you're thinking about?'
Zahir husked. 'Or will I just tell you what *I'm* thinking about?'

'Let me go!' she gasped.

He freed her hair and rolled back.

Low in her pelvis something clenched almost painfully while her nipples tingled into throbbing beads.

'You want me to take care of this myself?' He gestured towards where his erection was evident beneath
the sheet, shameless in his enjoyment of her most mor-
tifying yet moment of recollection as if he had somehow
worked out exactly what was on her mind.

No, she wanted to flatten him to the bed, kiss her
way down the roped muscles of his stomach *and*... With
a stifled sound of distress, Saffy leapt off the bed as
though she had been bitten and fled from the room to
the bathroom. He had *kidnapped* her, deprived her of
her freedom and she had been lying there in that bed
tempted to reach for him, touch him, caress him with
her mouth, watch him reach a climax with pride and
satisfaction, the only satisfaction she had ever known in

the bedroom, an entirely one-sided stunted thing born of her inability to engage in intercourse.

He was cruel; no, he was gorgeous. She couldn't make her mind up to the extent that in the grip of that struggle she felt semi-insane and, refusing to think, she took care of her more pressing needs instead. A knock sounded on the door when she had finished brushing her teeth with the brand new battery-powered tooth-brush set out for her use. After a moment's hesitation, she yanked the door open. Sheathed in jeans and noth-ing else, Zahir handed her a pile of clothing.

'I was joking.'

'No, you weren't,' Saffy snapped.

Zahir lifted and dropped his lean brown hands and sudden amusement slashed his full sensual mouth. 'Well, I wouldn't have said no…first and foremost, I'm a man and I have some very hot memories of you.'

'H-hot?' Saffy stammered helplessly, taken aback by the word, certain he must have misused it.

Zahir stared at her, taking in the tousled golden hair hanging like a veil round her slim shoulders, the brighter than bright blue eyes, and acknowledged that the em-barrassment her entire stance telegraphed was not at all what he had expected from her. She wasn't an innocent any more, so why was she blushing?

'In that department you were very hot.'

Cold tainted her at the meaning of that sentence, the reminder that there had been others intimate with him since their divorce. 'Now that you can make com-parisons?'

'Don't take that angle—it's offensive,' Zahir ground out with sudden force. 'If I'd known what I was doing in our bed, we wouldn't have had problems!'

Consternation slivered through her taut length. 'Is that what you thought? That it was somehow *your* fault? You are so wrong, Zahir. There was nothing you could have done to make things any different between us,' she declared with fierce conviction, her innate sense of fairness making her speak up. 'I needed professional help.'

Saffy couldn't believe she was telling him her even a little piece of her biggest secret, but then he had been the only other person who had experienced her problems with her. It shook her that he had blamed his inexperience for *her* failure in the bedroom, but then how could he possibly have guessed what was really wrong with her? Was that why he had come up with the insane idea of kidnapping her? Was that why he still supposedly wanted her? Was that ferocious pride of his still set on rewriting the past and retrieving his masculine pride?

Zahir frowned, his surprise palpable. 'Professional help?'

'Never mind. Like you last night and your back… not something I choose to discuss,' Saffy fielded, because she was extremely reluctant to share her secrets, and indeed was already wondering if he might consider her in some way 'soiled' if he knew the truth. And just at that moment, quite ridiculously in the circumstances, she really *did* value the fact that, in spite of everything, Zahir was *still* attracted to her. It made her feel better about the past, and when she collided afresh with his mesmerising dark golden eyes she was beset by a stark sense of regret and loss. After all, when she stripped all the complications away one fact stood clear: he wanted her and she was still fiercely attracted to him, the guy she had fallen for as a teenager. Did that make her sad and pathetic? Was it the pull of first love that still made her want to reach out to him? Or simply that all-important element of sexual desire that she had not so far managed to find with another man?

And did it really matter? she asked herself, for at last the opportunity to move into the adult world and be a normal woman was being offered to her with no strings attached. If she had sex with Zahir, nobody would ever know about it and she would never see him again... Wasn't this finally the chance for her to achieve the intimacy that she had always longed to experience? Sex was a physical thing, she bargained with herself, and it didn't have to mean anything, didn't have to take place within a defined relationship. Her sister, Kat, was a bit of a prude and had raised her to have a very different outlook...but Saffy had done the serious thing, the marriage thing and the love thing and had ended up broken to pieces inside herself, enduring a pain and insecurity that she had still not managed to overcome. Simple sex would be enough for her, she reasoned in desperation, suppressing her uneasy feelings while telling herself that she was surely old enough and mature enough to follow her own instincts.

'Go back to bed,' Saffy murmured tautly, the momentous decision already made and it was a choice that she felt she could live with. 'I'll join you in a few minutes...'

Zahir's cloaking black lashes lifted on frowning dark eyes of incomprehension. 'What are you saying?'

Saffy shrugged a slender shoulder, putting on a face because her pride was too great to allow him to suspect how insecure and inexperienced she actually was. 'It's only sex, not something worth making a fuss about...'

Taken aback by that blunt statement, Zahir breathed in deep. 'Passion is always worth pursuing.'

'Not in my world,' Saffy countered doggedly, thinking of the many casual affairs she had seen begin and end among her friends, and she doubted that true passion-ripping-your-clothes-off passion—had driven many of them. Loneliness and lust would be a more honest description of their motivation.

Zahir stepped forward, lean brown hands reaching up to curve to her cheekbones and centre her gaze on him. 'If that's true, I find it sad. I want to give you passion.'

'No, you don't,' she whispered. 'You said it yourself. I'm the one who got away and you can't live with that.'

'It's not that simple,' Zahir growled, protest etched in every hard, angular line of his powerful bone structure while he clashed with her beautiful blue eyes, knowing that no other eyes had ever been so very deep a blue that they reminded him of the sky on a hot summer day.

'Don't make it complicated,' she urged, her breath hitching as he angled down his tousled dark head and her lips tingled like a silent invitation.

'It was always complicated with us,' Zahir argued, stubborn to the last.

And Saffy rose up on her toes and angled her lips up to his, eager to stop him talking and treading all over her memories with hob-nailed boots in that obstinate, all-male, infuriating way of his. He kissed her and her heart seemed to jolt to a sudden halt inside her chest. He stole her breath with a kiss of such unashamed passion that she felt light-headed and her legs went weak.

He carried her back to bed, yes, *carried,* her bemused mind savoured, for very few men were physically big enough or strong enough to lift five-foot-ten-inch Saffy off her feet as if she were of tiny and delicate proportions. He captured her mouth again with intoxicating urgency, his tongue delving deep between her lips, and her body sang. Even while doubts and fears about how she would react to what came next were circulating madly in the back of her head, she could feel the supersensitive awareness of desire infiltrating her, sending prickling spasms of warmth across her breasts and a kick of heat down into her pelvis.

'I assumed I would have to seduce you,' Zahir admitted, staring down at her with those amazing eyes and the kind of honesty she had once loved him for.

'It's no big deal,' Saffy countered a tad shakily, wondering if he would assume that she was a slut, always up for the possibility of a little fling with an attractive man when she was on her travels. But what did it matter what *he* thought? she demanded angrily of herself, because what she was planning to do was entirely for her own benefit and nothing whatsoever to do with him. That he would also be getting what he apparently wanted was only an accidental by-product of her decision. She was the one in control, *full* control. This was sex, nothing to do with the softer emotions, because she simply refused to let him screw up her emotions again.

Taken aback by that statement, Zahir frowned again, ebony brows drawing together.

'Call a spade a spade, Zahir!' Saffy snapped, out of all patience. 'Isn't this why you brought me here?'

'You've changed,' he condemned.

'Of course I have…I grew up, realised fairies and unicorns didn't exist, got divorced,' Saffy recited tightly.

And then he kissed her again, his mouth crashing down on hers with angry fervour and, even though she recognised the anger, she was exhilarated by his passion. He tugged her up into a sitting position and before she even knew what he was about he had swept the kaftan off over her head, leaving her naked but for the cloaking veil of her long blonde hair.

'You're still the most beautiful woman I've ever known,' Zahir declared.

And she still wasn't comfortable being naked around him, Saffy registered in dismay, fearful that the embarrassment enveloping her was only a small taster of the discomfiture she had felt in the past with her own body. Casual nudity was the norm behind the scenes at catwalk shows where fast changes of clothing were a necessity and that didn't bother her, but being naked in front of Zahir bothered her on a much more visceral level.

As he studied her a veil of hot red colour blossomed on her skin in a flush that ran from her breasts to her brow.

Long brown fingers lifted to the rounded perfection of pale breasts topped with distended pink nipples and he stroked the tightly beaded tips before he pushed her gently back against the pillows and bent his tousled dark head to put his sensual mouth there instead, suckling at the straining peaks until she gasped for breathe, shaken by even what she recognised to be a relatively minor intimacy. Even so, it was an intimacy that sent arrows of fire hurtling to her womb and her thighs trembled at the thought of what was yet to come. Let it be all right this time, she pleaded inside her head, snapping her eyes shut, seeking to blank out her thoughts lest the old panic take hold of her again.

Zahir couldn't quite believe that this was Sapphire, lying there, admittedly passive but not freaking out. It felt just a little like all his fantasies rolling up in one go and that disturbed him. He didn't know what he had expected and could only recognise how much she had changed while wondering with dark, forbidding fury which of her men had succeeded where he had so comprehensively failed. That mystery burned through his bloodstream like acid and he had to fight it, suppress it and exert iron control not to ask questions and demand answers. On the other hand, what if she was acting like a human sacrifice because that was how she felt?

He tasted her lush mouth with driving hunger, tried and failed to squash that inner question and lifted his head again. 'If you don't want this, tell me,' he told her.

Consternation filled Saffy to overflowing as she registered that evidently she wasn't putting on a very good impression of being a relaxed and experienced lover. She sat up with a start, her pale hands fixing to his smooth bronzed shoulders, blue eyes wide. 'I want this...I want you.'

'Then touch me,' he growled low in his throat, his hunger unconcealed in his star-bright gaze.

And on the edge of fright and uncertainty, she did, smoothing her hands over his warm golden skin, feeling the rope of muscles beneath his hard, flat stomach and his sudden driving tension as she found him with her fingers. Hard and silky and so velvety smooth and large. She gulped at the very thought of what he was going to do with it...*if* she managed—and she *had* to manage, had to be normal for the sake of her own sanity and his.

Zahir groaned with unashamed sensuality, lying back against the pillows, his black hair in stark contrast to the pale linen, eyes half closed and screened by his outrageous black lashes. 'Not too much,' he warned her unevenly. 'I'm too aroused.'

So, she stayed with the touching, her hand trembling slightly while she felt her body progressively warm in a great surging wash of desire. She needed him to touch her, needed that so badly that it hurt yet she was terrified that she might lose her nerve, her control. He hooked a long thigh over hers, nudging her legs apart, and she stopped breathing as if she were a candle being snuffed out, for this was the acid test, the one she couldn't really call and couldn't afford to fail. Long brown fin-

gers smoothed down her thigh as if he knew on some
level that, even hungry as she was, she was scared as
no adult woman should be scared. After all, it wasn't
as though he had ever physically hurt her. She regu-
lated her breathing, cleared her head of such dangerous
thoughts, for thinking that way was surely like inviting
her phobia back in. He skated through the crisp golden
curls on her mound and she bit her tongue so badly she
tasted blood in her mouth and she was trembling, all
hyped up with expectation, wanting and not wanting in
that moment to test her boundaries. *New* boundaries,
she reminded herself resolutely.

He kissed her again and she squirmed against him,
insanely conscious of that exploring hand touching
where she had never been touched in adult memory,
rubbing over that wildly sensitive little button that she
hadn't even known existed for more years than she cared
to recall. Sensation sparked through her, startling in its
very intensity, sending another cloud of heat through
her quivering length. Before she even guessed what he
was about to do, he eased a finger into her and she didn't
go off into a panic attack, didn't jackknife back from
him as though he had assaulted her. It felt strange to be
touched like that, by someone else rather than by herself, but it didn't hurt and it didn't make her feel sick
or frightened, and hope rose in a heady gush inside her
that she was going to be all right, after all, and the scene
was not set for another disaster.

With so much frantic reflection taking place inside
her head, it took a minute at least for Saffy to register

that she *liked* what he was doing, the sweet rise of sensation fanning through her lower body as his mouth toyed with an achingly sensitive nipple and his fingers delved into the tender wetness of her body. She hadn't expected to like it, she acknowledged, had simply regarded it as something she had to get through, the mountain of her virginal state at nearly twenty-four years of age a complex challenge that had to be conquered solely for her own benefit.

'I want you so much but you're very tight, *aziz*.' Zahir groaned, snaking down her body, and she didn't know what he was doing and almost yelped in dismay when he put his carnal mouth between her parted thighs instead, caressing the sensitive pink folds of her femininity.

Saffy lay there like a stone dropped to the bottom of a very deep well, so far out of her depth she felt lost, indeed shattered by the gathering waves of increasingly powerful sensation that he was wringing from her untried body. The wave gathered her up and kept on pushing her higher until she was pulsing and throbbing and aching with an excitement that she had never known existed. Her hips were rising, her back was arching and then suddenly, with very little warning, the instant she had most feared was there: his bold shaft was nudging against her for penetration and she tensed, struggling not to freeze, but every skin cell in her body was gripped by nerves that her body might bottle out and let her down at the worst and most unforgivable moment.

And then she experienced the delicious friction of his entry eased by the slick dampness of her arousal.

He was pushing, stretching her inner sheath with the hard, demanding pressure of his entrance and she was briefly amazed at what he felt like inside her. Instinctively she lifted her pelvis and he plunged forward and then it was done, a sharp stinging pain flashing through her so that her eyes widened and she gritted her teeth together, contriving to rein back a cry of pain. She pushed her face up into his shoulder to further conceal her reaction. He had no entitlement to the privilege of learning that, against all odds, he had become her first lover, and there was not much she would not have withstood to keep him from that knowledge. On that ungenerous thought a spasm of intense pleasure took her quite by surprise as her inner muscles tightened their grip on his intrusion.

With a low growl of satisfaction that vibrated his chest against her soft breasts, he began to move, pulling out, pushing back in. The strange seductive sensations built and she gasped, feeling her control sliding against the onslaught of a wild excitement she hadn't anticipated. Excitement roared through her, her heart hammering while she panted for breath. He lifted her legs over his shoulders, rising up over her like a conquering god, his lean darkly handsome face flushed and taut with driving desire and uninhibited satisfaction while he drove into her hard and fast with a pagan rhythm that put her every sense on overload.

Nothing had ever felt so good or so necessary to her. Had he stopped she would have screamed. He touched the tiny button below her mound again, rubbing fast, and the golden light already expanding inside her burst through into brilliance and exploded in a series of violent aftershocks throughout her body. The waves of hot, sweet pleasure racked her with compulsive shivers of disbelief and a certain amount of awe, for she had never dreamt that he might make her feel so much. He shuddered over her with a moan of intense masculine satisfaction and then fell still, letting her legs fall back down on the bed and rolling off her to pull her close.

'That was absolutely amazing,' Zahir breathed, his diction ragged, his accent pronounced, his chest still heaving against her as he pulled her close, their bodies damp with perspiration and sliding against each other.

But Saffy's sense of perfect peace lasted for only a few seconds. What struck her as *most* amazing at that moment was how much other women must have taught him, how much practice he must have had in other beds to have gained the sexual expertise he had just demonstrated. That fast she wanted to thump him hard and kick him out of bed and her hands knotted into fists of restraint below the sheet. Careful, she told herself in fierce and bemused rebuke, for she didn't recognise the feelings bombarding her. He was her ex-husband, not her lover, and she wasn't jealous or possessive where he was concerned. He meant absolutely nothing to her and she didn't understand why he was still holding her and pressing a kiss to her delicate jaw bone as though they had shared something special. After all, she had just used him to have sex for the first time and he had been good…well, *amazing,* to borrow his word. But that was an acknowledgement that only made her fists knot tighter and her temper flare even higher, for nothing could have been more different from the tentative and inexperienced young husband she remembered than the uninhibited demonstration of raunchy sex he had just treated her to.

Without hesitation, indeed reacting on pure gut instinct, Saffy pulled free of Zahir and slid off the bed in one strong movement, a mane of rumpled golden hair falling round her pale slender length like a veil. 'Do I qualify for a car to the airport now?' she asked thinly, blue eyes cold as the polar wastes.

Raking long brown fingers through his black hair, Zahir sat up in the tangled sheets, the white linen providing a striking foil for his golden skin. He tensed and swore and, assuming his reaction was the result of her sudden exit from the intimacy of the bed, she flicked him a bitter glance. Yes, he was still unquestionably gorgeous, but she hated him, totally hated him, wanted to be gone now as fast as possible, escaping the scene of the crime. No doubt he thought *he* had used her but it was the other way round and she would have liked the freedom to tell him that, but was still not prepared to spill her deepest secrets to him.

'I want you to stay until tomorrow,' Zahir admitted in a low-pitched tone evocative of anticipation.

Her blue eyes flashed. 'No. I'm done here. I want to go home right now.'

Zahir, gloriously unaccustomed to being in receipt of a negative female response since his divorce, stared back at her with faint but perceptible hauteur while he wondered what had gone wrong. 'I don't do one-nighters.'

Her lovely face without expression, Saffy dealt him an impatient glance, eyes as unemotional as stones. 'I do and, as I said, I'm done.'

Determined not to meet his gaze, Saffy focused on the neat pile of freshly laundered clothes sitting on a chair and wondered when they had arrived, where they had contrived to get washed and ironed and when they had been returned, for all of those inconsequential thoughts were safer than thinking about the insane passion she had just shared with Zahir. She scooped her clothes up and headed at a brisk pace for the bathroom.

Zahir leapt out of bed and reached the door a step ahead of her, one brown hand bracing on the door to keep it shut. 'There's something I should tell you first.'

Refusing to look directly at him, Saffy grimaced. 'What?' she asked impatiently.

'The condom I used broke…I suspect I was too passionate. I assume that you're on the contraceptive pill and that there's no risk of conception?' he pressed with the evident belief that that was the natural order for a woman like her.

For a split second her eyes narrowed and she paled as she assimilated that shocking information, suddenly grasping what had most probably provoked his curse mere minutes earlier, and although a chill of dismay gripped her she nodded immediate agreement. 'Of course,' she lied, wanting him to believe that she was already taking that precaution against pregnancy because she slept with other men, for that belief best conserved her pride. And she also knew how much that belief would annoy him...for he was possessive to his backbone. At least, he *had* been when she knew him, she qualified grimly, but who could say what drove him now? Five years' separation, a lot of other women and possession of a throne had changed him: of course, they had. It would be very naïve of her to think otherwise.

'I'll organise transport,' Zahir breathed grittily. 'And see that the film shot of the commercial is also delivered to you before you depart.'

'Is that my reward?' Saffy enquired drily, concealing her relief that he was willing to hand over the film, well aware that the film crew and her clients would be going mad over its confiscation.

His handsome features clenched. 'If you choose to see it that way—'

'Oh, I do,' Saffy asserted, watching gold glimmer like a flame in his dark as midnight eyes and loving the burn of it, knowing she had annoyed him as he threw open the door for her to leave the bedroom section of the tent. 'And while I remember it, I would advise you to look more closely into the disappearance of that five million pounds you mentioned—because I'm telling you now, I didn't receive a penny of it!'

Zahir inclined his arrogant dark head in grudging acknowledgement. 'I will have the matter investigated,' he conceded, coldly formal in tone.

Was he offended that she hadn't appeared to want a repeat of their intimacy? Saffy stepped into the shower and washed her skin clean of the scent of him. She felt sore, every movement of her lower limbs reminding her of his passionate possession. It was done. She was no longer a virgin. She had surmounted her fears. She was *finally* a normal young woman and now in a condition to consider a relationship as a potential part of her future. That was good, she told herself firmly. She forced her stiff facial muscles into a determined smile and had just wrapped a towel round her dripping body when a knock sounded on the door and heralded Zahir's reappearance, his lean bronzed body still clad only in boxer shorts.

'Yes?' Saffy prompted tightly, not having wanted to see him again because seeing him hurt, made her think of the other women he had been with and, even though it wasn't fair or even rational when she had been unable to consummate their marriage while they were together and they were now divorced, she hated him for having found pleasure and satisfaction when she could not.

'I must have hurt you…there's spots of blood on the sheet,' Zahir informed her grimly. 'Why didn't you tell me?'

Hot colour flew into her cheeks like a banner of scarlet. It had not occurred to her that there might be any detectable physical proof of her innocence and she was mortified by his discovery. 'You didn't hurt me…er, it's been a while for me, so perhaps that explains it,' she muttered awkwardly through clenched teeth of discomfiture.

'Why has it been a while for you?' Zahir demanded bluntly. 'You live with a man.'

Somehow he contrived to voice that statement in a manner and tone that implied she regularly sold her body on street corners. 'That's my business,' Saffy responded flatly, her eyes veiled.

'You should see a doctor,' Zahir informed her curtly. 'I can contact someone—'

'No, thanks.' Her cup of humiliation now truly running over and threatening to drown her, Saffy moved towards him and opened the door for his exit. 'Excuse me, I'd like to get dressed.'

'Sapphire...' Frustration stamped on his lean dark features, Zahir glowered down at her, smouldering golden eyes alight. 'Why are you behaving like this? Is this a habit of yours? Do you often indulge in casual sex?'

She refused to look at him and her lush mouth compressed so hard that her lips turned bloodless. 'That would be kissing and telling, which I definitely *don't* do.'

CHAPTER FIVE

SAFFY RESTED BACK in her cream leather reclining seat in Zahir's incredibly opulent private jet, but beneath the skin her every muscle was tense and she could not relax.

Even so, Zahir had certainly ensured that she was travelling back to London in style. She frowned at the acknowledgement because she would have preferred to consign every image and conversation of the past twenty-four hours to a mental dustbin sealed with a good strong lid. She had slept with her ex, no big deal, she told herself with rigorous resolve. It was only a major event for her because having sex had been something she had, until relatively recently, been afraid she couldn't ever do. *She* had used *him*. That was how she had to look on what had happened. If he knew that his temper would have gone nuclear because Zahir expected everything on his own terms. In that spirit he had married her and in the same spirit he had decided to divorce her again. Nothing had ever been equitably discussed: he had been happy to make his mind up for both of them.

Five years ago, they had landed in Maraban as a newly married couple and that too had been very much on his terms, with her not having the first clue about the dysfunctional royal family she had joined. His father, King Fareed, had been livid that his younger son had married a foreigner and had initially refused to even meet her. She had met Zahir's older brother, Omar, and his wife, Azel. Omar had died in a car crash a few months after Saffy arrived. As Omar and his wife had been childless, Zahir's importance to his father had mushroomed once he became the heir-in-waiting and Saffy had seen even less of her husband as he was forced to take on the ceremonial roles that had once been his brother's.

Staying in the royal palace just outside the city limits, Saffy had been sentenced to a very boring and hidden existence. As her father-in-law refused to accept her as part of the family and was determined to keep the presence of a Western blonde in the palace a secret, she had not been allowed to go out and about in Maraban and explore freely. Indeed aside of a few stolen shopping expeditions in the company of her widowed sister-in-law, Azel, Saffy had barely gone out at all. Zahir had declared that *eventually* his father would accept her as his wife but that she would have to be patient. But twelve months living like the invisible woman had convinced Saffy that her marriage had been a major mistake, particularly when things between her and Zahir had gone badly awry as well.

'You're very unhappy here,' Zahir had acknowledged the very last time she saw him during their marriage.

'You've been telling me that you wanted a divorce for the past six months and now I must agree.'

'Just like that you *suddenly* agree?' Saffy had yelled at him incredulously, shock at his change of heart winging through her in sickening waves as she realised he had clearly had enough of her and their marriage. 'But you swore that you still loved me, that we could work it out...'

'But now I want you to go home to London as soon as it can be arranged. I want to divorce you and set you free,' Zahir had countered as stonily as though she had not spoken.

It was true that for weeks whenever they argued she had hurled the threat of a divorce at him on a fairly frequent basis. But she had never really *meant* it, had simply been dramatising herself and struggling to make her young husband take her unhappiness seriously. But she had somehow still expected Zahir to continue to refuse to even consider divorce as the answer to their problems. Coming at her out of the blue like that, his volte-face had shocked her and pleading in the face of his clear determination to get rid of her had been more than she could bear. For so long, regardless of their difficulties, she had clung to her conviction that Zahir still loved her no matter what and that what they had together was still worth fighting for. Deprived of that consolation and cruelly rejected by the divorce that swiftly followed, Saffy had been heartbroken and not surprisingly had felt abandoned.

Her older sister, Kat, who had raised her from the

age of twelve, had tried to comfort Saffy, pointing out that King Fareed's opposition to their marriage must finally have worn Zahir down while reminding Saffy that neither she nor Zahir had foreseen the very real difficulties that would arise in Saffy's struggle to adapt to life in a different country, far from family and friends. Saffy didn't want to remember how appallingly she had missed Zahir after she left Maraban or how many months had passed before she could enjoy the freedom she had reclaimed and stop thinking about Zahir at least once every minute. She had genuinely loved him and it hurt to appreciate that he had moved on from her so much more easily than she had moved on from him. Maybe he had never really loved her, Saffy conceded painfully. Maybe it had *always* been about the sex and only the sex. Certainly, given his behaviour in shipping her out to the desert for seduction, that looked like the most viable explanation. It was equally agonising to admit that had she been capable of doing what she had just done with him five years earlier they might still have been together. Or *would* they have been? Was that just fantasy land? Perhaps all along she had only been a fling in the form of a wife for Zahir.

But didn't she have rather more pressing concerns in the present? What about that contraceptive accident they had had? Saffy tensed, her appetite evaporating in front of the beautiful lunch she had been served as her skin chilled with complete fright at the idea of being faced with an unplanned pregnancy. Once she had believed she would never have children because she wasn't able

to have sex or even handle the concept of artificial in-
semination. Now she knew differently and knew her future had opened up another avenue once barred to her.
So, if she did fall pregnant, what would she do about it?
She had friends who would rush to request the morning-
after pill after such a mishap to ensure that no conception took place, but if against all the odds new life did
begin inside her, Saffy registered that she was totally
unwilling to consider a termination. In that moment she
was suddenly realising with a heart that felt full enough
to burst that a baby would mean the sun, the moon and
the stars to her and that there was nothing she would
cherish more. It might be a disaster as far as her current
clients were concerned, but it would only be a short-
term one and surely her earning power wouldn't die
overnight. She breathed in deep and slow, both terrified
and enervated by the risk she was prepared to take with
her own body. If conception happened, she decided, it
would happen and she would embrace it without regret.

Having dropped off the film of the shoot with the exceedingly relieved production company, Saffy caught
the tube back to the two-bedroom apartment she had
bought with Cameron. Cameron, a keen cook, was in
the kitchen dicing vegetables, but it was the sight of the
small brunette perched on the counter chatting nineteen
to the dozen to him that startled Saffy.

'Saffy!' Topsy cried, velvety somber eyes full of
warmth as she leapt off the counter like a miniature
whirlwind and threw herself exuberantly into her much
taller sister's arms. At slightly less than four feet eleven

inches tall, Topsy was tiny. 'I wish you hadn't been away this week. I wanted to go out with you to celebrate the end of my exams!'

Saffy's eyes stung as she gratefully accepted her youngest sister's affectionate hug. Topsy always wore her feelings on her sleeve. At eighteen years of age, having just finished school, Topsy was much less damaged by their disturbed childhood and more outgoing than her older sisters. She was also exceptionally clever and overflowing with an irrepressible joie de vivre that few could resist. Yet as Saffy studied the younger woman she saw shadows below her eyes and a tension far removed from Topsy's usual laid-back vibe and she wondered what was wrong.

'How did you find out that I was back so quickly?' Saffy prompted.

'She's been phoning here every day...I texted her after you called me from the airport,' Cameron, a tall attractive man with close-cropped dark curls, told her from his position by the state-of-the-art cooker.

'I assumed you'd want to stay on at Kat's with Emmie,' Saffy remarked.

'No, Kat and Mikhail are hosting a big dinner tonight and I wasn't in the mood to play nice with loads of strangers,' Topsy confided with a slightly guilty wince. 'And Emmie has already gone home again.'

Saffy's heart sank at that news because it was obvious to her that once again her twin had chosen to dodge meeting her. Her estranged twin was *still* avoiding her, Saffy acknowledged unhappily, wounded by Emmie's reluctance to even be in her company. Was she that bad? Was she truly so hateful to her twin? Or was it a simple if unpalatable fact that her past sins were beyond forgiveness?

'Emmie's gone back to Birkside?' she checked, referring to Kat's former home in the Lake District, the farmhouse her elder sister had inherited from her late father.

Kat was the daughter of their mother Odette's first marriage, the twins the daughters of her second marital foray while Topsy was the result of their mother's short-lived liaison with a South American polo player. By the time the twins reached twelve years of age they were a handful and Odette had placed all three girls in foster care. Kat, then in her twenties, had made a home at Birkside for all three of her sisters and Odette had had very little to do with her children since then. In every way that mattered, Kat had become the loving, caring mother her sisters had never really had.

'*Should* Emmie be on her own up there?' Saffy questioned the younger woman anxiously. 'I mean, it's a lonely house and now that she's pregnant…?'

Topsy rolled her eyes. 'Emmie always does her own thing and she has friends up there and a job,' she pointed out breezily. 'I also think that just at the minute Kat and Mikhail being so lovey-dovey makes them hard for Emmie to be around.'

Even while Saffy adored the fact that Kat had found happiness with a man who so obviously loved her, she too had felt like a gooseberry more than once in the couple's company. If her twin's solo pregnancy was the result of a recent relationship breakdown, Emmie was probably feeling a great deal more sensitive to that loving ambiance.

'Dinner will be ready in ten minutes,' Cameron announced.

'I've got time to get changed, then?'

'Yes. Let's go into your room,' Topsy urged, tugging at Saffy's arm.

A frown indented Saffy's brow at her sister's obvious eagerness to get her alone. 'What's up?' she asked as she closed her bedroom door.

Topsy, all liveliness sliding from her expressive face, sank down on the edge of the bed, hunched her shoulders and muttered, 'I found out something I wasn't prepared for this week and I didn't want to bother Kat with it,' she admitted.

Saffy dropped down on the stool by the dressing table. 'Tell me…'

'You'll probably think it's really silly,' Topsy confided.

'If it's upset you, it's not silly,' Saffy declared staunchly.

Topsy pulled a face. 'I don't know if I am upset. I don't know how I feel about it—'

'How you feel about what?' Saffy prompted patiently.

'A few weeks ago, my dad, Paulo, asked me to agree to a DNA test. I'm eighteen. We didn't need Kat's permission,' Topsy explained as Saffy raised her brows in astonishment at the admission. 'Apparently Dad had always had doubts that I was his child and since he got married he and his wife have had difficulty conceiving—'

'Your dad's got married? Since when? You never told us that!' Saffy exclaimed.

Topsy sighed. 'It didn't seem important. I mean, I've only met him a half-dozen times in my whole life. With him living in Brazil, it's not like we ever had the chance to get close,' she pointed out ruefully. 'Anyway, his new wife and him went for testing when she didn't fall pregnant and it turns out he's sterile.'

Saffy stiffened at the news. 'Hence the DNA testing...'

'And it turns out that I couldn't possibly be his kid,' Topsy confided with a valiant smile. 'So, I went to see Mum—'

Saffy gave her a look of dismay, for Odette was a challenging and devious personality. 'Please tell me you didn't!'

'Well, she was the only possible person I could approach on the score of my parentage,' Topsy pointed out ruefully. 'First of all she tried to argue that in spite of the DNA evidence I *was* Paulo's kid—'

'I doubt if she wanted the subject dug up after this length of time,' Saffy remarked stiffly, cursing their irresponsible and selfish mother and hoping she had dealt kindly with her youngest daughter.

'She definitely didn't,' Topsy admitted with a grimace of remembrance. 'She just said that if Paulo wasn't my father, she didn't know who was. Did she really sleep with that many men that she wouldn't know, Saffy?'

Saffy reddened and veiled her eyes. 'There were periods in her life when she was very promiscuous. I'm sorry, Topsy. That was an upsetting thing for you to find out. How did Paulo react?'

'I think he had already guessed. He didn't seem surprised. Let's face it, I don't look the slightest bit like him. He's over six foot tall and built like a rugby player,' Topsy reminded her companion ruefully. 'Now I'll probably never find out who my father is but why should that matter to me? After all, you and Emmie have a father who lives right here in London but who still takes no interest in you.'

Saffy groaned. 'That's different. Mum and him had a very bitter divorce. She dumped him because he lost all his money. When he built a new life and remarried and had a second family he didn't want anything more to do with us.'

'Does that bother you?'

'No, not at all. You can't miss what you've never had,' Saffy lied, for that was another rejection that still burned below the layer of emotional scar tissue she had formed. When she and her twin had been at their lowest ebb, their father, just like their mother, had turned his back on them and had said he wanted nothing to do with them.

'You're evil...just like your mother. Look what you've done to your sister!' he had told Saffy when she was twelve years old, and even the passage of time hadn't erased her memory of the look of dislike and condemnation in his gaze.

'Sorry to land you with all this,' her kid sister muttered guiltily.

Beyond the door Cameron called them for dinner and Saffy seized the chance to give her kid sister a comforting hug, wishing she had some clever reassurance to offer Topsy on the topic of absent father figures. Unfortunately, not having normal caring parents left a hole inside you and even Kat's praiseworthy efforts to fill that hole for her sisters had not proved entirely successful. Saffy had simply learned that when bad things happened you had to soldier on, hide your pain and deal with the consequences in private.

Only when Topsy had returned to Kat and Mikhail's home for the night with her spirits much improved did Cameron turn with a concerned look in his shrewd eyes to ask Saffy suspiciously, 'What—or should I say *who*—kept you unavoidably detained in Maraban?'

Saffy visibly lost colour. 'It's not something I want to talk about right now.'

'You know that's not a healthy attitude,' Cameron, who was a firm believer in therapy, warned her.

'Talking about anything personal will never come easily to me,' Saffy admitted tightly. 'I spent too many years locking everything up inside me.'

She was extraordinarily tired and she went to bed and lay there with her eyes wide open in the darkness, struggling to suppress the images of Zahir stuck inside her head. Fighting thoughts teemed alongside those unwelcome images. She would get over that little desert rendezvous in Maraban and leave Zahir behind her... in the past where he truly belonged.

* * *

Ten days later, Saffy wakened because while she had slept she had slid over onto her tummy and her breasts were too tender to withstand that pressure. With a wince, she sat up, wondering if it was time to use the pregnancy kit she had bought forty-eight hours earlier, but she was still strangely reluctant to put her suspicions to the test. Could she have enjoyed intimacy just one time and conceived when her unfortunate sister, Kat, had been trying without success to fall pregnant for many months? It struck her as unlikely and she had only bought the test in a weak moment of dreaming about what it might be like to become a mother.

Such silly dreams, *childish* dreams for a grown woman to be indulging in, she scolded herself impatiently, dreams full of fluffy, fantasy baby images and not a jot of reality. Somewhere deep down inside her a voice was telling her that a baby would be one little piece of Zahir that she could have and cherish, but she was intelligent enough to know that the reality of single parenthood was sleepless nights, cash worries and nobody else to share your worries and responsibilities with. Frustrated by her own rebellious brain, she got up and did her morning exercises, desperate to think of something else. When that didn't work she changed into her sports gear and went out for a run, returning to the apartment drenched in perspiration and on legs wobbly from over-exertion. Stripping, she walked into the shower and washed. She was towelling herself dry when she heard the doorbell buzz. She pulled on her robe and padded across the hall to answer.

She looked through the peephole first and froze, looked again, her heart rate kicking up a storm. *Zahir? Here in London?* Her teeth gritting, she undid the chain and opened the door.

'What do you want?' she demanded sharply.

CHAPTER SIX

'INVITE ME IN,' Zahir commanded.

Saffy was uneasily aware of the two security men standing by the lift, of the status and level of protection Zahir now required as the ruler of Maraban, and the very idea that he was now at risk of becoming a target for attack gave her stomach a sick jolt. She swallowed hard, mustering her defences such as they were. 'No.'

'Don't be juvenile,' Zahir urged, his handsome mouth tightening, his air of gravity lending a forbidding edge to the smooth planes of his lean dark absolutely gorgeous face. 'We have business to discuss.'

'*Business?*' Saffy parroted, suddenly wishing she hadn't opened the door with wet hair and a face bare of make-up for, deprived of her professional grooming, she felt defenceless.

'I told you that I would investigate the trust fund I set up for you.' Impatience edged his dark deep drawl, energised his stunning dark deep-set eyes with sparks of gold, and as she watched him her mouth ran dry as a bone. 'I have now done so.'

'Oh, the missing money,' she muttered in weak comprehension, and she stepped back with stiff reluctance to open the door, for she didn't want him inside her personal space, didn't want one more memory or association with him to further colour her existence.

'Yes, the money,' Zahir said drily, in a tone that suggested that he could have no other reason to roll up on her doorstep.

She studied him, in a split second memorising sufficient to commemorate his image for life, and she turned away, colour crawling up painfully over her cheekbones as she led the way into the living room. He wore a business suit, a beautifully tailored designer effort that showcased his height and breadth and long powerful legs. He had had his hair cut since she had last seen him, jet black hair feathering back from lean strong features to brush the collar of his shirt, the inevitable stubble shadowing his sculpted mouth and stubborn jaw line because he needed to shave twice a day. She felt like a vulture swooping down greedily on every tiny intimate detail of him and her tummy hollowed with a sense of dread, for she had never felt so vulnerable.

Zahir focused on the fluid sway of her hips encased in colourful silk as she moved ahead of him. He guessed she had just stepped out of the shower and was naked beneath those swirling folds of fabric and he was assailed by a slew of highly erotic images that sent a surge of lust shooting straight to his groin. He gritted his even white teeth and flung his arrogant dark head high. He knew what he was doing; he knew exactly what he was doing *this* time. He might have ditched his sense of honour but he had made a decision he could live with. Nobody was perfect, nobody followed every rule… Imperfection had suddenly become newly acceptable to him.

Saffy turned round and regarded him expectantly, her gaze slanting out of a direct meeting with his shrewd eyes and focusing on his wide sensual mouth instead. Instantly she felt hunger flare like a storm in her pelvis and perspiration beaded her short upper lip as she fought the weakness and tried to crush it out. But her body, it seemed, had discovered a treacherous life all of its own and she was suddenly aware of the heaviness of her tender breasts and the straining, aching peaks.

'That five million you told me about?' she prompted with deliberate tartness of tone, keen for him to take his leave again.

'My London lawyer set up the fund with your solicitor. But five years ago nobody involved was aware that your solicitor was in the early stages of senile dementia and, sadly, he didn't do his job properly,' Zahir explained grimly. 'You were not informed about the fund as you should have been and when your solicitor took early retirement through ill health, his son took over his legal practice. When the son realised that you were ignorant of the money accumulating every month, he committed fraud.'

'*Fraud?*' Saffy parroted, her bright blue eyes widening.

'He's been syphoning off the funds for his own benefit ever since. I have put the matter in the hands of the police,' Zahir informed her grimly. 'I owe you an apology for accusing you of having excessively enriched yourself since our divorce.'

Saffy lifted her chin. 'Yes, you do.'

'In spite of everything, I did intend for you to have that money as security and I am very angry that you did not receive it,' he admitted shortly. 'It is possible that you would never have become a model had you known that you were already financially secure.'

Saffy blinked in surprise at that suggestion. 'I doubt that. Had I known about the fund, I would have refused to accept it. We were married for such a short time that I didn't feel that you owed me anything.'

'You were my wife and my responsibility. I felt differently,' Zahir disagreed with unblemished cool.

'If you'd still had a large financial stake in my future, I wouldn't have felt free to put our marriage behind me,' Saffy admitted with quiet dignity as she began moving back to the door with obvious intent. 'But since I didn't know about the fund, it hardly matters now. I'm just relieved you've managed to sort it out. Now, if that's all you have to say—'

'No, it's not all. I have something else I wish to discuss.'

Saffy froze in her tracks and slowly turned back to him. 'If it's anything to do with the recent past, it's unwelcome and I don't want to hear it.'

Zahir regarded her with glittering dark golden eyes. 'Tough,' he told her. 'I'm here and you'll listen.'

'Look, that kind of attitude may go down well in Maraban but it leaves me cold!'

'But I don't…leave you cold,' he affixed as if she might be in some doubt as to his meaning.

A flush of pink washed from her long slender throat up in a wave of burning mortification, for to have him throw that in her face was an affront of no mean order. 'I'm not listening, Zahir… I'm going to show you out. I want you to leave.'

Instead he stalked towards her like a prowling jungle cat cornering a prey. 'No, you don't. You're being stubborn. You don't like the tables being turned but you put this ball into my court—'

'No, I didn't!' Saffy exclaimed in angry vexation.

'You came to me willingly—'

'I said I wasn't going to talk about this!' Saffy flung back at him furiously.

Zahir sent the door behind her crashing shut with an imperious shove of one strong hand. 'I have a proposition I want you to consider—'

'No…*no.*' Saffy whipped up her hands to press them against her ears in desperate defiance. 'I'm not listening. You've got nothing to say that I could want to hear.'

Zahir grabbed her hands and yanked them down, retaining a firm hold on her wrists. 'I've already bought you an apartment here in London. You'll move out of this one into it and I will visit you there whenever I am free…'

As simple shock winged through Saffy in a tidal wave her hands went limp in his grasp and she stared up at him wide-eyed with astonishment and no small amount of incredulity. 'An apartment? What on earth are you suggesting?'

'That you leave your current lover and become mine,' Zahir spelt out with barely leashed ferocity. 'I don't want you here with him. I don't care what arrangement you have. I will only come to you if you are mine alone!'

Saffy blinked rapidly, processing his words in disbelief. 'You're insane. Five years ago, you divorced me and cast me off like an old shoe you'd outgrown!' she condemned rawly. 'And now you're asking me to be your mistress?'

Brilliant dark eyes narrowed and he freed her hands. 'That's an emotive label and rather outdated.'

'And yet you've got the nerve to suggest such a demeaning relationship might suit me?' Saffy hissed at him furiously.

'Yes, I have the nerve,' Zahir declared in a driven undertone, his accent very thick. 'I want you to the edge of madness but I won't share you with other men.'

'My goodness,' Saffy said in a sharp and brittle voice. 'Was I that good in the tent?'

'Stop it,' Zahir urged harshly, stroking a stern finger across her parted lips, leaving a tingle in the wake of his warning. 'Don't reduce us both to that level with that tongue of yours. There is no sin in us indulging ourselves in pleasure. Who would it harm? We would be discreet. I would spend as much time with you as I can find to spare.'

But Saffy was still stunned by what he was proposing. A mistress? A kept woman in the background of his life, a *dirty* secret? *Her?* He had to be kidding. Her pride and independence would never allow her to accept such a relationship. Of course, how could he know that? At eighteen she had been loving, clingy and needy and that was probably how he still saw her. Back then marriage and a man she loved had been the zenith of her ambitions. But the more she thought of it the insult of what he was prepared to offer her in the present cut very deep indeed and she could not credit that he would believe even for a second that she could agree to be any man's secret mistress!

'It really is time that you go,' Saffy snapped, throwing her head back, damp golden hair rippling back from her taut cheekbones. 'You've said what you wanted to say and my answer is no. No, no, *no!* I like my life just the way it is.'

'Look at me and tell me you don't want me,' Zahir growled.

And she looked and lingered on those lean, darkly handsome features and lost, blue eyes fearlessly clashing with smouldering gold, and then it was as if a knot were unfurling faster and faster inside her, unleashing a disturbing blast of emotions and responses that shook her inside out. But even then in the midst of that gathering storm she knew that no way would she ever sink low enough to become his mistress. Yes, she wanted him, but no, she would never take what he was offering because the price was too high.

Saffy parted her lips. 'I don't want you enough for that...'

Zahir glowered down at her. 'Liar.'

Saffy tossed her head. 'You can't bully me into giving you the answer you want—'

'I don't bully you. I have never bullied you,' Zahir countered wrathfully.

'You've very domineering.'

'You like it,' he told her with a roughened edge to his voice, lush black lashes low over his gaze as he watched the tip of her tongue snake out to moisten her lower lip.

'I like my men civilised,' Saffy shot back scornfully.

'But you still want me,' Zahir framed with hungry intensity.

'As I said…not enough to become your personal, private slut,' she spelt out succinctly, but her breathing pattern was fracturing, her tension so great as he came closer that it was like a tightening band constraining her lungs.

'Prove it,' he said, backing her up against the wall, winding long brown fingers into her golden hair to anchor her in place, and drew her head up.

Saffy trembled, pink flying into her cheeks. 'No kissing, no anything,' she warned him. 'I won't let you do this to me—'

And being Zahir, who had a lot in common with an express train when he was set on a goal, he simply ignored her, bending his head, nuzzling her throat, licking a delicate path along her collarbone with such erotic skill that the pulse there went crazy. Her hands knotted into fists at her side to prevent herself from touching

him even while the lips he had so far ignored tingled
and burned for attention.

'And how dare you offer me *that* option?' Saffy continued heatedly, her rancour on that point unforgotten.

'He who does not dare *loses,*' Zahir traded with assurance, welding his hard, demanding mouth to hers in
an explosion of passion that sent her heart racing and the
blood pumping insanely fast through her veins.

'What the heck are you playing at?' she gasped
strickenly, appalled by the insidious weakness spreading through her lower limbs and the glow of heat and
yearning firing up low in her pelvis.

'I'm not playing,' Zahir said thickly, returning to
plunder her mouth, sliding his tongue in and out between her parted lips and then delving deep in a sensual
assault that made tiny shudders rack her tall, shapely
frame. He pressed her back against the wall and even
through the barrier of the suit she could feel him hard
and urgent and ready. 'I want you. I have wanted you
every day since you left Maraban... I can't sleep for
wanting you!'

And although words were easy to say and often
empty, something still quickened and tightened inside
Saffy's chest when he admitted that she exerted that
much influence over him. Her robe came undone as he
jerked it loose, sliding a hand below it to trail his fingers up her inner thigh. Instantly every sense went on
red alert. In that moment she wanted him to touch her
more than she had ever wanted anything and she went
rigid with anticipation, unable to breathe for longing.

She burned; she *ached*. And then with one stroke of
his clever fingers he found her and an agonised moan
was wrenched from her as he toyed with her tender
flesh, rubbing the tiny bud that controlled her until she
strained against him, whimpering, quivering, helpless
with need while he explored the slick, hot heat between
her legs and she gasped under his marauding mouth.
Time had no meaning for her. Indeed it felt as if the
world had speeded up because she was so frantically
impatient, every skin cell reaching for the climax her
body was so desperate to experience.

Zahir paused and she heard the sound of a zip, the
crackle of foil and she blinked like someone coming out
of the dark into the light, but her hunger didn't abate
even a little when she met stunning coal-black-fringed
golden eyes alight with desire. She trembled, tried to
reason and discovered that she was quite incapable of
logic in the grip of the uncontrollable need clawing at
her like a kind of madness…terrifying and overwhelming, utterly shameless in its single-minded focus.

'I cannot take you to another man's bed,' Zahir
growled, snaking one arm round her waist to lift her
off her feet. 'Wrap your legs round me,' he urged.

And she did, hungry for him to put his mouth back
on hers, unbearably hungry for him to touch her again.
Her arms locked round his neck to steady herself and
he braced her against the wall while he angled his hips
and lowered her until she felt the smooth, hot crown of
his bold shaft pushing against her most tender flesh. Her
eyes widened to their fullest, her head rolling back on

her shoulders as he slowly, strongly pressed his passage up into her tight sheath. Her excitement went into a tail-spin as he stretched her with his fullness, his grunt of all-male satisfaction vibrating sexily in her ear. He angled her back, withdrew from her achingly tender flesh and then brought her down again hard, sending shock-waves of sensation pounding through her lower body.

'You're so tight,' he growled through gritted teeth, repeating the movement until he was fully seated inside her. 'You feel *so* good. I would kill for this!'

'Don't stop!' she cried, shivering as another wild, exhilarating wave of pleasure-pain pulsed through her pelvis, pushing the excitement higher until it was all-consuming and she was battered by both frustration and uncontrollable need.

'I *couldn't*...' Zahir husked, positioning his hips, grinding against her and withdrawing before driving home again hard. Over and over he repeated that movement until she was literally roused to screaming point.

And the first throbbing upsurge of climax splintered through her like a lightning bolt then and she cried out as the successive spasms of intense pleasure rippled through her. He came with a shudder and a shout and slowly, gently, lowered her legs back down to the floor, which was unfortunate because her legs didn't want to hold her up. She tipped forward as he balanced her, hands strong on her slim shoulders, and he kissed her breathless in the interim before lifting his tousled dark head and saying with typical practicality, 'Where's the bathroom?'

She told him and had to stagger back against the wall to stay upright. She was feeling horribly dizzy. Shock was tearing through her every bit as powerfully as the orgasm had. He had had her against the wall and it had been hideously, horribly thrilling but she didn't want to accept that she had not only let that happen but urged him on to commit that sin. Her knees wanted to give way but she wouldn't let them. With shaking hands, she tied the sash on her robe and covered herself up. A little late, a snide voice remarked in her brain and she squashed it. Her body was still pulsing from his possession and she was weak as water, drained by disbelief at what she had allowed to take place between them.

'Are you OK?' Zahir asked huskily from the doorway.

Saffy shot him a look from below her tumbled hair that would have slaughtered a weaker man where he stood. 'Not really,' she answered truthfully.

'You're very pale—perhaps you should sit down.'

Saffy dropped down onto the nearest sofa, lowered her head and breathed in slow and deep while she fought to reclaim her composure. Her head was swimming, her skin damp with perspiration and she felt slightly sick.

'When would you like to move out?' Zahir enquired smoothly. 'Give me a date and I will have all the arrangements made for you. There will be no hassle, no inconvenience—'

'*Move out?*' Saffy questioned blankly. 'I'm not moving anywhere!'

'You can't continue to live here with McDonald.'

With unsteady hands Saffy caught up her trailing hair and shoved it back from her clammy face as she clumsily sat up. 'What just happened was a bad idea. A *really* bad idea and letting you keep me in an apartment somewhere as a mistress is never going to happen, Zahir. Just accept that.'

'I will not accept it.'

Saffy sprang up on a surge of temper and just as suddenly the room seemed to spin violently around her. Disorientated, she swayed sickly, so dizzy she couldn't focus and she couldn't combat the rising tide of darkness that engulfed her as she fainted.

With a sharp imprecation, Zahir snatched her limp body up from the wooden floor and he settled her down on the sofa. Saffy recovered consciousness quickly and blinked in confusion to find him on his knees beside her. 'What happened?'

'You just dropped where you stood,' Zahir breathed tautly. 'Did I hurt you? Are you ill?'

Her lashes fluttered in bemusement as she dimly registered the sound of the front door slamming. 'No,' she whispered weakly. 'But I think the real problem may be that I'm pregnant...'

'*Pregnant?*' Zahir exclaimed, his strong bone structure pulling taut below his olive skin. 'When did you get pregnant?'

'Oh, dear,' a familiar voice interposed from the door, which Zahir had left ajar. 'Is this one of those moments when I walk out and come back in making more noise so that you know that I'm here?'

'Cameron?' Saffy craned her neck and began to sit up as her flatmate stared at her anxiously from across the room. Her brain felt as lively as sludge. She had not meant to blurt out her suspicion that she might be pregnant; she had simply spoken her thoughts out loud and now felt exceedingly foolish. 'I fainted. I've never done that in my life before.'

'There's a first time for everything,' Cameron said soothingly.

'Pregnant,' Zahir said again as though he could not get past that single word, and he studied Cameron grimly. '*Your* child?'

'No, you can leave me out of this little chat. I bat for the other team,' Cameron confided with a wry smile. 'You need to make an urgent appointment with the doctor, Saffy.'

Zahir's brow indented. 'What do you mean?' he queried.

'I'm her gay best friend and you can only be Zahir,' Cameron responded ruefully. 'The guards at the front door and the limo flying the little flag parked outside are a dead giveaway.'

'You're gay?' Zahir murmured wrathfully, and he fixed brilliant dark golden eyes accusingly on Saffy. 'Why didn't you tell me that?'

'It was none of your business.'

'And the baby?' Zahir prompted tautly.

'Excuse me,' Cameron said quietly, and he walked back out of the room, carefully closing the door in his wake.

Sitting up then because she no longer felt light-headed, Saffy swung her feet down onto the floor and swivelled round to face Zahir. 'Look, I don't even know yet if I am pregnant,' she admitted heavily. 'I have a test but I haven't used it yet. My suspicions may just be my imagination.'

His face granite hard, Zahir studied her intently like a male struggling to concentrate on only one thing at a time. 'If he's gay, why do you live with him?'

'Because he's my friend and we both were keen to buy an apartment at the same time. We get on very well,' Saffy told him wryly, wishing she had bitten her tongue out of her head before letting drop the fact that she suspected that she might be pregnant, for such a threat—and she had no doubt that he would see it as a threat—would only create more stormy waves in her dealings with Zahir.

'If McDonald's gay, why do people believe you and he are a couple?' Zahir persisted.

Saffy sighed. 'Cameron was raised by elderly grand-parents and he's very attached to them. He doesn't think they could accept his sexuality and he says he won't come out of the closet until they're gone.'

'So, in the meantime he uses you for cover.'

'We use each other,' Saffy parried without hesitation. 'I get bothered less by aggressive men as long as Cameron appears to be part of my life. Now can we please leave my friend out of this discussion?'

Zahir gritted his even white teeth together. 'Pregnant,' he repeated afresh.

'Maybe, maybe not,' Saffy muttered wearily. 'Look, I'll go and do the wretched test now and we'll see if there's anything to worry about.'

'If it is true, how will we know whether or not it is mine?' Zahir demanded icily.

'Don't make me slap you, Zahir. I haven't the energy right now,' Saffy sighed unhappily, moving past him.

Long brown fingers snapped round her wrist to hold her still. 'Do you have any idea how major an event this could be for a man in my position?' he raked down at her.

'No and, right now, I don't want to think about it. I only want to find out if there is anything for us to worry about. You shouldn't have come here, Zahir. You should have kept your distance. What happened between us in Maraban ended there. You're screwing up my life,' Saffy condemned, dragging her arm angrily free.

'It won't be at an end if you're carrying my child.'

Without another word, Saffy trudged through the hall to the bathroom, retrieved the test kit from the cupboard and pulled out the instructions. Minutes later she stood at the window holding the wand, waiting to see the result. She still felt shell-shocked by the explosive passion that had erupted between them, had never dreamt that she could lose control of her own body to such an extent, had not even suspected that the desire for sex might so badly betray her principles. Of course it had not occurred to her either that she would see him again, that he would deliberately seek her out in London or tell her that he couldn't sleep for *wanting* her. At least she wasn't the only one of them tossing and turning sleepless in the dark of the night, she thought wretchedly. But without the smallest warning, everything had changed. She had believed she could shrug off their encounter in Maraban; she had tried to tell herself that she had used him. In short, she reflected painfully, she had told herself a whole lot of face-saving rubbish in an effort to persuade herself that she was fully in control of events and now reality was banging very loudly at her door.

Almost absent-mindedly she looked down at the wand in her hand and her entire body froze. She gulped in a breath, checked her watch, gazed down transfixed at the line that had formed just as the instructions had explained. Her legs suddenly felt so woolly she had to perch on the side of the bath. *Be careful of what you wish for*...for according to the test result, she was pregnant. For a split second a rush of joy consumed her and then she recalled Zahir's hard, forbidding expression and she groaned out loud, for nothing but complications lay ahead. Zahir and an accidental pregnancy would be a very dangerous combination: Zahir liked to plan everything; Zahir had to be in control; Zahir had been raised in a culture in which such a development was totally unacceptable, socially, morally and every other way there was.

Why, oh, why had she opened her silly mouth and told him? Regret touched her deep. Now whether she liked it or not he was involved and it would have been much better for both of them if he was not. She didn't want him involved. Even less did she want him to be hostile to her condition. She might never before have allowed herself to dream of having a baby, but she would never, ever have chosen to have a child by a man who couldn't possibly want either of them.

Saffy walked back into the living room where Zahir was drinking coffee—Cameron evidently having played host in her absence—and staring moodily out of the window. He didn't like cities: he felt claustrophobic in them. Why did she still remember that? Hearing her entrance, he swung round, stunning dark golden eyes shooting straight to her pale, tight features.

And he knew, that fast he knew, read the defensiveness there and the reluctance to get any closer to him. Why? Was she afraid of him now? Did she think that in some way he meant her harm? Her golden hair had dried into loose, undisciplined waves round her lovely oval face and her eyes were incredibly blue against her pallor. Even with strain etched in every line of her visage she was hauntingly beautiful.

'We do have something to worry about,' she confirmed.

Zahir released his breath in a slow hiss, not a muscle moving on his lean bronzed face. 'I thought you were taking the contraceptive pill.'

'You assumed I was. I saw no reason to tell you otherwise because I didn't think this situation would arise,' Saffy admitted doggedly, determined to be honest now because matters had become too serious for her to risk even half-truths.

'Why were you not taking precautions to protect yourself against this development?' he demanded.

'I had no reason to. I wasn't having sex with anyone, so you don't need to wonder whose child it is,' she told him tightly, colour mantling her cheekbones.

'Naturally I will wonder. I have no wish to offend you but I was certainly under the impression that you had other lovers,' Zahir countered flatly.

'Don't believe all that you read in the papers,' Saffy advised, lifting her head high, her blue eyes guarded.

'I don't but, even allowing for a fair amount of exaggeration and invented stories, there is room for me to doubt the likelihood that in one brief encounter I have fathered your child,' Zahir fielded very quietly.

'I didn't think it was very likely either, but we're both young and healthy, it was the wrong time of the month for me to have an accident and clearly you have killer sperm,' Saffy told him drily.

'Don't make a joke of it,' Zahir growled.

'I can't prove it's your baby until after it's born,' Saffy murmured ruefully. 'DNA testing is too risky during pregnancy. On the other hand you could think back sensibly to that day in the tent and appreciate that ironically you are the only lover I've *ever* had.'

Zahir frowned, winged ebony brows pleating above questioning dark as night eyes flaring with disbelief. 'That is not possible.'

'Forget the newspaper stories and your prejudices and think about it rationally,' Saffy urged with quiet dignity, determined not to allow him to continue to cherish doubts about who had fathered her child. 'You're not stupid—I know you're not. I was a virgin.'

All colour bled from below his olive-toned complexion as he stared back at her with smouldering golden force and she recognised the exact moment when he recalled the blood stains on the bed because he suddenly swore in Arabic, tore his stunned gaze from hers and half swung away from her, his lean brown hands clenching into fists. 'If that is true, I have greatly wronged you,' he bit out rawly.

'We wronged each other a long time ago,' Saffy cut in. 'I *chose* to share that bed with you. It was my decision and this is my...er, problem.'

'If it's my child, it's mine too and I don't see our child as a problem,' Zahir retorted with a harsh edge to his dark deep voice. 'We'll remarry just as soon as I can arrange it.'

'Remarry?' Saffy gasped in wonderment. 'You have to be joking!'

'Our child's future is too serious to joke about and it can only be secured through marriage.'

'And we all know how that turned out the last time,' Saffy returned doggedly, fighting to think logically because his proposal had shaken her to her very depths. Was he serious? Was he really serious?

'When my father died and I took the throne, everything changed in Maraban,' Zahir declared levelly. 'We would be able to lead normal lives now. You're pregnant. Of course, I want to marry you.'

Saffy was reeling from a dozen different reactions:

disbelief, scorn, anger, frustration among them. Zahir was set on taking charge as usual. He wasn't reacting on a personal level, he was reacting as a public figure, keen to hide an embarrassing mistake within the respectability of marriage.

'I don't want to marry you just because I'm pregnant.'

'And what do you think your child would want?' Zahir shot that icily controlled demand back at her. 'If you don't marry me, you will deprive that child of a father and of the status in life he or she has a right to enjoy. Without marriage, the child will have to remain secret and it will be almost impossible for me to establish a normal relationship with him or her.'

In one cool statement, Zahir had given Saffy a lot to think about, but then faster than the speed of light her child had gone from being a line on a test wand to a living, breathing being, who might well question her decisions at a later date. For the first time she appreciated that she could not continue to put her own wants and needs first because, whatever she chose to do, she would, one day, have to take responsibility for the choices she had made on her child's behalf.

'We could get married just to ensure that the baby was legitimate...and then get another divorce,' she suggested tautly.

Brilliant dark eyes flamed golden as flames. 'Is that really the very best you can offer? Is the prospect of being my wife again such a sacrifice?'

Saffy studied the floor. She thought of the wicked forbidden delight of his passion, recognising that on that level everything between them had radically changed. She looked up, feeling the instant mesmeric pull of him the moment she saw his lean dark face. Her heart hammered inside her, her mouth running dry.

'Couldn't you give our marriage a second chance?' Zahir asked huskily.

'It's too soon to consider that,' Saffy argued. 'The first thing I need to do now is see my doctor and confirm that I *am* pregnant. Then we'll decide what to do. Look at this from my point of view. When you arrived here, you asked me to be your mistress...now suddenly you're talking marriage, but I don't want to get married purely because you accidentally got me pregnant.'

Zahir surveyed her with stormy intensity and the atmosphere thickened as though laced with cracked ice. 'I believe in fate, not accidents. What is meant to be will be.'

Saffy rolled her eyes, compressed her lips and stood up. 'You shipped me out to the desert for seduction, not fatherhood. You brought this roof down over our ears—you sort it out!'

'Marriage will sort it out,' he contended stubbornly.

'Oh, if only it were that simple.'

'But it is.' Before she could even guess his intention, he had closed a hand over hers. His brilliant gaze sought and held hers by sheer force of will. 'Right now, it's the best choice you can make. Let go of the past. Trust me to look after you and my child. I will not let you down.'

'And would you agree to a divorce at a later date?'

Saffy prompted shakily, more impressed than she wanted to be by his promise of good intentions.

'If that's what you wanted, if you were unhappy as you were before, yes,' Zahir agreed grittily, not choosing to add the unpleasant realities that would accompany any such decision on her part. Complete honesty was not possible. What really mattered was getting that ring back on her finger and securing their child's future. 'This is not about us, this is about our child, what he or she needs most.'

'If you really mean that…' Saffy drew in a ragged breath, terrified of the confusing thoughts teeming through her head. She was trying very hard to put the welfare of her child first and not muddy the waters with the bitterness of the past and the insecurity of the present. He would keep his promise: she knew that. On that level she trusted him and she quite understood that he wanted their child to have the very best start in life possible. They owed their child that chance.

'I do,' Zahir confirmed levelly.

'Then on that basis, I agree.' So great was the stress of making that announcement that Saffy felt light-headed again as all the little devils in her memory banks began queuing up to remind her of how vulnerable she would be if she put herself in Zahir's power again.

Zahir released her hand. 'I'll organise it.'

He got as far as the door before Saffy called him back to say tautly, 'I want a *proper* wedding.'

'Meaning?' Zahir sought to clarify.

'No hole-in-the-corner do in the embassy for me this

time,' Saffy spelled out with scorn. 'I want a bridal gown and a family occasion with my sisters as bridesmaids and all the rest of the wedding hoopla.'

Taken aback by the admission, Zahir literally paled.

'Those are my terms and I won't budge on them,' Saffy completed doggedly.

CHAPTER SEVEN

'ARE YOU REALLY sure about doing this?' Kat looked tense and anxious and Saffy immediately felt guilty.

What had she been thinking of when she dragged her family into all of this? A shotgun wedding, no less. Her sister, Kat, didn't need the stress but she had insisted on organising the wedding within the space of one incredibly short week and had proven that if sufficient money was thrown at a challenge, it could be done. Saffy studied her reflection in the mirror. Her gorgeous designer wedding dress was a classic, nipped in at the waist for shape and falling in fluid folds to her satin-clad feet. She wasn't wearing a veil: the hairdresser had piled her hair up and topped it with the magnificent sapphire and diamond tiara Zahir had sent to her. Matching drop earrings sparkled with every movement she made.

'Saffy?' the attractive redhead pressed. 'You know, it may be your wedding day but it's still not too late to change your mind. You don't *have* to marry Zahir. You don't have to do this to please anybody.'

Looking reflective, Saffy breathed in deep. 'I really do want to give our baby the chance to have two parents. None of us ever had that. My sisters and I had you and you were a brilliant stand-in Mum,' she told Kat warmly. 'But I'd like to try it the old-fashioned way before I try to go it alone.'

Kat frowned. 'You're not in a very optimistic mood for a new bride.'

'I'm being realistic. Zahir will commit to being a father—I know that about him and I respect him for it. If marriage works for us, it works, and if it doesn't work, at least I'll have tried,' Saffy muttered ruefully.

'I just can't believe you got involved with him again. It's like fatal attraction without the bunny boiler. I mean, five years ago Zahir broke your heart and I don't want him doing it again.' Her sister sighed unhappily. 'Mikhail has checked him out and he says Maraban is stable now and that Zahir seems to be one of the good guys.'

'I could've told you that,' Saffy interrupted heatedly.

'And there's no sleazy stories about him either,' Kat added in a suitably quiet undertone. 'Obviously there's been women but not in the kind of numbers you need to worry about.'

Saffy ground her teeth together in silence, wishing that her Russian billionaire brother-in-law had minded his own business when it came to Zahir. Even as she thought it she knew she was wronging the man. Undoubtedly Kat's concerns about her sister's bridegroom had prompted Mikhail's investigation into Zahir's reputation. 'He would never be sleazy,' Saffy declared, suppressing her recollection of that invitation to be his mistress.

'Are you upset about Emmie refusing to come today?' Kat asked ruefully.

'No.' Saffy lied sooner than add additional worry to Kat's caring heart. 'I can understand her not wanting to get into a bridesmaid's frock when she's so pregnant and I can also understand her saying that she's not in the mood.'

'Some day soon, you two need to sit down and talk and sort out the aggro between you.'

'Easier said than done with Emmie always avoiding me like the plague,' Saffy countered ruefully. 'I phoned her and said I understood her not wanting to be a bridesmaid but would love her to come just as a guest and she said she wasn't feeling well enough to travel.'

'Well, she has had a pretty tough time being pregnant, so that probably wasn't a lie,' Kat conceded. 'It makes me wonder if I'm wise to be considering IVF in case that kind of sickness and nausea in pregnancy runs in the family.'

'I'm not feeling sick…not yet, anyway,' Saffy pointed out bracingly, smiling as Topsy bounced into the room, bubbling with excitement in her glittering green bridesmaid's dress and quite unaware of the serious chat her older sisters had been involved in. It seemed natural to the three sisters that neither Saffy's mother nor her father were taking part in the coming ceremony. Saffy had had virtually nothing to do with her mother, Odette, or her father since they had abandoned her to foster care when she was twelve years old. Her parents had divorced when she was much younger and the bitterness of their estrangement had had an inevitable effect on her father's attitude to his twin daughters. He had left them behind and moved on. Although Kat had encouraged Saffy to foster a forgiving attitude towards their mother, Saffy had too many memories of childhood neglect to do so. Odette simply wasn't a loving parent and never had been.

The wedding took place at the church only a few doors down from Kat and Mikhail's London home. The church's rather gloomy interior had been transformed with an abundance of white and pink flowers and knotted ribbons. Saffy walked down the aisle on Cameron's arm, her heart banging like a drum at a rock concert when she finally got close enough to see Zahir's imperious dark head at the altar. How did he feel about this? How did he *really* feel? Throughout the past crazy busy week while she packed up her life in London her only contact with Zahir had been by phone. She had rung him after the doctor had confirmed her pregnancy. He had rung her several times to find out about the wedding schedule. There had been nothing intimate about those exchanges.

She had also ploughed through a half-dozen frustrating meetings with her agent and various clients as the reality of her condition forced the need for urgent rethinks on previously planned shoots. A couple of clients had taken the opportunity to drop her because her pregnancy meant that she was in breach of contract.

Desert Ice, however, had retained her services because they were more than halfway through their campaign. She was grateful for that because it was mainly her earnings from the cosmetics company that funded the orphanage she supported.

Zahir's stunning black-fringed golden eyes met hers as she drew level with him and she felt painfully vulnerable, which she didn't like at all. Unfortunately wounding memories of their first wedding were assailing her, reminding her of a day when she had not had a doubt in the world about becoming a wife, had indeed innocently overflowed with feelings of love and happiness. The wedding ring slid onto her finger and she breathed in deep, conscious that Zahir retained a hold on her hand. It was done, the die was cast, she told herself soothingly. What was she afraid of happening? What was there to fear now? That he didn't love her—well, she knew he didn't love her, didn't she? Unfortunately the awareness that he was marrying her to give their baby a name and a home was no more welcome to her heart or her pride.

On their passage back down the aisle, Zahir pressed a supportive hand to her spine. 'You feel very shaky,' he admitted when she cast him an enquiring glance.

And it was true, she did feel shaky, had ridden roughshod over her misgivings to marry him, trying at every step to put her child's needs ahead of her own.

Zahir participated in the photographs in silence. Sapphire was pale as death and silent and her family, aside of the little bouncy one in green, who had smiled brightly at him, were clearly hostile and suspicious. No doubt her family had taken their cues from Sapphire. She didn't want to be married to him again; he could feel it in the tension that gripped her every time he touched her. That made him angry and bitter, roused memories better left buried. But he had royally screwed up by allowing his primal instincts to triumph and there was always a price to be paid for recklessness, he reminded himself darkly. He had got her back. That was, at least, a beginning, and only time would tell whether or not she would continue to hold the threat of a divorce like a gun to his head.

'You look stunning,' Zahir told her belatedly as she scrambled into the limo that would whisk them from the church to the embassy to undergo a Muslim marriage ceremony. 'How are you feeling?'

'I'm not ill, only pregnant,' Saffy countered defensively, wishing he hadn't reminded her of her condition, reluctant to be viewed as in any way in need of special treatment.

The second ceremony was brief, witnessed by embassy officials and a posed photograph was taken afterwards. They returned to Mikhail and Kat's house where a reception was being held in the ballroom. After the wedding breakfast, they circulated. Surrounded by the familiar faces of the models she often worked with, Saffy began to relax a little, bearing up well to comments about how quiet she had been about her supposed long-term relationship with Zahir and striving to behave more like a normal bride.

'Of course, I shouldn't mention it,' trilled Natasha,

a six-foot-tall Ukrainian blonde, well on her way to su-permodel status. 'But Zahir was mine first.'

It was said so quietly and with such a sunny smile that it took several seconds for that spiteful confession to sink in on Saffy. She stared back into Natasha's very pale blue eyes and murmured, 'Really?' as politely as if the other woman had commented on the weather.

'Yes, a couple of years ago now. A fling at a film festival,' Natasha confided with a little shrug of a designer-clad shoulder. 'But he was hard to forget.'

'Yes,' Saffy acknowledged, passing on as soon as she could into less aggressive company, anger licking like fire at her composure. Mine first? No, he had been hers, her husband and then her ex-husband before he became anyone else's. But the truth that he had sought amusement in other beds could still slash like a knife turning in her breast. She glanced back at Natasha, beautiful and reputedly sexually voracious, struggling not to picture Zahir entwined in her arms, and the nausea she had never experienced until that moment turned her stomach into a washing machine and sent sickness hurtling up her throat. Her skin clammy with perspiration, she rushed off to the cloakroom and made it just in time. She was horribly sick and it took a few minutes for her to freshen up and lose the unsteadiness that afflicted her in the aftermath.

When she emerged, Topsy was waiting for her. 'Are you OK? Zahir saw you leaving and asked me to check.'

Zahir didn't miss much, Saffy reflected wretchedly.

'I think I just got bitten by morning sickness.' And a very tall shrewish blonde.

But Saffy was no fan of ducking reality and she knew she had to deal with life as it was. Zahir had been with other women when he was no longer married to her and that was his business, not hers. His past was his own, just as hers would have been had she lived a little more dangerously since their first marriage. But unfortunately there had not been a cure for the fact that she had still found Zahir and her memory of him far more attractive than other men. What did that say about her? He was like a habit she had never managed to shake, her one and only fantasy, and the men who had pursued her over the years had never managed to cause her a single sleepless night. With the exception of Zahir, she had never pined for a phone call or a smile from a man, had truly never contrived to rouse that much interest, and perhaps that was why she had fallen so easily back into bed with him. Was it a kind of persistent physical infatuation? Had he somehow spoiled her for other men? She stared at him as she crossed the floor of the ballroom.

He was lithe, powerfully built and supremely sophisticated in his light grey morning suit with his luxuriant ebony hair fanning back from his brow; his dark deep-set eyes were riveting in his lean, bronzed face. He was drop-dead gorgeous and always had been a very hard act to follow. But as her body stirred with responses far removed from nausea, her breasts swelling and peaking beneath her bodice and a dull ache expanding in her pel-

vis, she was furious with herself for being so susceptible
to a male who neither loved nor even truly wanted her.

'What's wrong?' Zahir asked softly.

'Why would anything be wrong?' she traded tartly,
ice in her cool scrutiny and edging her voice. 'You tell
me…film festival two years ago, Ukrainian blonde by
the name of Natasha, ring any bells?' That scornful and
provocative question just leapt off Saffy's tongue before
she was even aware she was going to voice it.

The faintest hint of colour edged Zahir's chiselled
cheekbones but his dark golden gaze did not waver from
hers. Indeed if anything he stood a little straighter. 'I
will never lie to you.'

Even when you should, she almost screamed at him,
wanting, needing to know and yet fearing what knowing more would do to her.

'There weren't many and there was nothing serious,'
Zahir breathed in a harsh undertone. 'This is not a conversation I want to have on our wedding day.'

'It's not something I want to talk about either!' Saffy
launched back at him, her eyes a very bright blue lit
with anger.

His stubborn jaw line squared. 'Before you judge me,
ask yourself if you have any idea of what state I was in
after our divorce.'

Saffy came over all defensive. 'How would I know?'

'When you're ready to tell me what changed you out
of all recognition in the bedroom, I'll tell you why I
did what I did.' His brilliant dark eyes glittered. It was

a challenge, blunt and simple, and it only made Saffy angrier than ever.

He had divorced her. *He* had made that choice. He could not expect her to accept the consequences or feel responsible for a situation that had not been of her making. As for what had changed her into a normal sexually able woman, that was not something she was willing to share with him. It was too private, too personal, might well affect the way he looked at her and that very possible outcome made her cringe.

'Are you two actually arguing?' Kat came up to demand in dismay.

'We always did have a fiery relationship,' Zahir admitted.

'Not so different from our own,' Kat's husband, Mikhail, teased his wife. 'It takes time to adjust to living with another person.'

'Time and buckets of patience,' Zahir added, an authoritative look stamped on his lean dark face that only made Saffy want to slap him hard.

'Your guests are waiting for the bride and groom to start the dancing,' Kat informed them more cheerfully.

Saffy wasn't in the mood to dance, especially not with Natasha smirking at the side of the floor, but she owed her sister too much to risk upsetting her and she gave way with good grace.

Zahir was a great dancer with a natural sense of rhythm but Saffy felt as if someone had welded an iron bar to her spine and she was stiff in the circle of his arms, holding herself at a distance. Glimpses of Natasha watching them did not improve her mood. Yes, she had known he had made love to other women, but actually having a face to pin to one of those anonymous women was another turn of the torture screw. She had never thought of herself as the jealous type and now she was finding out different. Once Zahir had been hers, entirely hers, and even though things had gone wrong in the bedroom she had rather naively trusted him not to stray. Now she was wondering crazy things, such as how she compared to his other lovers, and she was regretting her lack of experience and her honesty on that score. Yet how could she have lied when her child's paternity hinged on telling the complete truth? That reminder cooled the fizz in her blood, settled her down and made her seek another topic of conversation.

'I thought you might have invited your brother and sister and possibly even Azel to the wedding,' she remarked gingerly.

'One of Hayat's children is in hospital with complications following on from a bout of measles. Akram is standing in for me at an OPEC meeting and my sister-in-law, Azel, no longer lives with us. She remarried last year and now lives in Dubai,' Zahir explained. 'You will meet what remains of my family tomorrow.'

'I'll look forward to it,' Saffy said politely. 'Do they know about the baby?'

'Only my siblings. When we chose to marry in such haste, it made sense to be honest,' Zahir said wryly.

Hot pink burned like a banner across her cheeks at the thought that his strictly raised siblings might assume that she was a total slut for succumbing so quickly and easily to their brother's attractions.

'You know, when you blush, the tip of your nose turns pink as well,' Zahir husked. 'It's cute as hell.'

'You know what happened in the desert...the baby,' Saffy said sharply. 'It's *all* your fault.'

A sizzling, utterly unexpected smile played across Zahir's wide sensual mouth and startled her. 'I know. But out of it I gained a very beautiful wife and we have a baby in our future and I can't find it within my heart to regret anything we did.'

Her eyes prickled and she blinked rapidly, knowing that her acid and pointless comment had not deserved so generous a response. Suddenly her tension gave and she rested her head down on his broad shoulder, drinking in and loving the familiar scent of him—warm clean male laced with an evocative hint of sandalwood. She was momentarily weak with the sheer amount of emotion pumping through her and so confused, still so desperately confused about what she felt, what she truly thought. With every passing moment, her feelings seemed to swing to one side and then violently to the other. So much had happened between them in such a short time frame that she was mentally all over the place.

Saffy was half asleep by the time they left for the airport. She had changed into a very elegant shift dress and jacket almost the same colour as her eyes and let her hair down to flow round her shoulders in a golden mane. Relaxation was infiltrating her for the first time that day.

Drowsily she studied the platinum ring on her finger. They were married again: she couldn't quite believe it.

'I think I'll sleep all the way to Maraban,' Saffy told him apologetically as they boarded the private jet.

'It's been a long day and it is after midnight,' Zahir conceded wryly. 'But first there's something I'd like to tell you.'

Alert to the guarded note in his dark deep drawl, Saffy felt her adrenalin start to pump. The jet took off and drinks were served. She undid her belt, let the stewardess show her into the sleeping compartment where she freshened up, and then she rejoined Zahir, made herself comfortable and sipped her fresh orange juice. 'So?' she prompted quietly, proud of her patience and self-discipline while she wondered what he had to unveil. 'What is it?'

Zahir straightened his broad shoulders and settled hard dark eyes on her without flinching. 'I've bought the Desert Ice cosmetics company.'

CHAPTER EIGHT

SAFFY BLINKED IN astonishment, for of all the many surprises she had thought Zahir might want to disclose that one staggering confession had not figured. She set down her glass and stood up, her mind in a bemused fog. 'You bought the company? But why? Why the heck would you do that?'

'It *was* a good investment.' Zahir loosed a sardonic laugh that bluntly dismissed that explanation. 'But I bought it only for your benefit. I knew the company had a cast-iron contract with you and I didn't want anyone putting pressure on you while you were pregnant.'

Eyes slowly widening, Saffy stared back at him in rampant disbelief, while she wondered what strings he had pulled to learn the contract terms she had been on with the company. 'I can't believe that you would interfere in my career to that extent!' she admitted in stunned disbelief, anger steadily gathering below the surface of that initial reaction. 'Nobody was putting pressure on me at the meeting I attended with their campaign manager this week.'

Cynicism hardened Zahir's expressive mouth, making him look inexpressibly tough in a way far different from the younger man she remembered. It was a look that was hard, weathered and unapologetic and she refused to be intimidated by it. 'Naturally not. By that time, I was the new owner, so of course there was no pressure. They can film your face as much as they like while you're pregnant but they'll be doing it in Maraban.'

'In…*Maraban?*' Saffy parroted as though he had suggested somewhere as remote as the moon.

'I don't want you forced to travel thousands of miles round the globe now that you're pregnant. It would be too stressful for you.'

'And what would you know about that?' Saffy demanded hotly. 'What do you know about what a pregnant woman needs?'

'I don't want you exhausted,' Zahir asserted grimly. 'I appreciate that the baby is a development that wasn't planned or, indeed, expected, but adjustments have to be made to your working schedule.'

'You're not the boss of me!' Saffy hissed back at him in helpless outrage. 'You know, the one phrase I heard you speak most clearly was, *"I don't want…"* This is about you, your need to clip my wings and control me. Isn't it enough that I married you? What about what I want? What about what I need? This isn't all about you!'

'I'm not trying to control you.' Eyes now smouldering with anger, Zahir gazed back at her, his hard jaw line set at an unyielding angle. 'But the security needs alone that are now required to ensure your safety would be impossible to maintain in some of the exotic locations where you have recently travelled.'

'I don't have security needs!' Saffy flung at him in a bitterly aggrieved tone of fury. 'It's taken me five years to build my career and I didn't get where I am by being difficult!'

Zahir didn't bat a single absurdly long eyelash. He stared steadily back at her, those twin black fringes round his remarkable eyes merely adding to the intensity of his scrutiny. 'As my wife, you have security needs. Just as I could be a target, you could be as well. I will not allow your headstrong spirit to tempt you into taking unnecessary risks. This is not about your career. This is about you accepting that your new status will demand lifestyle changes. You are no longer Sapphire Marshall, you are a queen.'

'I don't want to be a queen!' Saffy sobbed in a passionate rage at the logic he was firing at her. Memories were flooding back to her of long-buried quarrels during which she had raged while Zahir shot down her every argument with murderous logic and practicality. 'You never told me that. I just thought I'd be your wife, your consort, your plus one or whatever you want to call it!'

'The last queen was my mother, who died when my younger brother was born,' Zahir commented grimly. 'It is time you saw sense. You can't have thought you could marry me and ignore who and what I am.'

Saffy was so worked up she wanted to scream. Over the past week she had thought of many, many things, like dresses and wedding breakfasts and guest lists and babies, but not once had she pondered her future status in Maraban. In fact she hadn't wanted to think about Maraban at all because once she had been very unhappy there.

'I didn't think about it,' Saffy muttered in indignation, furious with him, wondering in a rage how on earth he had broken the news about the Desert Ice company and then contrived to roll over his indefensible interference in her career to put her on the defensive with the news that she was apparently a queen. 'I don't want to be a queen. I'm sure I'm not cut out for it. In fact I bet I'm totally unsuitable to be royal.'

'With that attitude you probably will be,' Zahir shot back at her with derision. 'I think you tried harder at eighteen to fit in than you are willing to try now as an adult.'

Saffy's lush mouth dropped open as temper exploded in her like a grenade. 'I was a doormat at eighteen, a total stupid doormat! I wanted to please you. I wanted to please your family. I was so busy trying to be something I'm not—*and* getting no thanks for it! I had no space to be me!'

'Times have changed. Maraban has been transformed and brought into the twenty-first century. But I have changed as well,' Zahir breathed on a taut warning note, his gaze burning gold in its force. 'I will tell you now how things are and I won't keep secrets from you again.'

'*Secrets?*' Saffy shot back at him jaggedly, entrapped by that one word of admission, her nervous tension seizing on it. '*What secrets?*'

'Five years ago, I kept a lot from you in an attempt to protect you. I didn't want to hurt you but this time I will employ no lies and no half-truths. I will tell it like it is…'

Other women, Saffy was thinking in despair, a sharp wounding pain piercing her somewhere in the chest region. What else could he be talking about? When he had found no satisfaction in the marital bedroom he had gone elsewhere. Maybe out to that remote desert palace where his late father had kept his personal harem, *very* discreet. Hey, Saffy, you dummy, a little voice piped up at the back of her mind…maybe he wasn't on army manoeuvres all those times he was gone. Maybe he was off the leash having fun, the kind of fun you couldn't give him then. And what shook Saffy most at that moment was that instead of confronting him on that score and demanding an explanation, she instead wanted to stay silent and withdraw, conserve some dignity, protect herself from painful revelations that she did not at that moment feel strong enough to bear. Every atom of ESP she possessed urged her to leave the past where it belonged.

Saffy lifted her golden head. 'I'm tired. I'm going to bed but thanks for making our wedding night almost as dreadful as the first we had,' she murmured with stinging scorn.

And she saw right then in his lean darkly handsome face that he had forgotten it was their wedding night. And really that said it all, didn't it? She had already travelled from being the object of intense desire to being the pregnant wife, apparently shorn of attraction.

Zahir gritted his teeth and resisted the urge to talk back to her in a similar vein. Had she really thought he would stage their wedding night on a plane when she was exhausted and already under strain from all the challenges of the past weeks? He suffered a hollow sensation of horror even recalling that first catastrophic wedding night, her sickness, fear and distress, his own incomprehension and sense of defeat. She had been too young, far too young and naïve at eighteen, he knew that now. Guilt assailed him as Saffy ducked into the cabin, her lovely face taut and pale awakening memories he would have done anything to avoid. So much for honesty, so much for trying to clear the air, he reflected bitterly.

That last comment of hers had been a low blow, Saffy conceded in shame. It wasn't either of their faults that their first wedding night had been catastrophic and he had been incredibly kind and patient and understanding even though she knew he didn't understand any more than she did then what was wrong with her. Hitting out at him like that had been unjust, a mean retaliation to the reality that Zahir had made her feel small and stupid with his talk of security concerns and queens. She didn't look much like a queen, she thought wretchedly, studying herself with wet pink eyes in the mirror, noting the mascara and eyeliner smudged from tears. She had panicked when he mentioned that because she was so terrified of not meeting his expectations again. Hadn't she *already* done that to him once? She didn't want to let him down or embarrass him but what did she know about being royal? Certainly she had learned absolutely nothing during their last marriage when only the servants knew she existed and she was virtually the invisible woman.

He didn't love her, didn't want her, probably had no faith in her ability to act like a royal wife either, Saffy thought painfully, tears streaming down her cheeks as she forced her convulsed face into a pillow. Why did she care so much about what he thought of her? Why did it hurt so much that she felt she couldn't stand it? And why more than anything in the world did she now want him to come in and put his arms round her to comfort her the way he had once done without even thinking about it? She had married him to give their baby a better start in life. That was the only reason and she didn't know why she was getting so worked up, sobs shuddering through her body like a storm unleashed on her without warning.

I am not in love with him. I am *so* not in love with him, she told herself urgently. That is not why I'm suddenly looking for more from him than he ever promised to deliver. And in that guarded state of mind she finally fell asleep.

The stewardess wakened her with breakfast and the announcement that the plane would be landing in an hour. Noting that she had slept alone in the bed, Saffy lifted her chin, knowing he had spent the night in one of the reclining seats. Why was she wondering whether he had been unfaithful to her when they had last been married? What did it matter? How was that relevant?

The last thing she needed was to get bound up in the problems of a long-dead past. They weren't the same people any more. Showered and elegantly attired in a print dress and a fine cashmere cardigan, she emerged from the sleeping compartment, feeling as brittle as bone china.

Zahir, sheathed in the beige and white pristine desert robes that accentuated his height and undeniably exotic attributes, gave her a smile that was a masterpiece of civility while wishing her good morning. She almost laughed but, once again, their shared past rattled like a skeleton locked in a cupboard: Zahir was superb at plastering over the cracks and pretending nothing had happened and that last night's divisive dispute had not occurred. Time and time again he had done that to her when they were first married when she tried to have serious talks with him and he shrugged them off, changed the subject, refused to be drawn. Stop it, *stop it,* she urged her disobedient brain, determined not to bring those memories of his evasiveness into the present when so much else had altered.

'We had a row,' she reminded him out of pure spite and resentment of his poise.

'I should never tackle a serious conversation after midnight when we're both tired.' His eyes glittered with unexpected raw amusement and the sheer primal attraction of him in that instant sent a flock of butterflies dancing in her tummy and clenched her muscles tight somewhere a great deal more intimate. Pink flushed her cheeks as he sipped at his coffee, the very image of cool control and sophistication. 'Coffee?'

Saffy served herself from the coffee pot on the table and sat down. 'What you said—'

Zahir shifted a fluid brown hand in a silencing motion. 'No, leave it. It was the wrong time and we have all the time in the world now.'

Saffy tried to steel herself to resist the command note in that assurance and then wondered if perhaps he was right. In any case, did she want confessions if what she suspected was true? Did she really want to stir up the past and perhaps damage the future relationship they might have before this marriage even got off the ground? Such patience, such careful concern felt unfamiliar to her in Zahir's presence, for once she had said whatever she liked to him with absolutely no lock on her tongue. And she wanted that freedom back, she recognised dimly, wanted it back almost more than she wanted anything.

'It's not like you to be so quiet.'

'The Queenie bit pulverised me,' she muttered tightly.

'You're more than up to the challenge,' Zahir asserted smoothly. 'You're accustomed to being in the public eye and right now you look...*wonderful.*'

'Do I?' Saffy hated the sound of that question, her gaze welded to his in search of falsehood, fake flattery, the smallest hint of insincerity.

'You always did and still do. And sadly, although it shouldn't matter, such beauty does impress people,'

Zahir murmured ruefully. 'I've never understood why you're not vain.'

'Other people work and train to do much more important and necessary things than I do but I got where I am because of my face and figure, not my brain or my skills,' Saffy pointed out flatly. 'It's not something to boast about.'

'But you're so much more—you always were,' Zahir declared, reaching for her fingers where they curled in discomfiture on the table top and enclosing them in his warm hand. 'And in Maraban, you will be able to show how much more you are capable of.'

'What does that mean?' Saffy prompted, touched by that hand round hers, energised by the conviction with which he spoke.

'That the woman who gives most of her earnings to an orphanage in Africa will have free rein to raise funds for good works in my country. Yes, I found out about that fact, quite accidentally through your crooked solicitor,' Zahir admitted. 'It made me feel very proud of you.'

Saffy tensed and reddened, wary of praise on the score of one of her biggest secrets. 'The children had so little and I wanted to help them. It made my career seem less superficial when I could feel that I had a worthwhile cause to work for.'

A wary sense of peace had settled over her by the time the plane landed at Maraban's splendid new airport. But when she stepped out of the plane to the music being played by a military band, and a smiling older man stepped up to bow and address Zahir while a little girl in a fancy dress stepped nervously forward to present a bouquet of flowers to Saffy, she realised that he had been right to warn her that her life would radically change. Zahir introduced her and the man bowed very low. He was the prime minister of Maraban. A discovery that startled Saffy and embarrassed her, for she knew she should have spent more time boning up on the changes in the country that was to be her new home. She had assumed Zahir was a feudal king like his late father, but evidently Maraban now had an elected government as well.

The little girl was the prime minister's daughter and spoke English and Saffy, always at her best with children, bent down to chat to her, suddenly wondering whether the child she carried would be a boy or a girl. A little boy with Zahir's amazing eyes and love of the outdoors and action. Or a little girl, who liked to experiment with hair and make-up and clothes. Or a mix of both of them, which would be much more likely, Saffy acknowledged abstractedly.

A limousine carried them through the city streets, lined on either side by excited crowds, peering at the car. 'Do I have to wave or anything?' she asked uneasily.

'No, only smile to look as happy as a bride is popularly supposed to be,' Zahir murmured with a wry note in his dark deep voice, and she suspected that he was recalling the night they had just spent apart.

'Your people seem to be celebrating the fact that you've got married,' Saffy remarked.

'People are reassured by the concept of family and

continuity, as long as it doesn't include a man like my late father,' Zahir imparted drily, and then turned to look at her. 'Why do you never mention yours? I noticed he was not at the wedding and didn't like to ask because you never ever mentioned him five years ago. Is he dead?'

'No. Alive with a second wife and family. His divorce from my mother was very bitter,' Saffy confided. 'And he hasn't had anything to do with me since I was twelve years old when I did something…' her voice slowed and thickened with distress '…something he couldn't forgive.'

His black brows drew together and he regarded her keenly. 'What could you have done that would excuse such an outright rejection from a father of his own child? I can't believe you did anything worthy of such a punishment.'

Saffy was very pale and she compressed her lips. 'Then you'd be wrong.'

'Tell me…you can't give me only half of the story.'.

It was her second most shameful secret, Saffy reflected wretchedly, but one that there was no reason for her to keep from him as he was part of her family now and everyone else knew the facts. 'As you know, life was pretty rough where I grew up and my sisters and I were often left without supervision, so of course we got in with the wrong crowd,' she confided tightly, her skin already turning clammy with never-forgotten shame and guilt. 'I went joyriding in a stolen car with my twin. I didn't steal it *or* drive it but the car crashed. Her leg was badly damaged and she was left disabled and scarred for several years afterwards. She went through hell as a teenager. Luckily she was able to have surgery when she was older and she can walk normally again now. But the joyriders were my friends first and it was my fault. I'm the older twin and I should have been looking after her.'

'Saffy...' and it was the very first time he had used the family diminutive of her name, which made his intervention all the more effective as she turned her head in surprise, her clouded blue eyes meeting his. 'You were twelve years old. You did something wrong and you paid a heavy price—'

'No, *Emmie* did—' Saffy protested vehemently. 'Every morning for years she had to wake up and see her identical twin, walking, unscarred, *perfect* and, even though she's completely healed now, she's never been able to forgive me for what she went through during that period of her life. We both know I was to blame and that it should have been me who got hurt.'

'But you *were* hurt,' Zahir murmured gently. 'She was hurt in the body and you were hurt in the mind. You've carried the guilt for what happened ever since, haven't you?'

Tears were swimming in Saffy's eyes and she didn't trust herself to speak, so she nodded vigorously in agreement. All those years she had stood by watching her twin suffer, first in a wheelchair, then on crutches, struggling to fit in with other teenagers when she couldn't play sport or dance or do almost anything that they could.

'Accidents happen,' Zahir continued. 'You learned from the experience, didn't you?'

Saffy nodded wordlessly, a soundless sob thickening her throat and making it impossible to swallow.

'So what did your father do?'

'He said…he said I was evil and that he didn't want to know me any more.'

'And how did he treat Emmie?'

'He cut her out of his life as well. So, you see, that was my fault too.'

'No. He was a father and perhaps he used your mistakes as an excuse to absolve himself of responsibility for his twin daughters. No decent man would stay away from an injured child merely to punish her sibling.'

That was a truth that had evaded Saffy all her life to that point and it shook her because when Zahir put the episode in that light, she saw his view of it and it altered her own. Her father had conveniently rejected both his daughters. Although Emmie had been hurt, he hadn't even visited her in hospital, nor had he intervened when the twins were forced to enter foster care because their mother refused to take further responsibility for them. It had been Saffy's sister, Kat, who had been the three sisters' saviour, giving them a proper home and a loving caring environment, the first any of them had ever known.

'I appreciate you viewing the episode that way,' Saffy breathed in a muffled undertone. 'But Emmie can't see it like that. She still doesn't want anything to do with me.'

'As I've never met her, you'll have to talk to her about that. Put it out of your mind now,' Zahir urged, stunning dark golden eyes welded to her troubled face, a smile slashing his wide sensual mouth. 'and stop blaming yourself for something that was outside your control.'

Her spirits picked up as if a bubble of happiness had been released inside her. He knew what she had done and it hadn't shocked him or made him see her as a cruelly irresponsible and selfish person. And most miraculously of all, he had made her feel better with one smile. She gazed back at him, her heart thumping hard inside her chest, an agony of feeling squeezed tight inside her. She wanted so badly to touch him, could feel her breasts heavy, the tender tips straining inside her bra while a warm honeyed heat built between her legs. It was pure lust, she told herself defensively, watching his eyes flame gold, and lust was a practical basis for a practical marriage.

'If we weren't in view of hundreds of people, you would be horizontal,' Zahir purred hungrily, the erotic note in his sensual drawl tugging at her senses.

'As you said, we have all the time in the world,' Saffy burbled, relieved that he could still respond to her, *want* her. 'I did think that the way you behaved yesterday meant that, now that I'm pregnant, I had lost my appeal,' she told him baldly.

Zahir laughed with rich appreciation. 'Is that a joke?'

Saffy stiffened. 'No.'

'Knowing that's my baby inside you makes me want you more than ever,' he breathed with a husky sensual edge to his voice, surveying her in a way no woman could have misunderstood or doubted, his hunger unashamed.

Although her colour heightened, Saffy relaxed, reassured that she was still an object of desire. In reality, she wanted a great deal more from him, she acknowledged inwardly, but it was early days and she could be patient. After all, she loved him. She couldn't lie to herself any longer about that. She had married him because she wanted to be his wife again, not only because of the child she carried. She wasn't quite the clear-headed, unselfish person she had pretended to be inside her own mind, putting her child's needs first. She wanted Zahir, she *loved* Zahir, and somehow she was going to make their marriage work so well that he found her indispensable. Furthermore, she wasn't going to cripple herself with wounding suspicions about other women, past infidelities or indeed anything from that era, she swore fiercely to herself. This marriage was a new beginning, not a rerun of mistakes and misunderstandings made long ago.

CHAPTER NINE

THE ROYAL PALACE was a vast building dating back hundreds of years and extended and renovated by every successive generation of Zahir's family. Even from the outside Saffy could see changes everywhere she looked because the massive courtyard fronting the palace entrance, once a parking area for military vehicles and limousines, had been transformed into beautiful gardens full of graceful trees being industriously watered to keep them healthy in the heat. Glorious flowering shrubs bloomed in every direction and fountains fanned water to cool the air in terraced seating areas. The gardeners at work fell still and lowered their heads respectfully as the limo passed by. When the late King Fareed had driven past, everyone had fallen down on their knees at his insistence and she was relieved that Zahir had clearly brought an end to that kind of exaggerated subservience.

'It looks so different,' she commented as the limo drew up outside the huge arched entrance. 'Much more welcoming.'

'It's so big we initially thought of knocking it down

and constructing something more fit for purpose. After all, I don't live like my father with hundreds of servants and guards, but it *is* an historic building and, since the family only requires part of it to actually live in, the government uses one wing and official events are staged here. We will still have total privacy though,' he asserted. 'Don't worry about that. And, of course, you'll be free to redecorate and do anything you like with our wing of the palace. I want you to feel at home here this time.'

Saffy decided that she would pretty much come to like and accept any place Zahir called home. Besides, their baby had been conceived in a tent. A palatial tent, to be sure, but a tent nonetheless. Her lush mouth quirked at the recollection. That was a secret that would probably never be shared.

The domestic staff greeted them at the end of the long hall and she was given more flowers, which were in turn taken from her as if she could not be expected to carry anything for herself. Zahir closed a relaxed hand round hers and walked her into a big reception room where a man and a woman awaited them.

'Hayat...' Saffy greeted his sister, several years his senior, warmly, registering that the delicate youthful brunette she had once met was now a more rounded woman in her thirties, but she still had the same warm, friendly smile. Hayat was quick to kiss her on both cheeks and offer good wishes. Saffy had never got to know the older woman that well because when she had first been married to Zahir, Hayat and her husband had been living in Switzerland.

'And since he was only a boy when you last met him, this is my younger brother Akram.'

She would have known Zahir's brother immediately by his close resemblance to her husband, but she was not impervious to the look of hostility in his rather set face as he murmured a strictly polite welcome that was neither sociable nor encouraging. But Saffy kept the smile on her face, reminding herself that it was early days and that, after the divorce five years earlier, Akram might consider her a particularly bad match for his brother, the king. Or maybe Akram was less than impressed by the fact that she was already pregnant, although if that was the case he ought to remember that conception took two people, not one, she thought ruefully.

Zahir carried her off again, one hand closed round hers as if he was keen to retain physical contact and, certainly, she had no objection retaining that connection. She had never been in the wing of the palace he took her to, was happy to be invited to explore and was pleasantly surprised by how contemporary the décor was there. Back in the old dark days of King Fareed's occupation, the parts of the palace she had known had rejoiced in a preponderance of over-gilded furniture, brightly coloured wallpaper, fussy drapes and half-naked statues. But now all that was tasteless and garish had been swept away as though it had never been.

'Did your father ever live here?' she asked awkwardly.

'No,' Zahir said succinctly. 'I didn't want to occupy his wing at the front…too many bad memories. It's government offices now.'

'This is beautiful,' Saffy confided, brushing back filmy drapes and opening French windows that led out into a spacious garden courtyard full of lush colourful plants. 'It will be perfect for the baby to play in.'

'One last place to show you,' Zahir murmured, tugging her impatiently back indoors to walk her down the corridor, while she tried to compute the sheer number of rooms that she now had the right to regard as part of her new home. He flung open the double doors at the foot like a showman. 'Our room. I had it freshly decorated.'

Our room, she repeated inwardly, thinking that phrase, which once had unnerved her, now had a good, solid, reassuring sound to it. The big room was breathtaking in the morning sunshine, furnished with a simply huge bed dressed in white and covered with more pillows and cushions than anyone would ever want to move before slipping between the sheets. Masses of white flowers filled several vases and perfumed the air with their abundance. The effect was light, bright and designer chic. Twin bathrooms led off the bedroom, one with a family-sized Jacuzzi in the corner.

'I'm already picturing you in there,' Zahir muttered huskily from behind her, his breath warming her cheek as he settled his lean hands on her rounded hips.

'Are you indeed?' Sliding round to look up at him, Saffy lifted her hands to his face and curved them to his exotic cheekbones. Dear heaven, those eyes of his got to her every time, she conceded dizzily as he bent his handsome dark head and circled her lush mouth slowly, teasingly with his own and her heart skipped a beat. 'I'll only get in with company.'

His cell phone hummed and Zahir winced. 'Hold that thought,' he urged, digging it out of his pocket to speak in his own language.

And that fast the moment of intimacy was over. He inclined his head at an apologetic angle and told her that something needed his attention and he would see her later. Saffy suppressed her disappointment, conceding that their lives would often be interrupted by his duties and knowing she would have to get used to the fact. She returned to exploring their wing of the palace. A manservant brought her luggage. There was a complete dream of a clothing closet installed in the room next door and she smiled, smoothing shoe shelves and glancing into what could only be custom-built units. Knowing Zahir must have ensured that so much was prepared for her in advance gave her a warm feeling deep down inside.

A maid brought her tea and tiny cakes and she sat out in the tranquil courtyard garden below the shade of the palm trees, enjoying the fading afternoon heat and the play of shadows through the palm fronds. For the first time in a long time she felt at peace. Acknowledging her feelings for Zahir had eased her worst insecurities and put paid to her frantic changes of mood because now she knew what lay behind her reactions. They were husband and wife and she was carrying their first child and she was happy. Happy, she thought wryly, unable to recall when she had last felt so happy or indeed an intensity of any emotion: only around Zahir. Had she always still loved him? Had it been his haunting image that prevented her from ever experiencing a strong attraction to another man? Regardless of what had happened between them, she had retained past memories of Zahir that were still clear as day in her mind. He had referred to her once as his 'first love' and she knew she wanted to be his first and *only* love, but the clock still couldn't be turned back. And nor in many ways would Saffy have wanted to achieve that impossibility, not if it meant returning to the uninformed, bewildered teenager she had been, incapable of consummating her marriage and having to live within the confines of the repressive regime of the late King Fareed.

Zahir phoned her full of apologies to say that he could not join her before dinner. He reappeared, vital and startlingly handsome, to study her where she sat reading on the terrace. She smiled at him, blue eyes sparkling, and his winged brows pleated in surprise. 'I thought you'd be furious with me for leaving you alone all afternoon,' he admitted ruefully.

And Saffy laughed. 'I'm not eighteen any more,' she reminded him gently. 'And I understand that you have responsibilities you can't escape.'

'But not the very first day you arrive. In that spirit, I have blocked off two weeks at the end of the month purely for us,' Zahir told her, his features suddenly very serious in cast. 'We can travel, stay here, do whatever you like, but there will no other demands on our time.'

Saffy was impressed that he had already foreseen the necessity for them to formally make space in their schedules to spend time together as a couple. It was an effort and an opportunity he had not tried to organise five years earlier and she appreciated it. A pretty fabulous three-course meal was served to them in the dining room. There was evidently a chef in charge of the kitchens and one out to impress. While they ate, Zahir shared his ambition to promote Maraban as a tourist destination and he asked her if she would be interested in helping to put together a public relations film to show off some of Maraban's main attractions.

'We have beaches, archaeological sites, mountains,' Zahir told her persuasively. 'You could present it. You're accustomed to being in front of the cameras.'

'Not in a speaking role, at least only occasionally.' But Saffy was pleased to be offered the chance to do something useful. 'I haven't been to any of those places though.'

Zahir frowned at the unspoken reminder that his father's determination to conceal their marriage had left her virtually imprisoned within the palace walls. 'Your eyes will be fresh then, your observations and expectations more realistic. We have a lot to learn about what tourists want. We don't have many marketing people here,' he confided. 'In fact Maraban would still be floundering and trapped in past mistakes if thousands of our former citizens hadn't responded to my appeal to come home after my father's regime fell. Many professionals returned from abroad to enable us to tackle the challenge of bringing our country into the twenty-first century.'

'It's wonderful that people chose to come back and help,' Saffy murmured, loving the gravity of his lean strong face, the warmth and concern he could not hide when he spoke about the country of his birth.

'But not half as wonderful as having you here with me again,' Zahir countered, dark golden eyes welded to her as he rose from his chair. 'Will you come to bed with me now, Your Majesty?'

'Call me Queenie—I'm never going to get used to the other. In answer to your question, I don't know…' Saffy angled her head to one side, pretending to think it over even though her heart was racing like a marathon runner's. 'Last night you were a no-show.'

Faint colour darkened his cheekbones. 'On board our flight, I didn't think I'd be welcome.'

'Put it this way—I wouldn't have kicked you out of bed,' Saffy confided, turning pink.

With a flashing smile of satisfaction, Zahir crossed the room and snatched her bodily up off the carpet into his arms to carry her down the corridor, a process accompanied by much giggling from Saffy. Halfway towards their bedroom he started kissing her and an arrow of sweet, piercing heat slivered between her thighs, smothering her amusement and awakening her body to desire.

'Being alone with you is all I've thought about all

day,' Zahir admitted, settling her down on the gigantic bed, which she noted was already clear of cushions and turned down in readiness for their occupation. Evidently the staff might be well acquainted with the habits of newly married couples.

As he cast off his robes and she kicked off her shoes Saffy smiled at his honesty. 'One-track mind.'

'*Always*...with you.' Zahir nuzzled against her slender throat, kissing and licking a sensitive spot below her ear that made her quiver and tightened her sensitive nipples. Then he groaned. 'I need a shave—'

Saffy grabbed him before he could spring back off the bed. '*Not* right now,' she told him squarely.

Zahir laughed. 'I don't want to scratch you.'

'Face facts. I won't agree to you going anywhere right at this minute,' Saffy told him, smoothing appreciative palms up over his broad muscular chest and then down very, very slowly and appreciatively over his six-pack abs. 'This is my time and I'm holding on tight to you.'

In the moonlight, Zahir's lean features were taut. 'You mean that?'

Saffy's fingers trailed daringly lower and closed around his bold erection.

With a roughened groan of satisfaction, Zahir flung himself back against the pillows. 'You're absolutely right. Nothing would move me right now.'

Saffy leant over him, her mane of hair trailing across his abdomen. He said something in Arabic. She pressed her lips to the tiny brown disc of a male nipple and moved in a southerly direction, taking her time as she kissed and stroked her way down his beautiful bronzed body.

'This is our wedding night…' Zahir muttered thickly. 'I should be doing this to you.'

'My turn later…right now, I'm in charge,' Saffy whispered just before she found him with her mouth and his hands lodged firmly into her hair, his hips rising to assist her, and an exclamation of intense pleasure was wrenched from him. Proud of her own boldness, no longer ashamed of the desire he roused in her, Saffy was thoroughly enjoying herself.

She loved having him in her power, revelled in every response he couldn't control and experienced a deep sense of achievement when he could no longer stand her teasing caresses and he dragged her up to him and flipped her over to ravage her lush lips with an almost savage kiss.

Making love to Zahir turned her on and no sooner had he registered that fact than he rose over her, all masculine, dominant power and energy, and thrust his engorged shaft into the silky wet tightness of her inner channel. She cried out in delight and then he was moving and stretching her, ramping up her level of excitement to an almost unbearable degree. It had never occurred to her that slow and deep could be as thrilling as fast and hard, but he wouldn't let her urge him on and control the pace.

'No, this we do *my* way,' Zahir growled, flexing his hips, sending a shiver of exquisite sensitivity over her entire skin surface, her nipples straining as he shifted position and angle to torture her more.

He kept her straining on the edge of climax for a long time and the ripples of growing excitement were engulfing her like a flood when, in receipt of one final driving thrust, she found a wild, scorching release that shattered her into shaking, sobbing weightlessness, utterly drained by the joy of the experience. She lay there for a long time afterwards, wrapped in his arms, steeped in pure pleasure, marvelling that they were together again.

'Now perhaps you'll consider telling me what or *who* transformed you in the bedroom from the terrified girl I remember into the woman you are now,' Zahir urged in a roughened undertone that nonetheless shockwaved through her like a sudden clap of thunder.

In receipt of that request, a little shudder of repulsion travelled through Saffy's suddenly ferociously tense body. No, she could not do that; no, she could not risk sharing what had happened to her lest it destroy the new bonds they had created. She could feel him waiting for her to speak, literally *willing* her to speak in that dreadful expectant silence. As the silence continued and she failed to respond the strong, protective arms wrapped round her tensed, loosened and then carefully withdrew and he shifted his lean, powerful body away from hers, forging a separation between them that she could feel aching through every fibre she possessed.

Zahir wasn't giving her a choice and he wasn't about to conveniently drop the subject for the sake of peace either, she recognised wretchedly. He wanted to know;

he was determined to know and he had a will of iron that would chip away at her obstinacy day after day. He wouldn't let it go and the distance that would create between them would provide fertile ground in which suspicion might well fester. Would he then start to doubt that he was truly her baby's father? Would he wonder if he had really been her only lover?

Stinging tears stung Saffy's eyes and trickled down her cheeks in the darkness. He was always so honest; he never seemed afraid of anything, never seemed to worry about how other people saw him. Why couldn't she be the same? Why couldn't she just spill it all out and stop worrying about how it might damage his view of her? But Saffy couldn't find an answer to the never-tell-anyone barrier that existed inside her mind. The therapist had had a lot of trouble getting her to talk and finally she had had hypnotherapy to overcome what she was too afraid and ashamed to remember, and only then, in possession of full knowledge, had she found it possible to move forward...

CHAPTER TEN

BREAKFAST FOR SAFFY and Zahir the following morning was an almost silent affair. Zahir, being Zahir of course, was scrupulously polite and yet in every glance, every intonation Saffy imagined she heard condemnation, suspicion, doubt that she could be trusted as he believed he should be able to trust his wife. Nausea stirred in her stomach as she contemplated the piece of toast clasped between her fingers and with a stifled apology she fled for the nearest bathroom to lose what little she had eaten.

Afterwards, weak and with hot, perspiring skin she lay down on the bed, relishing the restorative coolness of the air conditioning wafting over her.

Zahir strode through the bedroom door, stunning dark golden eyes intent on the picture she presented. 'With all the flowers surrounding you here you look like the Sleeping Beauty...'

Saffy parted pink lips. 'But this doesn't feel like a fairy tale,' she whispered apologetically because if there had ever been a romantic male, it was Zahir. And how on earth could a romantic male ever come to terms with something as ugly as her biggest secret?

'I've phoned Hayat's obstetrician.'

'Why the heck did you do that?'

'You're sick. You need medical attention,' Zahir informed her with a stubborn angle to his jaw line.

'Being sick in early pregnancy is very common and not something to make a fuss about,' Saffy countered steadily.

'I shouldn't have tired you out last night,' Zahir responded tight-mouthed, his beautiful eyes shaded by his outrageously lush black lashes.

Saffy thrust her hands down onto the mattress to lift herself up into sitting position. 'That's got nothing to do with this—this is only my body struggling to adapt to being newly pregnant and it's normal.'

'I will stop worrying only when the doctor tells me to do so. I'm responsible for looking after you,' Zahir asserted, unimpressed by her argument. 'And while I realise that you're not feeling like it, you must make an effort to eat some breakfast to keep your strength up.'

And the boss has spoken, Saffy tagged on in silence to that speech as Zahir stalked out of the door again. He did *care* that she wasn't feeling well, she assured herself ruefully. It wasn't love but it was concern, but for how long would she even retain that hold on him if she continued to keep her secrets? Naturally he was curious, naturally sooner or later he would need to know the truth about her past. For the first time she accepted

that telling Zahir the truth was unavoidable and a bridge
she would eventually have to cross.

Zahir's sister, Hayat, accompanied the consultant,
who had tended her through her pregnancies. A well-
built older man with a studious manner, he was calm
and practical and exactly what Saffy needed to reinforce
her belief that a little nausea was not serious cause for
concern.

'The baby's father is very worried about your health,'
the doctor declared. 'It is a challenge of civility to tell
a king he must not worry unduly.'

Hayat was waiting outside to ask Saffy to join her for
tea. Dressed in a light summer dress in shades of blue,
Saffy accompanied her sister-in-law to the rear of the
palace complex where she and her husband and children
lived. Her husband, Rahim, was a senior doctor at the
city hospital and their three little girls occupied much
of Hayat and Saffy's conversation until a maid arrived
to take the children out to the gardens to play.

Tea with tiny sweet cakes was served on a shaded
balcony.

'My brother needs to learn to say no,' Hayat told
Saffy firmly. 'The same day he brings you home a bride
he was immediately dragged into some government
squabble about security concerns and forced to abandon you. You will quickly discover that Zahir doesn't
know how to say no to the demands made on his time.'

Saffy simply smiled, warmed by the frank tongue
that Hayat appeared to share with her brother. 'Zahir

was always very conscientious. Thank you for being so welcoming, Hayat. I appreciate it.'

'I know how much you and Zahir went through when you were married five years ago and our people now have a very good idea as well,' Hayat commented, her brown eyes level and serious. 'Zahir was wise when he chose to issue a public statement, admitting that he was remarrying the woman whom his father once forced him to divorce.'

Saffy stiffened in surprise at that revelation. 'I had no idea there had been any statement made about our marriage!' she exclaimed.

'Or that now my brother, the king, is forced to tell *lies* in public to protect *you?*' another louder voice interposed from the doorway behind them and both women's heads whipped around in astonishment at the interruption.

'Akram!' Hayat snapped in a warning tone at her youngest brother before turning back to Saffy with her face flushed and her expression uneasy to say, 'Please excuse me for a moment.'

But Zahir's volatile kid brother had worked up too much of a head of steam to be denied the confrontation with his brother's wife that his temper clearly craved. He concentrated his attention on Saffy, who was already starting to rise from her chair in dismay. 'You walked out on my brother—you *deserted* him after all he had endured to keep you as a wife against our father's wishes!' he accused with loathing. 'Zahir was imprisoned, tortured and beaten for your benefit and then you threw your marriage away by divorcing him when he needed your loyalty most!'

Her expression distraught, Hayat was pleading with her angry brother to keep quiet while simultaneously yanking on his arm in an unsuccessful effort to physically drag him away.

Saffy could barely part her numb lips. She was in serious shock from Akram's ringing condemnation of her behaviour. And what on earth was he talking about? Imprisoned, tortured, *beaten? Zahir?*

'I will deal with this…' and another more familiar voice intervened, cutting across the row going on between Hayat and Akram with commanding force.

Trembling, Saffy focused on Zahir where he stood like a bronzed statue in the centre of the light, airy reception room, coldly surveying his squabbling siblings. He spoke in his own language at length to Akram and Hayat backed off, dropping her head apologetically. Whatever Zahir told his brother, Akram turned his head in consternation to stare back at Saffy with frowning disbelief. He took a half-step towards her and muttered uncomfortably, 'I am very sorry. It seems I got everything wrong.'

'Yes, Zahir divorced me,' Saffy pointed out ruefully.

'Even so, I should never have spoken to you in that way or approached you in a temper. It was not my business,' Akram mumbled, his face very flushed, his discomfiture in Zahir's thunderous presence pronounced. 'Over the years it seems I reached the wrong conclusions and, as my brother has reminded me, I was never party to the true facts of what happened between you.'

An uneasy silence fell. Zahir was still glaring angrily at his kid brother.

'No harm done,' Saffy said awkwardly, keen to dispel the tension. 'I assume that Zahir has told you what really happened and that you no longer think so badly of me. Now, if you would all excuse me…'

'Where are you going?' Zahir demanded.

'Only for a walk. I'd like to be alone for a while,' she muttered tightly.

'I will accompany you,' Zahir pronounced.

'No…I only want a minute alone,' Saffy whispered pleadingly, because she was thinking about what Akram had hurled at her and reaching the worst possible conclusions. Zahir had been punished by his father for defying him by marrying her? Why had that possibility never occurred to her before? Why had she been so wrapped up in her own misery that it had never occurred to her that Zahir might be dealing with bad things too? But, imprisoned, tortured, beaten…surely not? Was that possible? Would his father have subjected his son to such brutal intimidation? According to his reputation, King Fareed had been responsible for many atrocities. She thought of Zahir's appallingly scarred back and a sense of cold fear of the unknown and of such cruelty infiltrated her. But if Zahir had suffered like that, why hadn't he told her?

When Saffy actually focused enough to recognise where her wandering feet had carried her, she realised that she was back in the old part of the palace where she had once lived. She walked down a dim corridor and cast open the door of the room that had once been theirs. It shook her that it was still furnished the same, untouched by time or alteration, and she walked in with a compulsive shiver of remembrance of the past.

A thousand images engulfed her all at once and she reeled from memories of Zahir watching her with wary eyes, his silences, sudden absences and his refusal to answer questions. Had he been hiding stuff from her that she should have guessed? Was Akram telling the truth? She couldn't bear that suspicion, wasn't sure she could ever live with any discovery that painful...

'I should have had this place cleared...' Zahir murmured from behind her. 'But I used to come here to think about you.'

Saffy turned round, her face pale as milk, her eyes nakedly vulnerable. 'When? After the divorce? I think you need to start talking, Zahir...and maybe I do too,' she acknowledged unevenly.

'After I married you, my brother Omar asked me if I was insane to challenge our father to that extent,' Zahir admitted with curt reluctance. 'But at first I genuinely had no idea what I was dealing with: Omar had protected me too much. He kept a lot of secrets. I was the younger son, the junior army officer, and I wasn't part of the inner circle of people who knew what a monster my father had become on a diet of unfettered power.'

'So, you must have regretted marrying me rather quickly,' Saffy assumed, searching the lean strong features she loved for every passing nuance of expression and sinking down on the edge of the bed where she had often cried her heart out with loneliness.

His handsome mouth hardened. 'I only ever regretted the unnatural lifestyle which our marriage inflicted on you. I had no regrets on my own behalf.'

'That's a kind thing to say but it can't be the way you really felt.'

'I loved you more than life,' Zahir breathed starkly. 'My mistake was in rebelling against my father and bringing you back here to become the equivalent of a hostage. I should have married you and left you in London where you would be safe, but I was too selfish to do that.'

Loved you more than life. The declaration rippled through her like an unexpected benediction, steadying her nerves. 'I loved you too. You weren't selfish. I wouldn't have agreed to being left behind in London.'

'But you didn't know what you were getting into here any more than I did.' Face grave, Zahir compressed his lips. 'Omar had been married five years and he still had no child. Our father was impatient to see the next generation in the family born.'

'That must have put a lot of pressure on Omar and Azel.'

'More on Omar for the lack of fertility was his, *not* hers but I didn't learn that until shortly before Omar... *died.*' He spoke that last word with curious emphasis. 'My older brother's secret was that he had discovered he was unable to father a child and he was afraid to tell our father lest he was passed over in the succession stakes in favour of me. Omar was always the ambitious one,' Zahir told her heavily. 'Unfortunately for him, our father had run out of patience. He demanded that Omar either set Azel aside or take a second wife.'

Saffy was shocked. 'And that was the background to *our* marriage?'

'Our father was doubly enraged when I married you without permission because my marriage to a suitable woman would have been the next step on his agenda.'

'And of course I got in the way of his plans,' Saffy completed. 'Yet you thought he would eventually accept me.'

'I was wrong,' Zahir admitted grittily. 'I was much more naïve than I thought I was about what our father was really like. I never dreamt he would be as vicious with his sons as he was to some of our people. How adolescent was such innocence in a grown man?'

'Everybody wants to think the best of their parents,' Saffy told him with rueful understanding. 'I don't blame you for getting it wrong.'

'The year we were married was the year my father went over the edge. Although I was unaware of it, he had become a regular drug user and suffered from violent rages. From the first day you arrived he wanted me to divorce you...and the sensible act would have been to surrender to greater force, but I was never sensible about you.'

Her heart was beating in what felt uncomfortably like the foot of her throat. 'Greater force?' she queried suspiciously. 'If even half of what Akram suggested happened to you, I have the right to know about it. *Were* you imprisoned? Tortured? *Beaten?*'

Zahir stared levelly back at her, not a muscle moving on his bronzed handsome face, his mouth an unsmiling line. 'I could curse Akram, though he spoke out of ignorance. This is a conversation I never wanted to have with you…'

Saffy was trembling. 'You're telling me that your father—your own father—did do that stuff to you?' she prompted sickly. 'That you weren't away on army manoeuvres when you disappeared for weeks on end?'

Zahir gave confirmation with a grudging jerk of his chin.

And Saffy just closed her eyes, because all of a sudden she couldn't bear to look at him when she had excelled at being such a blind, childish fool all the months they had been man and wife the first time around. He had reappeared after those apparent military trips, filthy, often visibly bruised and cut, always having lost weight…and not once had she questioned the condition he was in, not once had she suspected that he had been brutally ill-treated while he was away from her and prevented from returning from her. In her little cocoon the very fact he was a prince had made entertaining such a suspicion too incredible to even consider. She had assumed that soldiers led a rough and ready life and that such trips were organised to be as realistic and tough as real warfare. And he had never told her, never once breathed a word of what was being done to him, never once sought her sympathy or support...

'Why didn't you tell me?' she asked thickly, tears thickening her throat and creating a huge lump there.

'I didn't want to upset you. There was nothing you could have done to stop it. Omar was correct. I should never have brought you to Maraban. Our father was a madman and he was out of control, incapable of accepting any form of opposition. It was all or nothing and once I defied him he was determined to break me.'

'And all over *me*...all because you married me,' Saffy muttered, her distress growing by the second as she looked back on her colossally ignorant and oblivious self at the age of eighteen. Little wonder he had ducked her questions, embraced silence, never knowing when he would be with her or torn from her side again.

'That whole year you were the only thing that kept me going,' Zahir informed her harshly. *'Look at me.'*

'No!' Saffy unfroze finally and flew upright. 'I have to think about this on my own!'

As she tried to brush past him he closed a hand round a slim forearm. 'I told you I would tell no more lies or half-truths but I never wanted you to know about that period of my life!'

'Oh, I know that...Mr Macho-I-suffer-in-silence!' Saffy condemned chokily, her increasing distress clawing at her control. 'So when you came back here to me after suffering gross mistreatment and allowed me to shout at you and complain that I was bored and lonely?

Just what I need to know to feel like the biggest bitch ever created!'

And, tears streaming down her distraught face, Saffy fled, in need of privacy. How could he do that to her? How could he not have told her? How could he have allowed her to find out all that from his resentful brother? She had known King Fareed wasn't a pleasant or popular man, but she had had no idea that he was a drug-abusing tyrant capable of torturing his own son if he was disobedient! What an idiot she must have been not to have guessed that something so dreadful was going on! How could she ever forgive herself for that? *You were the only thing that kept me going.* Why was he still trying to make her feel better by saying that sort of rubbish? He'd been stuck in a virtually sexless marriage while being regularly punished for rebelling against his father's dictates. And not once had she suspected anything. Was she stupid, utterly stupid, to have been so unseeing?

Saffy took refuge in their new bedroom, which was comfortably removed from the suffocating memories of the older accommodation they had once occasionally shared. She was remembering the condition of Zahir's back, thinking, although she didn't want to, of him being whipped, beaten up, *hurt* and all on her behalf. Zahir with his pride and his intrinsic sense of decency! She ran to the bathroom and heaved but nothing came up and she hugged the vanity unit to stay upright, surveying her tousled reflection with stricken accusing eyes.

How could you not know? How could you not see what he was going through?

'This is why I never wanted you to know. I didn't want to see you hurt because all of it was my fault…'

Saffy spun round. He stood in the doorway, lean and bronzed and gorgeous in black jeans and a white shirt, so much the guy she loved and admired and cared about. 'How was it your fault?' she scissored back at him incredulously.

'I married you. I brought you back here with me. I placed both of us in a foolish and vulnerable position,' Zahir stated grimly. 'I will never forgive myself for that.'

'You should've divorced me the minute the punishments started!' Saffy launched back at him. 'How could you be so stubborn that you went through that just for me?'

A faint shadow of a smile that struck her as impossible in the circumstances curved his wide sensual mouth. 'I loved you…I couldn't give you up.'

'I wouldn't have let you go through that if I'd known! How could you still want me?' she sobbed in disbelief. 'I wasn't even able to give you sex!'

'The sex was the least of it. Believe me, at the time, consummating our marriage was not my biggest challenge.' His stunning golden eyes lowered from her shaken face and he held out a hand until she grasped it, allowing him to pull her closer. 'But I couldn't seek help or advice for us either. Had anyone known we had those problems my father would have had yet another reason to want you out of my life…'

Saffy dragged in a quivering breath, still reeling from what she had learned. Eyes wet, she pushed her face against his shoulder, drinking in the scent of his sun-warmed flesh, the faint evocative tang that was uniquely his, which made her feel vaguely intoxicated. She was addicted to him, so pathetically *addicted*. 'Thank heaven you finally had the sense to divorce me and give the dreadful man what he wanted.'

'That was probably the one and only unselfish thing I ever did while I was married to you, the only thing I *ever* did solely for you and not for me,' Zahir muttered roughly above her down-bent head, his lips brushing across her brow in a calming gesture. 'I'm not the saint you seem to think. I made appalling errors of judgement.'

Her forehead furrowing, she looked up at him 'Such as?'

'Bringing you into Maraban five years ago,' he specified. 'Three months after Omar's death, I found out that he had been murdered...'

'What?' Shattered by that statement, she stared up at him.

'One of the generals told me the truth because the most senior army personnel were becoming nervous about my father's reign of terror. Omar was beaten up by my father's henchmen and he died from a head injury. The car crash was simply a cover-up. It was then that I realised that my father really had gone beyond the hope of return,' Zahir revealed rawly.

'Oh…my…word,' Saffy framed sickly. 'Are you sure?'

'One hundred per cent.' Zahir compressed his lips. 'That's when I appreciated that keeping you in Maraban was sheer insanity when my father wanted rid of you. I didn't have the power to protect you. I was putting your life at risk by refusing to divorce you. I was making you a target in my father's eyes. I'm ashamed it took Omar's death to make me accept that if I couldn't keep you safe, I *had* to let you go….'

Saffy's heart was beating very loudly in her eardrums and she drifted dizzily away from him on weak legs to drop heavily down on a sofa in the corner of their room. 'So, that's why the divorce came out of nowhere at me. You honestly thought I was in danger. Why didn't you tell me the truth then, Zahir?'

'The truth would have terrified you and I was ashamed that I could not even keep myself safe, never mind my wife. But that was also the moment that, in losing you, my father finally lost my loyalty. I could never have forgiven him for what he had done to Omar, but losing you was excruciating,' he completed gruffly, dropping down on his knees in front of her and momentarily lowering his dark head down onto her lap. 'You have no idea how much I loved you, what strength it took to give you up, knowing, having to accept that it was the *only* thing I could do…'

As he admitted that stinging tears were rolling down Saffy's face. She had never dreamt that she could feel such pain on someone else's behalf and yet when Zahir

talked of how much it had hurt to divorce her, it was as
if a giant black hole of unhappiness opened up inside her
and cracked her heart right down the middle. Her fingers
delved into his luxuriant black hair, delving, smoothing.
'I loved you too…I loved you so much. I don't think I
even understood how much I needed you in my life until
we were forced apart,' she confided jaggedly.

'I tried to contact you after my father died and the
fighting was finished,' Zahir told her grimly as he lifted
his handsome dark head and leapt back upright to pace
restively. 'I spoke to your sister, Kat.'

Saffy was stunned. 'She didn't tell me.'

Zahir grimaced. 'Kat pleaded with me to leave you
alone. She said you had just got your life back together,
that you were working, making friends and that the last
thing you needed was to see me again,' Zahir recalled,
tight-mouthed at the recollection.

Saffy felt as if someone had walked over her grave.
How could the sister she loved have got her so wrong?
The divorce had broken her heart but she had still loved
Zahir and would have moved heaven and earth to see
him again. 'She shouldn't have interfered.'

'On that score we'll have to disagree.' Zahir surprised
her with that response. 'Sadly, even though I didn't like
what Kat had to say, she was right.'

'No, she was wrong,' Saffy contradicted.

'You were far too young to deal with what I was dealing with then on top of the other problems we had and
Maraban had. You needed the time to live the normal
life you should have enjoyed before we married,' Zahir

contended. 'I can see that now but I couldn't see it at the time. I simply wanted you back the minute it would have been safe to bring you back...'

Tears trickled down Saffy's cheeks. 'I would've come back to you,' she whispered shakily.

'You would've walked away from those magazine covers and your face everywhere?' Zahir prompted dubiously.

'Yes, it was never that important to me. It was the means to make a living and not be a burden on my sister.'

Zahir bent down and grasped her hands to raise her. 'But we work better now because we're older and wiser.'

A shadow crossed her lovely face. 'And, of course, you're much more experienced.'

He paled, his strong bone structure tightening. 'After our *mutual* failure, I was afraid I had become...impotent. I had lost all confidence,' he confided in a grudging undertone, tension and shame etched in every line of his strong face. 'I knew I had to get past my obsession with you because you were no longer mine. My father sent me abroad before the civil war broke out. Ironically he was trying to reward me for divorcing you...'

Saffy lifted her fingers and gently smoothed the stubborn angle of his jaw. 'It's all right. I can't say I don't mind because that would be a lie, but I understand why it happened.'

His beautiful dark eyes narrowed and centred intently on her solemn face. 'Then isn't it time you explained how that miracle happened for you? You insist there hasn't been another man but—'

'That was the truth.' Her wandering fingers strayed to his wide sensual lower lip to silence him. 'I wanted to be normal in the bedroom and I went to see a specialist to find out what was wrong with me. I was told that I suffered from a condition called vaginismus, which is an involuntary tightening of the pelvic muscles, often triggered by some trauma in the past. My inability to relax, the panic attacks when you tried to touch me were all part of it,' she explained, doggedly pushing herself on to spill what had lain behind her deepest vulnerability. 'I went for therapy but it wasn't until I had hypnotherapy that I discovered what had triggered my phobia about that part of my body...'

Zahir held her back from him, his shrewd gaze welded to her troubled face and the sheen of perspiration already dampening her upper lip. 'Tell me—there should be nothing you can't tell me.'

'I was abused by one of my mother's boyfriends when I was a child,' Saffy framed shakily, tears welling up in her eyes because she could not bring herself to look and see how he was reacting to that unsavoury news. 'I suppose I was lucky he didn't rape me, but then he was never able to get me alone for very long. He threatened me. He said that if I told Mum, she wouldn't believe me, and he said Emmie and Topsy would have to take my place.'

Zahir swore in his own language and gripped her

shoulders. 'Please tell me that you went to your mother for help.'

A taut expression set Saffy's face. 'I did but my abuser was right—Mum refused to believe me and punished me for even opening the subject. My abuser was a well-off professional man with a name for being a womaniser and there was no way my mother was going to give him up or suspect him on only the strength of my word.'

Zahir pushed up her chin. 'What age were you?'

'Seven.' Saffy gazed up into his furious eyes and shivered. 'I couldn't stop him, Zahir, but I knew it was wrong.'

Zahir almost crushed her in his arms. 'Is that the impression I'm giving you? That it was somehow your fault that some filthy pervert abused your trust? That's *not* how I feel. I'm furious the bastard got away with it, furious your mother wouldn't listen to you, furious I wasn't there to prevent it happening in the first place!' he spelt out in a savage undertone.

'You're angry.'

'But *not* with you, with the people who have hurt you and let you down, even though I'm one of their number,' he muttered, his breathing fracturing as he scooped her up and brought her carefully down on the bed with him, holding her close to every line of his long, lean physique. 'Facing the fact that you'd been abused must have been very difficult for you.'

'Apparently it's quite common for children to suppress memories of that kind of assault,' Saffy whis-

pered unevenly, reassured by the solid thump of his
heart against her breast and the reality that he was hugging her without demonstrating any symptoms of re-
vulsion towards her. 'I felt horrible but, on one level,
it was a relief to find out what had made me the way I
was. I knew I'd never be able to have another relationship until I could overcome my problems.'

'I wish I'd known. What treatment did you have?'

'I had loads of supportive counselling and then a
physical intervention,' Saffy explained hesitantly. 'I had
muscle relaxants injected to prevent the contractions
and a dilator was inserted while I was still unconscious.
For a long time I slept with it inserted overnight...' As
Zahir looked down at her, her face was burning. 'I had
to learn to accept my own body and to touch myself.
I'd always avoided that without ever wondering why. I
assumed I was just very fastidious, I didn't know I suffered from an actual phobia until we got married and it
all went wrong. But after I had completed the treatment
I did hope to find a lover once I'd worked through all
the recovery steps.'

'And why didn't you do that?' Zahir demanded, stunning dark golden eyes pinned to her. 'I shouldn't have
thought that would have been a challenge.'

'You'd be surprised. I not only wanted a man who attracted me, but also one whom I *cared* something about.
Having waited so long and gone through so much to find
the answer to my problems, I didn't want just anyone!'
Saffy explained with spirit. 'Unfortunately the right
guy didn't appear. To most of the men I met, I would

only have been a trophy. I wanted more than that from a man. I believed I deserved more than that.'

His lush black lashes semi-screened his glittering scrutiny, colour lying in a hard line along his fabulous cheekbones. 'Then how on earth did you contrive to settle for me again?'

Saffy stiffened. 'I was still very attracted to you… don't know why,' she dared to pronounce, watching his amazing eyes smoulder at that challenge into glowing golden flames. 'I told myself that being with you didn't mean anything to me emotionally and that I was simply using you to get rid of my virginity.'

Zahir nodded very slowly and then bent his head to steal a kiss that made her head spin, and her fingers clutched frantic handfuls of his luxuriant black hair. The pressure of his mouth combined with the penetration of his tongue was an intoxicating thrill, so that when he lifted his head again, separating them, she frowned.

'I told myself a lot of lies that night in the tent as well. I couldn't admit how I still felt about you,' he confided with a hard twist of his mouth. 'In fact in the time we were divorced I had grown unreasonably and unjustly bitter.'

'Bitter?' she queried.

'Bitter that I'd loved and lost you and that you appeared to be having a hell of a good time without me. Even worse, I couldn't forget you,' he confessed harshly. 'There you were in my sister's magazines, which she was always leaving lying around, seemingly enjoying a party lifestyle with various different men. I was angry and jealous… There, I have said it at last! I wanted you back from the moment I lost you and I never changed towards you. I loved you five years ago and I love you even more now…'

'You…*do?*' Saffy was enchanted by that admission and the ferocious fervent force with which he spoke and studied her.

'I love you and I always will.' Zahir groaned because the wife he adored was not a patient woman and she was stroking her hand down his taut, powerful thigh with rousing intent.

'I love you too… I didn't stop loving you either,' Saffy confided. 'But I was too proud to admit that. At first, I wanted you to believe I'd had other lovers.'

'It wouldn't have mattered if you had had. I would still love you. I've grown up too,' Zahir declared. 'Circumstances tore us apart.'

'But you brought us back together again.' Saffy scored a fingernail along the rippling muscle of one thigh, loving his instant response to her provocation. 'You kidnapped me.'

'I also asked you to be my mistress. I'm ashamed of that,' he said bluntly. 'But I wanted you any way I could get you… I couldn't face losing you again but my behaviour was inexcusable.'

Saffy stared down at him and suddenly grinned, unable to hide her amusement. 'But that behaviour was very much *you.* You can't fight what you are inside: direct, bold, passionate. I couldn't believe you still wanted me that much after our disastrous year together.'

'I honestly did believe that it was *I* who had failed *you* in the bedroom,' Zahir told her tautly. 'I assumed my clumsiness and ignorance had scared you, that I'd hurt you, given you a *fear* of intimacy.'

'No…no, it wouldn't have mattered who I was with, it would have been the same, but another man might not have had your patience,' she argued, her eyes not leaving his for a second as, drawn like a moth to a flame, she slowly lowered her mouth to his. 'You were very kind and understanding when you must have been hugely sexually frustrated.'

It was Zahir's turn to smile. 'No, you took care of me in other ways and I had few complaints.'

Saffy tensed. 'Doesn't knowing about the…er… abuse turn you off?'

'No, it makes you even more worthy of being the love of my life. I know how strong you must be to have got through that and dealt with it.' With gentle fingers he smoothed a stray strand of golden hair from her brow. 'I know how hard I had to work coming to terms with what was done to me while I was imprisoned by my father…'

'I still can't stand the thought of that,' she admitted chokily, her eyes filming over.

'Omar and I were raised like spoilt little rich kids with titles. Being powerless and a victim taught me a lot that I needed to learn for the benefit of others,' Zahir delivered wryly, rolling over to slide a long, hard thigh between hers and nudge her knees apart. 'I want to make love to you…I want to know that you're mine forever.'

Loving the weight of him against her, Saffy gave him

a teasing smile. 'I hope you do appreciate that you will be stuck with me for ever.'

'I was terrified that that might not be the case,' Zahir sliced in, claiming a hungry driving kiss that left her breathless. 'Afraid that you were keeping your options open and planning to ask me for a divorce some day.'

'As long as you can kiss me like that, you're pretty safe,' Saffy teased, watching heat flare in his gaze.

He made love to her with all the scorching passion of his temperament and when she finally subsided in the strong circle of his arms, alight with happiness and the glorious aftermath of incredible physical pleasure, she snuggled close to him. 'I'm not going anywhere away from you ever again,' she swore vehemently.

Zahir grinned, splayed long fingers over her still-flat tummy and gently stroked it. 'So, you'll sleep in a tent with me next time I ask?'

'As long as it has electric and hot and cold running water,' Saffy specified. 'You're really happy about the baby, aren't you?'

A slashing smile scythed across his lean bronzed features. 'Of course I'm excited about the baby, the next generation. We'll be a family as I always dreamt. I still remember the first time I saw you in that store,' he confided huskily. 'And people don't believe in love at first sight.'

'I do...' Lacing her fingers into his thick, tousled black hair, Saffy looked up into his gorgeous eyes with a heart beating like a drum. 'And after what we've been through together and apart, I also believe that a love like that can last for ever...'

'For ever,' Zahir repeated, wrapping both arms round her and pulling her close, knowing that, having lost her once, he would never take the smallest risk of losing her again.

Two years on from that conversation, Saffy soothed her son, Karim, as he fell off his toddler bike for at least the third time and roared with temper and frustration. As soon as his mother set him down again on his sturdy little legs, Karim streaked back to the bike, determined to master the art of riding it so that he could race around the gardens in the company of his female cousins. As she watched her little boy tell the bike off for not doing his bidding, she laughed.

'He doesn't give up easily,' her sister, Kat, commented.

'No, he's like Zahir in that.' Saffy smiled at her sibling, loving the fact that she and Mikhail had come to stay with them in Maraban but aching for the couple at the same time. Kat had recently gone through IVF in Russia in an attempt to conceive but, sadly, the procedure hadn't worked. In another month the couple were set for a second try and Saffy was praying that the treatment would deliver a successful result, for if any woman deserved a child of her own it was Kat, who had raised her three sisters with so much love and support.

'The servants wait on him hand and foot,' Kat commented. 'You'll have to watch that.'

'I do. He tidies up his own toys. Zahir doesn't want him spoiled the same way he was.'

'The way your husband spoils you?' Kat laughed, secure in the knowledge that Saffy was deliriously happy in Maraban.

'Spoiling me gives Zahir a kick,' Saffy confided with a grin, thinking of the vast selection of jewels and luxuries she was continually showered in.

More importantly, Saffy had found a real role to keep her busy in her husband's country. She had participated in making a promotional film of Maraban and had impressed everybody with her skill as a presenter. But then she had thoroughly enjoyed the personalised tour of the various sites of interest with Zahir by her side and had become almost as knowledgeable about his country of birth as he was in the process. The warm welcome of the locals had increased her identification with Maraban as her new home. She had got involved with local charities, now sat on the board of the newest hospital in the city and regularly visited educational institutions. But most precious of all on her terms had been spending an entire week with Zahir and Karim at the orphanage school in South Africa, which she had long supported.

As a rule she usually went to London to see her sisters. Topsy was at university, studying hard and rarely free for more than a weekend, but Emmie often visited London to shop and the twins now got together as often as they could contrive it. Rediscovering her relationship with her sister meant a great deal to Saffy and the process was helped by the reality that both women now had much more in common.

Zahir strode through the door with Mikhail a mere step in his wake. Kat's husband, a Russian billionaire, was currently advising the Marabani government on how best to invest the oil revenues that kept the country afloat. Zahir swept his son off the bike a split second before the child fell again.

'He won't stop trying,' Saffy told her handsome husband. 'He won't give up. He's so like you.'

'But he has your eyes and impatience,' Zahir remarked appreciatively as he set his squirming son down again and watched him head straight back to the demon bike that still wouldn't do what he wanted it to do.

Zahir linked his fingers with Saffy and walked her out onto the terrace. Overhead the sun was sinking in a peach and orange blaze of colour and soon they would sit down to dinner by candlelight and talk long into the night. Just for a moment, even though she was very much enjoying having her sister and her husband as guests, she wished she were alone with Zahir.

He looked down at her with smouldering dark golden eyes and butterflies leapt in her tummy and her mouth ran dry. 'We should get dressed for dinner,' he murmured lazily.

A smile tugging at her lush lips, Saffy leant back against his lean powerful body in an attitude of complete trust, knowing they would end up in bed, loving the fact that he found it as hard to keep his hands off her as she did him. She was deliriously happy in her marriage and Karim's arrival had enriched and deepened the ties between her and Zahir. 'I love you,' she whispered.

'I love you too,' Zahir purred, pressing his mouth hungrily to the base of her throat and making her shiver against him.

* * * * *

THE SHEIKH'S SON

KRISTI GOLD

Kristi Gold has a fondness for beaches, baseball and bridal reality shows. She firmly believes that love has remarkable healing powers and feels very fortunate to be able to weave stories of love and commitment. As a bestselling author, a National Readers' Choice Award winner and a Romance Writers of America three-time RITA® Award finalist, Kristi has learned that although accolades are wonderful, the most cherished rewards come from networking with readers. She can be reached through her website at www.kristigold.com or through Facebook.

One

If a woman wanted a trip to paradise, the gorgeous guy seated at the bar could be just the ticket. And Piper McAdams was more than ready to board that pleasure train.

For the past twenty minutes, she'd been sitting at a corner table in the Chicago hotel lounge, nursing a cosmopolitan while shamelessly studying the stranger's assets, at least those she could readily see in the dim light. He wore an expensive silk navy suit, a pricey watch on his wrist and his good looks like a badge of honor. His dark brown hair seemed as if it had been intentionally cut in a reckless—albeit sexy—style, but it definitely complemented the slight shading of whiskers framing his mouth. And those dimples. She'd spotted them the first time he smiled. Nothing better than prominent dimples on a man, except maybe…

The questionable thought vaulted into Piper's brain like a bullet, prompting her to close her eyes and rub her temples as if she had a tremendous headache. She chalked up the reaction to her long-standing membership in the Unintentional Celibacy Club. She wasn't necessarily a prude, only picky. She certainly wasn't opposed to taking sex out for a spin before saying, "I do," in the context of a committed relationship. She simply hadn't found the right man, though not from the lack of trying. But never, ever in twenty-six years had she considered ending her sexual drought with a complete stranger...until tonight.

The sound of laughter drew her gaze back to said stranger, where the pretty blond bartender leaned toward him, exposing enough cleavage to rival the Grand Canyon. Oddly, he continued to focus on Blondie's face, until his attention drifted in Piper's direction.

The moment Piper met his gaze and he grinned, she immediately glanced back to search for a bathroom or another blonde but didn't find either one. When she regarded him again and found his focus still leveled on her, she started fiddling with her cell phone, pretending to read a nonexistent text.

Great. Just great. He'd caught her staring like a schoolgirl, and she'd just provided a big boost to his ego. He wouldn't be interested in her, a nondescript, ridiculously average brunette, when he had a tall, well-endowed bombshell at his disposal. He could probably have any willing woman within a thousand-mile radius, and she wouldn't be even a blip on his masculine radar. She took the mirror out of her purse and did a quick check anyway, making sure her bangs were smooth and her mascara hadn't gone askew beneath her eyes.

And going to any trouble for a man like him was simply ridiculous. History had taught her that she more or less attracted guys who found her good breeding and trust fund extremely appealing. Nope, Mr. Hunky Stranger would never give her a second look....

"Are you waiting for someone?"

Piper's heart lurched at the sound of his voice. A very deep, and very British, voice. After she'd recovered enough to sneak a peek, her pulse started to sprint again as she came up close and personal with his incredible eyes. Eyes that were just this shade of brown and remarkably as clear as polished topaz. "Actually, no, I'm not waiting for anyone," she finally managed to say in a tone that sounded as if she was playing the frog to his prince, not the other way around.

He rested his hand on the back of the opposing chair, a gold signet ring containing a single ruby circling his little finger. "Would you mind if I join you?"

Mind? Did birds molt? "Be my guest."

After setting his drink on the table, he draped his overcoat on the back of the chair, sat and leaned back as if nothing out of the ordinary had occurred. Then again, this was probably the norm for him—picking up someone in a bar. For Piper, not so much.

"I'm surprised you're not keeping company with a man," he said. "You are much too beautiful to spend Saturday night all alone."

She was surprised she hadn't fainted from the impact of his fully formed grin, the sexy half-moon crescent in his chin and the compliment. "Actually, I just left a cocktail party a little while ago."

He studied her curiously. "In the hotel?"

She took a quick sip of her drink and nearly tipped

the glass over when she set it down. "Yes. A party in honor of some obscenely rich sheikh from some obscure country. I faked a headache and left before I had to endure meeting him. That's probably a good thing, since for the life of me, I can't remember his name."

"Prince Mehdi?"

"That's it."

"I happened to have left there a few moments ago myself."

Lovely, Piper. Open mouth, insert stiletto. "Do you know the prince?"

"I've known him for a very long time. Since birth, actually." He topped off the comment with another slow smile.

She swallowed around her mortification while wishing for a giant crevice to open up and swallow her whole. "I'm sorry for insulting your friend. I just have an aversion to overly wealthy men. I've never found one who isn't completely consumed with a sense of entitlement."

He rimmed his finger around the edge of the clear glass. "Actually, some would say he's a rather nice fellow."

She highly doubted that. "Is that your opinion?"

"Yes. Of the three Mehdi brothers, he is probably the most grounded. Definitely the best looking of the whole lot."

When Piper suddenly realized she'd abandoned her manners, she held out her hand. "I'm Piper McAdams, and you are?"

"Charmed to meet you," he said as he accepted the handshake, and then slid his thumb over her wrist before letting her go.

She shivered slightly but recovered quickly. "Well, Mr. Charmed, do you have a first name?"

"A.J."

"No last name?"

"I'd like to preserve a little mystery for the time being. Besides, last names should not be important between friends."

Clearly he was hiding something, but her suspicious nature couldn't compete with her attraction to this mysterious stranger. "We're not exactly friends."

"I hope to remedy that before night's end."

Piper hoped she could survive sitting across from him without going into a feminine free fall. She crossed one leg over the other beneath the table and tugged at the hem of her cocktail dress. "What do you do for a living, A.J.?"

He loosened his tie before lacing his fingers together atop the table. "I am the personal pilot for a rich and somewhat notorious family. They prefer to maintain their privacy."

A pretty flyboy. Unbelievable. "That must be a huge responsibility."

"You have no idea," he said before clearing his throat. "What do you do for a living, Ms. McAdams?"

Nothing she cared to be doing. "Please, call me Piper. Let's just say I serve as a goodwill ambassador for clients associated with my grandfather's company. It requires quite a bit of travel and patience."

He inclined his head and studied her face as if searching for secrets. "McAdams is a Scottish name, and the hint of auburn in your hair and beautiful blue eyes could indicate that lineage. Yet your skin isn't fair."

She touched her cheek as if she had no idea she even

owned any skin. "My great-grandparents were Colombian on my mother's side. My father's family is Scottish through and through. I suppose you could say I'm a perfect mix of both cultures."

"Colombian and Scottish. A very attractive combination. Do you tan in the summer?"

A sudden image of sitting with him on a beach—sans swimwear—assaulted her. "I do when I find the time to actually go to the beach. I'm not home that often."

"And where is home?" he asked.

"South Carolina. Charleston, actually." She refused to reveal that she currently resided in the guesthouse behind her grandparents' Greek Revival mansion.

He hesitated a moment as if mulling over the information. "Yet you have no Southern accent."

"It disappeared when I attended an all-female boarding school on the East Coast."

He leaned forward with obvious interest. "Really? I attended military academy in England."

That certainly explained his accent. "How long were you there?"

His expression turned suddenly serious. "A bloody lot longer than I should have been."

She suspected a story existed behind his obvious disdain. "An all-male academy, I take it."

"Unfortunately, yes. However, the campus was situated not far from a parochial school populated with curious females. We were more than happy to answer that curiosity."

No real surprise there. "Did you lead the panty raids?"

His smile reappeared as bright as the illuminated beer sign over the bar. "I confess I attempted to raid a few panties in my youth, and received several slaps for my efforts."

She was consumed by pleasant shivers when she should be shocked. "I highly doubt that was always the case."

"Not always." He leaned back again, his grin expanding, his dimples deepening. "Did you fall victim to the questionable antics of boarding-school boys?"

She'd fallen victim to playing the wallflower, though she hadn't exactly been playing. "My school was located in a fairly remote area, and the rules were extremely strict. The headmistress would probably have shot first and asked questions later if a boy ever dared darken our doorstep."

His eyes held a hint of amusement. "I'm certain a woman with your looks had no difficulty making up for lost time once you escaped the confines of convention."

If he only knew how far off the mark he was with that assumption, he'd probably run for the nearest exit. "Let's just say I've had my share of boys darkening my doorstep. Most had last names for first names and more money than sexual prowess, thanks to my grandfather's insistence I marry within his social circles."

"Not a decent lover among them?"

Only one, and he'd been far from decent. She imagined A.J. would be a seriously good lover. She'd seriously like to find out. "Since I'm not into kissing and telling, let's move off that subject. Do you have a significant other?"

"I did have an 'other' almost a year ago, but she is no longer significant."

"Bad breakup?"

"Let's just say it took a while to convince her we did break up."

His sour tone told Piper that topic was also off-limits. On to more generic questions. "When I first spotted you at the bar, I was sure you're Italian. Am I right?"

Luckily his pleasant demeanor returned. "No, but I am quite fond of Italy, and I do know Italian, courtesy of a former teacher."

"My second guess would be you're of French descent."

"Je ne suis pas français, mais je peux bien embrasser à la francaise."

A sexy devil with devastating dimples and a wry sense of humor—a deadly combination. "I'm sure the parochial girls appreciated your French-kissing expertise. But you didn't exactly answer my question about your heritage."

"I am not of French, but I am impressed you speak the language."

She laid a dramatic palm over her breast and pulled out her best Southern speak. "Why, sugar, we're not all dumb belles. I know French and German and even a little Japanese."

"Should you find yourself in need of an Italian translator, I would be happy to accommodate you."

She would be thrilled if he did more than that. "I've never been to Italy but I've always wanted to see Rome."

"You should make that a priority. I personally prefer Naples and the coast...."

As he continued, Piper became completely mesmerized by his mouth, and began to ridiculously fantasize about kissing him. Then her fantasies took major flight as she entertained thoughts of his mouth moving down her body. Slow and warm and, oh, so...

"...large pink salmon walk down the streets texting on their smartphones."

She rejoined reality following the odd declaration. "I beg your pardon?"

"Clearly I bored you into a near coma while playing the travel guide."

He'd inadvertently drawn her into a waking sex dream. "I'm so sorry," she said. "It must be the booze."

He reached over and without an invitation took a drink from her glass, then set it down with a thud. "That is bloody awful," he said. "What is in this unpalatable concoction?"

Piper turned her attention to the drink and momentarily became preoccupied with the fact his lips had caressed the glass. And that was probably as close to his lips she would get...unless she took the plunge and turned the good girl to bad. "Basically vodka and cranberry juice, but the bartender made it fairly strong. It's gone straight to my head." And so had he.

He pushed his half-full glass toward her. "Try this."

She picked up the tumbler and studied the amber liquid. "What is it?"

"Twenty-year-old Scotch. Once you've sampled it, no other drink will do."

She would really like to sample him, and if she didn't stop those thoughts in their tracks, she might derail her common sense. "I'm not sure I should. I don't want to have to crawl to the hotel room."

"If you need assistance, I'll make certain you arrive safely."

Piper returned his wily smile. "Well, in that case, I suppose I could have a small sip."

The minute the straight liquor hit her throat, she truly wanted to spit it out. Instead, she swallowed hard and handed the tumbler back to him.

"You don't like it?" he asked, sounding somewhat insulted.

"Sorry, but it's just not my cup of tea. Or cup of alcohol, I should say. But then, I can't claim to have good drinking skills."

"How are your kissing skills?" Right when she was about to suggest they find out, he straightened, looked away and cleared his throat again. "My apologies. You are too nice a woman to endure my habit of spewing innuendo."

"Why do you believe I wouldn't appreciate a little harmless innuendo?"

He streaked a hand over his jaw. "You have a certain innocence about you. Perhaps even purity."

Here we go again.... "Looks can be deceiving."

"True, but eyes do not deceive. I've noticed your growing discomfort during the course of our conversation."

"Have you considered my discomfort stems from my attraction to you?" Heavens, she hadn't really just admitted that, had she? Yes, she had. Her gal pals would be so proud. Her grandfather would lock her up and toss away the key.

"I'm flattered," he said without taking his gaze from hers. "I must admit I find you very attractive as well, and I would like to know you better. Because of that, I have a request. You are under no obligation to agree, but I hope you will."

The moment of truth had arrived. Would she be willing to hurl caution to the wind and sleep with him? Would she really take that risk when she knew so little about him, including his last name? Oh, heck yeah. "Ask away."

When A.J. stood and offered his hand, her heart vaulted into her throat. She held her breath and waited for the ultimate proposition, the word *yes* lingering on her lips.

"Piper McAdams, would you do me the honor of taking a walk with me?"

Sheikh Adan Jamal Mehdi did not take women on long walks. He took them to bed. Or he had before he'd taken that bloody vow of celibacy eight months before in order to be taken more seriously by his brothers. A vow that had suddenly lost its appeal.

Yet Piper McAdams wasn't his usual conquest. She was witty and outgoing, while he normally attracted sophisticated and somewhat cynical women. She was only slightly over five feet tall, he would estimate, were it not for the four-inch heels, when he usually preferred someone closer in height to his six feet two inches. She also had surprisingly long legs and extremely full breasts for someone so small in stature, and he'd had trouble keeping his eyes off those assets for any length of time. The oath of restraint had not silenced his libido in any sense, especially now.

They strolled along the walkway bordering the lake for a good twenty minutes, speaking mostly in generalities, until Adan felt strangely at a loss for words. Conversation had always been his forte, and so had kissing.

He thought it best to concentrate on the first. "Do you have any siblings?"

When a gust of wind swirled around them, she pulled her hem-length black cashmere sweater closer to her body. "One. A twin sister whose official name is Sunshine, but she goes by Sunny, for obvious reasons."

He was immediately struck by the familiar name. "Sunny McAdams, the renowned journalist?"

Her smile showed a certain pride. "That would be her. We're actually fraternal twins, as if you couldn't figure that out from our obvious physical differences."

Yet neither woman lacked in beauty despite the fact one was blond and the other brunette. "Piper and Sunshine are both rather unusual names. Did they hold some significance for your parents?"

Her expression turned somber. "It's my understanding my mother named Sunny. Unfortunately, we don't know our father. Actually, we don't even know who he is, and I'm not sure my mother does, either. You could say we were a thorn in her socialite side. Our grandparents basically raised us for that reason."

That explained her sudden change in demeanor. But due to his own questions about his heritage, he believed discussing family dynamics in-depth should be avoided at all costs. "You said your mother named your sister. Who named you?"

"My grandfather did," she said with a smile. "He adores bagpipes."

Her elevated mood pleased him greatly. "I learned to play the bagpipes at school, but I quickly determined the kilts weren't at all my style."

She paused to lean back against the railing. "Tell

me something. Is it true that men wear nothing under those kilts?"

"A man needs some reminder that he is still a man while wearing a skirt." Being so close to this particular woman served to remind him of his manhood at every turn.

She laughed softly. "I suppose that's true. Why did your parents send you to boarding school?"

He'd asked that question many times, and he'd always received the same answer that he'd never quite believed. "I was an incorrigible lad, or so I'm told, and my father decided I could use the structure a military academy provides."

"Guess he wasn't counting on the panty raids."

Hearing the word *panty* coming out of her pretty mouth did not help his current predicament in the least. "He never learned about them as far as I know." His father had never really been close to his youngest son, if the truth were known.

"I'm sure if you'd ask him today," Piper said, "he'd probably admit he knew everything. Fathers and grandfathers have an uncanny knack of knowing your business."

He moved to her side, faced the lake and rested his hands on the railing. "My father passed away not long ago. My mother died some time ago."

"I'm sorry, A.J.," she said. "I didn't mean to be so thoughtless."

"No need to apologize, Piper. You had no way of knowing." Nor did she know he hailed from Middle Eastern royalty, and that bothered him quite a bit. Yet she had clearly stated she loathed men with fortunes,

and he had a sizable one. For that reason, he would continue to keep that information concealed.

Tonight he preferred to be only the pilot, not the
prince. "Did you attend university?" he asked, keeping his attention trained on the less-interesting view in
order to keep his desire for her in check.

"Yes, I did. In South Carolina. An all-women's university. Evidently my grandfather believed I couldn't
handle the opposite sex. But since he was footing the
bill, I put up with it long enough to get the dreaded
business degree."

He shifted to face her, one elbow braced on the top
of the railing. "Since business is apparently not your
chosen field of expertise, what would you do if you
weren't playing the ambassador?"

"Art," she said without the slightest hesitation.
"Painting is my passion."

He knew all about passion, only his involved planes.
"Then why not pursue that dream?"

She sighed. "I have several reasons, most having to
do with obligation."

"To your grandfather?"

"Yes."

Not so unlike his obligation to his legacy. "What
about remaining true to yourself and your own happiness, Piper?"

A span of silence passed before she spoke again.
"It's complicated."

Family dynamics always were, especially in his case.

When he noticed Piper appeared to be shivering,
Adan cursed his thoughtlessness. "Obviously you're
cold. Do you wish to return to the hotel now?"

She shook her head. "I'm fine. Really."

"You're wearing little more than a glorified sweater, and I suspect your teeth are chattering behind that beautiful mouth of yours."

Her laugh drew him further into her lair, as did the pleasant scent of her perfume. "Maybe a tad. It's rather nippy for April."

"Let me remedy that for you."

When Adan began to slip the buttons on his overcoat, Piper raised both hands as if to ward him off. "Heavens, no. I don't want to be responsible for you freezing to death."

Her smile alone generated enough heat in Adan to fuel half the city of Chicago. "Are you sure? I am accustomed to extreme temperatures."

"Seriously, I'm okay."

Without waiting for another protest, he shrugged out of his coat, wrapped it around her shoulders and took a step back. "Better?"

"Much better, but now you're going to be cold."

Not likely. Not while she stood before him with her dark hair blowing in the breeze, her bright blue eyes reflecting the light above them and her coral-painted lips enticing him to kiss her. Answering the invitation was a risk he didn't dare take.

She inhaled deeply then released a slightly broken breath. "I need something else from you, A.J."

He hoped she meant something warm to drink, a good excuse to retire back inside the hotel before he hurled wisdom to the blustery wind. "What would that be?"

"I need you to kiss me."

Bloody hell, what could he to say to that? Should he answer "absolutely not" when he wanted to blurt out a resounding yes? He brushed away a strand of hair from her cheek and ran his thumb along her jaw. "I'm not certain that would be a banner idea." Many times he had heard that phrase, but never coming out of his own mouth.

Disappointment called out from her eyes. "Why not?"

"Because if I kiss you, I would not want to stop with only a kiss."

She sent him an angel's smile. "Do you have issues with maintaining control?"

He prided himself on control when it came to flying jets and yes, wooing women. Still, there was something about this particular woman that told him he could end up losing the war he now waged with his libido.

Before he could respond, she wrapped her hand around his neck and lowered his lips to hers. He immediately discovered the angel kissed like the devil, and he liked it. He liked the way she tasted and the silken glide of her tongue against his, and he definitely liked the way she pressed her entire body against him. He would like it better if they were in his hotel bed without the hindrance of clothing. He did not particularly care for the warning bells sounding inside his brain.

Gathering every ounce of strength he still possessed, Adan pulled away and stepped back before he did something they might both regret. The dejected look on Piper's face gave him pause, and the urge to come up with some viable excuse. "You, lovely lady, are too much of a temptation for even the most controlled man."

Her expression brightened. "No one has ever accused me of that before."

"Apparently you have not been with anyone who appreciates your finer points."

Now she looked somewhat coy. "But you appreciate them?"

If she could see the evidence of his appreciation, she would not have posed the question. "I more than appreciate them, as I also appreciate and respect you. Therefore I am going to escort you back to the hotel and bid you good night." Or crush his determination to refrain from sex for three more months.

Piper pretended to pout. "But the night is still young, and I'm still cold."

"All the more reason to deliver you safely inside the hotel."

"Your room or mine?"

She seemed determined to make this incredibly hard on him...in every sense of the word. "Your room, and then I will retire to mine."

She sighed. "All right, if that's what you really want."

If he said that, he would be lying. "It's not a question of if I want you. The question is, would it be wise to continue this?"

"And your answer?"

"Completely unwise."

"Maybe we should ignore wisdom and do what comes naturally. We're both of age and free to do as we please, so why not take advantage of the opportunity?"

Just as he opened his mouth to issue another unenthusiastic argument, she kissed him again. Deeper this time, more insistent. He slid his hand down her back, cupped her bottom and brought her up against his erection, hoping to discourage her. The plan failed. She made a move with her hips and sent him so close to the edge that he considered lifting her skirt, lowering his pants and dispensing with all propriety.

The last thread of his coveted self-control prevented him from acting on his desire. He refused to succumb to animal instinct. He could not discard the vow, or his common sense, for one night of unbridled passion with someone he was clearly deceiving. He would remain strong, stay grounded, ignore the fact that he had a beautiful, sensual woman at his disposal and…

Whom was he attempting to fool? "Let's retire to my room."

Two

She had always strived to be the good twin. Straight as an arrow. Boring as hell. Never before had she demonstrated such assertiveness toward a man.

Now remarkably Piper found herself alone in an elevator with that man, with only one goal in mind—ending her self-imposed celibacy in a virtual stranger's hotel room. Oddly A.J. kept his distance and remained silent as they traveled all the way to the top floor. After the doors sighed open and they stepped out of the car, she expected to see a corridor containing a line of rooms. Instead she noticed only one double mahogany door flanked by two massive, stoic guards. If a pilot warranted this much security, then he must work for an incredibly powerful family or some high-ranking politician.

A.J. lightly clasped her elbow to guide her forward

before stopping at the entry to mutter something in what she assumed to be Arabic. One of the men turned immediately, slid a card key in the lock and opened the doors. As soon as they were safely sequestered inside, Piper took a moment to survey the area—exquisite dark wood floors, towering windows revealing the Chicago skyline, even a baby grand piano in the corner. An opulent penthouse designed for the rich and infamous. Her current companion was one lucky employee.

Piper started to comment on that very thing, but her words never made it to her open mouth. A.J. did, and the kiss he gave her had the impact of a firebomb. Somehow she ended up with her back against one wall with A.J. pressed against her, her face bracketed in his palms. When he shrugged the sweater from her shoulders, slipped it away and tossed it behind him, her heart rate began to run amok. Any concerns flittered away on the heels of a heat she'd never felt before with any man. But this man knew what he was doing, right down to the way he brushed kisses along the line of her jaw and her neck before he brought his mouth to her ear. "The bedroom," he whispered. "Now."

Okay, that would be the next step. A daring step. A step Piper had never taken with a man she barely knew. "Lead the way."

No sooner had she said it than he clasped her hand and guided her toward another closed door where he paused to kiss her again. When his palms roved along her rib cage before they came to rest on her bottom, she found it very difficult to breathe.

He suddenly broke all contact and took a step back. "There is something I need to say before we go any further."

Piper managed to break through the sensual fog and back into reality. "You're married."

"Of course not."

That left only one scenario as far as she could see. "If you're worried that I'm making some alcohol-induced decision, you're wrong. Yes, I've had a couple of drinks, but I'm not drunk. And yes, this strangers-in-the night scenario is a first for me. In fact, I've only had one lover, and even calling him that is a stretch."

He seemed totally confused by that concept. "How is that possible for such an appealing woman?"

"Believe me, it is possible because I'm very particular."

"I am flattered, yet I still question whether you are giving this enough thought."

She didn't want to think, only do. "Look, in a perfect world, I'd suggest we spend a few days getting to know each other before we take this step. But unfortunately I was informed only a few hours ago that I'm traveling to some obscure Middle Eastern country to schmooze with sheikhs for the sake of trying to win a water conservation contract."

His expression went stone-cold serious. "Are you referring to the Mehdis?"

"Yes, and I realize they're your friends, but—"

"We need to talk."

That meant only one thing—party's over. "All right," she muttered, unable to mask the disappointment in her voice.

A.J. led her to the white sofa set out in the middle of the room. After they settled on the cushions side by side, he took both her hands into his. "You are one of the most beautiful, intelligent and intriguing women I have met in a very long time. Quite simply, you're special. For that reason, I do not want to take advantage of you."

Take advantage of me, dammit, she wanted to say, but opted for a more subtle debate. "I'm not special at all. However, I'm sure you normally require an experienced partner, and if it's that's your concern, I'm much more adventurous than I seem. I think my being in your hotel room is a sure sign of that."

He released her hands and leaned back. "As much as I would like to find out, I'd prefer not to complicate matters, which leads me to what I need to tell you. I pilot the Mehdis' plane."

Her eyes widened from sheer shock. "Why didn't you tell me this in the beginning?"

"It didn't matter until you said you'd be working with them. If the king learned I was bedding a prospective client, he would, simply put, go ballistic."

Figured. "Leave it to some well-heeled royal to spoil my good time. That's why I have no use for that kind of man."

His gaze wandered away. "He would be justified in his condemnation. I have a responsibility to the Mehdis and a need to be taken seriously by them."

"At all costs?"

"I'm afraid that is the case at this point in time."

In other words, thanks but no thanks, or at least that was what Piper heard. Feeling somewhat humiliated, she came to her feet. "It's been a pleasure to meet you, A.J. Thank you for a very lovely and eye-opening evening."

Before she had a meltdown, Piper headed away, only to be stopped by A.J. bracing her shoulders from behind before she could open the door.

He turned her to face him, his expression extremely solemn. "Piper, there are two things you must know about me. First, I have been taught that a man is only as good as his honor, and I am trying to honor you, even if I would like to take that black dress off you and carry you to my bed. Despite my concerns about my job, you also deserve the utmost respect and regard. And once you have time to consider my decision, you will thank me for saving you from a possible mistake."

For some reason that made Piper a little miffed. "Do you honestly believe I don't know my own mind?"

"I believe you're too trusting."

Now she was just plain mad. "I'm an adult, A.J., not some naive adolescent. And in case you're worried, I'm not a prude, I'm picky. Last, the only mistake I made tonight was thinking you could be the man who would be worth the wait. Obviously I was wrong."

He softly touched her face. "You are not wrong. When it comes to us—" he twined their fingers together, sending a message that wasn't lost on Piper "—making love, I assure you that would definitely be worth the wait. And that is what I'm proposing, waiting until we have the opportunity to know each other while you are in Bajul."

Piper's anger almost disappeared. Almost. "That would depend on whether you're everything you seem to be, because I believe honesty *and* honor go hand in hand. Now, what was the second thing you wanted me to know?"

A strange look passed over his face. "I still believe in chivalry. Will you allow me to walk you to your room?"

She shook her head. "No, thanks. I'm a big girl and I can find my way."

"As you wish." After he escorted her into the corridor, A.J. executed a slight bow. "If I don't see you tomorrow on the plane, Ms. McAdams, then I will make it a point to seek you out in Bajul."

She boarded the extremely large and lavish private plane less than five minutes before their scheduled departure, due to the rush-hour traffic and an apathetic cabdriver. When the five-man survey crew settled into the vacant beige leather seats at the front of the plane, she walked the aisle past what she assumed to be staff and press members. Despite the size of the plane, it appeared the back half had been cordoned off to passengers. Most likely it held a series of conference rooms and perhaps even living quarters. She might ask A.J. to give her the grand tour, provided she actually encountered him before they landed.

She paused in the aisle to address a middle-aged, professor-like man with sparse graying hair, wire-rimmed glasses and kind brown eyes. Hopefully he spoke English, and that the last remaining spot was available. "Is this seat taken?"

"It is reserved for Miss McAdams," he replied. "Is that you?"

Fortunately a language barrier wouldn't exist during the lengthy flight. "Yes, that's me."

"Then the seat is yours."

After sliding in next to the man and settling her red tote at her feet, she shifted toward him and stuck out her hand. "Hello, I'm Piper McAdams. I'm traveling to Bajul with the GLM engineers."

He gave her hand a soft shake. "Mr. Deeb."

Not a lot to go on there. Time for a fishing expedition. "Are you a friend of the sheikh's?"

"I am serving as his attaché on this trip."

"I'm sure that's a very interesting duty."

He pushed his glasses up on the bridge of his nose. "Managing Prince Adan's schedule can be challenging at times, evidenced by his absence at the moment."

A good thing, since she might have missed the flight if the guy had been punctual. "He has a habit of being late, does he?"

"He occasionally suffers from tardiness, among other things."

Piper wanted him to define "other things" but then she noticed a commotion toward the front of the plane. Assuming the mysterious monarch had finally arrived, she came to her feet along with the rest of the passengers and leaned slightly into the aisle to catch a glimpse. She spotted only A.J. dressed in a crisp, white shirt covered by a navy blue suit emblazoned with gold military-like insignias. Not a sheikh in sight.

She regarded Mr. Deeb again and lowered her voice. "He must be some kind of pilot to earn that reception."

He cleared his throat and glanced away. "Yes, he is quite the aviator."

After everyone settled into their seats, Piper followed suit, well aware that her pulse had unwittingly picked up speed as she noticed A.J. stopping in the aisle to speak to one man. A man who oddly addressed the pilot as Prince Adan.

Reality soon dawned, along with the sense that she might have been completely betrayed by blind faith. She turned a frown on Mr. Deeb. "He's not the plane's pilot, is he?"

Again the man refused to look at her directly. "Yes, he is the pilot, as well as commander in chief of Bajul's armed forces."

"And a Mehdi?"

Deeb gave her a contrite look. "The third Mehdi son in line to inherit the throne."

And a major liar, Piper realized as she watched the sheikh disappear into the cockpit. She thanked her lucky stars she hadn't made the mistake of climbing into bed with him. Then again, he'd been the one to put an end to that with his fake concerns over being only a royal employee, not a royal prince. And all that talk of honor. Honorable men didn't deceive unsuspecting women about their identities.

Fuming over the duplicity, Piper pulled a fashion magazine from her bag and flipped through the pages with a vengeance during takeoff. She didn't have to deal with the situation now, or ever for that matter. She didn't have to spend even one minute with A.J. or Adan or whatever his name was. He would be nothing more to her than a cute meet that had gone nowhere, a precautionary tale in the book of her life, a man she would endeavor to immediately forget....

"May I have a moment with you in the aft lounge, Ms. McAdams?"

She glanced up and immediately took in A.J.'s damnable dimples and his sexy mouth before visually traveling to his remarkable dark eyes. "Is the plane flying itself, *Prince* Mehdi?"

He tried on a contrite look. "I have turned the controls over to the copilot for the time being so we can converse."

And if she spent one second alone with him, she

might find herself caught up in his lair once more. "I do believe the seat belt sign is still on, and that means it's not safe to move about the cabin."

Of course said sign picked that moment to ding and dim, robbing her of any excuse to avoid this confrontation. Nevertheless, he happened to be resident royalty, not to mention he could hold the power to grant—or reject—her grandfather's bid. For that reason, she shoved the magazine back into the carry-on and slid out of the seat, putting her in very close proximity to the fibbing prince. "After you," she said in a tone that was borderline irritable, to say the least.

As the princely pilot started toward the rear of the plane, Piper followed behind him with her eyes lowered in an attempt to avoid the two female attendants' curious stares. He paused to open a sliding frosted-glass door and gestured her forward into a narrow corridor before he showed her into a lounge containing dark brown leather furniture.

"Make yourself comfortable," A.J. said as he closed the sliding door behind her.

Comfortable? Ha! Piper chose the lone chair to avoid inadvertent physical contact, while the sneaky sheikh settled on the opposing sofa.

He draped his arm casually over the back cushions and smiled. "Have you enjoyed your flight so far?"

In an effort to demonstrate some decorum, she bit back the harsh words clamoring to come out of her mouth. "Since it's been less than fifteen minutes into the flight, I prefer to reserve judgment until landing."

He gave her a lingering once-over. "You look very beautiful today, Piper."

She tugged the hem of her black coatdress down to

the top of her knees. Unfortunately she couldn't convert the open collar to a turtleneck. "Thank you, but if you believe compliments will put you in the clear after you lied to me, think again."

"I am being completely sincere in my admiration."

"Forgive me if I question your sincerity. And by the way, what am I supposed to call you?"

"What would you like to call me?"

He'd walked right into that one. "Jackass?"

He had the audacity to grin. "I believe I have been called that before."

She had the utterly stupid urge to kiss that grin off his face. "I don't doubt that a bit. And where did you come up with A.J.?"

"My given name is Adan Jamal. My classmates called me A.J., but as an adult I do prefer Adan."

"I would have preferred you explain all of this to me last night."

His expression turned serious. "When I discovered you were involved with the water project, I was completely thrown off-kilter."

Not a valid excuse, in her opinion. "And after learning that, did you seriously believe you could hide your identity from me indefinitely?"

He sighed. "No. I had hoped to speak with you before takeoff. Unfortunately, traffic detained our driver on the way to the airport and I had to adhere to the original flight plan."

She couldn't reject that defense when she'd experienced the same delays. Still... "You still should have told me before I left your room, at the very least."

He leaned forward, draped his elbows on his parted knees and studied the carpeted floor. "Do you know what it's like to be judged by your station in life even though it has nothing to do with who you really are?"

Actually, she did—the rich girl born to a spoiled, partying socialite and an unknown father. "I can relate to that in some ways."

He finally raised his gaze to hers. "Last night, I wanted you to see me as an average man, not a monarch."

There was absolutely nothing average about him. "I don't base my opinions on a person's social status."

He straightened and streaked a palm over his shadowed jaw. "I believe I recall you mentioning you have an aversion to wealthy men, and specifically, the Mehdis. Is that not so?"

Darned if he wasn't right. "Okay, yes, I might have said that. My apologies for making generalizations."

"And I apologize for deceiving you. I promise it will not happen again, as soon as I tell you something else I omitted last evening."

Just when she thought she might be able to trust him. "I'm listening."

"I've been celibate since my eldest brother's wedding."

"When was that?" she asked around her surprise.

"Eight months ago and approximately two months following the dissolution of my relationship."

Piper couldn't imagine such a vital, viral man could go that long without sex. "Your breakup must have been really devastating."

"Not exactly," he said. "My brothers have always seen me as being less than serious when it comes to my role in the family. I decided to prove to them that my entire life does not revolve around seeking the next conquest."

She so wanted to believe him, yet wasn't certain she could. "I admire your resolve, but I'm still having a hard time with the trust issue where you're concerned."

Adan came to his feet, crossed the small space between them, clasped her hands and pulled her off the chair. "I must see to my responsibility now as captain of this ship. But before I go, I have a request."

Who knew what that might entail? "Go ahead."

"If you will allow me to serve as your personal host in Bajul, I will prove to you that I am not only a man of my word, but I am an honorable man."

That remained to be seen. But right then, when Adan Mehdi looked at her as if she deserved his utmost attention, she couldn't manufacture one reason to refuse his hospitality. And if she didn't keep a cool head, she worried he could convince her of anything.

"Ms. Thorpe is here to see you, Emir."

Great. He'd barely walked into the palace with Piper at his side only to be greeted by an unwelcome visit from his past in the form of a persistent, self-absorbed ex-paramour.

The entire travel party scattered like rats on a sinking ship, including the turncoat Deeb. Only the messenger of doom remained, an extremely perplexed look splashed across his bearded face. "Did you know she was coming, Abdul?"

The man revealed his discomfort by wringing his hands. "No, Emir. I attempted to ask her to return tomorrow, yet she would not hear of it. She is currently in the study with…uh…those who accompanied her. It would be in your best interest to speak with her."

Leave it to Talia to bring an entourage. And if she created a scene, he would never earn Piper's trust. Therefore he had to find a way to keep the two women separated.

With that in mind, Adan turned to Piper and gestured toward the towering staircase leading to the upper floors. "This shouldn't take too long, Ms. McAdams. In the meantime, Abdul will show you to your quarters and I will meet you shortly in the third-floor sitting room. Abdul, put her things in the suite across from mine."

After Abdul picked up her luggage, she didn't make a move other than to give Adan a decidedly suspicious stare. "I have a room reserved at the inn in the village, so it's best I keep those arrangements, Your Highness," she said, prompting the houseman to set the bags back down.

He had to encourage her to stay at the palace, and he had limited time to do so. After signaling Abdul to gather the bags again, he regarded Piper. "The inn is small and will not allow you to have what you need in terms of your business. They currently do not have internet access or an office center. We have all that here."

Abdul bent slightly as if prepared to return the luggage to the floor while Adan tamped down his impatience over Piper's delay in responding. "I suppose you have a point," she finally said. "As long as it's not an inconvenience for your staff."

He would be inconvenienced if he didn't have her nearby, and in deep trouble if the old girlfriend suddenly made an appearance. "I assure you, the staff is accustomed to guests. So if you will follow Abdul—"

"It's about time you finally showed up, you inconsiderate arse."

Adan froze like an iceberg at the sound of the familiar voice. Trouble had definitely arrived.

He could pretend he hadn't heard her, or he could face the unavoidable confrontation like a man. Taking the second—and least palatable—option, he turned to discover Talia Thorpe standing at the entry to the hallway wearing a chic white dress, hands propped on her narrow hips and her green eyes alight with fury.

A compliment should help to diffuse the possible verbal bloodbath. Or so he hoped. "You're looking well, Talia."

She rolled her eyes. "Why haven't you returned my emails or calls? I've sent you at least a hundred messages over the past month alone."

He ventured a fast glance at Piper, who appeared to be somewhat taken aback, and rightfully so. "Might I remind you, Talia, we broke off our relationship a year ago."

Talia tossed a lock of her long platinum hair back over one shoulder. "*You* broke it off, and it's been ten months. If you hadn't ignored me, I wouldn't have been forced to disrupt my schedule and make this beastly trip."

When he'd told her they were done after their on-and-off six-year relationship, he'd meant it. "Perhaps we should continue this conversation somewhere more private."

She flipped a manicured hand in Piper's direction. "Are you worried your new chicky will be exposed to all the dirty details?"

As a matter of fact... "For your information, Ms. McAdams is here on business."

"Well, so am I," Talia said. "Serious business."

He wouldn't be at all surprised if she tried to sue him over the breakup. "I find that somewhat difficult to believe, Talia, yet I am curious. What business of yours would concern me?"

She turned around and clapped her hands. "Bridget, you may come in now and bring it with you."

Talia went through personal assistants as frequently as she went through money, so Adan wasn't surprised when he didn't recognize the name. He was mildly concerned over the "it" comment. But he was nothing less than astounded when the meek-looking plump brunette strolled into the room...gripping a baby carrier. Myriad concerns began rushing through his mind. Unthinkable possibilities. Unimaginable scenarios.

Yet when Talia took the carrier and turned it around, and he saw the sleeping baby with the tiny round face and the black cap of hair, he would swear his heart skipped several beats, and he began to sweat.

"Adan, meet Samuel, your new son."

Three

Piper wouldn't be a bit surprised if Adan Mehdi keeled over from shock. Instead, he assumed a rigid posture and a stern expression, hands fisted at his sides. "Talia, if you believe I will simply take you at your word about this, you are completely daft."

The woman swept her manicured hand toward the infant. "Just look at him, Adan. You can't deny he's yours. Dark hair and golden skin. He even has your dimples. Despite all that, I do have proof in the form of a DNA test."

"How did you get my bloody DNA?" he asked.

Talia crossed her arms beneath her breasts and lifted her chin. "It's all over my Paris flat, Adan. And you happened to leave your toothbrush the night you tossed me to the gutter."

The sheikh's defenses seemed to disappear right before Piper's eyes. "We were always careful to prevent pregnancy."

Talia tapped her chin. "I do recall that one night last year in Milan—"

"That was one blasted night, Talia," he replied, his tone fraught with anger.

"Once was quite enough." The woman handed the carrier off to a bewildered Bridget. "Anyway, I have a photo shoot in a remote location in Tasmania, which will give you an opportunity to get to know your kid. We'll discuss the custody particulars when I get back next month."

Adan narrowed his eyes in a menacing glare. "We will discuss this immediately."

Talia checked her watch. "My flight leaves in less than an hour."

"You will not take one step out this door until we talk," Adan demanded. "Into the study. Now."

After the sheikh and his former girlfriend exited, Piper looked around to find Abdul had disappeared, leaving her in a quandary over what to do next. She occupied her time by surveying the beige stone walls, the ornate gold statues and the unending staircase leading to the top of the massive structure. A baby's cry would definitely echo loudly throughout the building.

With that in mind, Piper sought out Bridget, who'd taken a seat on the gold brocade cushioned bench set against the wall, the carrier at her feet. She smiled at the woman, who managed a slight, albeit shaky return of the gesture. But when the baby began to fuss, the presumed au pair looked completely alarmed.

Not good. Piper launched into action, crossed to the carrier, unfolded the yellow blanket, picked up the crying infant and held him against her shoulder. After he quieted, she regarded the wide-eyed Bridget. "You aren't a nanny, are you?"

"No, I am not," she finally responded, her tone hinting at a slight British accent and a lot of disdain. "I'm Talia's personal assistant. The last nanny quit yesterday when she learned she'd have to make the trip here. Traveling with Talia isn't pleasant under normal circumstances, let alone with a child in tow."

Piper claimed the vacant spot on the bench, laid the swaddled baby in the crook of her arm and studied his cherub face. "You're beautiful, little man, although you don't look like a Samuel. Sam fits you better."

"Don't let Talia hear you call him that," Bridget warned. "She fired the first nanny over that very thing."

That didn't exactly surprise Piper after what she'd witnessed upon meeting the model. "Then she's very protective of him, huh?"

Bridget frowned. "Not really. She hasn't held him more than a handful of times since his birth."

Piper couldn't contain her contempt, a product of her own experience. "Good mothers hold and care for their babies. They certainly don't foist their children off on someone else."

Bridget reached over and touched the infant's arm. "You're right, but unfortunately Talia isn't maternal. She's consumed by her modeling career and staying in shape. All I've heard since his birth is how hard she's had to work to regain her figure. I truly believe that's why she waited four weeks to bring the baby here."

Vanity, thy name is Talia. She was beginning to like her less and less. "At least now he'll have the opportunity to bond with his father."

"I am not prepared to raise a child, Talia."

So much for bonding, Piper thought at the sound of the sheikh's irritated tone.

The self-centered supermodel breezed into the room with one impatient prince following close on her heels. "At least you didn't have to suffer through thirteen hours of horrible labor last month. And just imagine pushing a soccer ball out your todger. Besides, you have a whole staff to assist you while I had to hire several useless nannies over the past month. Good help is hard to find."

"Perhaps that's because you have no idea how to treat the help," Adan muttered as he strode into the vestibule.

Talia turned and set an oversize light blue bag next to the carrier, affording Piper only a cursory glance. "Bridget gave him a bottle three hours ago, so no doubt he'll be hungry again very soon. There's enough nappies, bottles and cans of formula in here to get you by until tomorrow, plus a few outfits. After that, you're on your own. Let's go, Bridget."

Without giving the baby even a passing glance, much less a kiss goodbye, Talia headed for the door with poor Bridget cowering behind her. Piper practically bit a hole in her tongue against the urge to deliver a seething diatribe aimed at the woman's disregard for her child. Instead, she shifted Sam back to her shoulder and remained silent as Adan followed the two women to the entry and accompanied them out the door.

When the baby began to whimper again, Piper assumed he was probably in need of another bottle. Fortunately, feeding an infant wasn't an issue, even if it had been a while since her teenage babysitting days— the one job her grandparents had allowed her to accept, but only in a limited capacity, and exclusively for those parents who'd run in their social circle.

Piper laid Sam vertically in her lap, rummaged through the bag, withdrew a bottle and uncapped it. He took the nipple without hesitation and suckled with great enthusiasm, complete with soft, yummy noises that brought about her smile. After he drained the formula in record time, she set the empty bottle beside her, returned him to her shoulder and rubbed his back to successfully burp him. Then she cradled him in the crook of her arm and stroked his cotton-soft cheek. For a time he stared at her with an unfocused gaze before planting his right thumb in his rosebud mouth.

As his eyes drifted closed, Piper experienced sheer empathy for this precious little boy. She couldn't fathom how anyone would reject such a gift. Couldn't imagine how any mother worth her salt would simply drop off her child with a man who hadn't even known he had a son. Then again, why should she be surprised? Her very own mother had abandoned her and Sunny with their grandparents shortly after their birth. As far as she was concerned, women like Talia Thorpe and Millicent McAdams should not be allowed to procreate.

Despite her poor maternal example, Piper had always dreamed of having children of her own. So far she hadn't found a suitable candidate to father her future offspring, and she certainly wasn't going to settle for anything less than a loving relationship with a man who had the same wants and desires. A gentle, caring man. Grounded. Settled…

"I am officially moving to Antarctica."

After the declaration, Adan strode past Piper and disappeared into the nearby corridor adjacent to the

towering staircase. Again. Granted, she enjoyed holding baby Sam, but she hadn't signed on to be the royal
nursemaid. And apparently the sheikh hadn't signed up
for fatherhood, either.

A few moments passed before Adan returned with a
petite, attractive older woman wearing an impeccable
navy tailored blazer and skirt, her salt-and-pepper hair
styled in a neat bob. Yet when she caught sight of Piper
and the baby, her pleasant demeanor melted into obvious confusion. "May I help you, miss?"

"This is Piper McAdams," Adan said. "She has accompanied the survey crew, and while she's here, she
will be my guest. Piper, this is Elena Battelli, my former governess who now governs the entire household."

Piper came to her feet and smiled. "It's very nice to
meet you."

"And I, you." Elena leaned over and studied the baby.
"What a lovely child you have. Boy or girl?"

"He's Talia's child," Adan interjected before Piper
had a chance to respond.

Elena's initial shock melted into an acid look. "Is
that dreadful woman here?"

"She has departed for now," Adan said. "And she left
this infant in my charge before she left the premises."

Now the governess appeared completely appalled.
"She expects you to care for her child?"

The sheikh looked somewhat contrite before he re-
gained his commanding demeanor. "He is mine, Elena."

Piper really wanted to take the baby and bail before the verbal fireworks began. "If you two would like
some privacy—"

"You have no reason to leave," Adan said. "You have
already witnessed the worst of the situation."

Elena's features turned as stern as a practiced head-mistress. "How long have you known about this child, *cara?* And how can you be certain that woman is being truthful?"

Adan streaked a palm over his neck. "I didn't know until today, and she provided the test results that prove I am his father. Now, before you begin the lecture, I have a few things I need you to do."

The woman straightened her shoulders and stared at him. "This is your bed, Adan Mehdi, and you will lie in it. So if you expect me to raise your son—"

"I do not expect that at all," Adan replied. "In fact, I intend to take complete control over his care until his mother returns."

Provided the missing model did come back, Piper's major concern. But at the moment, she had a more pressing issue that needed to be addressed. "Do you think you might like to hold your son first, Your Highness?"

Uncertainty called out from Adan's brown eyes as he slowly approached her. "I suppose that would be the most logical next step."

Piper turned the baby around and placed him in his father's arms. "I promise he's not going to break," she added when she noted his slight look of concern.

While the sheikh held his son for the first time, the former governess stood next to him, one hand resting on Adan's shoulder. "He looks exactly like you did at his age, *cara,*" she said in a reverent tone. "Such a *bella* baby. Does he have a name?"

"Sam," Piper chimed in without thought. "Actually, Samuel, but I think he looks more like a Sam. Or maybe Sammy." When she noticed Adan's disapproving glance, she amended that decision. "Sammy definitely doesn't work. Of course, what you call him is solely up to you."

"He will eventually be renamed in accordance with tradition," Adan said, sounding very authoritative and princely. "Right now I must see to his comfort, including finding him a suitable crib."

"The nursery is still in order," Elena said. "And since your brother and Madison are currently residing at their home in the States, you may use it. We still have several bottles in the pantry, and a few items in the cupboard in the nursery, but I'm afraid we have no diapers or formula since the twins have moved past that stage. But the cribs are still there and fully equipped with blankets and such."

Adan appeared somewhat perplexed. "The nursery is down the hall from my quarters. I will not be able to hear him if he needs me during the night."

The governess took the baby without permission, and without protest, from the fledgling father, a sure sign of her close bond with the youngest Mehdi son. "There is something known as a baby monitor, *cara*. You will be able to see and hear him at any time when you are in your suite."

"Have the monitor set up in my room," he said. "I will see to the supplies tomorrow. You mentioned Zain is in Los Angeles, but you have not said anything about Rafiq."

Rafiq Mehdi, the reigning king of Bajul, and reportedly a hard case, according to her grandfather. Piper would buy tickets to see his reaction to the current scandal. Then again, maybe not. She'd had enough drama for one day.

Elena continued to stare at the baby with the reverence of a grandmother. "Rafiq has been with his wife at the resort for the past week. They will not be returning for two more days."

Adan shrugged out of his jacket and hung it on an ornately carved coat tree in the vestibule before returning to them. "Make certain Rafiq knows nothing about this until I have the opportunity to speak with him."

When she recognized a serious problem with that request, Piper decided to add her two cents. "Can you trust the household staff to keep this quiet?"

"The staff knows to exercise complete confidentially," Elena said.

"Or suffer the consequences," Adan added gruffly before turning to the governess. "Please have Abdul deliver the monitor and our bags to our rooms, and watch him while I show Ms. McAdams to her quarters."

Elena kissed the baby's forehead. "I have no reason to watch Abdul, *cara*. I trust he'll do as he's told."

After Adan muttered something in Arabic that didn't sound exactly pleasant, Piper stifled a laugh and considered an offer. "I have no problem watching the baby while you settle in, Your Highness."

"That will not be necessary, Ms. McAdams," Elena said as she handed the baby back to Adan. "If you are bent on being a good father to your son, then you should begin immediately."

Adan looked slightly panicked. "But—"

"No buts, Adan Mehdi." The governess snatched the empty bottle from the bench before addressing Piper again. "Ms. McAdams, it was certainly a pleasure to meet you, even under such unusual circumstances. I shall go instruct Abdul while the royal pilot becomes accustomed to paternity. Please let me know if you need any assistance with the boy."

Piper returned her smile. "Luckily I babysat quite a few times in my youth, so we'll be fine."

"Actually, I was referring to my former charge, the prince."

The two women shared a laugh before Elena walked away, leaving Piper alone with Adan and his son.

"She treats me as if I still wear knickers," he said, frustration evident in his tone.

Piper moved to his side and peeked at the still sleeping infant. "Evidently the two of you are very close, and I honestly believe she has your best interests at heart."

He released a rough sigh. "I suppose she does, at that. Now, if you're ready, I shall escort you to your room before I settle the baby into the nursery."

Piper almost insisted on returning to the inn, yet when she saw a trace of doubt in Adan's eyes, the touch of awkwardness as he held his child, the sympathy bug bit her. "Why don't we put him in the carrier while we climb the stairs?"

"No need," he said. "If you'll be so kind as to gather his things, I'll show you to the private elevator."

Piper couldn't help but smile over Adan's decision not to relinquish his son. Maybe she'd underestimated his ability to move into his new role after all.

He had untold riches at his disposal. He could fly jets at warp speed, navigate treacherous mountain slopes on skis and answer a woman's most secret fantasies with little effort. Yet he had no idea what to do with an infant.

As he studied the child in his arms, Adan's own paternal experience fueled his drive to succeed in this endeavor. He'd often wondered if the man who'd claimed him—and in many ways discarded him—had actually been his biological father. That question had always haunted him and always would. He vowed to give his son everything he would ever need, including his undivided attention.

His son. He'd never believed he would be in this position at this point in his life. Yet he was, and he had no one else to blame for his carelessness. No one to truly count on but himself.

"Is this where we get off, Your Highness?"

Until Piper had spoken, he hadn't noticed the car had come to a stop. "It is." After he moved through the open doors, he faced her in the corridor. "I respectfully request you call me Adan when we're in private."

She shifted the tote's strap to her shoulder. "All right, as long as you don't mind me referring to your son as Sam."

Clearly the woman was a born negotiator. "If that pleases you, I agree. I, however, will call him Samuel until he is renamed."

She sent him a satisfied smile. "It greatly pleases me, Adan."

Under different circumstances, he would definitely like to please her in other, more intimate ways. Then his son began to whimper, reminding him those carefree days were all but over. "Do you think he is hungry again?"

"I think he's probably wet," she said. "I also think we should stop by the nursery first and check it out."

A good plan. At least she could assist him when he took his first venture into diaper changing.

Piper followed behind him as he traveled the lengthy

hallway past several unoccupied guest suites. He stopped immediately right of the staircase landing and opened the door to the nursery that he had once occupied with his two brothers almost thirty years ago. The room had been left much the same, with two cribs and a small single bed set against the sand-colored walls, a large blue trunk holding the toys from his early childhood positioned in the corner. The miniature round table and chairs were still centered in the room, the place where Elena had taught the boys lessons as well as her native language, Italian. Where she had read to them nightly before bedtime in lieu of the mother Adan had never known. But that had lasted only until he'd turned six years old, when he'd been unceremoniously shipped off to boarding school.

The baby's cries began to escalate, thrusting the bittersweet memories away. He stepped aside to allow Piper entry, plagued by a sudden sense of absolute helplessness when he couldn't think of a blasted thing to do to calm his son. He hated failure in any form, and he'd worked hard to succeed in nearly everything he'd endeavored. Yet somehow this miniature human had left him virtually defenseless.

Piper crossed the room to the dressing table and set the tote and carrier at her feet. "Bring him over here."

"Gladly."

After he laid the infant on the white cushioned surface, Samuel continued to wail at a decibel that could possibly summon the palace guards. Piper seemed willing to speed up the process by sliding the yellow-footed pajama bottoms down the infant's legs. She then leaned down to retrieve a diaper that she set on the end of the table. "You can take it from here."

While the child continued to cry, Adan surveyed the plastic contraption and tried to recall a time when he'd watched his sister-in-law change one of the twins. Sadly, he could not. "I am not well versed in proper diaper-changing procedure."

Piper sighed. "First, you need to remove the wet diaper by releasing the tapes. But I need to warn you about something first."

He suspected it wouldn't be the last child-rearing caution he would hear. "Take care not to flip him on his head?"

She frowned. "Well, obviously that, and make sure you're ready to hold the diaper back in place if he's not done. Otherwise, you could find yourself being anointed in the face."

He certainly had never considered that. "How do you know these things?"

She withdrew a white container from the bag and opened it to reveal some sort of paper wipes. "I learned the hard way. I used to babysit for a family with three boys, and two of them were in diapers."

This woman—who had been a stranger to him twenty-four hours ago—could very well be his savior. After he lowered the diaper and didn't have to dodge, he readied for the next step. "Now what?"

"Gently grasp his ankles with one hand, lift his bottom, then slide the diaper from beneath him with your free hand."

Adan had earned a degree in aeronautics, yet this task seemed astronomical. Fortunately the boy found his thumb to pacify himself while his fumbling father figured out the process. And thankfully his hand easily circled both the infant's ankles, and raising his legs was akin to lifting a feather. Once he had the diaper re-moved and the baby lowered, he turned back to Piper. "Piece of cake."

She took the plastic garment from him and discarded it in the nearby bin. "True, but he's still little. Just re-alize there will soon come a time when he'll be much more mobile, and a lot less cooperative."

The image of his child vaulting from the dressing table assaulted him. "Will I need to strap him down?"

Piper laughed. "You'll have enough experience by then to handle him. And you'll probably want to change him in a place that's a little lower to the ground."

He shook his head. "I had no idea that caring for someone so small would require so much knowledge. I am ill equipped for the task."

"You're more than equipped, Adan." She handed him a damp paper cloth, set the container aside, then grabbed the clean diaper and unfolded it. "But right now your son requires that you finish this task. After you clean him up a bit, repeat the first step, only this time slide the diaper underneath him."

Piper displayed great patience as he followed her instructions to the letter. Once he had the infant redia-pered and redressed, he noticed that his son had fallen asleep.

"Grab the bag and we'll put this little guy to bed," Piper said as she lifted the baby, crossed the room and placed him on his back in one of the two cribs.

Tote in hand, Adan came to her side. As he watched his child sleep, he experienced a strong sense of pride. "I must say he's quite something."

"Yes he is," she replied in a hushed tone. "Now let's

go so he can have a decent nap before it's feeding time again."

After one last look at his son, Adan guided Piper into the corridor, leaving the nursery room door ajar. "Do you think it's all right to leave him all alone in an unfamiliar place?"

She patted his arm and smiled. "He's going to be fine for the next hour or so. And I'm sure Elena will have the monitor in place very soon so you can track his every move. But you will need to send out for supplies tomorrow."

"I prefer to take care of the supplies myself," he said on a whim. "However, I could use some counsel on what to purchase, if you would be so kind as to accompany me into the village. I can also show you the sights while we're there."

"Aren't you afraid someone might recognize you?"

He was more afraid she would reject his plan to spend more time with her. "I have ways to disguise myself to avoid recognition. We would appear to be tourists exploring the town."

She hid a yawn behind her hands. "I could probably do that. But at the moment, I could use a nap. Jet lag has taken hold of me."

What an inconsiderate buffoon he'd become. "Of course. If you'll follow me, I will show you to your quarters."

Adan guided Piper toward the suite opposite his, situated two rooms down from the nursery. Once there, he opened the door and she breezed past him, coming to a stop at the end of the queen-size bed. He stepped inside and watched as she surveyed the room before facing the open windows that revealed the mountains in the distance.

"This is a beautiful view," she said without turning around.

"Yes, it is." And he wasn't referring to the panoramic scenery. She was beautiful. Incredibly beautiful, from the top of her hair that ruffled in the warm breeze, to her man-slaying high heels, and all points in between. What he wouldn't give to divest her of that black dress, lay her down on the purple silk bedspread and have his wicked way with her....

"That peak is really prominent."

She had no idea, and he was thankful she hadn't turned around to find out. After regaining some composure, he crossed the room and moved behind her. "The largest mountain is called Mabrúuk. Legend has it that it blesses Bajul with fertility."

She turned, putting them in close proximity. "Fertile as in crops?"

"Actually, livestock and village offspring. We've come to know it as the baby-making mountain."

She smiled. "Did its powers reach all the way to Milan?"

"Perhaps so."

Her smile disappeared, replaced by self-consciousness. "I'm sorry. I shouldn't have brought that up. Obviously you were shocked over learning you had a son."

An understatement of the first order. "Yes, but I am in part responsible. If I had answered Talia's messages, I would have known much sooner. But I frankly did not have the desire to speak with her after we broke off the relationship. Six years of Talia's antics had been quite enough."

"And that brings me to a question," she said, followed by, "if you don't mind me asking."

After all his talk of honor, she deserved to grill him as much as she would like. "Ask away."

"Why were you with Talia all that time if you found her intolerable?"

A very good question. "In all honesty, my attraction to her was purely physical. But in defense of Talia, she has not had an easy life. She practically raised herself in the back alleys of London after her mother died and her father drowned his sorrows in the local pubs. Beneath that tough and somewhat haughty exterior resides a lost little girl who fears poverty and a loss of pride."

Piper released a caustic laugh. "Sorry, but that doesn't excuse her for bringing a baby into the world and basically ignoring him after the fact."

He recalled the recent conversation he'd had with Talia in the study. "She told me she had considered giving Samuel up for adoption, but she also felt I had a right to decide if I wanted to be a part of his life."

"And she thought springing him on you was the way to handle that?"

"Talia is nothing if not spontaneous. And as I've said, I refused to answer any correspondence."

She sighed. "Look, I know it's really none of my business, but I suspect she could be using Sam as a pawn to get you back into her life."

"Or perhaps for monetary gain," he said, regretfully voicing his own suspicions.

Piper reacted with a scowl. "She wants you to buy your own son from her?"

"She did not exactly say that, but it is a possibility. And if that proves to be true, I would willingly give her any amount of money for the opportunity to raise my child without her interference."

Her features brightened. "I admire your conviction, Adan. Sam is lucky to have you as his dad."

She could have offered him an accommodation for bravery in battle and it would not have meant as much. "And I appreciate your faith in me, Piper. Yet I am well aware of the challenges ahead of me."

She favored him with a grin that traveled to her diamond-blue eyes. "Just wait until you have to give him a bath this evening."

That sent several horrific images shooting through his muddled mind. "Bloody hell, what if I drop him?"

She patted his cheek. "You won't if you're careful. And I'll be there to show you how it's done."

He caught her hand and brought it against his chest. "You have been a godsend, Piper McAdams. And you now hold the distinction of being the most attractive tutor I have ever encountered."

"Then we're even," she said, her voice soft and overtly sensuous.

He tugged her closer. "In what way?"

She wrested out of his grasp and draped her arms around his neck. "You happen to be the best kisser I've ever encountered to this point."

He wanted to kiss her now. Needed to kiss her now. And he did—without any compunction whatsoever, regardless of his responsibility to his sleeping son. With a bed very close at hand and her heady response to the thrust of his tongue, all reasoning flew out the open windows.

"Excuse me, Emir."

Abdul's voice was as effective as having ice water

poured down one's pants, thrusting Adan away from Piper. He tried to clear the uncomfortable hitch from his throat before facing the servant. "Yes, Abdul?"

"I have Ms. McAdams's luggage."

"Then bring it in."

The man set the bags at the end of the bed, then executed a slight bow before hurrying away and closing the door behind him, something Adan should have done to avoid the predicament.

He sent Piper an apologetic look. "I am very sorry I did not see to our privacy."

She touched her fingertips to her lips. "We really shouldn't be doing this."

The declaration sent his good spirits into a nosedive. "Why not?"

"Because I can't help but wonder exactly how much you really knew about Talia's pregnancy."

This time when she called his honor into question, he responded with fury. "I did not even remotely suspect she might be pregnant. Otherwise this issue would have been resolved in the beginning. And it pains me to know you hold me in such low esteem that you think I would abandon my own child."

"I'm sorry," she said quietly. "That was an unfair assumption since you seem so willing to care for your son."

His anger diminished when he noted the sincerity in her voice. "You do have every right to doubt me, Piper, in light of my initial fabrications. But I swear to you again that I will do everything in my power to prove my honor."

She answered with a slight smile. "After meeting that

man-eater, Talia, I now understand why you might be driven straight into celibacy."

That vow was the last thing on his mind after he'd kissed Piper. "As I've said before, she had little to do with that decision. I am determined to demonstrate my ability to maintain control over baser urges."

"Then we should probably avoid situations where we're going to lose our heads and do something we both might regret."

He could not argue that point, but he would have no regrets when it came to making love to her should they arrive upon that decision. He might regret any emotional entanglement. "I suppose you're correct, but chemistry is very hard to control."

"We'll just have to learn to control it for the time being."

Easier said than done. "And let us both hope we can maintain control."

"Believe me, you'll have enough distractions taking care of Sam."

Perhaps while caring for his son that would be true, but she served as his primary distraction in private, the reason why he began backing toward the door— and away from these foreign feelings for Piper that had little to do with physical attraction. "Speaking of my son, I should go see about him. In the meantime, you should rest."

She yawned again and stretched her arms above her head. "A nap would be fantastic. So would a shower. Is there one nearby?"

Old habits reared their ugly heads when he almost offered his personal facilities—and his assistance— but instead he nodded to his right. "You have an en suite bathroom through that door. And my room is right across the hall, should you find you require anything else from me."

Her grin returned. "I'm sure I'll manage, but thank you for everything."

"My pleasure, and I do hope you get some much-needed sleep filled with pleasant dreams."

No doubt he would be having a few pleasant—and inadvisable—dreams about her.

Four

At the sound of a crying baby, Piper awoke with a start. She tried to regain her bearings only to discover the room was too dark to see much of anything, leading her to fumble for the bedside lamp and snap it on.

Since she hadn't bothered to reset her watch after she showered, she didn't know the exact time, nor did she know how long she'd been sleeping. She did know that her once-damp hair had dislodged from the towel and her pink silk robe was practically wrapped around her neck.

After pushing off the bed, she immediately strode to the dresser to untangle her hair with a brush and to select appropriate clothing before setting off to see about Sam. But the continuous cries had her tightening the robe's sash as she left the room and plodded down the hall on bare feet.

She paused at the nursery to find the door ajar and a disheveled sheikh pacing the area, a very distressed son cradled in his arms. She strolled into the room, feeling slightly uneasy over her state of dress—or undress as the case might be. While she wore only a flimsy robe, he was dressed in a white T-shirt and faded jeans, his feet also bare. He looked tousled and sexy and, oh, so tempting…and she needed to shift her brain back into an appropriate gear. "Having problems?"

Adan paused the pacing to give her a forlorn look. "I have fed him twice and diapered him more times than I can possibly count, and he still continues to cry at the top of his lungs."

Taking pity on the prince, she walked up to him, took Sam from his grasp and began patting the baby's back. "Did you burp him?"

He lowered his gaze. "Actually, no, I did not."

"Then it's probably just a bubble in his tummy." She sat down in a nearby rocker, draped the baby horizontally over her knees and rubbed his back. "Did Talia happen to mention anything about colic?" she asked, and when he seemed confused, she launched into an explanation. "It's an odd occurrence that happens to some babies at the same time every night. Basically a stomachache that can't quite be explained. On a positive note, it eventually resolves itself, usually when they're around three months old."

He slid his hands into his pockets and approached her slowly. "I highly doubt Talia would have known if he had this problem. Are you certain it's not dangerous?"

He sounded so worried her heart went out to him. "No, it's not dangerous. But it's probably wise to have him checked out by a doctor as soon as possible, just to make sure he's healthy and growing at the right rate. And please tell me Talia left some sort of medical records with you."

"That much she did," he said. "My sister-in-law, who also happens to be the queen and head of our ministry of health, is a physician. I will have her examine Samuel as soon as she returns at the end of the week."

Although Sam's sobs had turned into sniffles, she continued to gently pat the baby's back in hopes of relieving his tummy distress. "It's good to have a doctor in the family. How do you think the king will take the news about Sam?"

Adan leaned a shoulder against the wall. "He is no stranger to scandal, so he has no reason to judge me."

She recalled reading a bit about that scandal during a pretravel internet search. "I remember seeing something about him marrying a divorced woman."

"Maysa is a remarkable woman," he said. "And say what you will about Rafiq's reputation for being rigid, at least he has been willing to bring the country into the twenty-first century. He had the elevator installed."

Piper thanked her lucky stars for that modern convenience. She also experienced more good fortune when the baby lifted his little head and let out a loud belch. "I believe Sam could use a warm bath now that his belly problem's solved. I can do it if you're too exhausted to take that on."

Finally, he smiled. "As long as you are there to guide me, I am a willing student."

Piper shifted Sam to her shoulder, pushed out of the chair and nodded toward the cupboard angled in the corner. "Elena said there are still some baby things in there. Take a look and see what we have available."

Adan strode to the large cabinet and opened the double doors, revealing shelves that housed numerous infant outfits and supplies. "If we do not have what we need here, then it does not exist."

She crossed the room to survey the bounty. "You could be right about that. And I see exactly what we need on the top shelf. Grab that blue tub and two towels. And next to that you'll see a small container with all the shampoo and stuff. Get that, too."

After Adan complied, he turned around, the bathing provisions balanced precariously in his arms. "Anything else?"

"Just show me to the sink and we'll bathe your little boy."

"In here," Adan said as he opened a door to his immediate right.

Piper stepped into the adjacent bath that was right out of an Arabian dream. The large double sink, with ornate gold fixtures, appeared to be made of copper. The shower to her left was composed of rich beige stones, much like the one in her guest suite, only she had access to a deep marble soaking tub. For a nursery she would deem it way over the top, but functional enough to bathe an infant.

"Lay the towels out on the vanity and put the tub in the sink," she instructed Adan. "Always make sure you have everything within reach."

"In case he climbs out of the bath?"

This time she laughed. "He won't, at least not at this age. Once he's too big for this setup, you'll bathe him in a regular tub."

He frowned. "I greatly look forward to that time."

"And it will be here before you know it." After he

had the supplies set out, she handed Sam to him. "Now lay him down and undress him while I test the water."

With the bath moderately filled and the baby undressed, she slid her hands beneath Sam and laid him gently in the tub. "You're on, Daddy."

Sam seemed to be thoroughly enjoying the process. His father—not so much. Yet Piper admired the care in which he bathed his son, though at times he seemed somewhat tentative, especially when it came to removing the infant from the tub.

"He's soaking wet," he said. "What if I drop him?"

In consideration of his inexperience, she picked up Sam beneath the arms, careful to support his head with her fingertips, and wrapped him securely in the hooded towel. "See how easy that was?"

"Easy for you," he said. "I will definitely need more practice."

"You'll definitely get that."

After carrying the baby back to the dressing table, Piper outfitted him in one-piece white footed pajamas. Sam was wide-eyed and more awake than she'd seen him to this point, and she automatically leaned over to kiss his cheek. "You're a happy baby now, aren't you, sweetie? You smell so good, too."

"And you are a natural mother, Piper McAdams."

She straightened to find Adan staring at her, a soft smile enhancing his gorgeous face. "I don't know about that, but I do love kids."

Without any prompting, he picked up his son and set him in the crook of his arm. "And I would say this lad is fairly taken with you. I cannot say that I blame him."

Piper felt heat rise to her face over the compliment and his nearness. "You're a great father, Adan. The two of you will make a good team for many, many years to come."

The pride in his expression was unmistakable. "I am determined to do my best by him. Yet I already sense bedtime could be an issue. He does not appear at all ready to sleep."

Piper checked the clock on the wall and noted the time at half past nine. "I had no idea it was that late. I slept through dinner."

He gestured toward the door. "By all means, return to your quarters and I will have a tray sent up."

She truly hated to leave him all alone on his first night as a father. "Are you sure? I'm really not that hungry." A patent lie. Sam's half-full bottle of formula set on the table was starting to look appetizing.

"I have to learn to do this by myself eventually," he said. "You need food and sleep to sustain you during our shopping trip tomorrow."

She sincerely looked forward to the outing. "All right, but please let me know if you need help with Sam at any point during the night."

He reached over and pushed a damp strand of hair from her cheek. "You have done more than your share, Piper. I cannot express how much I appreciate your guidance."

He had no idea how much she appreciated his willingness to take on raising a baby on his own. "It was my pleasure. And before I turn in for the night, I'll make a list of things you'll need for the baby."

He grinned, showing his dimples to full advantage. "Perhaps I should purchase a pack mule while we're out."

She shrugged. "As long as you don't mind showing your ass all over town."

His laugh was gruff and extremely sexy. "I would rather show my son off all over town, so we will forgo the mule for the moment."

Piper wanted to argue against creating too much attention to his newly discovered child, but Adan seemed so proud of Sam, she didn't dare discourage him. In twenty-six years, her own mother had never expressed that devotion, nor would she ever.

Besides, the possibility of another scandal would fall on the royal family's shoulders, and they'd most likely dealt with those issues before. And if they played their cards right, no one would discover the prince in disguise in their midst.

Piper would swear the store clerk had recognized Adan, even though he wore a New York Yankees baseball cap covering his dark hair, sunglasses covering his amber eyes, khaki cargo pants, black T-shirt and heavy boots. Not to mention he hadn't shaved that morning, evident by the light blanket of whiskers along his chin, upper lip and jaw. She definitely liked that rugged, manly look. A lot. And maybe that was what had garnered the young woman's attention—Adan's sheer animal magnetism.

Yes, that had to be it. Why else would she giggle when Adan leaned over the counter and handed her the supply list? Unfortunately Piper couldn't understand a word they were saying, which left her to guess. And she'd begun to assume the sheikh might be making a date.

The baby began to stir in the stroller they'd pur-

chased on their first stop, drawing Piper's attention and
giving her a valid excuse to interrupt the exchange. "I
believe Sam is going to want a bottle very soon."

He pushed away from the counter and glanced at
Sam, who looked as if he might be in precrying mode.
"I believe you are correct. We should be finished here
soon."

After Adan spoke to the clerk again, she disappeared
into a back room and returned a few moments later with
a scowling, middle-aged man carrying three cardboard
boxes. He set the boxes down hard on the counter, then
eyed Adan suspiciously before he sent Piper a clear look
of contempt. She had no idea what they had done to
warrant his disdain, but she was relieved when he disappeared into the back area again. After the young woman
placed the clothing, toys and other provisions they'd se-
lected into several bags, Adan counted out cash—a lot
of cash—then smiled when his admirer fumbled with
the receipt before she finally set it in his open palm.

Ready for a quick escape before the love-struck clerk
fainted, Piper flipped her sunglasses back into place—
and immediately saw a problem with transporting the
items since the driver had parked in an alley two blocks
away to avoid detection. "Looks like we're going to
have to make several trips to get all of this to the car."

"I'll take care of that," Adan replied as he headed
out the exit, leaving her behind with a fussy baby and
a smitten cashier.

Piper could easily remedy one problem by giving
Sam a bottle. While she was rummaging through the
diaper bag to do that very thing, she noticed the grumpy
guy standing behind the counter, staring at her. She
immediately glanced down to make sure the sundress

hadn't slipped down and exposed too much cleavage. Not the case at all. And when she scooped the baby from the stroller to feed him, he continued to look at her as if she was a scourge on society.

Fortunately Adan returned a few moments later, three teenage boys dressed in muslin tunics and pants trailing behind him. He handed them each a few bills, barked a few orders, and like a well-oiled human machine, the trio picked up the supplies, awaiting further instruction.

After opening the door, Adan made a sweeping gesture with one hand. "After you, fair lady."

"Thank you, kind sir, and please bring the stroller and the bag."

With Sam in her arms and the secret sheikh by her side, they stepped onto the stone sidewalk and traveled past clay-colored artisan shops and small eateries. The luscious scents of a nearby restaurant reminded Piper they hadn't yet had lunch. The way people stared at them reminded her of the overly stern guy in the store. "Did you notice how that older man in the boutique kept looking at us?" she asked Adan as she handed him the empty bottle, then brought Sam up to her shoulder.

He dropped the bottle back into the bag resting in the stroller without breaking his stride. "Some of Bajul's citizens are not particularly fond of foreigners."

That made sense. Sort of. "He actually seemed angry."

"Perhaps he noticed you were not wearing a ring and assumed we are unmarried with a child."

"He would be wrong on all counts."

Piper experienced a sudden melancholy over that fact. She'd learned long ago not to chase unattainable dreams, and wanting more from Adan would definitely qualify. She still wasn't sure she could entirely trust him, although he seemed to be making an effort to earn it. Even so, she was clearly in danger of becoming too close to the baby—and the baby's father.

As they rounded the corner and entered the alley, a series of shouts startled the sleeping baby awake. Sam began to cry and Piper began to panic when a crowd of people converged upon them on the way to the car. Most members of the press, she surmised when she noticed the microphones being thrust in Adan's face. She hadn't been able to understand the questions until one lanky blond English-speaking reporter stepped forward. "Whose child is this, Sheikh Mehdi?"

Overcome with the need to protect Adan, Piper responded without thought. "He's mine."

She managed to open the car door as the driver loaded the trunk, escaping the chaos. But she'd barely settled inside before the reporter blocked the prince's path. "Is the baby your bastard child?"

Adan grabbed the journalist by the collar with both hands. "The child is not a bastard," he hissed. "He is my son."

Piper saw a disaster in the making and had to intervene. "Adan, he's not worth it."

The reporter cut a look in her direction. "Is this woman your mistress?"

Adan pointed in her direction. "That woman is... She is...my wife."

"*Your wife?* What were you thinking, Adan?"

He hadn't been thinking at all, only reacting. But after spending a good hour sitting on the veranda outside the nursery, that was all he had been doing. "The bloody imbecile insulted my child, and then he insulted you."

Piper yanked the chair opposite his back from the table and sat. "Telling the press we're married was a bit extreme, don't you agree?"

That extreme stemmed from wrath over the circumstance. "Had you not begun this debacle by claiming to be Samuel's mother, then I would not have had to defend yours and my son's honor."

She sent him a withering look. "For your information, I was simply trying to protect you from answering questions you weren't prepared to answer. I had no idea you were going tell the world you're Sam's father, nor did I have a clue you were going to have us living in wedded bliss."

"I believe that would be preferable to confirming you're nothing more than a mistress who bore my *bastard* child."

"What would have been wrong with letting everyone believe he's mine and leave it at that?"

His anger returned with the strength of a tempest. "I will not deny my son to anyone. Under any circumstance."

She blew an upward breath that ruffled her bangs. "Okay, it's obvious we're not going to get anywhere by playing the blame game. The question is, what are you going to do now? I don't think moving to Antarctica is a viable option with a month-old child."

The trip was beginning to appeal to him greatly. "If I refuse to comment further, the rumors will eventually die down."

She leaned back and released an acerbic laugh. "By the time Sam turns twenty?"

He recognized the absurdity in believing any scandal involving the Mehdi family would simply go away. "You're right. I will have to come up with some way to explain the situation. But I will not retract my statement regarding my son."

She appeared resigned. "I understand that, but you have to be worried Talia might find out someone else is pretending to be your son's mother, not to mention your wife. If she decides to come forward, everyone will know Sam's the result of a relationship out of wedlock and you lied about our marriage."

Since his ex was the consummate publicity hound, handing her that bone could prove to be problematic eventually. "To my good fortune, she's unreachable at the moment. I highly doubt she will hear any of this until she returns to France."

"Possibly, but I'm sure the king has heard by now and—" she streaked both hands down her face "—if my grandfather finds out, he'll demand I board the next plane bound for the Carolinas."

Despite what had transpired an hour ago, he still did not want her to leave for many reasons. "As far as I know, you have not yet been identified."

"I saw camera flashes."

"And you were wearing sunglasses. You could be any number of women who've crossed my path." He regretted the comment the moment it left his stupid mouth.

"All your ex-lovers?" she asked, her voice surprisingly calm.

He grasped for anything to dig himself out of the hole. "I meant any woman, whether I've slept with her or not. When you are constantly in the spotlight, your reputation becomes completely overblown. My brother Zain could attest to that. His reputation preceded him before he married Madison."

"I recall Elena mentioning they're in Los Angeles," she said. "Is his wife from the States?"

"Yes, and she is unequivocally the best thing that has ever happened to him. I sincerely never believed he would settle down with one woman."

She leaned back against the seat and began to toy with the diamond pendant dangling between her breasts. "Well, since I'm apparently just any woman, I suppose I shouldn't be worried at all. However, if I know the press, it's only a matter of time before they learn who I am."

Adan pushed out of the chair and moved to the veranda's edge to stare at the mountainous panorama he had always taken for granted. "It would be better for Samuel if everyone believed you are his mother, not Talia. She has quite a few skeletons in her dressing room closet."

Piper joined him and folded her arms atop the ledge. "Haven't we all in some way?"

He turned and leaned back against the stone wall. "I would have a difficult time believing you have anything scandalous to hide."

She smiled. "Well, apparently I gave birth and I haven't been exposed to sex in quite some time. That would be some fairly heavy fodder for the gossipmongers."

He shook his head and returned her smile. "It's good to see your wit is still intact."

"Hey, if you can't immediately fix a terrible situation, you might as well find some humor in it."

A true optimist. He added that to his ever-expanding

list of her attributes. "Do you consider the thought of being wed to me so terrible?"

"Actually, I can think of a few perks being married to you would provide."

He inched closer to her. "What perks do you have in mind?"

She faced him and folded her arms beneath her breasts. "Living in a palace immediately comes to mind."

Not at all what he'd wanted to hear. "That's it?"

"Who wouldn't want to be waited on hand and foot?"

He reached out and tucked her hair behind her ear. "I'm disappointed that's the best you can do."

She frowned. "If you want me to include your expertise as a lover, I can't speak to that because I don't know. Not that I didn't try my best to convince you to show me in your hotel room."

He still wanted to be her lover. More than he'd wanted anything in quite some time, aside from being a worthy father to his son. "Since the rest of the world now believes we've conceived a child together, perhaps we should give lovemaking serious consideration."

Her grin rivaled the sun setting on the horizon. "Procreation in reverse. I kind of like the thought of that, but..." Her words trailed off along with her gaze.

"You still doubt my honor." He hadn't been able to mask the disappointment in his tone.

"You're wrong," she said adamantly. "I realize now only an honorable man would so obviously love a child he just met. I see it every time you look at Sam."

Every time he looked at her, he felt things he could not explain, and shouldn't be feeling. "Then what would stop you from exploring our relationship on an intimate level, particularly when you were so bent on doing so in Chicago?"

"I'm taking your need for celibacy into consideration."

That vow was quickly becoming the bane of his existence. "I do not believe that to be the case."

She sighed. "Fine. Truth is, I don't want to get hurt."

He slid a fingertip along her jaw. "I would never do anything to hurt you, Piper."

"Not intentionally," she said. "But if we take that all-important step, I worry it's going to be too hard to walk away. And we both know I'll be walking away sooner than later."

Letting her walk away wouldn't be one of his finest moments, either. But he could make no promises. "I propose we continue with our original plan and learn all we can about each other while you're here. Anything beyond that will happen only if we mutually decide it's beneficial for both of us."

She tapped her chin and pretended to think. "A prince with benefits. That does sound intriguing."

He had resisted her long enough was his last thought before he reeled her into his arms and kissed her. She didn't reject the gesture at all. She didn't push him away or tense against him. She simply kissed him back like a woman who had not been kissed enough. And as usual, his body responded in a way that would merit a serious scolding from his former governess.

Bent on telling her what she was doing to him, he brought his lips to her ear. "If we had no care in the world, and all the privacy we needed, I would lift up your dress, lower your panties and take you right here."

She pulled back and stared at him with hazy eyes. "I could think of worse things."

He could think of something much better. "You deserve a bed and champagne and candles our first time."

"You're certainly not lacking in confidence."

Subtlety had never been his strongest suit. "Provided we decide to take that next step."

"Provided we could actually find the time to do it while adhering to your son's schedule."

Right on time, the sound of a crying baby filtered out through the nursery's open window. "I shall go see about him," he said without removing his hold or his gaze from her.

"I'll do it," she answered without making a single move.

"I already have."

Adan glanced to his right to see Elena strolling onto the terrace, his son in her arms, sending him away from Piper. "We were on our way."

Elena rolled her eyes. "You were on your way, all right, but that had nothing to do with the *bambino*."

Caught by the former nanny like a juvenile delinquent stealing candy from the market. "We shall take charge of him now."

Elena moved in front of him and smiled. "I will watch him for a while until you and Miss McAdams return."

"Where are we going?" Piper asked before he could respond.

"Your presence is requested in the conference room. Both of you."

Perhaps the first information from the engineers, although he had a difficult time believing they'd have anything significant to report in such a short time. "Shouldn't we wait to meet with the conservation crew until after Rafiq returns?"

"Rafiq arrived a few minutes ago," Elena said. "He called the meeting."

Damn it all to hell. He'd been summoned to take his place in the king's hot seat. "Did he happen to mention anything about water conservation?"

"I would speculate he's interested in conserving the military commander in chief's reputation." Elena cradled the baby closer and patted Adan's arm. "Good luck, *cara*. You are absolutely going to need it."

Depending on what his brother had in store for him, he could very well need to call out the royal guard.

Five

Dead silence—Piper's first impression the minute she followed Adan into the conference room for the so-called meeting. And she had no doubt she knew exactly what was on the agenda—quite possibly her head delivered to her personally by the king of Bajul.

He wore a black silk suit, dark gray tie and a definite air of authority. His coal-colored eyes and near-black hair would qualify him as darkly handsome, and somewhat intimidating. *Very* intimidating, Piper realized when he pushed back from the head of the mahogany table and came to his feet. Adan might be an inch or so taller, but his brother's aura of sheer power made him seem gigantic.

The mysterious Mr. Deeb stood nearby, absently studying his glasses before he repositioned them over his eyes. "Please join us," he said, indicating the two chairs on each side of the stoic monarch.

Adan had already settled in before Piper had gathered enough courage to walk forward. She could do this. She could face Rafiq Mehdi with a calm head and feigned confidence. Or she could turn and run.

Choosing the first option for diplomacy's sake, she claimed the chair opposite Adan as the king sat and folded his hands before him on the tabletop. "It is a pleasure to meet you, Ms. McAdams," he began, "though I would have preferred to have done so under different circumstances."

She would have preferred not to meet him at all today, if ever. Sucking up seemed like a fantastic idea. "The pleasure is all mine, Your Excellency. My grandfather has said some wonderful things about your leadership. And you may call me Piper."

"And you may address me as Rafiq, since it seems you have become a part of the royal family without my knowledge."

Piper swallowed hard around her chagrin. "Actually, that's not—"

"Are you going to jump to conclusions without hearing our side of the story, Rafiq?" Adan asked, a serious hint of impatience in his tone.

The king leaned back and studied them both for a moment. "I am giving you the opportunity now."

"I have a son," Adan said. "That whole wife issue was simply a misunderstanding, and that is all there is to the story."

Rafiq released a gruff laugh. "I fear you are wrong about that, brother. I know this because I have heard the entire sordid tale. And I do believe that included you delivering the 'wife' proclamation yourself."

Piper noticed an immediate change in Adan's demeanor. He definitely didn't appear quite as confident as he had when they'd entered the room. She had to come to his defense due to her contribution to the mess. "Your Excellency, I'm in part responsible for—"

Adan put up a hand to silence her. "It was simply an error in judgment on both our parts. We were attempting to protect each other and my son."

"Yet instead you have created a scandal at a time when we are trying to convince our people this conservation project is worthwhile," Rafiq replied. "Their attention has now been diverted from the need to relocate some of the farms to an illegitimate child born to the man in charge of protecting our borders."

"Never use that word to describe my son again," Adan hissed. "I may not have known about him, but he is every bit a Mehdi."

Rafiq looked extremely surprised. "I never thought of you as being the paternal sort, Adan. That being said, it is my understanding his true mother is the narcissistic Talia Thorpe."

Evidently the royal family and staff held the model in very low esteem. "That's true," Piper interjected before she could be cut off again. "I was simply pretending to be the baby's mother to delay the questions over his parentage."

"Yet everyone now believes you are his mother," Rafiq replied. "That has created quite the dilemma."

"I promise you I will handle this," Adan said. "I will retract the marriage statement and explain that Samuel is my child from a previous relationship."

Rafiq straightened and scowled. "You will do no such thing."

Adan exchanged a look with Piper before bringing his attention back to his brother. "You would have us continue the lie?"

"As a matter of fact, that is exactly what you will do," Rafiq began, "until you find some way to be rid of the model, for both yours and your heir's sake. Naming her as the mother will only wreak more havoc. The woman is known for posing in the nude in several photographs."

The king's condescension ruffled Piper's artistic feathers. "Some do not find nudity offensive. It would depend on what the photographer was attempting to convey."

"Centerfold photos," Adan added. "She posed for several magazines, in print and online. Some of those publications are obscure and questionable at best."

That did change everything from an artistic standpoint. "Are they widely circulated here?"

Adan looked somewhat sheepish. "After word got out that we were involved."

The king turned his full attention to her. "Ms. McAdams, if you would kindly continue the charade until your departure, then we will make certain you are compensated."

She could not believe someone was offering to pay her for a humongous fib that could alter her own life. "No offense, Your Excellency, but I can't in good conscience accept money for my silence."

"Temporary silence," the king added. "And I was not suggesting a bribe. However, I will award the contract to your corporation upon review of the bid. Once you have returned to the States, we will issue a statement saying you felt it best that the marriage be dissolved on the basis of irreconcilable differences, and that you feel your son should live in his homeland."

"And what do you propose we do with Talia?" Adan asked. "Bind and gag her before she leaks the truth to the media?"

"*She* we will have to pay," Rafiq stated. "I am certain it will cost a fortune to have her relinquish her rights as well as execute a legal document forbidding her to have any claim on the child. Fortunately, you have the means to meet her price, however high that might be."

Adan released a weary sigh. "Rafiq, this could all backfire no matter how carefully we plan. Talia could refuse to meet our terms, and furthermore, the truth may surface no matter how hard we try to conceal it."

"I trust that you and Ms. McAdams will see that does not happen."

The man was making too many impossible demands as far as Piper was concerned. "How do you propose we do that when you risk someone within these walls leaking that information?"

"The staff normally practices absolute discretion," Rafiq said, mirroring Adan's words from the day they discovered Sam existed. "Yet it would be foolish not to believe someone with lesser responsibility in the palace could sell the information to the highest bidder. Therefore it is paramount you both act as if you are a wedded couple at all times. We will issue a press release stating you were married at an undisclosed location prior to the pregnancy."

As she regarded Adan, Piper couldn't quite contain her sarcasm. "Would that be all right with you, dear?"

He shook his head. "None of this is right, but I do believe it is a viable plan, at least for the time being."

She saw her control over the situation begin to slip away. "Do I have any say in the matter?"

"Yes you do," Rafiq said. "You are free to refuse and leave immediately. With your company's crew."

A not-so-veiled threat. She mulled over a laundry list of pros and cons while Adan and the king waited for her answer. If she didn't agree, they would lose the contract, and that could send the struggling business into a free fall. If she did agree, she would have to stay on for at least a month immersed in a massive lie. And most important, she would be charged with contacting her grandparents to break the news before someone else did. She could only imagine her grandfather's reaction to either scenario. Then again, if she went along with the marriage pretense, she'd have the opportunity to stand up to him once and for all if he gave her any grief. She could finally be her own person and control her own life—for at least a month. Not a bad thing, at that.

A few more seconds ticked off while she weighed her options. The one bright spot she could see coming out of this entire debacle had directly to do with Adan. Being his make-believe spouse could come with some serious perks.

She drew in a deep breath, let it out slowly and said, "I'll do it."

Adan looked caught completely off guard. "You will?"

"I will." She rose from the chair and managed a smile. "Now, if you gentlemen would please excuse me, this pretend wife needs to make a call to her very real grandparents."

Adan stood and returned her smile. "Feel free to use my private study next door."

"Thanks. I believe I will."

Piper did an about-face, strode into the hall and prepared to lie.

"Have you totally lost your ever-lovin' mind, sweet pea?"

Oh, how she hated her grandfather's pet name for her. But Piper had to admit she was enjoying his shock. She'd never seriously shocked anyone in her sheltered life up to this point, at least not to this extreme. "No, Poppa, I'm quite sane. I would have told you sooner about the marriage but it was rather spontaneous." And pure fiction.

"When did you meet this character?"

Lie number one. "Quite a while ago, when I was in the U.K. last year."

"And you didn't bother to tell me this when you knew full well I was sending you to his country? That dog just don't hunt."

Lie number two. "We've kept our relationship quiet because we didn't want other contractors thinking I could influence the bidding process."

"And you don't have an influence over the bid now that you've gotten yourself hitched to him, sweet pea?"

Lie number three. "Not at all."

A span of silence passed before he responded. "I guess there's nothing I can do about it now, but at least it's good to know he's got royal blood and money to burn."

Of course that would be Walter McAdams's main concern when it came to her choice in a life partner. It always had been. "I'm sure when you met him back in Chicago you realized he's a very charming man."

"A charming snake," he muttered. "Of course, your grandmother's all atwitter over this. She wants to talk to you, so hang on a minute."

Piper heard him put down the receiver, followed by muffled conversation before someone picked up the phone again. "My little sugar plum is a married woman!"

Enough with the overly sweet endearments, she wanted to say, but kept her impatience in check. "Yes, Nana, I finally took the plunge." Headlong into a humongous fabricated fairy tale.

"I saw a picture of him on the internet, Piper. My, my, he's a good-looking young man. When did you two meet?"

Piper was frankly sick to death of fibbing, so she decided to try on the truth. "In a hotel bar. I attempted to seduce him but he didn't take the bait. He's quite the gentleman."

As usual, her grandmother giggled like a schoolgirl, a good indicator she didn't believe what she'd heard. "Oh, child, you are still such a cutup when it comes to boys. And you don't have to tell me any details right now."

But she did have to tell her more truths. "Nana, Adan is a very public figure, so you might hear a few rumors that aren't exactly accurate."

"What kind of rumors?" she asked with obvious concern.

She could trust her grandmother with some of the facts, even if the woman was a little too steeped in Southern society. "First, you have to promise me that whatever I tell you, it has to remain strictly confidential."

"Sugar, you know how I abhor gossip."

An advantage for Piper in this gossip game. "All right. You're probably going to hear that we've had a baby together."

Nana released an audible gasp. "Did you?"

Heavens, the woman wasn't thinking straight. "Do you recall me even remotely looking pregnant over the past few months?"

"Well, no."

"Precisely, because I wasn't. Adan does have an infant son, but obviously I'm not his mother. That said, as far as the world knows, Samuel is my baby. The biological mother's identity is a well-kept secret and has to remain so for reasons I can't reveal."

"Is she an actress? Maybe a singer? Oh, wait. Is she a call girl?"

Piper had no idea Drusilla McAdams even knew what that was. "Don't worry about it. I just need you to refuse to comment on anything if any reporters track you and Poppa down, and keep everything I've told you to yourself. Can you do that, Nana?"

"I certainly can, sugar plum," she said. "And I'm so proud of you, sweetie. It's admirable you're willing to take another woman's child and raise it as your own."

"I learned that from you, Nana."

A span of silence passed before her grandmother spoke again. "I have never regretted raising you and your sister, Piper. I do regret that Millie could never be a decent mother to you. But that's mine and your Poppa's fault. We spoiled her too much, maybe even loved her too much. She never had a care in the world aside from herself."

She still didn't as far as Piper could tell. She'd barely even seen her fly-by-night mother over the past few years, let alone established a relationship with her. "You were very good to me and Sunny, Nana. Millie is responsible for her behavior, not you. And I don't believe you can ever love anyone too much."

"Only if they can't possibly love you back, honey."

Her grandmother's words gave her some cause for concern. If she happened to stupidly fall in love with Adan, she wondered if he had the capacity to return her feelings. Probably not, and she certainly didn't intend to find out. Sadly, sometimes intentions went awry. "Look, Nana, I have a few things to do, but first, do you have any questions for me?" Piper held her breath and hoped for a no.

"Yes I do. How is the sheikh when it comes to… you know?"

Regretfully Piper hadn't experienced "you know"… yet. "Nana, a girl's gotta have her secrets, so I'll only say I'm not at all disappointed." Should she and Adan take that lovemaking step, she would wager she wouldn't be disappointed in the least.

"That's a good thing, sugar plum. What goes on between the sheets better be good if you want to sustain a relationship. Your grandfather and I have been happily going after—"

"I'd better go." Before they wandered into too-much-information territory. "I'll talk to you both real soon."

"Okay, but your grandfather told me to deliver a message before you hang up, the old grump."

Lovely. "What is it?"

"Married or not, you still have a job to do, and he expects a full report on the survey crew's progress within the next two days."

So much for spending time with father and son. For the time being, Adan would just have to go it alone.

"Congratulations, Dad. Your baby is the picture of health."

Adan turned from the crib to face Maysa Barad Mehdi—Arabian beauty, American-educated premiere physician and current queen of Bajul. "Are you absolutely certain? He seems rather small to me."

His sister-in-law sent him a sympathetic look, much to his chagrin. "He's not quite five weeks old, Adan, so he's going to be small. Fortunately Ms. Thorpe had the foresight to include copies of his medical records since his birth. He's gaining weight at a favorable pace and I expect that to continue." She paused and sent him a smile. "And before you know it, he will have a playmate."

Clearly the woman had taken leave of her senses. "I have no intention of having another child in the near future, if ever." First, he would have to have a willing partner, and his thoughts immediately turned to Piper. With her he wouldn't be seeking procreation, only practice. As much practice as she would allow, if she allowed any at all after being thrust into Rafiq's harebrained scheme.

"Let me rephrase that," Maysa said. "Samuel will have a new cousin in a little less than eight months."

Adan let that sink in for a moment before he responded, "You're pregnant?"

"Yes, I am."

He gave her a fond embrace. "Congratulations to you, as well. How is Rafiq handling impending parenthood?"

Her expression turned somber. "He is worried to death, though he tries not to show it."

"That's understandable considering the accident." The freak car accident that had claimed Rafiq's former wife and unborn child. A horrific event that had turned his brother into a temporary tyrant. "I'm certain he will relax eventually."

She frowned. "Did you only recently meet Rafiq, Adan? The man does not know the first thing about relaxing. I only hope he calms somewhat before the birth. Otherwise we'll have a fretful child."

He couldn't imagine Rafiq remaining calm under such a stressful situation. "Perhaps having Samuel around will demonstrate that tending to an infant isn't rocket science. If I can manage it, then certainly so will he."

She patted his cheek. "And you are doing very well from what I hear."

Curiosity and concern drove him to ask, "What else have you heard?"

"If you're wondering if I know about the presumed marriage, I do. My husband told me you could not have chosen a more suitable counterfeit wife." She accentuated the barb with a grin.

He found little humor in the current state of affairs. "This entire situation reeks of fraud, and I find it appalling that I've drawn Piper into that web of deceit. She's a remarkable woman and deserves much better."

Maysa inclined her head and studied him a few moments. "You sound as if you care a great deal for her."

More than he would ever let on—to Piper or to himself. "I've only known her a few days, yet I admittedly
like what I do know."

"It shows," she said. "Your face lights up at the mention of her name."

A complete exaggeration. "Women always seem to
imagine things that aren't there," he muttered. "Just
because I am fond of her does not mean I see her as
anything other than my unwitting partner in crime."
But he could see her as his lover, as he had often in his
fantasies. "I certainly have no plans to make this marriage real."

"We'll see," Maysa said as she covered the now-
sleeping infant with the blanket. "One never knows
what will transpire once intimacy is involved."

"I am not sleeping with her, Maysa," he said, a little
too defensively. "And as it stands now, that is not on
the to-do list." At least not on the one he wasn't hiding.

Maysa flipped a lock of her waist-length hair over
one shoulder. "Adan, when you do not have an agenda
that includes bedding a woman, then the world has truly
spun on its axis."

If he had his way, someday people would see him as
more than a womanizer. They would see him as a good
father. "As always, dear queen, you are correct, at least
partially. I would be telling a tale if I said I had not considered consummating our relationship. She's beautiful
and intelligent and possesses a keen wit. She is also in
many ways an innocent. For that reason I have vowed
not to take advantage of her trusting nature."

"Perhaps you should explore the possibilities," she
said. "And I do not mean in a sexual sense. You should

take this time to get to know her better. You might be pleasantly surprised at what you learn."

Exactly as he had promised both himself and Piper—getting to know each other better before they took the next step. That was before he'd learned he had a son. "I see several problems with that prospect. Being charged with Samuel's care is taxing and time-consuming. Commanding the whole bloody Royal Air Force doesn't require as much attention."

Maysa began returning supplies to her black doctor's bag resting on the dressing table where she'd performed the examination on his son. "Then perhaps you will be happy to know my husband has instructed me to tell you to take your bride away for two days for a respite."

Adan firmly believed his brother had taken leave of his senses. "Why would he suggest that?"

She snapped the bag closed and turned toward him. "He's trying to buy more time, Adan. The media have already been hounding him for an interview with you, and it will only become worse once the palace releases an official statement later today. Rafiq feels that if he tells them you're away for a brief holiday, they'll let up for the time being. And considering Samuel's age, this would be the appropriate time for you to resume your husbandly duty."

He could not resume a duty he had yet to undertake. However, the prospect of spending more time with his presumed wife was greatly appealing, yet he could not ignore the obvious issues. "I cannot abandon Samuel."

"I am sure Elena would wholeheartedly step in while you're gone."

"Actually, she wouldn't," he said. "She's made it quite clear that she is handing all the responsibility to me."

"Then I will watch him until you return. And you are more than welcome to take your new wife to the resort."

He had his own secluded resort equipped with a pool where they could spend some quality time. Then again, swimming with Piper would involve very little clothing. Not a good scenario for a man who for months had engaged in sexual deprivation in order to build character. At the moment, he had enough character to rival philanthropists worldwide. "I certainly appreciate your offer, but I would not want to burden you with my responsibility."

"It's not a burden at all," Maysa said as she leaned over and touched the top of Samuel's head. "I consider it an opportunity to practice parenthood. Now, hurry along while you still have the better part of the day."

A plan began to formulate in Adan's brain. A good plan involving his favorite mode of transportation. Now all he had to do was convince Piper to come along for the ride of her life.

After the harrowing trip to the airbase, Piper would be out of her mind if she agreed to go on this little flying excursion in the miniplane built for two. "You don't really believe I'm going to climb into that sardine can, do you?"

Adan flipped his aviators up to rest atop his head and tried to grin his way out of trouble, which wasn't going to work on Piper. Much. "This happens to be a very solid aircraft," he said.

Solid, maybe. Too tiny. Definitely. "First, you make me wear a massive helmet, throw me onto the back of a motorcycle and travel at excessive speeds on skinny little back roads to get here—"

"That was designed to evade the press, and if my memory serves me correctly, you came along willingly."

Darn it, she had. "That's not the point. Now you want me to get into a plane equivalent to a golf cart with wings."

He moved in front of said wing and patted the white plane's belly as if it were a favored pet. "Do not let the propeller scare you away. This is a Royal Air Force training craft meticulously maintained by our best mechanics. And of course, you are in good hands with me as your personal pilot."

A personal pilot with great hands, and she sure would like to know how they would feel all over her body. Maybe today she might actually find out. Maybe squeezing into this plane would be well worth it. "Just show me to my seat."

He grinned and opened the miniature door. "Hand over your bag and I will assist you."

Piper relinquished the tote to Adan, as well as her coveted control. "Here you are, and be careful with it because it contains some breakable items."

His smile melted into a scowl. "This bag must weigh ten pounds. Did you pack all your worldly belongings?"

She playfully slapped at his biceps, well aware he had one heck of a muscle. "No, I did not. I just packed a swimsuit and a change of clothes, per your request. I also brought along a few toiletries and sunscreen and towels. And a small sketch pad and pencils, in case I want to immortalize our day together on paper."

His smile returned full force. "It is quite possible you will not have time to sketch."

That sounded very promising. "And why would that be, Your Highness?"

He leaned over and brushed a kiss across her cheek. "Well, my pretend princess, I have several activities planned to occupy our time."

She could think of only one activity at the moment that interested her. "Can you give me a hint?"

"No. I want you to be surprised." He executed a slight bow. "Now climb into my chariot, fair lady, and we will begin our adventure."

She managed a not-half-bad curtsy. "As you wish, good sir."

Luckily the step up into the two-seater plane wasn't all that steep, but the small space seemed somewhat claustrophobic once Adan took his place beside her.

After strapping himself in, he handed her a headset. "Put this on and we'll be able to hear each other over the engine noise."

Noisy engine—not good. "Are you sure this is safe?" she asked before she covered her ears.

"Positive. And don't look so worried. We'll barely be off the ground before it's time to land again."

"A planned landing, I hope," she muttered as she adjusted the bulky headphones.

From that point forward, Piper watched Adan in action as he guided the pitiful excuse for a plane to the airstrip adjacent to the fleet of high-powered jets. As he did a final check, the Arabic exchange between Adan and the air traffic controller sounded like gibberish to her. But once he began to taxi down the runway, she didn't care if the pilot was speaking pig Latin. She held her breath, fisted her hands in her lap, gritted her teeth and closed her eyes tightly.

During liftoff, her stomach dipped as if she were riding a roller coaster. She felt every bump and sway as they gained altitude, and even when the plane seemed to level off, she still refused to look.

"You are missing some incredible scenery."

Feeling somewhat foolish, Piper forced herself to peer out the window at the terrain now cast in the midmorning sun. She noticed only a few man-made structures dotting the landscape, but the approaching mountains looked as if she could reach out and touch them, and that did nothing for her anxiety.

As if sensing her stress, Adan reached over the controls and took her hand. "This is the best view of my country," he said. "And when I am flying, I feel completely at peace."

She wished she could say the same for herself. "I've got a swarm of butterflies in my belly."

"I had no idea you're such a nervous flier."

"Not usually," she said. "I've never been in an aircraft quite this small before."

"Try to think of this as being as close to heaven as you can possibly be."

"I'd prefer not to get too much closer."

He grinned and squeezed her hand. "I will have you earthbound in a matter of minutes. If you look straight ahead, you'll see where we are going to land."

She tried to focus on the horizon, and not the descent toward the ground. Or the fact Adan was guiding them toward what appeared to be no more than a glorified dirt road—and a rather large mountain not far away. Her stomach dipped along with the plane as they approached the makeshift runway, but this time she kept her eyes open. She still remained as tense as a tightrope when the wheels touched down and they bounced a time or two before coming to a stop.

Piper let out the breath she'd been holding and looked around to find a thick copse of odd-looking trees surrounding them, but no signs of human life. "Where are we?"

Adan removed his headset, then hers, and smiled. "I am about to show you my most favorite place on the planet, and an experience you will not soon forget."

Six

"Wow."

Piper's wide-eyed reaction to the mountain retreat greatly pleased Adan. He'd brought only one other woman there, and she'd complained incessantly about the lack of facilities. But then Talia wasn't fond of sacrificing creature comforts for nature's bounty.

"It's basically a simple structure," he explained as he led her farther into the lone living area. "It's comprised of native wood and powered by solar energy. The water comes from the nearby lake to the house through a filtering system."

She walked to the sofa and ran her fingertips along the back of the black leather cushion. "It's very comfortable and cozy."

Her code for small, he surmised. "It has all one would require in this setting. One loft bedroom and a bath upstairs, another bedroom and bath downstairs, and my study."

She turned and smiled. "No kitchen?"

He pointed to his left. "Behind the stone wall, and it's the most impressive part of the house. However, I rarely utilize the stove, but I do make good use of the refrigerator and microwave."

"No housekeeper available?"

"No, but I do have a caretaker. He and his wife look after the place when I'm away."

She dropped down onto the beige club chair and curled her legs beneath her. "What possessed you to build a place out in the middle of nowhere?"

"You will soon see." After setting her bag on the bamboo floor, Adan crossed the room and pushed aside the drapes, revealing the mountainous terrain.

"Wow again," Piper said as she came to his side. "A view and your own private pool. I'm impressed."

He slid double doors open, bringing the outdoors inside. "This greatly expands the living space. And you'll appreciate the scenery far better from the veranda."

She smiled. "Then lead the way."

When Piper followed him onto the deck containing an outdoor kitchen and several tables with matching chairs, Adan paused at the top of the steps leading to the infinity pool. "This glorified bathtub took two years to build."

"It's absolutely incredible."

So was this woman beside him. He sat on the first step and signaled her to join him. Once she complied, he attempted not to notice the way her white shorts rode up her thighs, or the cleavage showing from the rounded neck in her sleeveless coral top that formed to her breasts very nicely. "This has always been my sanctuary of sorts. A good place to escape."

She took her attention from the water and turned it on him. "Exactly what are you escaping, Adan?"

He'd asked himself that question many times, and the answers were always the same. "I suppose the drudgery of being a royal. Perhaps the responsibility of overseeing an entire military operation. At one time, my father."

The final comment brought about her frown. "Was he that hard on you?"

He sighed. "No. He wasn't particularly concerned with what I did. I once believed he'd never quite recovered from losing my mother." That was before he'd learned his father's secrets.

"You mentioned your mother when we were in Chicago," she began, "but you didn't say what happened to her. Of course, if it makes you uncomfortable to talk about it, I understand."

Oddly, he wanted to tell her about his mother, what little he knew of Cala Mehdi. He wanted to tell her many things he'd never spoken of to anyone. And eventually he would tell her their visit would be extended beyond the afternoon. "Her death was a mystery of sorts. She was found at the bottom of the mountain near the lake. Most believed she'd taken a fall. Some still wonder if she'd taken her own life due to depression following my birth. I've accepted the fact I'll never know the truth."

"Are you sure you've accepted it?"

It was as if she could see straight to his soul. "I have no choice. My father never spoke of her. But then, he rarely spoke to me. Perhaps I reminded him too much of her."

"At least you actually knew your real father."

"Not necessarily." The words spilled out of his stupid mouth before he'd had time to reel them back in.

She shifted slightly toward him and laid a palm on his arm. "Are you saying the king wasn't your biological father?"

He saw no reason to conceal his concerns now that he'd taken her into his confidence. "I only know I do not resemble him or my brothers. My hair is lighter and so are my eyes."

"That's not definitive proof, Adan," she said. "Maybe you look like your mother."

"I've seen a few photographs, and I see nothing of me in her. She had almost jet-black hair and extremely dark eyes, like Rafiq."

"If that's the case, then why would you think someone else fathered you?"

"Because my mother was reportedly very unhappy, and I suspect she could have turned to another man for comfort. Rafiq's former wife, Rima, did that very thing due to her own discontent with the marriage."

"Are you certain you're not speculating because of Rafiq's situation?"

He had valid reasons for his suspicions, namely his father's two-decade affair with the governess. Yet he had no intention of skewing Piper's opinion of Elena by revealing the truth yet. "My parents' marriage was arranged, as tradition ordained it. Marriage contracts are basically business arrangements, and in theory advantageous for both families. Unfortunately, when human emotions enter into the mix, the intent behind the agreement becomes muddled."

She frowned. "You mean emotions as in *love?*"

"Yes. The motivating force behind many of the world's ills."

"And the cure for many more."

She didn't sound pleased with his assessment. She had sounded somewhat wistful. "Spoken like a true romantic."

"Spoken like a diehard cynic," she said. "But your cynical days could soon be over now that you have a baby. There is no greater love than that which exists between parent and child, provided the parent is open to that love."

That sounded somewhat like an indictment to his character. "I have already established that bond with my son. But I have never welcomed romantic love for lack of a good example." And for fear of the inability to live up to unreasonable expectations.

She inclined her head and studied him. "Love isn't something you always have to work at, Your Highness. Sometimes it happens when you least expect it."

Piper sounded as if she spoke of her own experiences. "Have you ever been in love?" he asked.

"Not to this point." She glanced away briefly before bringing her attention back to him. "Do arranged marriages still exist in the royal family?"

Happily for him, the answer was no. "That requirement changed after Rafiq inherited the crown. Otherwise he would not have been able to marry a divorced woman. All the better. It was an illogical and worthless tradition, in my opinion."

She offered him a sunny smile that seemed somehow forced. "Well, I guess we really bucked tradition by arranging to have a fake marriage."

At the moment he'd like to have a fake honeymoon, yet he still had reservations. Piper had accommodated the king's wishes by joining in the ruse, and she'd selflessly helped care for his son. He never wanted her to believe he would take advantage of the situation. "Quite frankly, all this talk of family dysfunction is making me weary." He stood and offered his hand. "Would you care to go for a swim?"

"Yes, I most definitely would," she said as she allowed him to help her up. "But are you sure you're up to it? You look tired, and I suspect that has to do with Sam."

"He was awake quite a bit last night and I had the devil of a time getting him back to sleep after the two o'clock feeding. Yet I grew accustomed to little sleep while training for my military duties."

"Why didn't you wake me? I would have taken a shift."

"Because my child is my responsibility, not yours." He immediately regretted the somewhat callous remark and set out to make amends. "I definitely appreciate all that you've done, but I do not want to take advantage of your generosity."

She attempted a smile that failed to reach her blue eyes. "I really don't mind, Adan. What are fake mothers for?"

He could always count on her to use humor to cover her hurt. Hurt that he had caused. "We'll worry about Samuel's care when we return in two days."

Her mouth momentarily dropped open. "Two days? I thought you said this was an afternoon outing."

He endeavored to appear guileless. "Did I?"

She doomed him to hell with a look. "You did."

"My apologies. As it turns out, we have been in-structed by the king to remain absent from the palace for two days to avoid the media frenzy. I do think it's best we return tomorrow before sundown. I do not want to be away from Samuel two nights."

"But my grandfather ordered me to see that the en-gineers finalize the—"

"Bid, and that has been handled by Rafiq. He has accepted, and the contract will be couriered to your grandfather tomorrow. He has also arranged for the en-gineers to be transported to the States in the morning."

She threaded her lip between her teeth as she took several moments before speaking. "Then I guess ev-erything has been handled."

"Yes, which frees you to relax and see to your own pleasure. Nonetheless, if you insist on returning early, we shall."

This time her smile arrived fully formed. "Where should I change to get this two-day party started?"

He caught her hands and brushed a kiss across her knuckles. "Never change, Piper McAdams. I like you exactly the way you are."

She wrested away, much to his disappointment. "I meant 'change' as in clothes. I need to put on my swim-suit."

He preferred she'd go without any clothes. "You may use the bath downstairs. You'll find it between my study and the guest room, immediately past the kitchen. Or if you prefer, use the one upstairs adjacent to my bed-room. It's much larger."

"Where are you going to change?"

"I hadn't planned on wearing anything at all." He couldn't contain his laughter when he noticed her shocked expression. "I'm not serious, so do not look so concerned. My swim trunks are upstairs."

She began backing toward the entry. "I'll use the downstairs bath while you go upstairs. And I'd better not find you naked in that pool when I come back."

The word *naked* put specific parts of his anatomy on high alert. "At one time that might have been the case, but I have turned over a new leaf."

She paused at the doors and eyed him suspiciously. "A leaf from the player tree?"

He supposed he deserved that. "Believe what you will, but there have not been that many women in my life. None since I ended my relationship with Talia."

"Ah, yes. The celibacy clause. How's that working out for you?"

Not very well at the moment. Not when he knew in a matter of moments he would see her with very little covering her body. Or so he hoped. "I will let you know by day's end."

As soon as she returned to the pool, Piper found Adan staring out over the horizon. She couldn't see his face or eyes, but she sensed his mind was on something else—or someone else, namely his child. Her mind immediately sank into the gutter when she shamelessly studied all the details from his bare, well-defined back to his impressive butt concealed by a pair of navy swim trunks.

She approached him slowly, overwhelmed by the urge to run her hands over the patently male terrain. Instead, she secured the towel knotted between her breasts. "I'm fairly sure that mountain won't move no matter how long you stare at it."

He turned to her, his expression surprisingly somber. "If only I had that power."

Once she moved past the initial shock of seeing his gorgeous bare chest, she found her voice. "Are you worried about Sam?"

"I'm worried that my position will prevent me from being a good father to him. I'm also concerned that perhaps I would be wrong to ask Talia to give up all claims on him."

"No offense, Adan, but I don't see Talia as the motherly type."

"Perhaps so, but isn't any mother better than no mother at all?"

"Not really," she said without thought. "My so-called mother never cared about her daughters. Her own needs took precedence over ours. Luckily for us, my grandmother willingly stepped in and gave us all the love we could ask for, and more. Otherwise I don't know how we would have turned out."

He brushed his knuckles over her cheek. "You have turned out very well. And now if you would kindly remove that towel, we'll spend the afternoon basking in the Bajul sun."

That would be the logical next step—revealing her black bikini that left little to the imagination. A step that required some advance preparation. "Before I do that, you need to know I'm not tall and skinny like Talia. I'm short and I haven't been blessed with a lean build and—"

He flipped the knot with one smooth move and the towel immediately fell to the ground. Then he gave her a lingering once-over before raising his gaze back to her eyes. "You have been blessed with a beautiful body, Piper. You have the curves this man desires."

He desired her curves? Incredible. "Your physique is the thing fantasies are made of. But the question is, how well do you swim? I have to warn you, I'm pretty darned good at it."

And without giving her any warning, he strode to the far end of the pool and executed a perfect dive. He emerged a few moments later, slicked back his hair and smiled. "Now it's your turn to prove your expertise."

If only she could stop gaping at his dimples and get her feet to move. Finally she willed herself to follow his lead by moving to the same spot he had and doing a little diving of her own. After her eyes adjusted, she sought Adan out where he now stood in the shallow end. She remained underwater until she swam immediately in front of him and came up for air. "How's that?"

"Perfect," he said as he put his arms around her. "As are you."

She laughed even though she could barely concentrate while being up close and personal. "Not hardly, Your Majesty. I can be stubborn and I do have a little bit of a temper at times. I'm also a picky eater and I speed when I drive—"

He cut off her laundry list of faults with a kiss. A kiss so hot it rivaled the sun beating down on her shoulders. A down-and-dirty, tongue-dueling kiss that had Piper heating up in unseen places on her person. When he streamed his palms along her rib cage and grazed the side of her breast, she thought she might melt. When he returned his hands to her shoulders, she thought she might groan in protest.

He studied her eyes with an intensity that stole what was left of her breath. "Before this continues, I need to say something."

She needed him to get on with it. "I'm listening."

"I want to make love to you, more than anything I have wished for in some time. But you are under no obligation to honor that request."

Was he kidding? "If I remember correctly, I went to your hotel room in Chicago with that one goal in mind. Of course, where I wanted to end my celibacy, you were determined to hang on to yours."

"Not anymore," he said. "Not since the day I met you, actually. You are different from any woman I have ever known."

"Is that a good thing?"

"A very good thing."

"Then let's put an end to doing without right here and now."

He gave her an unmistakable bad-boy grin. "Take off your suit."

"You go first," she said, suddenly feeling self-conscious.

"All right." He quickly removed the trunks and tossed them aside, where they hit the cement deck with a splat. "Your turn."

After drawing in a deep breath, she reached back and released the clasp, then untied the bow at her neck. Once she had that accomplished, she threw the top behind her, her bare breasts no longer concealed by the water. "Better?"

"Yes, but you're not finished yet."

Time to go for broke. Piper shimmied her bottoms down her legs and kicked them away. Right then she didn't care if they were carried away by the pool pump's current and ended up in another country. "Are you satisfied now?"

"Not quite, but I will be," he said as he pulled her close, took her hand and guided it down his belly and beyond.

When Adan pressed her palm against his erection, Piper blew out a staggered breath. "I do believe I've located an impressive sea creature down below."

"Actually, it's an eel."

"Electric?"

"Highly charged." He brought her hand back to his chest. "But should you investigate further, I fear I will not be able to make it to the bed."

She stood on tiptoe and kissed the cute cleft in his chin. "What's wrong with a little water play?"

"If you're referring to water foreplay, then I am all for that." He wrapped one arm around her waist, then lowered his mouth to her breast while slipping his hand between her thighs simultaneously.

Piper gripped his shoulders and grounded herself against the heady sensations. She felt as if her legs might liquefy with every pass of his tongue over her nipple, every stroke of his fingertip in a place that needed his attention the most.

As badly as she wanted the sensations to go on forever, the climax came in record time. She inadvertently dug her nails into his flesh and unsuccessfully stopped the odd sound bubbling up from her throat.

Once the waves subsided, Piper closed her eyes and sighed. "I'm so sorry that happened so fast," she murmured without looking at him.

He tipped her chin up with a fingertip. "You have no

need to apologize. It has been a while for you, by your own admission."

"Try never."

As she predicted, he was obviously stunned by the truth. "You've never had an orgasm?"

She managed a shrug. "Not with anyone else in the room."

"You clearly have encountered nothing but fools."

Fool, singular. "I've only been intimately involved with one man, and he basically treated me like a fast-food drive-through. In and out as quickly as possible."

Adan released a low, grainy laugh. "I am glad to know you find some humor in the situation. I personally find it appalling when a man has no concern for his lover's pleasure."

She draped her arms around his neck and wriggled her hips. "That goes both ways, and I do believe you are greatly in need of some pleasure. Why bother with a bed when we have a perfectly good pool deck and a comfy-looking chaise at our disposal?"

He kissed her lightly. "True, but we have no condoms."

"I see where that would be a problem."

"A very serious problem. I have already received one unexpected surprise with my son. I do not intend to have another."

Piper wasn't certain if he meant another surprise pregnancy or simply another child, period. Or he could mean he didn't care to have a baby with her. But she refused to let haywire emotions ruin this little temporary piece of paradise, even if it was based on pretense. "Then I suggest you take me to bed, Your Machoness."

No sooner than the words left her mouth, Adan swept

her up into his arms and carried her into the house. She expected him to make use of the downstairs bedroom, but instead he started up the stairs with ease, as if she weighed no more than a feather. Far from the truth. Yet he had a knack for making her feel beautiful. She figured he'd probably earned pro status in the flattery department years ago.

Piper barely had time to look around before Adan deposited her in the middle of the bed covered in a lightweight beige spread. She did have time to assess all his finer details while he opened the nightstand drawer and retrieved a condom. He was evidently very proud to see her, and she was extremely happy to be there. But when he caught her watching, she grabbed the pillow from beneath her head and placed it over her fiery face.

She felt the mattress bend beside her right before he yanked the pillow away. "You're not growing shy on me, are you?" he asked.

No, but she was certainly growing hotter by the second. "I'm just feeling a bit exposed."

He smiled as he skimmed his palm down her belly and back up again. "And I am greatly enjoying the exposure." Then his expression turned oddly serious. "If you have any reservations whatsoever—"

She pressed a fingertip against his lips. "I want this, Adan. I have for a while now."

"Then say no more."

He stretched out and shifted atop her body, then eased inside her. She couldn't speak if she tried. His weight, his powerful movement, captured all her attention. The play of his muscles beneath her palms, the sound of his voice at her ear describing what he felt at that moment, sent her senses spiraling. His broken breaths, the way he tensed signaled he was barely maintaining control. When she lifted her hips to meet his thrust, he groaned and picked up the pace. Only a matter of time before he couldn't hold out, she realized. And then he shuddered with the force of his climax before collapsing against her breasts, where she could feel his heart beating rapidly.

Piper wanted to remain this way indefinitely—with a sexy, skilled man in her arms and a sense of pride that she'd taken him to the limit. She felt unusually brave, and incredibly empowered. Never before had it been this way with Keiler Farnsworth. And the fact that the jerk's name jumped into her brain made her as mad as a hornet. He couldn't hold a candle to Adan Mehdi. She suspected she'd be hard-pressed to find any man who would.

After a few blissful moments ticked off, Adan lifted his head from her shoulder and grinned. "I hope you don't judge me on the expediency of the act."

She tapped her chin and pretended to think. "I'll have to take a point off for that."

He frowned. "You are keeping score?"

"I wasn't until you mentioned it. However, I'm giving you back that point because you are just so darn cute. So no need to despair, because you've earned a perfect ten."

He rolled over onto his back, taking his weight away and leaving Piper feeling strangely bereft. "I will do much better next time," he said in a grainy voice.

Next time couldn't come soon enough for her.

Piper McAdams proved to be more enthusiastic than any woman before her. Adan had recognized that during their second heated round of lovemaking at midnight. And again a few hours ago, immediately before dawn, when she'd awakened him with a kiss before urging him to join her in the shower. They'd spent a good deal of time there bathing each other until he took her up against the tiled wall. Still he could not seem to get enough of her.

Making love to her a fourth time in twenty-four hours seemed highly improbable. He should be completely sated. Totally exhausted. Utterly spent.

"Smells like something good is cooking in the kitchen."

At the sound of her sensual morning voice, Adan glanced over one shoulder to find Piper standing in the opening, wearing his robe. The improbable became possible when his body reacted with a surprisingly spontaneous erection.

"I'm heating up the *ataif* that Ghania prepared." And attempting to hide his sins by paying more attention to the stove than his guest.

"What is *ataif*?" she asked.

Recipe recitation should aid in calming his baser urges. When goats sprouted wings. "*Ataif* is a Middle Eastern pancake dipped in honey and cinnamon and covered in walnuts. It is served with a heavy cream known as *kaymak*."

"Thank you for such a thorough description, Chef Sheikh. Now, who is Ghania?"

He was somewhat surprised she hadn't asked that question first. "Ghania is Qareeb's wife. They're the caretakers. She was kind enough to bring the food by a few moments ago."

"How nice of her."

He afforded her another fast glance before returning to his task. "I received news about my son. According to Maysa, he only awoke one time."

"You have cell towers all the way out here?"

"No. The message arrived by carrier pigeon."

"Very amusing," she said before he felt something hit the back of his head.

He looked down to see a wadded paper napkin at his feet. "No need for violence. If you care to communicate with someone, you may use the phone in my study. It's a direct line to the palace that I had installed in the event a military crisis arises."

"That's good to know, and I'd also like to know why you refuse to look at me. I know my hair's still damp and I don't have on a scrap of makeup, but it can't be all that bad. Or maybe it could."

If she only knew how badly he wanted her, with or without the feminine frills, she would not sound so unsure of herself. "For your information, you are a natural beauty, and I am trying to retain some dignity since it seems I am unable to cool my engine in your presence."

"Still revving to go, are you?"

Piper's amused tone sent him around to face her. And if matters weren't bad enough, she was seated on the high-back bar stool facing him, her shapely thighs completely uncovered due to the split in the white cloth. "Are you naked beneath the robe?"

She leaned back against the stainless steel island, using her elbows for support. "Yes, I am. I forgot to bring panties into the bath before I showered."

He was seconds away from forgetting himself and the food preparation. "Perhaps you should dress before we dine."

She crossed one leg over the other and loosened the sash enough to create a gap at her breasts, giving him a glimpse of one pale pink nipple. "Perhaps we should forgo breakfast for the time being."

That was all it took to commit a culinary cardinal sin by leaving the pan on the burner. But if the whole bloody kitchen went up in flames, it could not rival the heat he experienced at that moment.

Without giving her fair warning, Adan crossed the small space between them and kissed her with a passion that seemed to know no bounds. He untied the robe, opened it completely, pushed it down her shoulders and then left her mouth to kiss her neck. He traveled down her bare torso, delivering more openmouthed kisses, pausing briefly to pay homage to her breasts before continuing down her abdomen. What he planned next could prompt her to shove him away, but he was willing to take a chance to reap the reward—driving her to the brink of sexual insanity. A small price to pay for ultimate pleasure, as she would soon see, if she allowed it.

When Adan parted her knees, he felt her tense and noted apprehension in her eyes. "Trust me, *mon ange,*" he whispered.

She smiled weakly. "Considering I'm half-naked on a bar stool, that would indicate I'm no angel, Adan. But I do trust you. So hurry."

Permission granted, all systems go. He began by lowering to his knees and kissing the insides of her thighs until he felt her tremble. As he worked his way toward his intended target, she shifted restlessly and then lifted her hips toward his mouth in undeniable encouragement. He used gentle persuasion to coax her climax with soft strokes of his tongue, the steady pull of his lips. As she threaded her fingers through his hair and held on firmly, he sensed he would soon achieve his goal. He wasn't the least bit wrong. She released a low moan as the orgasm took over, yet he refused to let up until he was certain she'd experienced every last wave.

Only after he felt her relax did his own desires demand to be met, and so did the need to make haste. He quickly came to his feet, grabbed the condom she'd discarded on the island and ripped open the plastic with his teeth.

Adan had the condom in place in a matter of moments and then seated himself deep inside her. He tried to temper his thrusts, but when Piper wrapped her legs around his waist, restraint left the bungalow. He couldn't readily recall feeling so driven to please a woman. He could not remember the last time he had felt this good. His thoughts disappeared when his own climax came with the force of a missile and seemed to continue for an extraordinary amount of time.

Little by little, logic began to return, including the fact he'd probably turned the cakes into cinders. He lifted his head and sought Piper's gaze. "I fear I have failed in my chef duties."

She reached up and stroked his unshaven jaw. "But you didn't fail me in your lovemaking duties, and that's much more important than breakfast."

For the first time in his life, he'd needed to hear that declaration from a lover. He'd never lacked in confidence or consideration of his partners' needs, yet he had kept his emotions at arm's length with every woman— until now.

But as much as he wanted to please this beautiful woman in his arms, as much as he would like to give more of himself to her, he wasn't certain he could. And if his relationship history repeated itself, he would probably fail her, too.

Seven

After they arrived back at the airbase and boarded the blasted motorcycle again, Piper feared turning prematurely gray thanks to Adan's daredevil driving. Fortunately that wasn't the case, she realized when they entered the palace foyer and she sneaked a peek in the gold-framed mirror. Granted, her hair was a tangled mess, but she couldn't wait a minute longer to see baby Sam.

Adan obviously felt the same, evidenced by his decision to forgo the elevator and take the stairs instead. She practically had to sprint to catch up with him as Abdul, who insisted on carrying her bag, trailed behind them.

Once they reached the third floor, both she and the houseman were winded, while Adan continued toward the nursery as if he possessed all the energy in the world. He actually did, something she'd learned over the past forty-eight hours in his bed. In his shower. In his kitchen and the pool.

Before Adan could open the nursery door, a striking woman with waist-length brunette hair walked out, clearly startled by the sheikh's sudden appearance. "You took years off my life, brother-in-law."

"My apologies, Maysa," he replied, confirming she was the reining queen. "I'm anxious to see about my son."

Maysa closed the door behind her before facing Adan. "I have already put him down for the night and I advise you wait until he wakes. You seem as though you could use some rest." She topped off the comment with a smile aimed at Piper.

Taking that as her cue, she stepped forward, uncertain whether to curtsy or offer her hand. She opted to let the queen make the first move. "I'm Piper McAdams, and it's a pleasure to finally meet you, Your Highness."

"Welcome to the family," she said, then drew Piper into a surprising embrace. "And please call me Maysa."

Piper experienced a fraud alert. "Actually, I'm not really—"

"Accustomed to it yet," Adan interjected. "Given time she will take to the royal treatment as an electric eel takes to water."

Leave it to the prince to joke at a time like this. "I'm not in the market to be treated royally, but I have enjoyed my time in the palace so far."

"I am glad," Maysa said. "Now, if you will both excuse me, I am starving."

Adan checked his watch. "Isn't dinner later than usual?"

Maysa shrugged. "No, but Rafiq is waiting for me in our quarters."

He winked at Piper before regarding Maysa again. "Oh, you're referring to a different kind of appetite. Do not let us keep you from our king."

"You could not if you tried."

Following a slight wave and a smile, Maysa strode down the hallway and disappeared around the corner, leaving Piper alone with the shifty, oversexed sheikh. And she liked him that way. A lot.

He caught her hand and tugged her against him. "Have I told you how much I enjoyed our time together?"

"At least ten times, but I'll never grow tired of hearing it. I'm just sad it's over."

"It doesn't have to be, Piper. You can stay with me in my suite."

She could be entering dangerous emotional territory. "Maybe it should be, Adan. I'll be leaving in a few weeks."

"I know," he said, sounding somewhat disappointed. "All the more reason to spend as much time together before you depart. I am an advocate of taking advantage of pleasure at every opportunity."

How easy it would be to say yes. "I don't know if that's a good idea."

"Since we are to give the impression we are married, what better way than to share the same quarters?"

A false impression of holy matrimony. "We could do that without sleeping in the same bed."

He rimmed the shell of her ear with the tip of his tongue. "I don't recall mentioning sleep."

And she wouldn't get much if she agreed, for several reasons. "You have to consider Sam's needs over ours."

He pulled back and frowned. "Exactly as I intend to do, but he doesn't require all our time during the night."

"He requires quite a bit."

Framing her face in his palms, Adan looked as if his world revolved around her decision. "Stay with me, Piper. Stay until you must leave."

Spending time with this gorgeous Arabian prince, quality time, would be a fantasy come to life. Yet it could never be the real stuff fairy tales were made of. If she took wisdom into account, she'd say no. If she was willing to risk a broken heart, she'd say yes. And she suddenly realized this risk would be well worth undertaking now, even if it meant crying about it later.

"All right, Adan. I'll stay."

In the silence of his private quarters, the room illuminated by the soft glow of a single table lamp, Adan had never experienced such a strong sense of peace. He had the woman curled up next to him to thank for that. Granted, he still wanted Piper in every way imaginable—he'd proved that at his mountain retreat— yet he greatly appreciated the moments they'd spent in comfortable silence after retiring to his quarters.

That lack of conversation would soon end once he told her what he'd learned from his brother upon their arrival a few hours ago. "I have to go to the base tomorrow to oversee training exercises. It will require me to stay in the barracks overnight."

For a moment he'd thought she'd fallen asleep, until she shifted and rested her cheek above his heart. "Gee, thanks. You invite me to reside in your room and then promptly leave me for a whole night."

The teasing quality to her voice gave Adan some semblance of relief. "If I had to choose between sleeping in the barracks with twenty snoring men and sleeping with you, I would choose you every time. Unless you begin snoring—then I could possibly reconsider."

She lightly elbowed him in the rib cage. "If I did happen to snore, which I don't, you'd have no right to criticize me. I thought a freight train had come through the bedroom last night."

"Are you bloody serious?"

"I'm kidding, Adan," she said as she traced a path along his arm with a fingertip. "Your snore actually sounds more like a purr."

That did not please him in the least. "I prefer a freight train to a common house cat."

"Don't worry, Prince Mehdi. Snore or no snore, you're still as macho and sexy as ever."

He pressed a kiss against the corner of her smiling, sensual mouth. "You are now forgiven for the affront to my manhood."

She yawned and briefly stretched her arms over her head. "Have you ever been in live combat before?"

The query took him aback. "Yes, I have."

"Was it dangerous?"

He smiled at the zeal in her voice. "Does that prospect appeal to your daring side?"

"I'm not sure I actually have much of a daring side. I asked because we're presumed to be husband and wife, so I believe it might be prudent for me to learn all I can about you, in case someone asks."

That sounded logical, but not all his military experiences had been favorable. "I've been involved in a skirmish or two while protecting our no-fly zone."

"Bad skirmishes?"

This was the part he didn't speak of often, yet again he felt the need to bare his soul to her. "One turned out to be extremely bad."

"What happened?"

"I killed a man."

He feared the revelation had rendered her speechless, until she said, "I'm assuming it was justified."

"That is a correct assumption. If I hadn't shot down his plane, he would have dropped a bomb over the village."

"How horrible. Was he a citizen of Bajul?"

"No. He was a known insurgent from another country. Because the files are classified, I am not at liberty to say which country."

She lifted her head and kissed his neck before settling back against him. "You don't have to say anything else if you don't want to."

Oh, but he did, though he wasn't certain why. "It happened four years ago," he continued. "That morning I received intelligence about the threat, and I decided I would enter the fray. Later I found out my father was livid, but only because if I perished, he would be without a commander."

"He told you that?" Her tone indicated her disbelief.

"Rafiq informed me, but it doesn't really matter now. I assisted in thwarting an attack that could have led to war for the first time in Bajul's history, and that is what matters. But I never realized..."

"Realized what, Adan?"

He doubted she would let up unless he provided all

the details. "I never knew how affected I would be by sending a man to his death."

"I can imagine how hard on you that must have been."

"Oddly, I had no real reaction to the incident until the following day while briefing our governing council. Midway through the report, I felt as if I couldn't draw a breath. I excused myself and walked outside to regain some composure. That night I had horrible dreams, and they continued for several months."

"I'm so sorry," she said sincerely. "For what it's worth, I think you're a very brave and honorable man. Sam is very lucky to have you as his father."

He'd longed to hear her acknowledge his honor, but he didn't deserve that praise in this situation. "There is no honor in taking another life. And now that I have a son, I will stress that very thing to him."

"That attitude is exactly what makes you honorable," she said. "You were bothered by an evil man's demise to the point of having nightmares. That means you have compassion and a conscience."

If that were the case, he wouldn't have asked her to remain in his quarters for the duration of their time together. Yet he'd not considered anything other than his own needs. And he did need her—in ways he could not have predicted. Still, he couldn't get too close to her or build her expectations beyond what he could provide aside from being her lover. He wasn't suited for a permanent relationship, as his family had told him time and again. "We should try to sleep now. I suspect Samuel will be summoning me in less than two hours."

She fitted her body closer to his side. "I'll be glad to take care of Sam tonight while you get your rest."

"Again, that's not necessary."

"Maybe not, but I really want to do it, not only for you, but for me. We barely caught a glimpse of him tonight. Besides, I'll only have him a little longer, while you'll have him the rest of your life."

Piper's words filled Adan with unexpected regret. Regret that, in a matter of weeks, he would be forced to say goodbye to an incredible woman. In the meantime, he would make the most of their remaining hours together and grant her whatever her heart desired, not only as the provisional mother to his son, but as his temporary lover.

He rolled to face Piper, leaving nothing between them but bare flesh. "Since you have presented such a convincing argument, we will see to Samuel together. Before this, could I convince you to spend the next few hours in some interesting ways?"

She laughed softly. "I thought we were going to sleep."

Bent on persuasion, he skimmed his palm along her curves and paused at the bend of her waist. "We could do that if you'd like."

She draped her arm over his hip. "Sleeping is definitely overrated, so I'm willing to go wherever you lead me."

And she was leading him to a place he'd never been before—close to crashing and burning with no safe place to land. Tonight, he wouldn't analyze the unfamiliar feelings. Tonight, she was all his, and he would treat her as if she always would be.

What an incredible night.

A week ago, Piper would never have believed she

could find a lover as unselfish as Adan. She also couldn't believe her inhibitions had all but disappeared when they made love.

As she supported her cheek with her palm and studied him in the dim light streaming through a break in the heavy gold curtains, she wanted him desperately— even if she was a bit miffed he'd failed to wake her to help care for Sam. Apparently she'd been so relaxed in the postcoitus afterglow, she hadn't heard the baby's cries through the bedside monitor. Some mother she would make.

When Adan stirred, she turned her complete focus on him as he lay sleeping on his back, one arm resting above his head on the navy satin-covered pillow, the other draped loosely across his abdomen. She loved the dark shading of whiskers surrounding his gorgeous mouth, envied the way his long dark lashes fanned beneath his eyes and admired the intricate details of his hand as he slid his palm from his sternum down to beneath the sheet and back up again. The reflexive gesture was so masculine, so sexy, she fought the urge to rip back the covers and climb on board the pleasure express.

Then he opened his eyes and blinked twice before he presented a smile as slow as the sun rising above the mountains. "Good morning, princess."

Didn't she wish. "Good morning. Did you sleep well?"

"Always with you in my bed. How did you sleep?"

"Too soundly. I didn't even hear Sam last night, and evidently you either didn't wake me to help, or couldn't."

He frowned. "I didn't hear him, either."

Simultaneous panic set in, sending them both from the bed and grabbing robes as they hurried out of the bedroom. They practically sprinted toward the nursery and tore through the door, only to find an empty crib.

Piper's hand immediately went to her mouth to cover the gasp. "Someone took him."

"That is impossible," Adan said, a hint of fear calling out from his gold-brown eyes. "The palace is a virtual fortress. If someone kidnapped him, it would have to be an inside job. And if that is the case, I will kill them with my bare hands."

"No need for that, *cara.*"

They both spun around to discover Elena sitting in the rocker in the far corner of the lengthy room, the baby cradled in her arms, her expression tinged with disapproval.

Weak with relief, Piper hung back and immediately launched into explanation overdrive. "We never heard him last night. We were both very tired and—"

"The bloody monitor must not be working," Adan added. "Is he all right?"

Elena continued to calmly rock Sam in a steady rhythm. "He is quite fine. And judging from the weight of his diaper when I changed him, I would guess he simply slept all night."

Adan narrowed his eyes and glared at her. "You should have said something the moment we walked into the room."

"You should learn to be more observant of your surroundings when it comes to your son, Adan," she replied. "A hard lesson learned, but one that needed to be taught. When he is toddling, you must know where he is at all times."

Piper, in theory, didn't disagree with the governess's assertions, but she did question her tactics. "We were both expecting to find him in the crib, and needless to say we were shocked when we didn't."

Adan clasped his hands behind his neck and began to pace. "I've been in treacherous military situations less harrowing than this."

Elena pushed out of the chair and approached him. "Settle down, Adan, and hold your baby."

He looked as though he might be afraid to touch him. "I have to prepare for my duties today, but I will return to check on him before I depart for the base."

And with that, he rushed away, leaving Piper alone with the former nanny.

"Well, I suppose I should put this little one to bed for a nap," Elena said, breaking the awkward silence.

Piper approached her and held out her arms. "May I?"

"Of course."

After Elena handed her Sam, Piper kissed his cheek before carefully lowering him to the crib. She continued to study Sam's sweet face slack with sleep, his tiny lips forming a rosebud. He'd grown so much in only a matter of days, and in only a few weeks, she would say goodbye to him—and his father—for good. "He's such a beautiful little boy."

The woman came to her side and rested her slender hands on the top of the railing. "Yes, he is, as his father was at that age."

She saw the chance to learn more about Adan from one of the biggest influences in his life and took it. "Was Adan a good baby?"

"Yes. He was very little trouble, until he turned two,

and then he became quite the terror. He climbed everything available to him, and I didn't dare turn my back
for more than a second or he would have dismantled
something. I would try to scold him over his bad behavior, and then he would give me that charming smile,
and all was forgiven."

Piper could absolutely relate to that. "He was lucky
to have you after losing his mother."

Some unnamed emotion passed over Elena's care-
worn face. "I was fortunate to have the opportunity to
raise him. All the brothers, for that matter."

Time to broach the subject of the paternal presence.
"Was the king involved in his upbringing?"

Elena turned and crossed the room to reclaim the
rocker, looking as if all the energy had left her. "He did
the best that he could under the circumstance. Losing
his wife proved to be devastating to him, yet he had
no choice but to postpone his grief in order to serve
his country."

Piper took the light blue club chair next to Elena.
"Adan has intimated the king was a strict disciplinar-
ian."

"He could be," she said. "He wanted his sons to be
strong, independent men, despite their wealth and their
station. Some might say he was too strict at times."

"Would you say that?"

"Perhaps, but it was not my place to interfere."

"I would think you had every right to state your opinion in light of your relationship."

Elena stiffened and appeared quite stunned by the
statement. "Has Adan spoken to you about myself and
the king?"

Piper smelled a scandal brewing. "Not at all. I only

meant that since you were in charge of the children, you should have had some say in how they were treated."

Elena relaxed somewhat, settled back against the rocker and set it in motion. "The king was stern, but fair."

"I'm not sure how fair it was for Adan when he shipped him off to boarding school at such a young age." And she'd probably just overstepped her bounds by at least a mile.

"He did so to protect him."

The defensiveness in her tone did not deter Piper. "Protect him from what?"

Elena tightened her grip on the chair's arms. "I have already said too much."

Not by a long shot, as far as she was concerned. "Look, I don't know what you know, and frankly I don't have to know it. But Adan deserves the truth."

"It would be too painful for him, and would serve no purpose at this point in time."

She wasn't getting through to the woman, which meant she would have to play the guilt card. "Have you ever asked Adan if he would prefer to be kept in the dark? I personally think he wouldn't."

"And you, Ms. McAdams, have not known him all that long."

Touché. "True, but we have spoken at length about his father. Even though he's reluctant to admit it, Adan has a lot of emotional scars, thanks to the king's careless disregard for his youngest son's needs."

She saw the first real hint of anger in Elena's topaz eyes. "Aahil…the king loved Adan. He gave him the very best of everything money could buy, and the opportunity to do what he loved the most. Fly jets."

A perfect lead-in to confront the crux of the matter, yet asking hard questions could be to her detriment. But if Adan could finally put his concerns to rest, it would be worth the risk. "I personally believe he failed to give Adan the one thing he needed most, and that would be a father who paid more attention to him, instead of shipping him far from his home. For that reason, Adan honestly believes the king isn't his biological father."

Elena glanced away, a very telling sign she could be skirting facts. "That is a wrongful assumption."

Piper wasn't ready to give up just yet. "Are you being absolutely honest with me, Elena? And before you speak, keep in mind Adan deserves to know so he could put that part of his past to rest."

"I swear on my papa's grave that the king was very much Adan's biological father."

Even though Elena sounded resolute, Piper couldn't quite help but believe the woman still had something to hide. "Then you need to tell him that, Elena. And you'll have to work hard to convince him, because he's certain something isn't right when it comes to his heritage."

Elena gave her a surprisingly meaningful look. "Do you care for Adan, Ms. McAdams?"

It was her turn to be shocked. "It's Piper, and yes, as one would care for a very good friend." Now she was the one hiding the truth.

"Then I suggest you not worry about things that do not concern you for Adan's sake."

Piper's frustration began to build. "But in some ways they do concern me. I want to see Adan happy and at peace. He can't do that when he knows full well people are protecting secrets from the past. And no offense, but I believe you're bent on protecting the king and his secrets."

"Are you not protecting Adan and Samuel by masquerading as his wife?"

She had her there. "That's true, but this pretense isn't causing either one of them pain."

"Give it time, Piper," Elena said in a gentler tone. "I can see in Adan's eyes that he cares for you, as well. Perhaps much more than he realizes at this point. But when the fantasy ends and you leave him, reality will be a bitter pill for both of you to swallow. Adan is not the kind of man to commit to one woman, or so he believes."

If Adan did care for her, but he could never be more than her lover, that would possibly shatter her heart completely. But she could still foolishly hope that the man she was dangerously close to loving might change his mind. All the more reason to give him the gift of knowledge, whether he came around or not. "Elena, if you ever cared for Adan at all, I'm imploring you to please consider telling him what you know. Isn't it time to put an end to the mystery and his misery?"

Elena sighed and stared off into space for a few moments before regarding Piper again. "This truth you are seeking will forever change him. He might never accept the mistakes the people in his life have made, even if those mistakes resulted in his very existence."

Finally they were getting somewhere. "Then it's true the queen had an extramarital affair that resulted in Adan's birth."

"No, that is not the case, but you are on the correct path."

Reality suddenly dawned on Piper. "The king had an indiscretion?"

She shook her head. "He had the desire to give the queen what she could not have. A third child. That decision required involving another woman."

"He used a surrogate?" Piper asked, unable to keep the shock from her voice.

"Yes. In a manner of speaking."

"And you know the mother," she said in a simple statement of fact.

Elena knitted her hands together and glanced away. "Very well."

She doubted she would get an answer, but she still had to ask. "Who is she, Elena?"

The woman turned a weary gaze to her and sighed. "I am."

Eight

Piper's brief time in Bajul had been fraught with misunderstanding and mysteries and more than a few surprises. But this bombshell trumped every last one of them. "Who else knows about this?" she asked when she'd finally recovered her voice.

Elena pushed slowly out of the rocker and walked to the window to peer outside. "No one else until now."

All these years, Adan had been living under the assumption that he was another man's child. A supposition that had caused him a great deal of pain, though he had downplayed his burden. But Piper had witnessed it firsthand, and now she wanted nothing more than to finally give him the answers he'd been silently seeking for years. "You have to tell him, Elena."

She turned from the window, a despondent look on

her face. "I have pondered that for many years. I still am not certain it would be wise."

Wise? Surely the former nanny wasn't serious. "Adan deserves to know the truth from the woman who gave him life."

"And he will hate me for withholding that truth for his entire life."

"Why did you withhold it?"

Elena reclaimed the chair and perched on the edge of the cushioned seat. "The king requested that Adan's parentage remain a secret, for both my sake and his."

"You mean for the king's sake, don't you?" She hadn't been able to tamp down the obvious anger in her tone, but she was angry. Livid, in fact.

"For all our sakes," Elena replied. "And for the benefit of the queen, who was already suffering from the decision Aahil made to give her another child."

"But I thought she wanted another baby."

"She did, yet after Adan was born, she could not hold him. In fact, she wanted nothing to do with him. What was meant to give her solace only drove her deeper into depression."

Piper was about to step out on a limb, even knowing it could break the revelations wide-open. "When Adan was conceived, was it through artificial means?"

Elena shook her head. "That process would have included medical staff, and we could not risk involving anyone who might reveal the truth."

"Then Adan was conceived—"

"Through natural means." Once again her gaze drifted away. "And after all was said and done, I am somewhat ashamed to say Aahil and I fell in love during the process, though he continued to be true to the queen until her demise. We remained devoted to each other until his death, and until last year, I kept our relationship a secret."

That meant the king had slept with the governess for the sake of procreation to please his queen, resulting in a decades-long affair. A twisted fairy tale that needed to be untangled. "You said 'until last year.' Does that mean Adan knows you were involved with his father?"

"Yes," she said quietly. "All the boys know. But they do not know I am Adan's true mother."

"It's not too late to rectify the deception, Elena, especially now that Adan has a son. A grandson whom you can acknowledge if you'll just tell Adan the whole story."

Elena's eyes began to mist with unshed tears. "I could not bear to tell him the rest for fear he'll hate me."

Piper leaned forward and clasped Elena's hands. "You're the only mother Adan has ever known, and it's obvious he loves you very much. He might need time to adjust, but I'm sure he'll eventually forgive you."

"It is because of my love for him that I want to protect him from more pain. And you must promise me, Piper, that you will say nothing to him."

The woman drove a hard bargain that could force a wedge between Piper and Adan should he ever learn she'd continued the ruse. "I'll allow you to tell Adan, but—"

"Tell me what?"

Startled by Adan's sudden appearance, Piper quickly shot to her feet. "We were just discussing…actually…"

"We were discussing Samuel's care," Elena said as she gave Piper a cautioning look.

"Am I doing something wrong?" Adan asked, sounding somewhat frustrated.

The lies would surely taste as bitter as brine going down. But it honestly wasn't Piper's place to enlighten him. "You're doing a great job. I basically asked Elena to keep encouraging you when I'm no longer here."

His expression turned somber. "We will discuss that following your departure. At the moment, I need to say goodbye to my son."

Piper remained rooted to her spot as Adan walked to the crib and laid a gentle hand on Sam's forehead. He looked so handsome in his navy flight suit, sunglasses perched atop his head and heavy boots on his feet. He also looked like the consummate father. And when he turned and came to her side, she desperately wanted to blurt out the truth.

Instead, she maintained an overly pleasant demeanor that inaccurately reflected her mood. "I guess we'll see you tomorrow evening, right?"

"Yes, and hopefully not too late." Then he brushed a kiss across her lips, as if this make-believe marriage had somehow become real. She knew better.

"Keep her company, Elena," he said as he kissed her cheek, unaware he was showing affection to his mother. "And do not reveal to her all my bad habits."

Elena reached up and patted his face. "Godspeed, *cara mia*."

After Adan left the room in a rush, Piper regarded Elena again. "I'll give you my word not to say anything to him, as long as you promise you'll tell him the truth. If you don't, I will."

Elena oddly didn't seem at all upset by the threat. "I will tell him before you depart. And I sincerely hope you will tell him what you have been concealing from him, as well."

That threw Piper for a mental loop. "I'm not hiding anything from Adan."

"Yes, my dear, you are." She started for the door but turned and paused before she exited. "You love him, Piper. Tell him soon."

Long after Elena left the nursery, Piper stood there aimlessly staring at the sleeping baby as she pondered the former governess's words. Did she love Adan? Did she even dare admit it to herself, much less to him?

Yet in her heart of hearts she knew that she did love him, and she loved his son as she would have her own child. Regardless, nothing would come of it unless Adan felt the same way about her. Only time would tell, and time was slowly slipping away.

At half past midnight, Adan arrived at the palace initially exhausted from performing his duties. Yet the moment he entered the corridor leading to the living quarters, his fatigue began to dissipate as he started toward his first stop—the nursery to see his son. After that, he would retire to his bedroom in hopes of finding Piper waiting up for him. He certainly wouldn't blame her if she wasn't, considering the lateness of the hour. And if that happened to be the case, he would use creative kisses in strategic places to wake her.

He found the nursery door open and the room entirely vacant. An empty bottle on the table next to the rocker indicated someone had recently been there to tend to Samuel, and he suspected who that someone might be.

On that thought, he traveled down the hall at a quick

clip, and pulled up short at the partially ajar door when
he heard the soft, melodic sounds of a French lullaby.

*"Dodo, l'enfant do, l'enfant dormira bien vite. Dodo,
l'enfant do. L'enfant dormira bientôt."*

The lyrics alone indicated Piper could be having difficulty putting Samuel to sleep, but Adan imagined her
sweet voice would eventually do the trick. He stayed in
the hallway, immersed in faint memories of Elena sing-
ing him to sleep. Sadly he'd never had the pleasure of
recalling his own mother doing the same.

He wondered if Samuel would eventually resent him
for taking him away from Talia. Provided Talia actually
agreed to signing over her rights, and he didn't change
his mind about asking her to do that very thing.

The sudden silence thrust the concerns away and sent
Adan into the bedroom. He discovered Piper propped
up against the headboard, eyes closed, her dark hair
fanning out on the stack of white satin pillows beneath
her head, and his son, deep in slumber, cradled against
her breasts. Had she not been gently patting the baby's
back, he might have believed she'd fallen asleep, as well.

He remained in place, recognizing at that moment
how greatly he appreciated this woman who had stepped
in to care for his child without hesitation. He'd begun
to care for her deeply, more than he had any woman.
But to expect her to continue in this role much longer
would be completely unfair to both her and his child.
She had another life in another country, and she would
soon return to resume that life.

When Piper opened her eyes and caught his glance,
she smiled before holding a finger against her lips to
ensure his silence. He waited at the door as she worked
her way slowly off the bed and approached him at the

door. "I'll be right back," she whispered. "Unless he wakes again."

Unable to resist, he softly kissed the top of Samuel's head, remarkably without disturbing him, then leaned and kissed Piper's cheek, earning him another smile before she left the room.

In order to be waiting in bed for her return, Adan launched into action. He stripped out of his clothes on his way into the bathroom, turned on the water in the shower, then stepped beneath the spray and began to wash. He'd barely finished rinsing when the glass door opened—and one beautiful, naked woman with her hair piled atop her head boldly joined him.

Using his shoulders for support, she stood on tiptoe and brought her lips to his ear. "I missed you."

He framed her face in his palms. "I missed you, too."

All conversation ceased as they explored each other's bodies with eager hands as the water rained down over them. They kissed with shared passion, touched without restraint. Adan purposely kept Piper on the brink of orgasm with light pressure before he quickened the pace. She released a small moan, then raked her nails down his back with the force of her release. He soon discovered she was bent on reciprocating when she nudged him against the shower wall, lowered to her knees and took him into her mouth. He tipped his head back and gritted his teeth as she took him to the breaking point. Refusing to allow that to happen, he clasped her wrists and pulled her to her feet.

"Not here," he grated out, then swept her into his arms, carried her into the bedroom and brought her down on the sheets despite the fact they were soaking wet.

He slowed the tempo then, using his mouth to bring her more pleasure as she had done with him, until his own body demanded he hurry. In a matter of moments, he had the condom in place, and seated himself soundly inside her. She sighed when he held her closer, yet he couldn't seem to get close enough, even when she wrapped her legs around his waist.

All the unfamiliar emotions, the desperate desire, culminated in a climax that rocked him to the core. He had difficulty catching his breath as his heart beat a thunderous tempo against his chest. Piper began to stroke his back in a soothing rhythm, bringing him slowly back into reality. And that reality included an emotion he'd always rejected in the past. An expression he had never uttered to any lover. A word he dared not acknowledge now, for in doing so he would be completely vulnerable to a woman who was bound to leave.

He preferred to remain as he'd always been, immune to romantic love. Yet as Piper whispered soft words of praise, he wondered where he would find the strength to let her go. He would find it. He had no choice.

But not now. Not tonight.

Three weeks gone, one more to go.

As the first morning light filtered in from the part in the heavy gold curtains, Piper couldn't stop thinking about how little time she had left before she went home. And as she lay curled up in the empty bed, hugging a pillow, she also couldn't stop pondering Adan's abrupt change in mood.

For the past several days, he'd begun to spend more time with the baby when he wasn't at the base and a lot less time with her. She felt somewhat guilty for even questioning his paternal role, but she didn't quite understand why he'd started coming to bed in the middle of the night. Nor could she fathom why they hadn't made love in over a week when they hadn't missed a day since their first time together.

She questioned whether Elena had told him her secret, but she felt certain Adan would have told her if that had been the case. Blamed her for meddling, for that matter. Maybe the prince was simply preparing for their parting. Maybe the pretend princess would be wise to do the same. But lately she'd learned to lead with her heart, not her head. Her head told her to accept the certain end to their relationship. Her heart told her not to go down without a fight.

At the moment, her heart made more sense. For that reason, she climbed from beneath the covers to confront the missing sheikh, who she presumed was still in the nursery, tending to his son. After donning her robe, she padded down the hall to confirm her conjecture. And she did when she walked into the nursery and found Adan in the rocker, Sam cradled against his shoulder, both fast asleep.

All her previous concerns disappeared as she took in the precious sight. A scene worthy of being commemorated on canvas. Regrettably she didn't have one readily available, but she did have a sketch pad.

With that in mind, she hurried back to the bedroom she hadn't occupied in weeks, retrieved paper and pencil and then returned to the nursery. She moved closer to achieve a prime vantage point of father and son in the throes of blissful sleep. A souvenir to take with her that would enhance the wonderful memories…unless…

As she sketched the details with second-nature

strokes, a plan began brewing in her mind. A good plan. She quietly backed out the door and returned to Adan's quarters, closed the door, hid the pad in her lingerie drawer beneath her panties and picked up the palace phone. She expected Elena to answer, but instead heard an unfamiliar female voice ask, "May I help you?"

"Yes. This is…" The sheikh's fake spouse? The prince's bed buddy? She couldn't stomach lying again, even to a stranger. "With whom am I speaking?"

"My name is Kira," she said, her pleasant voice not even hinting at a Middle Eastern accent. "And you are the newest princess."

Apparently the woman thought Piper had forgotten her title. Bogus title. "Right. Is there someone available who could run an errand for me?"

"I will be up immediately."

Before she could offer to come downstairs, the line went dead, allowing her only enough time to brush her teeth and hair before she heard the knock.

After tightening the robe's sash, Piper opened the door to find a woman with golden-brown shoulder-length hair and striking cobalt eyes. She wore a navy blazer covering a white blouse and matching knee-length skirt, sensible pumps and a sunny smile. "Good morning, Princess Mehdi."

Piper would like to return the sentiment, but so far the morning hadn't started off well when she'd woken up alone. "Thank you for answering the summons so quickly, Kira, but this errand isn't really that pressing. I'm not even sure it's possible."

Kira straightened her shoulders and slightly lifted

her chin. "This is only my second day as a palace employee, and it is my duty to make this task possible."

Talk about pressure. "Okay, then. Is there a store that sells art supplies in the village?"

Kira seemed to relax from relief. "Thankfully, yes there is."

Things could be looking up after all. "Great. I need a canvas, the largest one available, and a basic set of oil paints today, if at all possible."

"I will gladly see to the purchase myself."

"Wonderful." Piper hooked a thumb over her shoulder. "I'll just grab my credit card and—"

"That is not necessary," Kira said. "The household budget covers all your expenses."

She didn't have the energy or desire to argue. "I truly appreciate that. And out of curiosity, are you from Bajul? I ask because you don't really have an accent."

"I was born and grew up here but I've been living in Montreal for the past few years. My mother was Canadian, and while she was working in Dubai, she traveled to the queen's mountain resort here one weekend, met my papa, fell madly in love and never left."

At least someone's whirlwind affair had turned out well. "That's a wonderful story. Now, if you don't mind, I have one more favor to ask."

"Whatever you wish, Princess Mehdi."

She really wished she would stop calling her that. "Please, call me Piper."

Kira looked just this side of mortified over the suggestion. "That would not be proper. I am a member of the staff and you are a member of the royal family."

Little did the woman know, nothing could be further from the truth. "How old are you, Kira, if you don't mind me asking?"

She looked a little confused by the question. "Twenty-seven."

"And I'll turn twenty-seven in three months. Since we're basically contemporaries, I'd prefer you address me by my given name while we're in private. If we're in a public forum, we'll adhere to all that ridiculous formality since it's expected. And in all honesty, I could use a friend in the palace. A female friend close to my age."

That brought the return of Kira's grin. "I suppose we could do that. A woman can never have an overabundance of friends."

Piper returned her smile. "Great. Now about that other favor." She gestured Kira inside the suite and closed the door. "Please don't say anything to anyone about the art supplies. I want to surprise Adan."

She raised her hand as if taking an oath. "I promise I will not say a word to the prince, even if it means residing in the dungeon while being subjected to torture."

"There's a dungeon?"

Kira chuckled. "Not that I have seen. And I apologize. At times I let my questionable sense of humor overtake my sound judgment."

"Well, Kira, since I'm prone to do the same, I believe that will make us fast friends. We can meet weekly and exchange smart remarks to enable us to maintain a certain amount of decorum."

They both shared in a laugh then, but all humor ceased when Adan came through the door without warning. He gave Piper a confused look before his gaze settled on Kira—and he grinned. "Are my eyes deceiving me, or has the caretaker's daughter come home?"

"No, Your Highness, your eyes are not deceiving you. I have returned, and I am now working in the palace with the sole intent to serve you."

He frowned. "Serve me grief no doubt, and what is with the 'Your Highness'? If I recall, I was the first boy to kiss you."

"And if I recall, I slugged you before you could."

This time Adan and Kira laughed, before he grabbed her up and spun her around, indicating to Piper this pair knew each other well. Possibly very well. She couldn't quell the bite of jealousy, even though she sensed nothing aside from camaraderie between the two. Or maybe she was just playing the ostrich hiding its head in the desert sand.

After Adan let Kira go, he kept his attention on her. "I thought you were engaged to be married."

"That didn't work out," she replied. "It's a long, sad story that is not worth telling. Luckily Mama and Papa mentioned my return to Elena, and here I am."

Adan finally regarded Piper. "Kira's parents were members of the household staff for many years."

"My father tended the palace grounds," Kira added. "My mother was the head chef at the palace."

Adan pointed at her. "And she was the resident holy terror in her youth."

Kira frowned. "If I were not your subordinate, I would possibly slug you again. But since I am, I will leave you both to your privacy as I have an important task to oversee. Princess Mehdi, it was a pleasure to meet you." She then did an about-face and left, closing the door behind her.

"She certainly left in a hurry," Piper said. "Evidently she had a very bad breakup."

Adan's good spirits seemed to dissolve right before Piper's eyes. "More often than not, relationships run their course and usually come to a less than favorable conclusion."

Piper's hope that he might have feelings for her beyond gratitude evaporated like early-morning fog. "I had no idea you were that cynical, Your Highness."

He disappeared into the closet and returned with khaki cargo pants, a navy T-shirt, socks and a pair of heavy boots. "I am a realist."

She leaned a shoulder against the bedpost as he shrugged out of his robe, finding it difficult to ignore his board-flat abdomen and the slight stream of hair disappearing beneath the waistband of his boxer briefs. "It seems to me both your brothers are happily married."

He tugged the shirt over his head, ruffling his dark hair in the process. "Perhaps, but they are the exception to the rule."

"Your relationship rules?"

He put on his pants one leg at a time and zipped them closed. "I didn't make the rules, Piper. I'm only acknowledging that failed relationships seem to be my forte."

"Are you referring to Talia?"

After rounding the bed, he perched on the mattress's edge to put on his boots. "Yes, among a few other nonintimate relationships, including my father."

Now they were getting somewhere. "You didn't fail him, Adan. He failed you."

"I suppose you're right. Apparently I never accomplished anything to suit him, no matter how hard I tried."

"Even learning to pilot jets wasn't good enough?"

He came to his feet and faced her. "I have no idea since he rarely mentioned my skills, even when he convinced the counsel to appoint me as the armed forces commander."

"Well, at least he had enough faith in you to believe you could handle the responsibility."

"Or he was possibly setting me up to fail. Fortunately I proved him wrong."

She smiled. "Yes, you did, at that. And if it's any consolation, I'm proud of your accomplishments, both military and paternal."

Discomfort called out from his eyes. "You never did say why Kira was here."

Time to lighten the mood. Or die trying. "She was seeking donations for the poor. I told her to take five or so of the watches in your extensive collection since I'm sure they'll go for a hefty price, and you probably wouldn't miss them."

From the sour look on his face, her efforts at levity had fallen flat. "Try again, Piper."

She folded her arms beneath her breasts and sighed. "If you must know, I sent her into the village for a few feminine unmentionables. But I'll be glad to show you the list if you're worried we were somehow plotting against you."

He held up both hands, palms forward. "That will not be necessary. I presently need to prepare for the day."

"Are you going to the base?"

"Not today. Following breakfast, I thought I would

take Samuel for a stroll around the grounds as soon as he wakes from his morning nap."

"Do you mind if I join you?"

"That is entirely up to you."

The lack of enthusiasm in his response told Piper all she needed to know—she wasn't welcome, and that stung like a bumblebee. "I'll let you and Sam have some father-and-son alone time. Besides, I have something I need to do anyway." Namely begin painting a portrait that would serve as a gift for the prince. A parting gift.

"That is your prerogative," he said in a noncommittal tone as he started to the door. "I'll tell the cook to keep your breakfast warm while you dress."

She wasn't hungry for food, but she was definitely starved for answers. "Before you leave, I have something I need to tell you."

Adan paused with his hand on the doorknob and turned to face her. "I'm listening."

She drew in a deep breath and prepared for the possibility of having her heart completely torn in two. "I'm in love with you."

He looked as if she'd slapped him. "What did you say?"

"Don't be obtuse, Adan. I love you. I didn't plan it. I really didn't want it. But it happened in spite of my resistance. My question is, how do you feel about me?"

He lowered his eyes to the floor. "I cannot be the man you need, Piper."

"That's my decision to make, not an answer."

His gaze snapped to hers. "You deserve someone who can give you the emotional support you require."

Meaning he didn't return her feelings. Or maybe he

refused to admit it. Only one way to find out. "What are you afraid of, Adan?"

"I'm not afraid, Piper. As I've said, I'm pragmatic."

"No, you're not," she said. "You're a risk taker, but you're scared to take a chance on us."

"I am only considering your well-being. I do care about you, Piper. Perhaps more than I've cared for any woman in my past. But I'll be damned if I break your heart because I cannot succeed at being faithful to one woman."

The surprising revelations took Piper aback. "Did you cheat on Talia during the six years you were together?"

"No."

"Have you cheated on any woman you've been with?"

"No, but—"

"Then why would you believe you would be unfaithful to me?"

"Because I could be genetically predisposed to adultery, compliments of my mother."

She could no longer allow him to think that his mother had taken a lover who resulted in his birth, in spite of her promise to Elena. Not when their future together could depend on the truth. "Adan, your mother was—"

The sharp rap suspended Piper's confession midsentence and caused Adan to mutter a string of Arabic words as he opened the door.

Piper expected a member of the staff. What she got was Adan's erstwhile lover, her platinum hair slicked back in a low chignon, her lithe body tightly encased in a blue silk jumpsuit, her makeup applied to perfection and her red painted lips curled into a snarl-like smile.

"Surprise, you bleedin' bastard. I'm back!"

Nine

The woman in the catsuit looked ready for a catfight, but Piper wasn't about to bite. "I'll leave you two with your privacy," she said as she targeted the door as her means to escape.

Talia stormed into the room, blocking her escape. "Oh, do stay, chicky. The party is only getting started."

Adan stepped to Piper's side and moved slightly in front of her. "Calm down, Talia. If anyone has cause to be irritated, it should be me. You might have had the courtesy of notifying me of your impending arrival."

"And you might have told me you married—" she pointed a finger at Piper "—this wench."

"Piper is not a wench," Adan stated with a touch of venom in his tone. "And your argument is with me, not her. If you will join me in my study, we will discuss our son."

Talia smirked. "Here seems fine. After all, you've obviously been taking care of the bonking business in the bedroom with her for quite some time, according to the press."

And Piper had only thought they'd covered all their media bases. "You can't believe everything you hear or read, Talia. Adan has done whatever it takes to protect Sam."

The woman nailed her with a seething glare. "Our son is not your concern."

"But he is my concern," Adan said. "And I am prepared to offer you a sizable settlement in exchange for retaining full custody of Samuel."

Talia flipped a hand in dismissal. "Your attorneys have already worked that out with my attorneys."

Adan's expression was a mixture of confusion and anger. "How is that possible when I have not consulted the palace barrister?"

"Maybe you should talk to your brother about that," Talia replied.

"The king knew you were coming?" Piper chimed in, earning a quelling look from Adan.

"Yes, he did," she said. "I had Bridgette call when I arrived back in Paris. Rafiq wouldn't let me speak to you, the duffer, so I hopped on a plane and came here. He practically met me at the door with the papers. I signed them and then I had to evade the houseboy on my way up here."

Piper knew very little British slang, but it didn't take much to interpret Talia's words. "Then I assume you're okay with giving Adan full custody," she said, sticking her nose in where it obviously didn't belong.

Talia screwed up her face in a frown. It wasn't pretty.

"No. I'm giving him to Adan. What would I need with a kid?"

A litany of indictments shot into Piper's brain, threatening to spill out her mouth. Luckily Sam's cry filtered through the monitor at that exact moment, supplying an excuse to bail before she blew up. "I'll take care of him." She brushed past Talia, resisting the urge to rip the expensive designer bag from her shoulder and stomp on it for good measure.

She took a few calming breaths as she quickly made her way to the nursery to see about the baby. The minute she walked into the room, Sam's cries turned into wails, as if he somehow sensed the stressful situation brewing down the hall.

"What's wrong, sweetie?" she said as she picked him up from the crib. "Did you have a bad dream or just need some company?"

His sobs turned to sniffles as she cradled him in her arms, and then she realized he was in dire need of a diaper change. After she saw to that task, she considered instituting Adan's plan to take the baby for a stroll around the grounds. She discarded that idea when she remembered she was still wearing her robe. Nothing like giving tabloid reporters more fuel for gossip should she get caught on camera. Of course, if any of the bottom-feeders had been hanging around in the past hour, which they had been periodically known to do since she'd arrived in Bajul, they would have a field day with Toxic Talia.

Her anger came back full throttle when she considered how the woman had agreed to relinquish her child without a second thought. Couldn't she see what a precious gift she'd been given? Of course she couldn't. She wasn't concerned about anything that didn't promote her personal gain...just like her own mother.

Piper refused to make this decision easy on the selfish supermodel, and with that goal in mind, she strode back down the hall with Sam in tow. She arrived at the open door to the suite in time to hear Talia say, "Now that everything's settled, I'll be on my way."

"You're not going anywhere yet," Piper said through gritted teeth. "Not until you take a good long look at what you're giving away."

Talia spun around and rolled her eyes. "For the last time, this is none of your business, ducky."

Undeterred, Piper walked right up to her and turned the baby around in her arms. "Look at him, Talia, and think about what you're doing. It's still not too late to change your mind."

Adan took a few steps forward. "It's no use, Piper. She's made her choice, and she chooses her career. She wants no part in raising him."

Ignoring Adan, Piper kept her gaze trained on Talia. "This is a life-altering decision. There's no turning back if you walk away now. Is that what you really want?"

A spark of indecision showed in Talia's eyes. "I can't raise him," she said, an almost mournful quality to her voice.

Piper's disdain lessened as she witnessed the woman's defenses began to crumble, one fissure at a time. "Are you absolutely sure?"

"If I were a different person, perhaps I could. But I'm never going to be good at it, and it would be unfair to him if I tried." Then she surprisingly reached out and touched Sam's fisted hand. "So long, little fellow. Be good for your daddy and your new mum."

Talia hurried out the door, but not before Piper caught a glimpse of tears in her eyes. "Maybe I misjudged her," she said as she placed Sam against her shoulder. "Maybe for the first time in her life, she's doing something unselfish."

Adan shoved a hand in his pocket, rubbed his neck with the other and began to pace. "Do you find it odd that all three of us have been betrayed by our mothers?"

In a way, he was right, but not completely. Piper had intended to tell him the truth before Talia's interruption. She now recognized she walked a fine line between breaking a promise and bringing him peace. Perhaps she could avoid crossing that line by handing him only a partial truth. "There are some things you don't know about your mother, and it's high time you do."

He faced her and frowned. "What are you talking about?"

"You need to ask Elena," she said. "She holds the answers, and she's prepared to tell you."

At least that was what she hoped.

A few moments later, Adan found himself standing outside Elena's private office, his mind caught in a maze of confusion. He had no idea what Piper had been talking about, yet he suspected he would soon find out, even if he wasn't certain he wanted to know.

When he rapped on the frame surrounding the open door, Elena looked up from her position behind the desk, obviously startled before surprise melted into a smile. "Come in, *cara*."

He entered, pulled back the chair opposite her and sat. "Am I interrupting anything?"

"Of course not. You are always welcome here."

He stretched out his legs in an attempt to affect a casual demeanor, when in truth his nerves were on edge. "Talia stopped by to sign over custody of Samuel."

"I heard," she said. "And I am very sorry that your son will not have the opportunity to know his mother. On the other hand, since I do know his mother's shortcomings, the decision she made was the best course of action in this case."

"Piper suggested it was an uncharacteristically unselfish act on Talia's part."

"Piper is correct, but then she has wisdom beyond her years."

The moment had arrived to transition into his real reason for being there. "And continuing on with the subject of motherhood, Piper also informed me you had information about my mother that she's convinced I should know."

Unmistakable panic showed in Elena's eyes. "I told her I would tell you in due time."

"Perhaps that time is now."

Elena hesitated for several moments, leading him to believe she might thwart his attempts at garnering information. "I suppose you are right."

"Then proceed," he said as he braced for the possibilities and prepared for the worst.

She picked up a stack of papers and moved them aside before folding her hands atop the desk. "First of all, I must clarify an incorrect assumption you have long held regarding your parents. Your mother always remained true to her husband during their marriage, and they both grew to love each other. Most important, Aahil Mehdi was your biological father, not some unknown man."

He had waited all his life for confirmation or a denial of his theory, yet something didn't quite ring true. "If that is a fact, then why was I the only son not raised and schooled here at the palace? Why was I the only brother sent away during my formative years?"

"To protect you, Adan."

"From what?"

"The chance someone could learn your true parentage, and you would suffer the consequences from being labeled the child of a concubine."

Anger began brewing immediately beneath the surface of his feigned calm. "Then you are saying my father was the adulterer and I am the product of his affair with a servant?"

"No. Your father was a good man, but you were the reminder of his failure to make his queen happy by giving her the baby she was not able to conceive." She sent him a wistful smile. "Yet you were the greatest joy in my life from the moment you came into this world."

Awareness barreled down on him with the force of a hundred wild horses. "*You* gave birth to me?"

"Yes, *cara,* as a favor to the king, and during the process of conception, your father and I fell in love. And as you already know, that love continued until his death, but I assure you we did not act on it until the queen's demise."

Questions continued to bombard his brain. He chose the one that took precedence over all. "Why did you wait to tell me this?"

"I promised your father I would never reveal the truth to anyone, even you."

Once the initial shock subsided, ire took its place.

"He had no right to ask that of you, and you had no right to keep this from me all these years."

"I realize that now," she said. "And had Piper not come to me and then pressed me to reveal the truth to you, I might have carried the secret to my grave."

Adan was torn between gratitude and resentment aimed toward both Elena and Piper. "How long has she known about this secret?"

"For a while."

One more betrayal in a long line of many. "She should have told me immediately."

"Do not blame Piper for not saying anything, Adan. I begged her to allow me to tell you."

"She should not have come to you in the first place."

"She did so because she loves you, Adan. She only wants what is best for you, and she believes with this information you'll find some peace."

Piper's declaration of love intruded into his thoughts, but he pushed it aside. "If that is so, then why would she subject me to this confession knowing it would cause such turmoil?"

"I suspect she recognizes that lies have the capacity to destroy relationships."

And so could the truth. His relationship with Piper had been fraught with lies from the beginning, and he wasn't certain he could trust her now.

Bent on a confrontation, he shoved the chair back and stood. "We will discuss this further after I have had time to digest this information."

Tears filled Elena's eyes. "Please tell me you do not hate me, Adan."

How could he hate the woman who had been the only

mother he had ever known? In reality, his real mother. "I could never hate you, Elena."

"But you might never forgive me," she said, resignation in her tone.

"I will try, and that is all I can promise at this moment," he said before he turned to leave.

"Where are you going, Adan?" Elena called after him.

"To have a serious conversation with my alleged wife."

"What possessed you to interfere in my life?"

Piper put down the art book she'd attempted to read in the common sitting area, moved to the edge of the uncomfortable chair and faced Adan's wrath head-on. "I assume Elena told you everything."

He released a caustic laugh. "You would be correct in that assumption, and you have yet to answer my question."

"Okay. You see it as interference, and I see it as making an effort to find the answers you've always longed for."

"I never sought those answers for a reason."

"And that reason is?"

"I knew nothing good would come of them, and nothing has."

She couldn't believe his attitude or his misdirected anger. "What's not good about finally knowing the identity of your real mother? Believe me, Sunny and I unsuccessfully tried to find our father, but we could only narrow it down to three prospects. One was in prison for insider trading, one was a money-hungry gigolo and the last was married with four children. With that field of prospects, we decided it wasn't worth pursuing. At least you now know you have a wonderful mother."

He ran a fast hand over his jaw. "I am not you, Piper. I had no desire to learn the truth. And now that I do know, I have been shown that even the most trustworthy person is capable of the ultimate betrayal."

She felt as if he'd placed her in that category, along with his biological mother. "Look, Adan, I don't agree with Elena concealing the truth for such a lengthy period of time, but on some level I did understand why she was afraid to reveal it. Seeing your reaction only validated her fears."

He paced back and forth like a caged animal before pausing before her. "How would you wish me to react, Piper? Should I be celebrating the lies I've been told my entire life? Or the fact that you knew the truth and concealed it?"

"Believe me, keeping it from you wasn't easy." A colossal understatement. "But it wasn't my place to tell you, although I would have before I left if Elena hadn't."

He narrowed his eyes into a hard glare. "It wasn't your place to go on a bloody fact-finding mission, either."

No matter how hard she tried to see it from his point of view, his condemnation hurt like the devil. Time to fight fire with fire. "Sometimes it's necessary to set a lie into motion to protect those you love, just like you're protecting Samuel by lying about our marriage."

"You are absolutely correct," he said, taking her by surprise. "And I plan to put an end to that fabrication immediately. Now that Talia has relinquished her rights, you have no cause to remain here any longer. I will make the arrangements for you to fly home as soon as possible."

As she came to her feet, she seriously wanted to cry, maybe even beg, but instead called on fury to give her strength. "So that's it, huh? I've served my purpose and now you're going to toss me out into the street like refuse?"

"I am not tossing you out," he said. "I am giving you back your freedom."

And he was going to hold her emotionally captive for a very long time. But deep down, hadn't she known all along this would happen? And she'd been an unequivocal fool to believe otherwise. "Shame on me for believing I meant more to you than just a quick fix to save your sterling reputation. And shame on you for leading me to believe you were honorable."

She could tell by the harsh look on his face she'd delivered a knockout blow. "I would be less than honorable if I kept you here any longer when we both know that I will never be able to give you what you need."

Battling the threatening tears, Piper snatched up the book and clutched it to her heart. "You're right, Your Highness. I need a man who can let down his guard and take a chance on love, even though I've recently discovered love is a risky business. But just remember, there's a little boy who's going to need all the love you can give him, since, like his father, he's never going to know his mother. Don't fail him because you're too afraid to feel."

Without giving him a chance to respond, Piper stormed down the hall to the make-believe lovers' hideaway, slammed the door behind her and started the process of packing. Only then did she let the tears fall at will and continued to cry until she was all cried out, though she inherently knew she was only temporarily done with the blubbering.

Not long after Piper finished filling the last of the suitcases, a series of knocks signaled a guest had come calling, the last thing she needed. Unless… On the way to answer the summons, she couldn't help hoping Adan had somehow come to his senses and decided to ask for a second chance. That he would appear on the threshold on bended knee with his heart in his hands and a declaration of love flowing from his gorgeous mouth. As if that fairy-tale scenario was going to happen. Most likely she'd find Abdul standing in the hall with his head slightly bowed, a live-to-serve look on his face while he declared his unwavering need to carry her luggage.

She discovered she'd been wrong on both counts when she opened the door to the ever-smiling Kira. "I'm so sorry to bother you, Your—" She sent a quick glance over her shoulder. "…Piper, but the art shop didn't have any canvases available and they only had colored chalk. They did offer to order the supplies for you."

She'd forgotten all about the painting she'd planned to give Adan. "That's okay. I won't be needing those supplies now." Or ever.

Kira appeared sorely disappointed. "But you seemed so excited over surprising your husband."

He's not my husband, she wanted to say, but opted for a partial truth. "I probably shouldn't mention this, but you'll know soon enough. The marriage isn't working out, so I'm returning home this afternoon."

Kira hid a gasp behind her hand. "I am so sorry, Piper. I was so certain seeing you and Adan together today that you were completely in love."

"Love isn't always enough, Kira," she said without thought.

"I know that all too well, Piper."

She sensed her newfound friend did, at that. "Oh, well. Nothing ventured, nothing gained, as they say. And I'm going to miss having the opportunity to get to know you."

"Surely I'll see you when you bring the baby to visit his father."

If only that were the case. Leaving Sam would be equally as difficult as leaving his father behind, never knowing what might have been. "Adan is going to have full custody. I travel a lot with my job and we both think it's important Sam grows up in his homeland with his people."

"But you'll be coming here to see him often, right?"

And now for the final, and most painful, lie. "Of course."

That prompted the return of Kira's smile. "That's wonderful. We can still have those smart-remark sessions when you're here."

"I'd offer to have one now, but I want to give Sam one last bottle before I go."

As Piper stepped into the hall to do that very thing, Kira drew her into a hug. "Goodbye for now, Piper. I wish you the best of luck."

"Same to you," she replied as she started toward the nursery, before she gave in to the temptation to tell Kira the truth.

As much as she wanted to see the cherished baby boy, Piper dreaded telling him goodbye. That didn't prevent her from lifting the sleeping Sam from his crib and holding him for the very last time. He opened his

eyes slowly and didn't make a sound, as if he understood
the importance of the moment. She walked around the
room as one more time she sang the lullaby she'd used
to put him to sleep. If only she could be his mother. If
only his father had loved her back. If only…

"The car is waiting, Your Highness."

Piper wanted to tell Abdul it would just have to wait,
but she saw no use in prolonging the inevitable farewell
to the second love of her life. She kissed Sam's forehead, laid him back in the crib and managed a smile.
"I love you, sweetie. I know you'll forget me once I'm
gone, but I will never forget you."

Or the man who had given him life.

After one last look at Sam, Piper turned to go, only
to discover Adan standing in the open door looking
somewhat remorseful. "I did not want you to leave before I expressed my gratitude for all that you've done
for myself and Samuel."

She truly wanted to tell him what he should do with
that gratitude, but she couldn't. She honestly wanted to
hate him, and she couldn't do that, either. "You're welcome, Your Highness. It's been quite the adventure."

He attempted a smile that didn't quite reach his eyes.
"Yes, it has. And I also want to assure you that I will
treat my son as he should be treated. I will make certain he has all that he desires."

Too bad he couldn't promise her the same. "Within
reason, I hope. I'd hate to think you'd buy him his first
plane on his first birthday."

He favored her with a dimpled grin. The same grin
she'd noticed the first time she'd laid eyes on him. "Rest
assured I will withhold that gesture until his second
birthday."

"Good idea. We wouldn't want him to be too spoiled."

A lengthy span of silence passed as they remained quiet, as if neither knew what to say next. Piper had already said what she'd needed to say when she'd told him she loved him, even if he hadn't done the same. Now all that remained was the final goodbye. "Well, I guess I need to get my things and take to the friendly skies. I'd like to say give me a call if you're ever in need of ending your celibacy, but that wouldn't be wise."

He streaked a palm over the nape of his neck. "I suppose it wouldn't be, at that."

"And just so you know, I don't regret the time we've spent together. I only regret this little fake fairy tale didn't have a happy ending. But that's life. Goodbye, Adan."

When she tried to make a hasty exit, Adan caught her arm and pulled her into an embrace that didn't last nearly long enough. "You are a remarkable woman, Piper McAdams. I wish for you only the brightest future with a deserving man."

She was convinced he could be that man, if only he believed it, which he didn't.

Piper began backing away, determined to leave him with a smile. "I'm going to forgo the whole man-hunting thing for a while, but I've decided I am going to further pursue a career in art."

"I am pleased to hear that," he said sincerely. "Perhaps you can send me some of your work in the future. I will pay top price."

How badly she wanted to run back into his arms, but her pride had already suffered too many hits as it was. "I'll certainly give that some serious consideration. In the meantime, take care, Adan."

"I wish the same to you, Piper."

She chose not to afford Adan another look for fear she might do something foolish, like give him another kiss. But after she climbed into the black limousine a half hour later, she glanced back at the red-stone castle and caught a glimpse of someone standing at the second-floor-terrace railing—the someone who had changed her life.

The sheikh of her dreams. A prince of a guy. The one who got away…with her heart.

Ten

"This arrived for you a little while ago."

Adan turned from the nursery window to find Elena holding a large rectangular box. "More gifts from some sultan attempting to insert themselves in the government with bribes for the baby?"

She crossed the room and handed him the brown-paper-wrapped package. "This one is from the United States. South Carolina, to be exact."

He immediately knew what it contained, though he never believed she would actually honor his request. Not after the way he had regretfully treated her.

While Elena looked on, Adan tore through the wrapping and opened the box to find what appeared to be a painting, exactly as he'd expected. Yet when he pulled it from the box, he didn't expect that the painting would depict a slumbering father holding his sleeping son in remarkable detail, right down to the cleft in his chin and Samuel's prominent left dimple.

"Oh, Adan," Elena began in a reverent voice, "this is such a *bella* gift."

He would wholeheartedly agree, if he could dislodge the annoying lump in his throat. The baby began kicking his legs in rapid-fire succession against the mattress as if he appreciated the gesture.

After resting the painting against the crib, Adan picked up Samuel and held him above his head. "You are quite the noisy character these days."

His son rewarded him with a toothless smile, something he'd begun doing the past month. A milestone that had given him great joy. Bittersweet joy, because Piper had not been around to share in it.

"You should call her and thank her, Adan."

He lowered Samuel to his chest and faced Elena with a frown. "I will send her a handwritten note."

She took the baby from his arms without invitation. "You will do no such thing. She deserves to hear from you personally. She also deserves to know that you have been mourning your loss of her since she departed."

"I have not been mourning," he said, sounding too defensive. "I have been busy raising my son and seeing to my royal duty."

Elena patted his cheek. "You can deceive yourself, but you cannot deceive me. You are so sick with love you could wilt every flower in the palace courtyard with your anxiety."

He avoided her scrutiny by picking up the painting and studying the empty wall above the crib. "I believe this is the perfect spot, right above Samuel's bed so he will go to sleep knowing I am watching over him throughout the night."

"Since it is obvious you are not getting any sleep, why not watch over him in person?"

He returned the painting to the floor at his feet. "I am sleeping fine."

"Ah, yes, and I am entering the marathon in Dubai two weeks from now."

That forced Adan around. "Would you please stop assuming you know everything about me?"

She kissed Samuel's cheek before placing him back in the crib, where he began kicking again at the sight of the colorful mobile above him. "I do know you, *cara,* better than most. When you were Samuel's age, I stayed up many nights while you were teething. When you were a toddler, I put you to bed every night with a book, the reason why you were always such a grand reader. When you were six, and you broke your right arm trying to jump the hedges, I was the one who fed you until you learned to eat with your left hand. And when you were twelve, I discovered those horrid magazines beneath your bed and did not tell your father."

He'd forgotten that incident, with good reason. "I realize you've been there for me through thick and thin, but that does not give you carte blanche to lord over me now that I am an adult."

"I agree, you are an adult."

"I am pleased to know you finally acknowledge that."

"An adult who has absolutely no common sense when it counts most."

He should have expected this as soon as he opened the box. "If you're going to say I made the wrong decision by allowing Piper to leave, I would have to disagree."

"And you would be wrong." Elena leaned back against the crib's railing and donned her stern face. "As I have told both your brothers, you all have a great capacity to love, but it would take a special woman to bring that out in you. Zain and Rafiq learned that lesson by finding that special woman, and so have you. Piper is your soul mate, *cara.* Do not destroy what you could have with her by being so stubborn you cannot see what was right in front of you and you foolishly let go for good."

He hated that she had begun to make sense. "I am not being stubborn. I am being sensible. If you know me as well as you say you do, then you realize I have never stayed involved with one woman longer than six years, and we know how well that turned out."

Elena glared at him much as she had when he'd been a badly behaved boy. "Comparing Talia to Piper is like comparing a cactus to a down comforter. It's true Talia gave you a precious son, but she also gave you continuous grief. Piper gave you not only this touching portrait but also the means to heal your wounds with the truth. And you repay her by not admitting how you feel about her."

"I'm presently not certain how I feel about anything." Other than he resented Elena for pointing out the error in his ways.

"And you, *cara mia,* are guilty of propagating the biggest lie of all if you do not stop denying your love for Piper."

"I have never said I love her." He was too afraid

to leave himself open to that emotion, more so now than ever.

She pointed a finger at his face and glowered at him. "Adan Mehdi, before your obstinate behavior destroys what could be the best thing that has happened to you, listen to me, and listen well. First of all, consider how Piper selflessly cared for your son. How she protected you and Samuel by putting her life on hold while pretending to be your wife, only to be dismissed by you as one would dismiss a servant."

"But I never—"

"Furthermore," she continued without regard for his attempts to halt the tirade, "should you finally regain some semblance of wisdom befitting of royalty and decide to contact her, you will beg her forgiveness for being such a rigid *cretino*."

The woman knew how to deliver a right hook to his ego. "I take offense to my own mother calling me an idiot."

Her expression brightened over the unexpected maternal reference. "It means everything to hear you finally acknowledging me as your mother."

He laid a palm on her cheek. "I suppose I have known that all along. Only a true mother would tolerate my antics."

"And only a true mother would agree to raise a child that is not her own, and love that child's father with all her being despite his shortcomings."

He recognized the reference to Piper, yet he couldn't quell his concerns. "What if I try to contact her and she rejects me? And what do I say to her?"

"You must speak from the heart."

"Something I have never truly mastered."

She sighed. "Adan, your father also viewed revealing emotions as a sign of weakness, and in many ways you have inherited that trait from him. But in reality, it's a brave man who shows vulnerability for the sake of love. I implore you to call on your courage and tell Piper your true feelings, before it is too late."

Admittedly, Elena—his mother—was right. He had never backed away from a battle, and he shouldn't avoid this war to win Piper back. Better still, he had the perfect weapons to convince her to surrender—his well-honed charm, and his remarkable son.

When she sensed movement in the corner of her eye, Piper tore her attention away from the painting of the red-stone palace and brought it to the window that provided natural light. And after she glimpsed the tall man pushing the stroller up the guesthouse walkway, she blinked twice to make sure her imagination hadn't commandeered her vision.

But there he was, the man who'd haunted her dreams for the past four weeks. He wore a crisp tailored black shirt and casual beige slacks, his perfect jaw covered by a shading of whiskers, his slightly ruffled thick dark hair as sexy as ever. And she looked like something the cat had dragged into the garage.

She barely had time to remove the paint-dotted apron and smooth the sides of her lopsided ponytail before the bell chimed. After drawing in a cleansing breath, she opened the door and concealed her shock with a smile. "To what do I owe this honor, Your Highness?"

Adan reached into the stroller and retrieved the baby who had stolen Piper's heart from the moment she'd first held him. "This future pilot insisted on paying a personal visit to the artist who presented us with such a fine painting."

She couldn't believe how cute Sam looked in the miniature flight suit and tiny beige boots. "He really said that, huh?"

"He did."

"Wow. I had no idea three-month-old babies could talk."

"He's an exceptional child."

Born to an exceptionally charming father. A charm he'd clearly passed on to his son, evident when Sam kicked his legs and smiled, revealing his inherited dimples. "Well, don't just stand there, boys. Come inside before you both melt from the heat."

Balancing Sam in one arm, Adan leaned over, retrieved the diaper bag from the basket behind the stroller and slipped the strap over his shoulder. "We are accustomed to the heat, but this humidity is excruciating, so I will gladly accept your offer."

Once he stepped into the foyer, Piper showed him into the small living area and gestured toward the floral sofa. "Have a seat, as soon as you give me the kid."

After he handed Samuel off to her, he claimed the end of the couch and set the bag at his feet. "This is a very comfortable yet quaint abode."

"A nice way of saying *small*," she said as she sat in the club chair across from him and gently bounced the baby in her lap. "But the rent is cheap. Actually, it's free. My grandparents live in the main house and this is the guest quarters."

"Yes, I know. Your grandfather greeted me as soon as we left the car."

Great. "Not with a shotgun, I hope."

He laughed. "Actually, he wasn't armed. In fact, he was quite cordial. He's still very pleased that he's been granted the water conservation project, and that's going quite well, by the way."

"So I've heard," she said. "I spoke with Rafiq a few days ago."

"He never mentioned that to me."

"He had no reason to mention it, Adan. He's well aware that once I met the terms of our arrangement I'd go back to business as usual."

"And I presume you've done that?"

"Actually, I'm giving a few private art lessons, and I'm looking for a place to open a small gallery. Interestingly enough, my grandfather is willing to invest in the venture."

"How did you convince him to let you leave the company?"

"I told him that it was high time I had a life of my own that included pursuing my personal aspirations. And then I bribed my grandmother into taking up the cause by helping her with a fund-raiser. Between the two of us, he finally caved."

"I'm glad you're happy, Piper," he said, a solemn note to his voice.

She could think of one other thing that would make her happy, but that was only a pipe dream. "I am, for the most part. Are you?"

He rubbed a palm over his jaw. "I'm happy that I have a son and a fulfilling career. Aside from that—"

When Sam began to fuss, Adan withdrew a bottle from the tote, uncapped it and handed to her. "It seems he's getting hungry more often these days. The books

I've read clearly state that an increase in appetite in an infant signals a growth spurt."

"Spoken like the consummate father," Piper said, bringing the return of Adan's smile.

"I am certainly trying my best."

"And you're succeeding," she said as she laid the baby in the crook of her arm and watched as he downed the formula with gusto. "He's definitely grown. Before you know it, he'll be riding a bike. I can't wait to see that." The statement left her mouth before she'd considered how unrealistic she sounded.

"Perhaps he should learn to walk first."

That drew her attention back to Adan. "Yes, you're right. Time is too short to wish it away." After a bout of awkward silence, she added, "How is Elena these days?"

He leaned back against the sofa and draped an arm over the back of the cushions. "She is doing well. We've had several discussions about my father. She insists he was proud of my accomplishments, and claims he had difficulty expressing his emotions. I'm going to endeavor not to do that with Samuel. He deserves to know that his father supports him at every turn."

"And I'm positive you'll manage that just fine."

"You always have had more faith in me than most." He studied her eyes for a long moment. "I didn't realize how much I would miss your company once you left. But I have missed you. Very much."

She had no idea what to say or how to react. She certainly knew better than to hope. "That reminds me. I never saw where you released the statement outlining the reasons behind my departure."

His gaze drifted away. "That is because I never issued that particular statement. We led the press to believe you were on a sabbatical in the States, visiting family."

That made no sense to her at all. "What was the point in delaying the truth? You're eventually going to have to explain why I left and never came back."

Finally, he brought his attention back to her, some unnamed emotion in his eyes. "Perhaps that will not be necessary."

She put the now-empty bottle on the side table and set Sam upright in her lap. "You're hoping that if you sweep it under the rug, everyone will forget I ever existed?"

"I am hoping after you hear what I have to say, you will realize my mission entails alleviating that necessity."

The man insisted on speaking in riddles. "By all means, continue. I'm waiting with bated breath for clarification."

He pushed off the sofa and stood before her. "And I pray I have not waited too long to do this."

As if she'd been thrust in the middle of some surreal dream, Piper watched in awe as Adan fished a black velvet box from his pants pocket and lowered to one knee. She couldn't catch her breath when he opened that box to reveal a massive princess-cut diamond ring. "Piper McAdams, I have never met a woman quite like you, and I have never been in love until you. I probably do not deserve your forgiveness for my careless disregard, but I sincerely believe we both deserve to be together." He tugged the ring from the holder and held it up. "Now, will you do me the honor of being my real wife, and a mother to my son?"

Heaven help her, the cat that had dragged her into

the garage now had hold of her tongue. She could only stare at the glistening diamond, awed by Adan's declaration of love and the knowledge the fairy tale could soon come true. But then came the questions. Should she take this leap of faith? Could she trust that he really wanted her as his wife, not only as a mother for his child? Or was she overanalyzing everything? Then suddenly the baby reached back, grabbed a wayward tendril of hair at her nape and tugged hard, eliciting her involuntary yelp and Adan's scowl.

"That was not the reply I had hoped for," he said gruffly.

She laughed as she extracted Sam's grasp and offered him her pointer finger. "Apparently he was tired of waiting for my answer."

"And I am also growing impatient."

She pulled Sam up from her lap and turned him to face her. "What do you think about this whole thing, little boy? Should I say yes?"

When the baby squealed in response, Adan said, "I do believe he agrees that you should."

She turned Sam around in her lap to face his father and held out her left hand. "I do believe you're right."

After Adan slid the ring into place, he stood and motioned for Piper to join him. Then with baby Sam nestled between them, he kissed her softly and smiled. "I do love you, Piper. More than my MiG-20 jet."

He could be such a cad. A very cute cad. "And I love you more than my purple fluffy slippers that you always found so comical."

His ensuing smile soon disappeared. "On a serious note, as soon as we are wed, I want you to legally become Samuel's mother."

"I would be honored," she said. And she would.

His expression remained overtly somber. "He has a right to know about Talia, although I am at a loss over what to tell him."

"That's simple. When he's old enough to understand, we'll say that his mother loved him enough to give him up because she felt it was the best thing for him. And if I've learned anything at all, I suppose in some way that's what my own mother did for me and Sunny. She wasn't equipped for parenthood."

"But you are," he said. "And I've come to realize that not knowing about Elena did not discount the fact she was always the best mother a man could ask for. She's also a very good grandmother, and she is dying to have you as her daughter-in-law."

Piper couldn't ask for more. "Any idea when we're going to take care of the wedding business?"

"As soon as possible. Perhaps before we return to Bajul."

"We could always hold the ceremony in the family backyard. I provide the groom, and my grandfather provides the shotgun."

Adan laughed as if he didn't have a care in the world. "No need for that. I am a willing participant in establishing a future with you."

And very soon she would no longer be his pretend wife. She would be the real deal.

Epilogue

If a woman wanted to live in a palace, the gorgeous guy standing a few feet away could be just the man to make that come true. And three months ago he had—in a civil ceremony surrounded by her grandparents' lush gardens, sans shotgun. Now Piper McAdams was more than ready to legitimately assume her role as his princess during the elaborate reception held in their honor.

For the past twenty minutes, she'd been schmoozing with wealthy strangers while shamelessly studying her husband's assets. He wore a navy suit adorned with military insignias, a pricey watch on his wrist and a wedding band on his left hand. His usually tousled dark brown hair had been neatly styled for the occasion, but it still complemented the slight shading of whiskers framing his mouth. And those dimples. She'd spotted them the first time she'd laid eyes on him six months ago in the Chicago hotel bar.

And as it had been that night, he was currently speaking to a lithe blonde wearing a chic red sparkling dress, only she didn't see this woman as a threat. In fact, she saw her as simply Madison Foster Mehdi, her sister-in-law and recent addition to Piper's ever-expanding gal-pal club.

Speaking of expanding, a woman dressed in flowing coral chiffon that didn't completely hide a baby bump stood at the ballroom's entrance. She'd come to call her Maysa while most called her queen, and aside from the duties that came along with the title, she served as Sam's stellar doctor and Piper's confidante. The man on her arm, also known as the king, hadn't been as easy to get to know, yet he'd been warming up to his youngest brother's wife, slowly but surely.

All in all, Piper couldn't be happier with her new family. And she couldn't be more pleased when her husband started toward her with that sexy, confident gait that threatened to bring her to her knees.

Once he reached her side, he leaned over and whispered, "I have another gift for you."

"Giving it to me now would be rather inappropriate, don't you think?" she whispered back.

He straightened and smiled. "I'll reserve that gift for later when we are safely ensconced in our room. But this particular present is totally appropriate for the occasion."

Piper took a quick glance at her left hand. "I really think the boulder on my finger is quite sufficient, and so was the wonderful honeymoon in Naples."

"Have you forgotten our time on the beach?"

She faked a frown. "All right, that thing you did to me on the beach was very unforgettable."

"I thought you enjoyed that thing."

She grinned. "I did!"

He pressed a palm against the small of her back and feathered a kiss across her cheek. "Remain here while I retrieve your surprise."

As he headed across the room, Madison came to Piper's side. "Where is he going in such a hurry?"

"He says he has a gift for me."

"Oh, that," Madison replied. "I was beginning to wonder when he was going to get to that."

Piper's eyes went wide. "You know what it is?"

"Yes, I do. In fact, I assisted in acquiring it. And don't look so worried. You'll love it."

Knowing Adan, she probably would. "I'm counting on it."

Madison momentarily scanned the crowd before bringing her attention back to Piper. "I haven't seen Elena yet. She promised she'd come down once she had the babies put to bed."

"She told me she wanted to read them all a book."

"Good luck with that," Madison said, followed by a laugh. "I'm not sure year-old twins and a six-month-old will fit in her lap."

"She enlisted Kira's help," Piper added. "And believe me, Kira is amazing. I'm not sure there's anything she can't do."

"Except hold on to a man," Madison said. "At least according to her."

"A worthless man, maybe. She told me all about her broken engagement. Too bad we snatched up all the Mehdi brothers. She'd make a great sister-in-law."

Madison grinned. "Maybe there's one hiding in

the closet somewhere. Of course, there is their cousin, Rayad, although he's all into the military thing."

Piper still had a lot to learn about the family. "You'd better hope there's not a secret Mehdi hiding out somewhere. That means you'd be in charge of handling that scandal."

"True." Madison pointed at the double doors to her left, where Adan now stood. "Your husband is about to reveal your surprise, so wait and watch and get ready to be wowed."

Piper kept her gaze trained on the doors, wondering what might actually come through them. A new sports car? A pet elephant? Maybe even a…sister?

The minute Sunny caught sight of Piper, she practically ran across the room and engaged her in a voracious hug. And as if they'd been propelled back into the days of their youth, they momentarily jumped up and down until Piper realized exactly where they were and who she now was.

She stopped the girlish celebration, but she couldn't stop her smile. "Sunny McAdams, what are you doing here?"

"Answering your new husband's invitation."

She noticed they'd gained the attention of a room full of dignitaries. "Thanks to our boisterous show of affection, these people are now convinced the new princess is nuttier than a squirrel's nest."

"If the glass slipper fits," Sunny said as she stepped back and surveyed Piper from head to high heels. "You clean up good, sugar plum. Aqua is definitely your color, but I'm clearly underdressed."

Piper smoothed a hand down the bling-embellished satin strapless gown and grinned. "If you'd walked in here wearing something other than black slacks and a white silk blouse, I'd be asking you to return to the mother ship and give me back the real Sunny McAdams."

They shared in a laugh until Adan interrupted the camaraderie. "Did I succeed in surprising you, fair lady?"

She gave him a grateful hug and an enthusiastic kiss. "An excellent surprise, good sir. I do believe you've thought of everything."

"He wanted to make up for me not being at the wedding," Sunny added.

"That's okay, dear sister. You can make it up to me by staying here a few days."

"Unfortunately, I'll be leaving tomorrow. I'm meeting up with Cameron in Africa to cover a few of the most recent uprisings."

Piper hated how her sibling insisted on putting herself in danger, but she was pleased that she seemed to have found her match. "So how's it going with Cameron the cameraman?"

Sunny shrugged. "We're hanging in there. He wants to settle down in suburbia and have a few kids, but I'm not ready for that."

"Take it from me," Madison began, "you can balance career and motherhood. I've managed it with twins."

"And a very accommodating husband." All eyes turned to Zain Mehdi as he slid an arm around his wife's waist. "It's good to see you again, Sunny."

Piper momentarily gaped. "You two have met?"

"Briefly in Nigeria," Sunny said. "But I didn't know who he was until much later, since he was traveling incognito at the time."

Must run in the family, Piper thought when she considered how Adan had concealed his identity. They'd come a long way in a very short time.

As casual conversation continued, Piper noticed a man standing alone a few feet away, his attention focused on the group. "Does anyone know who that man is to my left, holding up the wall?"

"What man?" Adan asked.

"The one who keeps staring."

Sunny glanced over her shoulder before focusing on Piper again. "That's Tarek Azzmar, a corporate investor who hails from Morocco and a billionaire probably ten times over. I met him in Mexico City a few years back when he was opening an orphanage. He's a man of few words and rather reclusive. An enigma wrapped in a mystery, as they say."

"And Rafiq invited him," Zain added. "Apparently he's building a mansion not far from the palace. We'll be able to see his estate when we're standing on the west-facing veranda."

"So much for privacy," Adan muttered. "And with that in mind, if you fine people will excuse us while I have a few moments alone with my wife?"

"By all means," Zain said. "The courtyard outside provides enough protection to begin your honeymoon, if you so choose. My wife will attest to that."

Piper caught a glimpse of Madison elbowing Zain in the side, earning quite a bit of laughter as her husband led her away.

Once in the corner of the deserted vestibule, Adan turned her into his arms. "How does it feel to be an honest-to-goodness princess?"

"Unreal. Surreal. Wonderful."

"I'm glad you are up to the task, and I'm hoping you are willing to take on another."

She suspected she knew where this could be heading. "Hold it right there, hotshot. We have plenty of time to make a sibling for Sam."

"I would like to get to that in the immediate future," he said, "but this task involves your painting skills."

"What would you like me to paint, Your Highness? And please don't tell me one of your planes."

He gave her that earth-shattering, heart-melting grin. "As tempting as that might be, I'm referring to capturing the entire family on canvas. Rafiq, with the council's support, wants to commission you as the official palace artist in order to preserve history."

Piper could think of nothing she would like better. Actually, she could, but she'd take care of that later in bed. "I'm absolutely honored, and I will do my best to prove I'm up to the challenge."

"It is going to be challenging, at that. You'll have to rely on photographs of my father to capture his likeness. And we'll hang that in the foyer."

"I can do that," she said, thankful Adan had thought of it first. "What about your mother?"

"Since she's here for the sitting, that should not be a problem."

Another feat accomplished—his acceptance of Elena. "We'll hang that one in the nursery, next to yours and Sam's."

"And will you be able to paint one of all three of us?"

"Certainly, and I'll make myself look much thinner."

He frowned. "No need for that. You are perfect in every way."

So was he. So was their life, and their love. "Now

that we've taken care of the details, why don't we go up and say good-night to your son?"

"*Our* son."

"You're right. As of this morning, he's legally mine." He brushed her hair back from her shoulder and kissed her gently. "He has been yours from the beginning, and I will be yours for all time."

In that moment, Piper realized she'd been very lucky to find the sheikh of her dreams. A prince of a guy. The one who got away…and came back, this time to give her his heart.

* * * * *

CAPTURED BY
THE SHEIKH

KATE HEWITT

After spending three years as a die-hard New Yorker, **Kate Hewitt** now lives in a small village in the English Lake District with her husband, their five children and a golden retriever. In addition to writing intensely emotional stories, she loves reading, baking and playing chess with her son – she has yet to win against him – but she continues to try. Learn more about Kate at kate-hewitt.com.

CHAPTER ONE

'SOMETHING'S WRONG——'

Elena Karras, Queen of Thallia, had barely registered
the voice of the royal steward behind her when a man in
a dark suit, his face harsh-looking and his expression inscrutable, met her at the bottom of the steps that led from
the royal jet to this bleak stretch of desert.

'Queen Elena. Welcome to Kadar.'

'Thank you.'

He bowed and then indicated one of three armoured
SUVs waiting by the airstrip. 'Please accompany us to our
destination,' he said, his voice clipped yet courteous. He
stepped aside so she could move forward, and Elena threw
back her shoulders and lifted her chin as she walked towards the waiting cars.

She hadn't expected fanfare upon her arrival to marry
Sheikh Aziz al Bakir, but she supposed she'd thought she'd
have a little more than a few security guards and blacked-
out cars.

Then she reminded herself that Sheikh Aziz wanted
to keep her arrival quiet, because of the instability within
Kadar. Ever since he'd taken the throne just over a month
ago there had been, according to Aziz, some minor insurgent activity. At their last meeting, he'd assured her it was
taken care of, but she supposed a few security measures
were a necessary precaution.

Just like the Sheikh, she needed this marriage to succeed. She barely knew the man, had only met him a few times, but she needed a husband just as he needed a wife.

Desperately.

'This way, Your Highness.'

The man who'd first greeted her had been walking beside her from the airstrip to the SUV, the desert endlessly dark all around them, the night-time air possessing a decided chill. He opened the door of the vehicle and Elena tipped her head up to the inky sky, gazing at the countless stars glittering so coldly above them.

'*Queen Elena.*'

She stiffened at the sound of the panicked voice, recognising it as that of the steward from the Kadaran royal jet. The man's earlier words belatedly registered: *something's wrong*.

She started to turn and felt a hand press into the small of her back, staying her.

'Get in the car, Your Highness.'

An icy sweat broke out between her shoulder blades. The man's voice was low and grim with purpose—not the way he'd sounded earlier, with his clipped yet courteous welcome. And she knew, with a sickening certainty, that she did not want to get in that car.

'Just a moment,' she murmured, and reached down to adjust her shoe, buy a few seconds. Her mind buzzed with panic, static she silenced by sheer force of will. She needed to *think*. Somehow something had gone wrong. Aziz's people hadn't met her as expected. This stranger had and, whoever he was, she knew she needed to get away from him. To plan an escape—and in the next few seconds.

She felt a cold sense of purpose come over her, clearing her mind even as she fought a feeling of unreality. *This was happening. Again, the worst was happening.*

She knew all about dangerous situations. She knew what it felt like to stare death in the face—and survive.

And she knew, if she got in the car, escape would become no more than a remote possibility.

She fiddled with her shoe, her mind racing. If she kicked off her heels she could sprint back to the jet. The steward was obviously loyal to Aziz; if they managed to close the door before this man came after her...

It was a better option than running into the dark desert. It was her only option.

'Your Highness.' Impatience sharpened the man's voice. His hand pressed insistently against her back. Taking a deep breath, Elena kicked off her heels and ran.

The wind streamed past her and whipped sand into her face as she streaked towards the jet. She heard a sound behind her and then a firm hand came round her waist, lifting her clear off the ground.

Even then she fought. She kicked at the solid form behind her; the man's body now felt like a stone wall. She bent forward, baring her teeth, trying to find some exposed skin to bite, anything to gain her freedom.

Her heel connected with the man's kneecap and she kicked again, harder, then hooked her leg around his and kicked the back of his knee so the man's leg buckled. They both fell to the ground.

The fall winded her but she was up within seconds, scrambling on the sand. The man sprang forward and covered her with his body, effectively trapping her under him.

'I admire your courage, Your Highness,' he said in her ear, his voice a husky murmur. 'As well as your tenacity. But I'm afraid both are misplaced.'

Elena blinked through the sand that stung her eyes and clung to her cheeks. The jet was still a hundred yards away. How far had she managed to run? Ten feet? Twenty?

The man flipped her over so she was on her back, his arms braced on either side of her head. She gazed up at him, her heart thudding against her ribs, her breath coming in little pants. He was poised above her like a panther, his eyes the bewitching amber of a cat's, his face all chiselled planes and harsh angles. Elena could feel his heat, sense his strength. This man radiated power. Authority. *Danger*.

'You would never have made it back to the plane,' he told her, his voice treacherously soft. 'And, even if you had, the men on it are loyal to me.'

'My guards—'

'Bribed.'

'The steward—'

'Powerless.'

She stared at him, trying to force down her fear. 'Who *are* you?' she choked.

He bared his teeth in a feral smile. 'I'm the future ruler of Kadar.'

In one fluid movement he rolled off her, pulling her up by a hand that had closed around her wrist like a manacle. Still holding her arm, he led her back to the cars, where two other men waited, dark-suited and blank-faced. One of them opened the rear door and with mocking courtesy her arrogant captor, whoever he really was, sketched an elaborate bow.

'After you, Your Highness.'

Elena stared at the yawning darkness of the SUV's interior. She *couldn't* get in that car. As soon as she did the doors would lock and she'd be this man's prisoner.

But she already was his prisoner, she acknowledged sickly, and she'd just blown her best bid for freedom. Perhaps if she pretended compliance now, or even fear, she'd find another opportunity for escape. She wouldn't even have to pretend all that much; terror had begun to claw at her senses.

She looked at the man who was watching her with cold amusement, as if he'd already guessed the nature of her thoughts.

'Tell me who you really are.'

'I already did, Your Highness, and you are trying my

patience. Now, get in the car.' He spoke politely enough, but Elena still felt the threat. The danger. She saw that cold, knowing amusement in the man's amber eyes, but no pity, no spark of compassion at all, and she knew she was out of options.

Swallowing hard, she got in the car.

The man slid in beside her and the doors closed, the automated lock a loud click in the taut silence. He tossed her shoes onto her lap.

'You might want those.' His voice was low, unaccented, and yet he was clearly Arabic. Kadaran. His skin was a deep bronze, his hair as dark as ink. The edge of his cheekbone looked as sharp as a blade.

Swallowing again, the taste of fear metallic on her tongue, Elena slipped them on. Her hair was a mess, one knee was scraped and the skirt of her staid navy blue suit was torn.

Taking a deep breath, she tucked her hair behind her ears and wiped the traces of sand from her face. She looked out of the window, trying to find some clue as to where they were going, but she could barely see out of the tinted glass. What she could see was nothing more than the jagged black shapes of rocks in the darkness, Kadar's infamously bleak desert terrain. It was a small country nestled on the Arabian Peninsula, its borders containing both magnificent coastline and deadly rock-strewn desert.

She sneaked a sideways glance at her captor. He sat with his hands resting lightly on his thighs, looking relaxed and assured, yet also alert. Who was he? Why had he kidnapped her?

And how was she going to get free?

Think, she told herself. Rational thought was the antidote to panic. The man must be one of the rebel insurgents Aziz had mentioned. He'd said he was the future ruler of Kadar, which meant he wanted Aziz's throne. He must have kidnapped her to prevent their marriage—unless he wasn't aware of the stipulations set out in Aziz's father's will?

Elena had only learned of them when she'd met Aziz a few weeks ago at a diplomatic function. His father, Sheikh Hashem, had just died and Aziz had made some sardonic joke about now needing a wife. Elena hadn't been sure whether to take him seriously or not, but then she'd seen a bleakness in his eyes. She'd felt it in herself.

Her Head of Council, Andreas Markos, was determined to depose her. He claimed a young, inexperienced woman such as herself was unfit to rule, and had threatened to call for a vote to abolish the monarchy at the next convening of the Thallian Council. But if she were married by then... if she had a husband and Prince Consort...then Markos couldn't argue she was unfit to rule.

And the people loved a wedding, wanted a royal marriage. She was popular with the Thallian people; it was why Markos hadn't already tried to depose her in the four turbulent years of her reign. Adding to that popularity with a royal wedding would make her position even stronger.

It was a desperate solution, but Elena had felt desperate. She loved her country, her people, and she wanted to remain their queen—for their sake, and for her father's sake, who had given his life so she could be monarch.

The next morning Elena had sent a letter to Aziz, suggesting they meet. He'd agreed and, with a candour borne of urgency, they'd laid out their respective positions. Elena needed a husband to satisfy her Council; Aziz needed to marry within six weeks of his father's death or he forfeited his title. They'd agreed to wed. They'd agreed to a convenient and loveless union that would give them the spouses they needed and children as heirs, one for Kadar, one for Thallia.

It was a mercenary approach to both marriage and parenthood and, if she'd been an ordinary woman, or even an ordinary queen, she would have wanted something different for her life. But she was a queen hanging onto her kingdom by a mere thread, and marriage to Aziz al Bakir had felt like the only way to keep clinging.

But for that to happen, she had to get married. And to get married, she had to escape.

She couldn't get out of the car, so she needed to wait. Watch. Learn her enemy.

'What is your name?' she asked. The man didn't even look at her.

'My name is Khalil.'

'Why have you taken me?'

He slid her a single, fathomless glance. 'We're almost at our destination, Your Highness. Your questions will be answered there, after we are both refreshed.'

Fine. She'd wait. She'd stay calm and in control and look for the next opportunity to gain her freedom. Even so terror caught her by the throat and held on. She'd felt this terrible, numbing fear before, as if the world were sliding by in slow motion, everything slipping away from her as she waited, frozen, disbelieving that this was actually happening…

No, this was not the same as before. She wouldn't let it be. She was queen of a country, even if her throne was all too shaky a seat. She was resourceful, courageous, *strong*.

She would get out of this. Somehow. She refused to let some rebel insurgent wreck her marriage…or end her reign as queen.

Khalil al Bakir glanced again at the woman by his side. She sat straight and tall, her chin lifted proudly, her pupils dilated with fear.

Admiration for the young queen flickered reluctantly through him. Her attempt at escape had been reckless and laughable, but also brave, and he felt an unexpected sympathy for her. He knew what it was like to feel both trapped and defiant. Hadn't he, as a boy, tried to escape from his captor, Abdul-Hafiz, as often as he could, even though he'd known how fruitless such attempts would be? Deep in the desert, there had been no place for a young boy to run or hide. Yet still he'd tried, because to try was to fight, and to fight was to remind yourself you were alive and had something to fight for. The scars on his back were testament to his many failed attempts.

Queen Elena would have no such scars. He would not be accused of ill-treating his guest, no matter what the frightened monarch might think. He intended to keep her for only four days, until the six weeks had passed and Aziz would be forced to relinquish his claim to the throne and call a national referendum to decide who the next sheikh would be.

Khalil intended to be that man.

Until that moment, when the vote had been called and he sat on the throne that was rightfully his, he would not rest easy. But then, he'd never rested easy, not since the day when he'd been all of seven years old and his father had dragged him out of his lesson with his tutor, thrown him onto the sharp stones in front of the Kadaran palace and spat in his face.

'*You are not my son.*'

It was the last time he'd ever seen him, his mother, or his home.

Khalil closed his eyes against the memories that still made his fists clench and bile rise in his throat. He would not think of those dark days now. He would not remember the look of disgust and even hatred on the face of the father he'd adored, or the anguished cries of his mother as she'd been dragged away, only to die just a few months later from a simple case of the flu because she'd been denied adequate medical care. He wouldn't think of the terror he'd felt when he'd been shoved in the back of a van and driven to a bleak desert outpost, or the look of cruel satisfaction on Abdul-Hafiz's face when he'd been thrown at his feet like a sack of rubbish.

No, he wouldn't think of any of that. He'd think of the

future, the very promising future, when he, the son his father had rejected in favour of his mistress's bastard, would sit on the throne of the kingdom he'd been born to rule.

Next to him, he felt Queen Elena tremble.

Twenty taut minutes later the SUV pulled up at the makeshift camp Khalil had called home for the last six months, ever since he'd returned to Kadar. He opened the door and turned to Elena, who glared at him in challenge.

'Where have you taken me?'

He gave her a cold smile. 'Why don't you come out and see for yourself?' Without waiting for an answer, he took hold of her wrist. Her skin was soft and cold and she let out a muffled gasp as he drew her from the car.

She stumbled on a stone as she came to her feet, and as he righted her he felt her breasts brush his chest. It had been a long time since he'd felt the soft touch of a woman, and his body responded with base instinct, his loins tightening as desire flared deep inside. Her hair, so close to his face, smelled of lemons.

Firmly Khalil moved her away from him. He had no time for lust and certainly not with this woman.

His right-hand man, Assad, emerged from another vehicle. 'Your Highness.' Elena turned automatically, and Khalil smiled in grim satisfaction. Assad had been addressing him, not the unruly queen. Even though he had not officially claimed his title, those loyal to him still addressed him as if he had.

He'd been surprised and gratified at how many were loyal to him, when they had only remembered a tousle-haired boy who'd been dragged crying and gibbering from the palace. Until six months ago, he had not been in Kadar since he'd been ten years old. But people remembered.

The desert tribes, bound more by tradition than the people of Siyad, had always resented Sheikh Hashem's rash decision to discard one wife for a mistress no one had liked, and a son he'd already publicly declared illegitimate.

When Khalil had returned, they'd named him sheikh of his mother's tribe and had rallied around him as the true ruling Sheikh of Kadar.

Even so, Khalil trusted no one. Loyalties could change on a whim. Love was capricious. He'd learned those lessons all too painfully well. The only person he trusted now was himself.

'Queen Elena and I would like some refreshment,' he told Assad in Arabic. 'Is there a tent prepared?'

'Yes, Your Highness.'

'You can debrief me later. For now, I'll deal with the Queen.' He turned to Elena, whose panicked gaze was darting in every direction, her body poised for flight.

'If you are thinking of running away,' he told her calmly, switching to English as the language they both knew, 'don't bother. The desert stretches for hundreds of miles in every direction, and the nearest oasis is over a day's ride by camel. Even if you managed to leave the camp, you would die of thirst, if not a snake or scorpion bite.'

Queen Elena glared at him and said nothing. Khalil gestured her forward. 'Come, have some refreshment, and I will answer your questions as I promised.'

Elena hesitated and then, clearly knowing she had no choice, she nodded and followed him across the camp.

Elena took stock of her surroundings as she walked behind Khalil. A few tents formed a rough semi-circle; she could see some horses and camels tethered to a post under a lean-to. The wind blew sand into her face and her hair into her mouth.

She held her hands up to her face, tried to blink the grit out of her eyes. Khalil pushed back the folds of the tent and ushered her inside.

Elena took a steadying breath, trying to compose herself. The only thing she could do now was learn as much as she could, and choose her moment well.

Khalil moved to the other side of the tent, gesturing to an elegant teakwood table and low chairs with embroidered cushions. The outside of the tent had been basic, but the interior, Elena saw as her gaze darted around, was luxurious, with silk and satin furnishings and carpets.

'Please, sit down.'

'I want answers to my questions.'

Khalil turned to face her. A small smile curved his mouth but his eyes were cold. 'Your defiance is admirable, Your Highness, but only to a certain extent. Sit.'

She knew she needed to pick her battles. Elena sat. 'Where is Sheikh Aziz?'

Irritation flashed across his chiselled features and then he gave a little shrug. 'Aziz is presumably in Siyad, waiting for you.'

'He'll be expecting me—'

'Yes,' Khalil cut her off smoothly. 'Tomorrow.'

'*Tomorrow*?'

'He received a message that you were delayed.' Khalil spread his hands, his eyes glittering with what felt like mockery. 'No one is looking for you, Your Highness. And, by the time they are, it will be too late.'

The implication was obvious, and it made her breathless with shock, her vision blurring so she reached out and grabbed the edge of the table to steady herself. *Calm*. She needed to stay calm.

She heard Khalil swear softly. 'I did not mean what you obviously think I meant.'

She looked up, her vision clearing as she gazed up at him. Even scowling he was breathtaking; everything about him was lean and graceful. Predatory. 'You mean you aren't going to kill me,' she stated flatly.

'I am neither a terrorist nor a thug.'

'Yet you kidnap a queen.'

He inclined his head. 'A necessary evil, I'm afraid.'

'I don't believe any evil is necessary,' Elena shot back.

She took another steadying breath. 'So what are you going to do with me?'

It was a question she wasn't sure she wanted answered, yet she knew ignorance was dangerous. Better to know the danger, the enemy. *Know your enemies and know yourself, and you will not be imperilled in a hundred battles.*

'I'm not going to do anything with you,' Khalil answered calmly. 'Except keep you here in, I hope, moderate comfort.'

One of the guards came with a tray of food. Elena glanced at the platter of dates and figs, the flat bread and the bowls of creamy dips, and then looked away again. She had no appetite, and in any case she would not eat with her enemy.

'Thank you, Assad,' Khalil said, and the man bowed and left.

Khalil crouched on his haunches in front of the low table where Assad had set the tray. He glanced up at Elena, those amber eyes seeming almost to glow. They really were the most extraordinary colour. With his dark hair and tawny eyes, that lean, predatory elegance, he was like a leopard, or perhaps a panther—something beautiful and terrifying. 'You must be hungry, Queen Elena.'

'I am not.'

'Then thirsty, at least. It is dangerous not to drink in the desert.'

'It is dangerous,' Elena countered, 'to drink in the presence of your enemies.'

A tiny smile tugged at the corner of his mouth and he inclined his head in acknowledgement. 'Very well, then. I shall drink first.'

She watched as he poured what looked like some kind of fruit juice from an earthen pitcher into two tall tumblers. He picked up the first and drank deeply from it, the sinuous muscles of his throat working as he swallowed.

He met her gaze over the rim of his glass, his eyes glinting in challenge.

'Satisfied?' he murmured as he lowered his glass.

Elena's throat ached with thirst and was scratchy from the sand. She needed to stay hydrated if she was going to plan an escape, so she nodded and held out her hand.

Khalil handed her the glass and she sipped the juice; it was both tart and sweet, and deliciously cool.

'Guava,' he told her. 'Have you had it before?'

'No.' Elena put the glass back down on the table. 'Now I am refreshed.' She took a deep breath. 'So you intend to keep me here in the desert—for how long?'

'A little less than a week. Four days, to be precise.'

Four days. Elena's stomach knotted. In four days the six weeks Aziz had been given to marry would be up. He would lose his right to his title, and Khalil must know that. He must be waiting for a chance to seize power.

'And then?' she asked. 'What will you do?'

'That is not your concern.'

'What will you do with me?' Elena rephrased, and Khalil sat down in a low-slung chair richly patterned with wool, regarding her with a rather sleepy consideration over the tips of his steepled fingers. Elena felt her frayed nerves start to snap.

'Let you go, of course.'

'Just like that?' She shook her head, too suspicious to feel remotely relieved. 'You'll be prosecuted.'

'I don't think so.'

'You can't just kidnap a head of state.'

'And yet I have.' He took a sip of juice, his gaze resting thoughtfully on her. 'You intrigue me, Queen Elena. I must confess, I've wondered what kind of woman Aziz would choose as his bride.'

'And are you satisfied?' she snapped. *Stupid*. Where was her calm, her control? She'd been teetering on a tightrope for her entire reign; was she really going to fall off now?

But maybe she already had.

Khalil smiled faintly. 'I am not remotely satisfied.'

His gaze held her and she saw a sudden gleam of masculine intent and awareness flicker in his eyes. To her surprise and shame, she felt an answering thrill of terror—and something else. Something that wasn't fear, but rather… anticipation. Yet, of what? She wanted nothing from this man but her freedom.

'And I won't be satisfied,' Khalil continued, 'until Aziz is no longer on the throne of Kadar and I am.'

'So you are one of the rebel insurgents Aziz mentioned.'

For a second Khalil's gaze blazed fury but then he merely inclined his head. 'So it would seem.'

'Why should you be on the throne?'

'Why should Aziz?'

'Because he is the heir.'

Khalil glanced away, his expression veiled once more. 'Do you know the history of Kadar, Your Highness?'

'I've read something of it,' she answered, although the truth was her knowledge of Kadaran history was sketchy at best. There hadn't been time for more than a crash course in the heritage of the country of her future husband.

'Did you know it was a peaceful, prosperous nation for many years—independent, even, when other countries buckled under a wider regime?'

'Yes, I did know that.' Aziz had mentioned it, because her own country was the same; a small island in the Aegean Sea between Turkey and Greece, Thallia had enjoyed nearly a thousand years of peaceful, independent rule.

And she would not be the one to end it.

'Perhaps you also know, then, that Sheikh Hashem threatened the stability of Kadar with the rather unusual terms of his will?' He turned back to her, raising his eyebrows, a little smile playing about his mouth.

Elena found her gaze quite unreasonably drawn to that mouth, to those surprisingly lush and sculpted lips. She forced herself to look upwards and met Khalil's enquiring gaze. There was no point, she decided, in feigning ignorance. 'Yes, I am well aware of the old Sheikh's stipulation. It's why I am here to marry Sheikh Aziz.'

'Not a love match, then?' Khalil queried sardonically and Elena stiffened.

'I don't believe that is any of your business.'

'Considering you are here at my behest, I believe it is.'

She pursed her lips and said nothing. The Kadaran people believed it was a love match, although neither she nor Aziz had said as much. People believed what they wanted to believe, Elena knew, and the public liked the idea of a royal fairy-tale. If it helped to stabilise their countries, then so be it. She could go along with a little play-acting. But she wasn't about to admit that to Khalil.

'Pleading the fifth, I see,' Khalil said softly. 'I grew up in America, you know. I am not the barbarian you seem to think I am.'

She folded her arms. 'You have yet to show me otherwise.'

'Have I not? Yet here you are, in a comfortable chair, offered refreshment. Though I am sorry you hurt yourself.' He gestured to her scraped knee, all solicitude. 'Let me get you a plaster.'

'I don't need one.'

'Such abrasions can easily become infected in the desert. A grain of sand lodges in the cut and, the next thing you know, it's gone septic.' He leaned forward, and for a moment the harshness of his face, the coldness in his eyes, was replaced by something that almost looked like gentleness. 'Don't be stupid, Your Highness. God knows I understand the need to fight, but you are wasting your energy arguing with me over such small matters.'

She swallowed, knowing he was right, and hating it. It was petty and childish to refuse medical care, not to mention stupid as he'd said. She nodded and Khalil rose from his chair. She watched as he strode to the entrance of the tent and spoke to one of the guards waiting outside.

Elena remained seated, her fists clenched in her lap, her heart beating hard. A few minutes later Khalil returned to the table with a cloth folded over his arm, a basin of water in one hand and a tube of ointment in the other.

'Here we are.'

To her shock he knelt in front of her and Elena pressed back in her chair. 'I can do it myself.'

He glanced up at her, his eyes gleaming. 'But then you would deny me the pleasure.'

Her breath came out in a rush and she remained rigid as he gently lifted the hem of her skirt over her knee. His fingers barely brushed her leg and yet she felt as if she'd been electrocuted, her whole body jolting with sensation. Carefully Khalil dampened the cloth and then dabbed the scrape on her knee.

'Besides,' he murmured, 'you might miss some sand, and I would hate to be accused of mistreating you.'

Elena didn't answer. She couldn't speak, could barely breathe. Every atom of her being was focused on the gentle touch of this man, his fingers sliding over her knee with a precision that wasn't sensual, not remotely, yet...

She took a careful breath and stared at the top of his head, his hair ink-black and cut very short. She wondered if it would feel soft or bristly, and then jerked her mind back to her predicament. What on earth was she doing, thinking about his hair, reacting to his hands on her skin? This man was her *enemy*. The last thing, the *very* last thing, she should do was feel anything for him, even something as basic as physical desire.

His hand tightened on her knee and everything inside Elena flared to life.

'I think that's fine,' she said stiffly, and tried to draw her leg away from Khalil's hand.

He held up the tube of ointment. 'Antiseptic cream. Very important.'

Gritting her teeth, she remained still while he squeezed some cream onto his fingers and then smoothed it over the cut on her knee. It stung a little, but far more painful was the kick of attraction she felt at the languorous touch of his fingers on her sensitised skin.

It was just her body's basic physical reaction, she told herself as he rubbed circles on her knee with his thumb and her insides tightened. She'd never experienced it like this before, but then she was inexperienced in the ways of men and women. In any case, there was nothing she could do about it, so she'd ignore it. Ignore the sparks that scattered across her skin and the plunging deep in her belly. Attraction was irrelevant; she would never act on it nor allow it to cloud her judgement.

Escape from this man and his plans to ruin her marriage was her only goal now. Her only desire.

CHAPTER TWO

KHALIL FELT ELENA'S body tense beneath his touch and wondered why he had chosen to clean the cut himself. The answer, of course, was irritatingly obvious: because he'd wanted to touch her. Because, for a moment, desire had overridden sense.

Her skin, Khalil thought, was as soft as silk. When had he last touched a woman's skin? Seven years in the French Foreign Legion had given him more than a taste of abstinence.

Of course, the last woman he should ever think about as a lover was Queen Elena, Aziz's intended bride. He had no intention of complicating what was already a very delicate diplomatic manoeuvre.

Kidnapping a head of state was a calculated risk, and one he'd had to take. The only way to force Aziz to call a national referendum was for him to lose his right to the throne, and the only way for that to happen was to prevent his marriage.

His father's will, Khalil mused, had been a ridiculous piece of legal architecture that showed him for the brutal dictator he truly had been. Had he wanted to punish both his sons? Or had he, in the last days of his life, actually regretted his treatment of his first-born? Khalil would never know. But he would take the opportunity his father's strange will offered him to seize the power that was rightfully his.

'There you are.' Khalil smoothed her skirt over her knee, felt her tense body relax only slightly as he eased back. 'I see your skirt is torn. My apologies. You will be provided with new clothes.'

She stared at him, studying him as you would a specimen or, rather, an enemy: looking for weaknesses. She wouldn't find any, but Khalil took the opportunity to gaze back at her. She was lovely, her skin like golden cream, her heavy-lidded eyes grey with tiny gold flecks. Her hair was thick and dark and gleamed in the candlelight, even though it was tangled and gritty with sand.

His gaze dropped to her lips, lush, pink and perfect. Kissable. There was that desire again, flaring deep inside him, demanding satisfaction. Khalil stood up. 'You must be hungry, Your Highness. You should eat.'

'I'm not hungry.'

'Suit yourself.' He took a piece of bread and tore off a bit to chew. Sitting across from her, he studied her once more. 'I am curious as to why you agreed to marry Aziz.' He cocked his head. 'Not wealth, as Thallia is a prosperous enough country. Not power, since you are already a queen. And we know it isn't for love.'

'Maybe it is.' Her voice was low, pleasingly husky. She met his gaze unflinchingly but he heard her breath hitch and Khalil smiled.

'I don't think so, Your Highness. I think you married him because you need something, and I'm wondering what it is. Your people love you. Your country is stable.' He spread his hands, raised his eyebrows. 'What would induce you to marry a pretender?'

'I think you are the pretender, Khalil.'

'You're not the only one, alas. But you will be proved wrong.'

Her grey-gold gaze swept over him. 'You genuinely believe you have a claim to the throne.'

His stomach knotted. 'I know I do.'

'How can that be? Aziz is Sheikh Hashem's only son.'

Even though he'd long been used to such an assumption, her words poured acid on an open wound. A familiar fury rose up in him, a howl of outrage he forced back down. He smiled coldly at this woman whose careless questions tore open the barely healed scars of his past. 'Perhaps you need to brush up on your Kadaran history. You will have plenty of time for leisure reading during your stay in the desert.' Although he knew she wouldn't find the truth in any books. His father had done his best to erase Khalil's existence from history.

She stared up at him unblinkingly. 'And if I do not wish to stay in the desert?'

'Your presence here, I'm afraid, is non-negotiable. But rest assured, you will be afforded every comfort.'

Elena licked her lips, an innocent movement that still caused a hard kick of lust he instantly suppressed. Queen Elena was a beautiful woman; his body, long deprived of sensual pleasures, was bound to react. It didn't mean he was going to do anything about it.

Perhaps the most attractive thing about her, though, was not her looks but her presence. Even though he knew she had to be frightened, she sat tall and proud, her grey eyes glinting challenge. He admired her determination to be strong; he shared it. Never surrender, not even when the whole world seemed to be against you, every fist raised, every lip curled in a sneer.

Had she faced opposition and hardship? She had, he knew, suffered tragedy. She'd taken the throne at nineteen years of age, when her parents had died in a terrorist bombing. She was only twenty-three now and, though she looked very young, she seemed older in her bearing, somehow. In her confidence.

She rose from her seat, every inch the elegant queen. 'You cannot keep me here.'

He smiled; he almost felt sorry for her. 'You'll find that I can.'

'Aziz will send someone to fetch me. People will be looking.'

'Tomorrow. By that time any tracks in the desert, any evidence of where you've gone, will have vanished.' He glanced towards the tent flap, which rustled in the wind. 'It sounds as if a storm is brewing.'

Elena shook her head slowly. 'How did you manage it? To get a false message to him, convince the pilot to land somewhere else?'

'Not everyone is loyal to Aziz. In fact, few are outside of Siyad. You know he has not been in the country for more than a few days at a time since he was a boy?'

'I know he is very popular in the courts of Europe.'

'You mean the country clubs. The gentleman playboy is not so popular here.'

Elena's eyes flashed gold. 'That's a ridiculous nickname, given to him by the tabloids.'

Khalil shrugged. 'And yet it stuck.' Aziz, the playboy of Europe, who spent his time at parties and on polo fields. He ran a business too, Khalil knew; he'd started up some financial venture that was successful, if just an excuse for him to party his way through Europe and avoid the country of his birth.

Aziz didn't even *care* about Kadar, Khalil thought with a familiar spike of bitterness. He didn't deserve to rule, even if he hadn't been a bastard son.

'No matter what you think of Aziz, you can't just kidnap a queen,' Elena stated, her chin jutting out defiantly. 'You'd be wise to cut your losses, Khalil, and free me now. I won't press charges.'

Khalil suppressed a laugh of genuine amusement. 'How generous of you.'

'You don't want to face a tribunal,' she insisted. 'How can you become Sheikh if you've committed a crime?

Caused an international incident? You will be called to
account.'

'You'll find that is not how things are done in my country.'

'My country, then,' she snapped. 'Do you think my
Council, my country, will allow its queen to be kidnapped?'

He shrugged. 'You were merely detained, Your Highness, as a necessary measure. And, since Aziz is a pretender to the throne, you should be grateful that I am
preventing a marriage you would undoubtedly regret.'

'Grateful!' Her eyes sparked with anger. 'What if your
plan fails?'

He smiled coldly. 'I do not consider failure a possibility.'

She shook her head slowly, her eyes like two grey-gold
pools, reminding him of a sunset reflected on water. 'You
can't do this. People don't— World leaders don't do this!'

'Things are different here.'

'Not that different, surely?' She shook her head again.
'You're mad.'

Fury surged again and he took a deep, even breath. 'No,
Your Highness, I am not mad. Just determined. Now, it is
late and I think you should go to your quarters. You will
have a private tent here and, as I said before, every comfort possible.' He bared his teeth in a smile. 'Enjoy your
stay in Kadar.'

Elena paced the quarters of the elegant tent Assad had escorted her to an hour ago. Khalil had been right when he'd
said he'd give her every possible comfort: the spacious tent
had a wide double bed on its own wooden dais, the soft
mattress piled high with silk and satin covers and pillows.
There were also several teak chairs and a bureau for clothes
she didn't even have.

Had they brought her luggage from the jet? She doubted
it. Not that she'd even brought much to Kadar. She'd only
been intending to stay for three days: a quiet ceremony, a

quick honeymoon and then a return to Thallia to introduce Aziz to her people.

And now none of it would happen. Unless someone rescued her or she managed to escape, prospects she deemed quite unlikely, her marriage to Aziz would not take place. If he did not marry within the six weeks, he would be forced to relinquish his claim to the throne. He wouldn't need her then, but unfortunately she still needed him.

Still needed a husband, a Prince Consort, and before the convening of the Council next month.

Elena sank onto an embroidered chair and dropped her head into her hands. Even now she couldn't believe she was here, that she'd actually been *kidnapped*.

Yet why shouldn't she believe it? Hadn't the worst in her life happened before? For a second she remembered the sound of the explosion ringing in her ears, the terrible weight of her father's lifeless body on top of hers.

And, even after that awful day, from the moment she'd taken the throne she'd been dogged by disaster, teetering on the precipice of ruin. Led by Markos, the stuffy, sanctimonious men of the Thallian Council had sought to discredit and even disown her. They didn't want a single young woman as ruler of Thallia. They didn't want *her*.

She'd spent so much time trying to prove herself to the men of her Council who questioned her every action, doubted her every word. Who assumed she was flighty, silly and irresponsible, all because of one foolish mistake made when she'd been just nineteen and overwhelmed by grief and loneliness.

Nearly four years on, all the good she'd done for her country—all the appearances she'd made, the charities she'd supported and the bills she'd helped draft—counted for nothing. At least, not in Markos's eyes. And the rest of the Council would be led by him, even in this day and age. Thallia was a traditional country. They wanted a man as their head of state.

Tears pricked under her lids and she blinked them back furiously. She wasn't a little girl, to cry over a cut knee. She was a woman, a woman who'd had to prove she possessed the power and strength of a man for four endless, stormy years.

It couldn't end now like this, just because some crazed rebel had decided he was the rightful heir to the throne.

Except, Elena had to acknowledge, Khalil hadn't seemed crazed. He'd been coldly composed, utterly assured. Yet how could he be the rightful heir? And did he really think he could snatch the throne from under Aziz's nose? When she didn't show up in Siyad, when the Kadaran diplomat who had accompanied her sounded the alarm, Aziz would come looking. And he'd find her, because he was as desperate as she was.

Although, considering she was being held captive in the middle of the desert, perhaps she was now a little more desperate than Aziz.

He could, she realised with a terrible, sinking sensation, find another willing bride. Why shouldn't he? They'd met only a handful of times. The marriage had been her idea. He could still find someone else, although he'd have to do it pretty quickly.

Had Khalil thought of that? What was preventing Aziz from just grabbing some random woman and marrying her to fulfil the terms of his father's will?

Elena rose from the chair and once more restlessly paced the elegant confines of her tent. Outside the night was dark, the only sound the sweep of the sand and the low nickering of the tethered horses.

She *had* to talk to Khalil again and convince him to release her. That was her best chance.

Filled with grim determination, Elena whirled around and stalked to the opening of her tent, pulled the cloth aside and stepped out into the desert night, only to have two guards step quickly in front of her, their bodies as impenetrable as a brick wall. She gazed at their blank faces, at the rifles strapped to their chests, and lifted her chin.

'I want to speak to Khalil.'

'He is occupied, Your Highness.' The guard's voice was both bland and implacable; he didn't move.

'With something more important than securing the throne?' she shot back. The wind blew her hair about her face and impatiently she shoved it back. 'I have information he'll want to hear,' she stated firmly. 'Information that will affect his—his intentions.'

The two guards stared at her impassively, utterly unmoved by her argument. 'Please return to the tent, Your Highness,' one of them said flatly. 'The wind is rising.'

'Tell Khalil he needs to speak to me,' she tried again, and this time, to her own immense irritation, she heard a pleading note enter her voice. 'Tell him there are things I know, things he hasn't considered.'

One of the guards placed a heavy hand on her shoulder and Elena stiffened under it. 'Don't touch me.'

'For your own safety, Your Highness, you must return to the tent.' And, pushing her around, he forced her back into the tent as if she were a small child being marched to her room.

Khalil sat at the teakwood table in his private tent and with one lean finger traced the route through the desert from the campsite to Siyad. Three hundred miles. Three hundred miles to victory.

Reluctantly, yet unable to keep himself from it, he let his gaze flick to a corner of the map, an inhospitable area of bleak desert populated by a single nomadic tribe: his mother's people.

He knew Abdul-Hafiz was dead, and the people of his mother's tribe now supported him as the rightful ruler of Kadar. Yet though they'd even named him as Sheikh of their tribe, he hadn't been back yet to receive the honour.

He couldn't face returning to that barren bit of ground where he'd suffered for three long years.

His stomach still clenched when he looked at that corner of the map, and in his mind's eye he pictured Abdul-Hafiz's cruel face, his thin lips twisted into a mocking sneer as he raised the whip above Khalil's cringing form.

'The woman is asking for you.'

Khalil turned away from the map to see Assad standing in the doorway of his tent, the flaps drawn closed behind him.

'Queen Elena? Why?'

'She claims she has information.'

'What kind of information?'

Assad shrugged. 'Who knows? She is desperate, and most likely lying.'

Khalil drummed his fingers against the table. Elena was indeed desperate, and that made her reckless. Defiant. No doubt her bid to speak to him was some kind of ploy; perhaps she thought she could argue her way to freedom. It would be better, he knew, to ignore her request. Spend as little time as possible with the woman who was already proving to be an unwanted temptation.

'It is worth investigating,' he said after a moment. 'I'll see her.'

'Shall I summon her?'

'No, don't bother. I'll go to her tent.' Khalil rose from his chair, ignoring the anticipation that uncurled low in his belly at the thought of seeing Queen Elena again.

The wind whipped against him, stinging his face with grains of sand as he walked across the campsite to Elena's tent. Around him men hunkered down by fires or tended to their weapons or animals. At the sight of all this industry, all this loyalty, something both swelled and ached inside Khalil.

This was, he knew, the closest thing he'd had to family in twenty-nine years.

Dimah was family, of course, and he was incredibly thankful for what she'd done for him. She had, quite literally, saved him: provided for him, supported him, believed in him.

Yes, he owed Dimah a great deal. But she'd never understood what drove him, how much he needed to reclaim his inheritance, his very self. These men did.

Shaking off such thoughts, he strode towards Elena's tent, waving the guards aside as he drew back the flaps, only to come up short.

Elena was in the bath.

The intimacy of the moment struck him like a fist to the heart: the endless darkness outside, the candlelight flickering over the golden skin of her back, the only sound the slosh of the water against the sides of the deep copper tub as Elena washed herself—and then the hiss of his sudden, indrawn breath as a wave of lust crashed over him with the force of a tsunami.

She stiffened, the sponge dropping from her hand, and turned her head so their gazes met. Clashed. She didn't speak, didn't even move, and neither did Khalil. The moment spun out between them, a moment taut with expectation and yet beautiful in its simplicity.

She was beautiful, the elegant shape of her back reminding him of the sinuous curves of a cello. A single tendril of dark hair lay against the nape of her neck; the rest was piled on top of her head.

As if from a great distance Khalil registered her shuddering breath and knew she was frightened. Shame scorched him and he spun on his heel.

'I beg your pardon. I did not realise you were bathing. I'll wait outside.' He pushed outside the tent, the guards coming quickly to flank him, but he just shook his head and brushed them off. Lust still pulsed insistently inside him, an ache in his groin. He folded his arms across his chest and willed his body's traitorous reaction to recede.

Yet, no matter how hard he tried, he could not banish the image of Elena's golden perfection from his mind.

After a few endless minutes he heard a rustling behind him and Elena appeared, dressed in a white towelling robe that thankfully covered her from neck to toe.

'You may come in.' Her voice was husky, her cheeks flushed—although whether from the heat of the bath or their unexpected encounter he didn't know.

Khalil stepped inside the tent. Elena had already retreated to the far side, the copper tub between them like a barrier, her slight body swallowed up by the robe.

'I'm sorry,' Khalil said. 'I didn't know you were in the bath.'

'So you said.'

'You don't believe me?'

'Why should I believe anything you say?' she retorted. 'You haven't exactly been acting in an honourable fashion.'

Khalil drew himself up, any traces of desire evaporating in the face of her obvious scorn. 'And it would be honourable to allow my country to be ruled by a pretender?'

'A *pretender*?' She shook her head in derisive disbelief, causing a few more tendrils of hair to fall against her cheek. Khalil's hand twitched with the sudden, absurd urge to touch her, to brush those strands away from her face. He clenched his hand into a fist instead.

'Aziz is not the rightful heir to the throne.'

'I don't *care*!' she cried, her voice ringing out harsh and desperate. Khalil felt any soft longings in him harden, crystallise into determination. Of course she didn't care.

'I realise that, Your Highness,' he answered shortly. 'Although why you wish to marry Aziz is not clear to me. Power, perhaps.' He let her hear the contempt in his voice but she didn't respond to it, except to give one weary laugh.

'Power? I suppose you could say that.' She closed her eyes briefly, and when she opened them he was surprised to see so much bleak despair reflected in their grey-gold depths. 'All I meant was, none of it really matters to me, being here. I understand this—this conflict is very important to you. But keeping me here won't accomplish your goal.'

'You don't think so?'

'No.' Her mouth twisted in something like a smile. 'Aziz will just marry someone else. He still has four days.'

'I'm aware of the time that is left.' He regarded her thoughtfully, the bleakness still apparent in her eyes, the set of her shoulders and mouth both determined and courageous. He felt another flicker of admiration as well as a surge of curiosity. *Why* had she agreed to marry Aziz? What could such a marriage possibly give her?

'So why keep me here?' she pressed. 'If he can fulfil the terms of his father's will with another woman?'

'Because he won't.'

'But he will. We barely know each other. We've only met once before.'

'I know.'

'Then why do you think he would be loyal to me?' she asked and he felt a sudden flash of compassion as well as understanding, because he'd asked that question so many times himself. Why would anyone be loyal to him? Why should he trust anyone?

The person he'd loved most in the world had betrayed and rejected him utterly.

'To be frank,' he told her, 'I don't think loyalty is the issue. Politics are.'

'Exactly. So he'll just marry someone else.'

'And alienate his people even more? They love the idea of this wedding. They love it more than they do Aziz. And if he were to discard one woman for another...' *As our father did.* No, he had no wish to divulge that information to Elena just yet. He took a quick breath. 'It would not be popular. It would destabilise his rule even more.'

'But if he's going to lose his crown anyway...'

'But he won't, not necessarily. Did he not tell you?' Uncertainty flashed across her features and Khalil curved his mouth in a grim smile. 'The will states that, if Aziz does not marry within six weeks, he must call a national referendum. The people will then choose the new sheikh.'

She stared at him, her eyes widening. 'And you think that will be you?'

He let out a hard laugh. 'Don't sound so sceptical.'

'Who *are* you?'

'I told you, the next ruler of Kadar.' Her gaze moved over his face searchingly, and he saw despair creep back into her eyes.

'But Aziz could still go ahead and marry someone else while I'm stuck here in the desert. What happens then?'

'If he does that, it might lead to a civil war. I don't think he wishes for that to happen. Admittedly, Your Highness, I am taking a risk. You are right in saying that Aziz could marry someone else. But I don't think he will.'

'Why not just meet him and ask him to call the referendum?'

He shook his head. 'Because he knows he won't win it.'

'And if it comes to war? Are you prepared?'

'I will do what I must to secure my country's rule. Make no mistake about that, Queen Elena.' She flinched slightly at his implacable tone and something in Khalil softened just a little. None of this was Elena's fault. She was a casualty of a conflict that didn't involve her. In any other circumstance, he would have applauded her courage and determination.

'I'm sorry,' he said after a pause. 'I realise your plans to marry Aziz have been upset. But, considering how they were made so recently, I'm sure you'll recover.' He didn't mean to sound quite so cutting, but he knew he did, and he saw her flinch again.

She looked away, her gaze turning distant. 'You think so?' she said, not really a question, and again he heard the bleak despair and wondered at its source.

'I know so, Your Highness. I don't know why you decided to marry Aziz, but since it wasn't for love your heart is hardly broken.'

'And you know about broken hearts?' she answered with another weary laugh. 'You don't even seem to have one.'

'Perhaps I don't. But you didn't love him?' That *was* a question, of a sort. He was curious, even if he didn't want to be. He didn't want to know more about Elena, to wonder about her motives or her heart.

And yet still he asked.

'No,' she said after a moment. 'Of course I didn't— don't—love him. I barely know him. We met twice, for a couple of hours.' She shook her head, let out a long, defeated sigh, and then seemed to come to herself, straightening again, her eyes flashing once more. 'But I have your word you will release me after four days?'

'Yes. You have my word.' She relaxed slightly then, even as he stiffened. 'You don't think I'd hurt you?'

'Why shouldn't I? Kidnappers are usually capable of other crimes.'

'As I explained, this was a necessary evil, Your Highness, nothing more.'

'And what else will be a *necessary evil*, Khalil?' she answered back. He didn't like the hopelessness he saw in her eyes; it was as if the spark that had lit her from within had died out. He missed it. 'When you justify one thing, it becomes all too easy to justify another.'

'You sound as if you speak from experience.'

'I do.'

'Your own.'

A pause and her mouth firmed and tightened. 'Of sorts.'

He opened his mouth to ask another question, but then closed it abruptly. He didn't want to know. He didn't need to understand this woman; he simply needed her to stay put for a handful of days. He was sorry, more or less, for her disappointment. But that was all it was, a disappointment. An inconvenience, really. Her future, her very life, was not riding on a marriage to a stranger.

Not like his was.

'I promise I will not hurt you. And in four days you will be free.' She simply stared at him and, with one terse nod, he dismissed her, leaving the tent without another word.

CHAPTER THREE

ELENA WOKE SLOWLY, blinking in the bright sunlight that filtered through the small gap in the tent's flaps. Her body
ached with tiredness; her mind had spun and seethed all
night and she hadn't fallen asleep until some time near
dawn.

Now she stretched and stared up at the rippling canvas
of the tent, wondering what this day would bring.

She'd spent hours last night considering her options.
She'd wondered if she could steal someone's mobile phone,
make contact. Yet who would she call—the operator, to
connect her to the Kadaran palace? Her Head of Council, who would probably be delighted by the news of her
capture? In any case, she most likely couldn't get a signal
out here.

Then she'd wondered if she could make a friend of one
of the guards, get him to help her. That seemed even less
likely; both of the guards she'd met had appeared utterly
unmoved by her predicament.

Could she cause a fire, so its smoke might be caught by
a satellite, a passing helicopter or plane?

Each possibility seemed more ludicrous than the last,
and yet she refused to admit defeat. Giving in would mean
losing her crown.

But the longer she stayed here, the more likely it was
Aziz would marry someone else, no matter what Khalil
said or thought. Or, even if he didn't, he wouldn't marry

her. Maybe he would call this referendum and win the vote. He wouldn't need her at all.

But she still needed him, needed someone to marry her in the next month as she'd promised her Council, someone *she* was willing to marry, to father her children...

The thought caused her stomach to churn and her heart to sink. Her plan to marry Aziz had been desperate; finding another groom was outlandish. What was she going to *do*?

Sighing, she rose from the bed. A female voice sounded outside her tent, and a second later a woman entered, smiling and bearing a pitcher of fresh water.

'Good morning, Your Highness,' she said, ducking a quick curtsey, and Elena murmured back her own greeting, wondering if this woman might be the ally she was looking for.

The sight of the water in the woman's hands reminded her of her bath last night—and Khalil seeing her in it. Even now she felt her insides clench with a nameless emotion at the memory of his arrested look. The heat in his eyes had burned her with both pleasure and pain. To be desired, it was a fearsome thing—exciting, yes, but terrifying too, especially from a man like Khalil.

It had been foolish, she supposed, to take a bath, but when the two surly, silent guards had brought in the huge copper tub and filled it with steaming water, Elena had been unable to resist.

She'd been tired and sandy, every muscle aching with physical as well as emotional fatigue, and the thought of slipping into the rose-scented water, petals floating on top, had been incredibly appealing. A good wash would clear her head as well as clean her body and Khalil, she'd assumed, would not see her again that night.

And yet he'd seen her... Oh, how he'd seen her. She blushed to remember it, even though logically she knew he couldn't have seen much. The high sides of the tub would have kept her body from his sight, and in any case her back had been to him.

Even so she remembered the feel of his stilled gaze on her, the heat and intensity of it and, more alarmingly, her own answering response, everything inside her tightening and tautening, *waiting…*

'Is there anything else you need, Your Highness?' the woman asked, her voice pleasantly accented.

Yes, Elena thought, *my freedom*. She forced a smile. She needed this woman to be her friend. 'This is lovely, thank you. Were you the one who arranged the bath last night?'

The woman ducked her head. 'Yes, I thought you would like a wash.'

'It was wonderful, thank you.' Elena's mind raced. 'Where do you get the water? Is there an oasis here?'

'Yes, just beyond the rocks.'

'Is it very private? I'd love to have a swim some time, if I could.'

The woman smiled. 'If Sheikh Khalil approves, then I'm sure you could. It is lovely for swimming.'

'Thank you.' Elena didn't know if the oasis might provide her with an opportunity either to escape or attempt some kind of distraction to alert anyone who might be looking for her, but at least it was an option, a chance. Now she just had to get Khalil to agree to let her have a swim.

'When you are ready, you may break your fast outside,' the woman said. 'Sheikh Khalil is waiting.'

That was the second time the woman had called Khalil 'sheikh'. Was he a sheikh in his own right, Elena wondered, or did she already consider him as having the throne of Kadar? She wanted to ask Khalil just what made him feel so sure of his position, but she knew she wouldn't. She didn't want to know more about this man or, heaven forbid, find some sympathy for him. Her physical awareness of him was alarming enough.

A few minutes later, dressed in a pair of khakis and a

plain button-down shirt that had been provided for her, her hair neatly plaited, Elena stepped out of her tent.

The brilliance of the desert sun, the hard, bright blue of the sky and the perfect clarity of the air left her breathless for a moment. She was dazzled by the austere beauty of the desert, even though she didn't want to be. She didn't want to feel anything for any of it.

Khalil was eating by himself under an awning that had been set up above a raised wooden platform. He rose as she approached.

'Please. Sit.'

'Thank you.' She perched on the edge of a chair and Khalil arched an amused eyebrow.

'Courteous today, are we?'

Elena shrugged. 'I choose my battles.'

'I look forward to the next one.' He poured her coffee from an ornate brass pot; it looked thick and dark and smelled of cardamom. 'This is Kadaran coffee,' he told her. 'Have you ever tried it?'

She shook her head and took a tentative sip; the taste was strong but not unpleasant. Khalil nodded his approval. 'Would you have taken on Kadaran ways, if you'd become Aziz's bride?'

Elena stiffened. 'I could still become his bride, you know. He might find me.'

The look Khalil gave her was arrogant and utterly assured. 'I wouldn't get your hopes up, Your Highness.'

'Yours certainly seem high enough.'

He shrugged, one powerful shoulder lifting slightly, muscles rippling underneath the linen *thobe* he wore. 'As I told you before, the people of Kadar do not support Aziz.'

Surely he was exaggerating? Elena thought. Aziz had mentioned some instability, but not that he was an unpopular ruler. 'Outside of Siyad, you said,' she recalled. 'And why wouldn't they support him? He's the Sheikh's only son, and the succession has always been dynastic.'

Khalil's mouth tightened, his tawny eyes flashing fire before he shrugged again. 'Maybe you should take my advice and brush up on your Kadaran history.'

'And is there a book you suggest I read?' She raised her eyebrows, tried to moderate her tone. She was not doing herself any favours, arguing with him. 'Perhaps one I can take out of the library?' she added, in a poor attempt at levity.

Khalil's mouth twitched in a smile of what Elena suspected was genuine amusement. It lightened and softened him somehow, made him even more attractive than when he was cold and forbidding. 'I have a small library of books with me. I'll be happy to lend you one, although you won't find the answers you're looking for in a book.'

'Where will I find them, then?'

He hesitated and for a moment Elena thought he was going to say something else, something important. Then he shook his head. 'I don't think any answers would satisfy you, Your Highness, not right now. But when you're ready to listen, and consider there might be more to this story than what you've been told by Aziz, perhaps I'll enlighten you.'

'I should be so lucky,' she retorted, but for the first time since meeting Khalil she felt a flicker of real uncertainty. He was so *sure*. What if his claim had some legitimacy?

But, no, he was an insurgent. An impostor. He *had* to be. Anything else was unthinkable.

To her surprise Khalil leaned forward, placed his hand over hers. Elena stiffened under that small touch and it seemed as if the solid warmth of his hand spread throughout her whole body. 'You don't want to be curious,' he murmured. 'But you are.'

'Why should I be curious about a criminal?' she snapped, and he just smiled and removed his hand.

'Remember what I said. There is another side to the story.' He turned to go and Elena stared at him in frustration; she'd completely missed her opportunity to ask him about the oasis.

'And what am I meant to do for four days?' she called. 'Are you going to keep me imprisoned in my tent?'

'Only if you are foolish enough to attempt to escape.' Khalil turned to face her, his voice and face both hard once more.

'And if I did?'

'I would find you, hopefully before you were dead.'

'Charming.'

'The desert is a dangerous place. Regardless of the scorpions and snakes, a storm can arise in a matter of minutes and bury a tent, never mind a man, in seconds.'

'I know that.' She pressed her lips together and stared down at her plate; Khalil had served her some fresh fruit, dates, figs and succulent slices of melon. She picked up a fork and toyed with a bit of papaya.

'So I may trust you won't attempt an escape?' Khalil asked.

'Do you want me to promise?'

'No,' he answered after a moment. 'I don't trust promises. I just don't want your death on my conscience.'

'How thoughtful of you,' Elena answered sardonically. 'I'm touched.'

To her surprise he smiled again, revealing a surprising dimple in one cheek. 'I thought you would be.'

'So, if I'm not stupid enough to try and escape, may I go outside?' she asked. 'The woman who brought me water said there was an oasis here.' She held her breath, tried to keep her face bland.

'You mean Leila, Assad's wife. And, yes, you may go to the oasis if you like. Watch out for snakes.'

She nodded, her heart thumping with both victory and relief. She had a plan. She could finally *do* something.

'Are you going somewhere?' she asked, her gaze slid-

ing to the horses that were being saddled nearby. If Khalil
was gone, all the better.

'Yes.'

'Where?'

'To meet with some of the Bedouin tribes in this area
of the desert.'

'Rallying support?' she queried, an edge to her voice,
and he lifted his eyebrows.

'Remember what I said about arguing?'

'How was that arguing? I'm not going to just give up, if
that's what you want. "Attack is the secret of defence",' she
quoted recklessly. '"Defence is the planning of an attack".'

Khalil nodded, a slight smile on his lips. '*The Art of
War* by Sun Tzu,' he said. 'Impressive.' She simply stared
at him, chin jutted out, and he quoted back at her, '"He
who knows when he can fight and when he cannot will
be victorious".'

'Exactly.'

He laughed softly, shaking his head. 'So you think you
can win in this situation, Your Highness, despite all I've
said?'

'"The supreme art of war is to subdue the enemy without fighting".'

He cocked his head, his gaze sweeping over her almost
lazily. 'And how do you intend to subdue me?'

Surely he hadn't meant those words to have a sensual
intent, a sexual innuendo, yet somehow they had. Elena
felt it in the warmth that stole through her body, turning
her bones liquid and her mind to mush.

Khalil held her gaze, his eyes glowing gold and she simply stared back, unable to reply or even think. Finally her
brain sputtered back into gear and she forced out, '"Let
your plans be dark and impenetrable as night".'

'Clearly you've studied him well. It makes me curious,
since your country has been at peace for nearly a thousand years.'

'There are different kinds of wars.' And the war she fought was scarily subtle: a murmured word, a whispered rumour. She was constantly on the alert for an attack.

'So there are. And I pray, Your Highness, that this war for the throne of Kadar might be fought without a single drop of blood being spilled.'

'You don't think Aziz will fight you?'

'I hope he knows better. Now, enough. I must ride. I hope you enjoy your day.'

With that he strode towards the horses, his body dark and powerful against the brilliant blue sky, the blazing sun. When he had gone Elena felt, absurdly, as if something was missing that she'd both wanted and enjoyed.

After Khalil had left, riding off into the desert with several of his men, great clouds of dust and sand billowing behind them, Elena went back to her tent. To her surprise, she saw a book—*The Making of Modern Kadar*—had been placed on her bedside table. Was Khalil being thoughtful, she wondered, or mocking?

Curious, she flipped through the book. She already knew the basics of Kadar's history: its many years of peace, isolated as it was on a remote peninsula, jutting out into the Arabian Sea. While war had passed it by, so had technology, and for centuries it had remained as it had always been, a cluster of tribal communities with little interest beyond their nomadic life of shepherding. Then, in the early 1800s, Sheikh Ahmad al Bakir, the great-great-grandfather of Hashem, had united the tribes and created a monarchy. He'd ruled Kadar for nearly fifty years, and since then there had only been peace and prosperity.

None of it told her why Khalil believed he was the rightful ruler and not Aziz, Hashem's only son. The book didn't even hint at any insurgency or civil unrest; if it was to be believed, nothing had caused so much as a flicker of unease in the peaceful, prosperous rule of the House of al Bakir.

She tossed the book aside, determined not to wonder any more about Khalil. She didn't need to know whether his claim had any merit. She wasn't going to care.

She just wanted to get out of here, however she could. Resolutely, she went in search of Leila. The guards outside her tent summoned her, and Leila was happy to show her the way to the oasis. She even brought Elena a swimming costume and a packed lunch. It was all so civilised, Elena almost felt guilty at her deception.

Almost.

Alone in her tent, she searched for what she needed. The legs of the table were too thick, but the chairs might do.

Kneeling on the floor of the tent, the sound muffled by a pillow, she managed to snap several slats from the back of a chair. She stuffed the slats in the bag with the picnic and with her head held high walked out of the tent.

The guards let her pass and Leila directed her down a worn path that wound between two towering boulders.

'"Threading the needle", it's called,' Leila said, for the path between the rocks was incredibly narrow. 'It is a beautiful spot. See for yourself.'

'And you're not worried I'll make a run for it?' Elena asked, trying to keep her voice light. Leila's face softened in sympathy, causing another flash of guilt that she ruthlessly pushed away. These people were her captors, no matter how kind Leila was being. And she *had* to escape somehow.

'I know this is difficult for you, Your Highness, but the Sheikh is a good man. He is protecting you from an unhappy marriage, whether you realise it or not.'

Now *that* was putting quite a spin on things. 'I wasn't aware that Khalil was concerned with the happiness of my marriage,' Elena answered. 'Only with being Sheikh.'

'He is Sheikh already, of one of the desert tribes,' Leila answered. 'And he is the rightful heir to the throne of

Kadar. A great injustice was done to him, and it is finally time to make it right.'

Again Elena felt that uncomfortable flicker of uncertainty. Leila sounded so sure…as sure as Khalil. 'What injustice?' she asked before she could think better of it. Leila shook her head.

'It is not for me to say. But if you had married Aziz, Your Highness, you would have been marrying an impostor. Very few people outside of Siyad believe Aziz should be Sheikh.'

It was what Khalil had said, yet Elena could not accept it. 'But *why*?'

Leila's forehead creased in a troubled frown. 'You must ask Sheikh Khalil—'

'He's not really Sheikh,' Elena interjected, unable to keep herself from it. 'Not of Kadar. Not yet.'

'But he should be,' Leila said quietly, and to Elena she sounded utterly certain. 'Ask him,' the older woman advised. 'He will tell you the truth.'

But did she want to know the truth? Elena wondered as she walked between the towering rocks towards the oasis. If Khalil had a legitimate claim to the throne, what did it mean for her—and her marriage?

Would she still marry Aziz if he wasn't the rightful Sheikh? Would her Council even want her to? The point, Elena reminded herself, was most likely moot—unless she got out of here.

After walking between the boulders she emerged onto a flat rock overlooking a small, shimmering pool shaded by palm trees. The sun sparkled on the water as if on a metal plate, the sky brilliant blue above. The air was hot, dry and still, perfect for a swim.

She glanced around, wondering if the guards had followed her, but she could see no one. Just in case, she made a show of putting down her bag, spreading her towel on the rock. She slathered herself with sunscreen before she stripped down to the plain black swimming costume Leila had provided.

She glanced around again; she was definitely alone. No one had followed her from the camp.

And why should anyone? She was but a five-minute walk from her tent, in the middle of the desert, the middle of nowhere. In every direction the desert stretched, endless sand and towering black rocks, both bleak and beautiful.

There was, Elena knew, nowhere to go, nothing to do but wait and hope that Aziz found her.

Or send a signal.

She reached for her bag and took out the slats she'd broken from the chair. A few weedy-looking plants grew by the oasis's edge, and she took them and made a small, rather pathetic-looking pile. She wasn't going to get much of a blaze from this, Elena realised disconsolately, but it would have to do. It was her only chance. If someone saw the smoke from her fire, they might investigate, might look for her.

Resolutely, she started rubbing the sticks together.

Fifteen minutes later she had blisters on both hands and the sticks were a little warm. She hadn't seen so much as a spark. Frustrated, she laid the sticks aside and rose from the rock. The air was hot and still and the shimmering waters of the oasis looked extremely inviting.

Balancing on her tiptoes, she executed a neat dive into the pool. The water closed around her, cool and refreshing, and she swam under water for a few metres before she surfaced, treading water, not knowing what was on the bottom and not particularly wishing to touch it with her bare feet.

Even if she managed to start a fire, she thought, what would distinguish it from any other camp fire? She'd have to get a really big blaze going for someone to take notice. She'd have to set the whole camp on fire.

Her plan, Elena realised, was ridiculous. The sense of purpose that had buoyed her all morning left her in a depressing rush. Yet even so she decided to try again. It wasn't as if she had many, or any, other options.

She swam to the side of the oasis and hauled herself, dripping, onto the rock ledge. Drying herself off, she knelt before the sticks again and started to rub.

Five minutes later she saw the first tiny spark kindle between the sticks. Hope leapt in her chest and she rubbed harder; some of the dried plants and leaves she'd gathered caught the spark and the first small flame flickered. She let out a cry of triumph.

'Don't move.'

Everything in Elena stilled at the sound of that low, deadly voice. She looked up, her heart lurching against her ribs at the sight of Khalil standing just a few feet away. His eyes were narrowed, his mouth thinned, everything about him tense and still.

Her heart started to pound and then it seemed to stop completely as Khalil slowly, steadily, raised the pistol he'd been holding and pointed it straight at her.

CHAPTER FOUR

THE SOUND OF the pistol firing echoed through the still air, bounced off the boulders and rippled the still waters of the oasis.

Dispassionately Khalil watched as the snake leapt and twisted in the air before falling a few feet away, dead.

He turned back to look at Elena and swore softly when he saw her sway, her face drained of colour, her pupils dilated with terror. Without even considering what he was doing, or why, he strode forward, caught her in his arms and drew her shuddering body to his chest.

'I killed it, Elena,' he said as he stroked her dark hair. 'It's dead. You don't need to be afraid now.'

She pushed away from him, her whole body still trembling. 'What's dead?'

Khalil stared at her for several seconds as the meaning of her question penetrated. He swore again. 'I shot the snake! Did you not see it, but three feet from you, and ready to strike?'

She just stared at him with wide, blank eyes, and forcibly he took her jaw in his hand and turned her head so she could see the dead viper. She blanched, drawing her breath in a ragged gasp.

'I thought…'

'You thought I was aiming at you?' Khalil finished flatly. His stomach churned with a sour mix of guilt and anger. 'How could you think such a thing?' He didn't wait for her answer, for he knew what it would be: *because you kidnapped me.* 'I promised you I wouldn't hurt you.'

'And you also said you didn't trust anyone's promises. Neither do I, Khalil.' She tried to move away from him but she stumbled, her body still shaking, and Khalil pulled her towards him once more. 'Don't—'

'You've had a shock.' He sat down on the rock, drawing her onto his lap. It was a jolt to his system, to feel a warm body against his, yet it also felt far too good, familiar in a way that made no sense, yet felt intrinsically *right*.

He felt the stiffness in her body, saw the way she angled her face away from him and knew that just as he was she was trying to keep herself apart, stand on pride. He saw so much of himself in her and it unnerved him. It touched him in a way he didn't expect or even understand. From the moment he'd met Elena she'd *done* things to him. Not just to his body, but to his heart.

Gently he stroked her damp hair away from her face. She let out a shuddering breath and relaxed against him, her cheek against his chest. Something deep and fierce inside Khalil, some part of him he hadn't thought still existed, let out a roar of both satisfaction and need.

He tucked a tendril behind her ear just as he'd wanted to yesterday. Her eyes were closed, her dark lashes sweeping her pale cheeks.

'You pointed that gun at me,' she whispered, her voice sounding distant and numb.

'I pointed it at the *snake*,' Khalil answered. He knew she was in shock, trying to process what had happened, but he still felt a flash of anger, a stirring of guilt. He should have made her feel safer. She should have been able to trust him.

This, when you trust no one?

'A black snake,' he continued, keeping his voice steady and calm. 'They can be deadly.'

'I didn't even see it.' He thought she was recovering

from the shock but then she let out a little shuddering sob and pressed her face against his chest.

His whole body jolted with the fierce pleasure of having her curl into him, seek his comfort. When had anyone ever done that? When had anyone wanted something real and tender from him? And when had he felt it in response, this yearning and protectiveness?

He could not remember a time, and it forced him to acknowledge the stark emptiness of his life, the years of relentless and ruthless striving, utterly without comfort.

'There, there, *habiibii*. You're safe now. Safe.' The words were strange to him, yet he spoke them without thinking, stroking her hair, his arms tight around her. He could feel her shoulders shake and he could tell from her ragged breathing she was doing her best to keep herself from crying. His throat tightened with emotion he hadn't felt in decades.

After a moment she pushed away from him, her eyes still dry, her face pale but resolutely composed.

'I'm sorry. You must think I'm being ridiculous.' She sat stiffly in his lap now, her chin lifted at a queenly angle. Already Khalil missed the feel of her against him.

'Not at all,' he answered. He suppressed the clamour of his own feelings, forced it all back down again. 'I realise that a great deal has happened to you in a short amount of time.' He hesitated, choosing his words with care, wanting and even needing her to understand. To believe him. 'I'm sorry for the fear and unhappiness I have caused you.'

For a second, no more, he thought she did. Her face softened, her lips parting, and then she gave a little shake of her head and scrambled off his lap. 'Even though it was entirely preventable?'

Their moment of startling intimacy was over and Khalil, half-amazed at his own reaction, felt a sudden piercing of grief at its loss.

* * *

Elena stood on the rock, trying to calm her thundering heart—and ignore the ache Khalil's touch had created in her. She couldn't remember the last time she'd been held so tenderly, spoken to so gently.

He's your captor, she reminded herself grimly. *He kidnapped you*. But in that moment he'd been incredibly kind, and her body and heart had responded to it like a flower unfurling in the sunlight.

When had someone comforted her, touched her, understood her? She'd lived such a solitary existence, first as an only child, then as an orphan queen. The one person she'd let close had betrayed her utterly.

Just as Khalil will betray you. At least he was honest about his intentions.

Khalil gazed at her, his expression inscrutable, any remnant of tenderness erased completely from his harsh features. He glanced at her pathetic pile of plants and broken chair slats; the tiny flame she'd been kindling had gone out. 'What on earth were you doing?' he asked. He turned back to her, his mouth twisting with bemusement. 'Were you building a *fire*?' She didn't answer and his mouth curved into a smile as he shook his head. She almost thought she heard admiration in his voice. 'You were building a signal fire, weren't you?'

Elena lifted her chin. 'And if I was?'

'It's the most pathetic signal fire I've ever seen.' Khalil smiled, inviting her to share the joke, his teasing gentle, compassion kindling in his eyes—a compassion she hadn't seen before and hadn't thought he possessed.

Elena felt an answering smile tug at her own mouth. It *was* pathetic. And it felt good to joke, to laugh, even with Khalil. Especially with Khalil. 'I know. I realised it wasn't going to work. It would be far too small if it had even caught at all. But I had to do something.'

Khalil nodded, his expression serious once more. 'I understand that, Elena,' he said quietly. 'You know, we are a lot alike. We both fight against what we cannot change.'

'It looks to me like you're trying to change something,' she retorted, and he inclined his head in acknowledgement.

'Yes, now. But there was a time when I couldn't. When I was powerless and angry but determined to keep fighting, because at least it reminded me I was alive. That I had something to fight for.'

And, God help her, she knew how that felt. The last four years, she'd felt that every day. 'If you know what that feels like,' she asked in a raw voice, 'then how can you keep me prisoner?'

For a second, no more, Khalil looked conflicted. Torn. Then his eyes veiled and his mouth firmed, everything about him hardening. 'We are not as alike as all that,' he said shortly. 'You might be a prisoner, Elena, but you are treated with respect and courtesy. You have every comfort available.'

'Does that really matter—?'

'Trust me,' he cut her off, his voice cold now, implacable. 'It matters.'

'When have you felt like a prisoner?'

He stared at her for a long moment then gave a little shake of his head. 'We should return to the camp.'

She still wanted answers, even if she shouldn't ask the questions, shouldn't get to know this man any more. Yet she did, because he understood her in a way no one else did. She wanted, she realised, to understand him. 'Why did you come looking for me?'

'I was worried about you.'

'That I'd escape?'

A tiny smile lightened his features. 'No, I'm afraid not. I was worried you might encounter a snake, and I was very nearly right. They like to sun themselves on these rocks.'

'You did warn me.'

'Even so.'

She shook her head, her throat suddenly tight because everything about this was so strange. Khalil was her captor. Her enemy. But he'd also treated her with more gentleness than any other human being that she could remember, and if he had a legitimate claim to the throne...

'What is it, Elena?' he asked quietly.

'I don't know what to think,' she admitted. 'I don't even know if I want to ask you.'

'Ask me what?'

She took a breath, let it out slowly. 'Your side of the story.'

Something flared in his eyes, something she couldn't name, but it had her body responding, heat unfurling low in her belly. Then it died out and his expression hardened once more. 'You don't want to change your mind.'

'You don't know what this marriage means for me, Khalil.'

'Then why don't you tell me?'

'What good would it do? Would you lose the chance of your crown so I can keep mine?'

He raised his eyebrows, his expression still uncompromising. 'Are you in danger of losing it?'

She didn't answer, because she'd already said too much and the last thing she wanted to do was admit to Khalil how shaky her throne really was. So far she'd managed to hide the threat Markos posed to her. If it became public, she knew it would just give him power. She could already imagine the newspaper headlines about the teenaged queen and the stupid mistake she'd made, trusting someone, thinking he loved her.

She wouldn't do that again.

And certainly not with Khalil.

Yet even so part of her yearned to tell him the truth, to unburden herself, have someone understand, sympathise and even offer advice.

Like Paulo had?

Why on earth was she thinking of trusting Khalil when she knew to trust no one? What about this man made her want to break her own rules?

Because he understands you.

'Like you said, we should return to the camp,' she said and with her head held high she walked past him, back through the boulders.

As soon as she got back to her tent, Elena stripped off her swimming costume and dressed in the clothes she'd been given that morning. She felt more trapped now than she had since Khalil had first forced her into the car, but the prison this time was one of her own making. Her own mind. Her own heart.

She knew it was the coward's way not to listen to Khalil, not to ask what his side of the story was. Would she really want to marry Aziz if he wasn't the rightful Sheikh?

And yet he had to be, she told herself as she sat down on the bed. *He had to be.*

Because if he wasn't…

It didn't even matter, she reminded herself with a gusty sigh, dropping her head into her hands. She wasn't going to marry Aziz. No matter how gentle and tender he'd been with her today, Khalil still intended keeping her until the six weeks were up. Soon Aziz would have no reason to marry her.

Whether she wanted to or not.

She looked up, her gaze unfocused as she recalled the way Khalil had held her; the soft words he had spoken; the way he'd stroked her hair; the thud of his heart against her cheek.

She felt deep in her bones that he'd been sincere, and the realisation both terrified and thrilled her. She didn't have real relationships. She didn't know how. She'd been shy as a child, her parents distant figures, her only company a nanny and then a governess. Even if she'd wanted, yearned, for such things, she hadn't known how to go about getting them—and then Paulo had broken her trust and destroyed her faith in other people and, even worse, her faith in herself and her own judgement.

Was she misjudging Khalil now? Was it simply her pathetic inexperience with men and life that made her crave more of that moment, more tenderness, more contact?

Nothing about their relationship, if she could even use that word, was real.

Yet it *felt* real. She felt as if Khalil understood and even liked her for who she was. Maybe that was just wishful thinking, but whatever her association with Khalil was she knew she needed to know the truth. To ask for his side of the story…and face the consequences of whatever he told her.

She let out a shuddering breath, the decision made.

A little while later Leila slipped into the tent, smiling and curtseying as she caught sight of Elena. 'I've brought fresh clothes and water for washing. Sheikh Khalil has invited you to dine with him tonight.'

'He has?' Surprise, and a damning pleasure, rippled through her. 'Why?'

Leila's smile widened. 'Why shouldn't he, Your Highness?'

Why should he?

His reasons didn't matter, she told herself. This could be her opportunity to ask Khalil about his claim to the throne. And if she felt a little flare of anticipation at seeing him, at spending time with him, then so be it.

'Look at the dress he has brought you,' Leila said and, opening a box, she withdrew a dress of silvery grey from folds of tissue paper.

It was both beautiful and modest, the material as delicate and silky as a spider's web. Elena touched it before she could stop herself.

'I'm not sure why I need to wear that,' she said sharply,

drawing her hand away as if the fragile material had burned her. The temptation to try it on, to feel feminine and beautiful, was overwhelming.

Leila's face fell and she laid the dress down on the bed. 'You would look beautiful in it, Your Highness.'

'I don't need to look beautiful. I'm being held captive in a desert camp.' *And she needed to remember that. To stay strong.*

She turned away abruptly, hating that she sounded petulant and childish, and hating even more that she was tempted to wear the dress and have dinner with Khalil.

Hear his side of the story.

Quietly Leila folded the dress and returned it to the box. Elena felt even worse. 'Shall I tell Sheikh Khalil you wish to remain in your tent tonight?'

Conflicted, Elena turned back to Leila. 'I don't—' She stopped, took a breath. She was being a coward, hiding in her tent. She needed to face her fears. Face Khalil. If she learned just what his side of the story was, she'd be able to make a more informed decision about her own future. She'd know all the facts. Know her enemy.

Even if he didn't feel like her enemy any more.

'You may tell Khalil I'll eat with him,' Elena said.

'Thank you, Leila.' She glanced down at the dress, an ache of longing rising in her. It was such a lovely gown. 'And you may leave the dress.'

An hour later Leila escorted Elena to Khalil's private tent. Her heart started thudding and her palms felt damp as she stepped inside the luxurious quarters.

She felt self-conscious in the dress Leila had brought, as if she were dressing up for a date, but she also enjoyed the feel of the silky fabric against her skin, the way it swirled around her ankles as she moved. And, a tiny, treacherous voice whispered, she liked the thought of Khalil seeing her in it.

Everything in her rebelled at the realisation. She shouldn't want to please Khalil. She *couldn't* start to feel something for him. It would be beyond stupid—it would be dangerous.

As she came into the tent, she saw candlelight flickering over the low table that had been set with a variety of dishes. Silk and satin pillows were scattered around it in the Arabic style of dining, rather than sitting in chairs as she was used to.

Khalil emerged from the shadows, dressed in a loose, white cotton shirt and dark trousers; he'd taken off the traditional *thobe* she'd seen him in before. With his golden eyes and midnight hair, his chiselled jaw glinting with dark stubble, he looked like a sexy and dangerous pirate. Dangerous, she told herself, being the operative word.

Elena swallowed audibly as Khalil's heated gaze swept over her. 'You look lovely, Your Highness.'

'I'm not sure what the point of this dress is,' Elena retorted. 'Or this meal.' She was feeling far too vulnerable already, and attack was her best defence. She'd learned that in the Council Room; it had helped keep the crown on her head for four years.

When Markos had mocked her plans for better childcare provision, saying how women didn't need to work, Elena had come back with the percentages of women who did. When he'd belittled her idea for an arts festival, she'd pointed out the increased tourist revenues such events would bring. She'd refused to back down, and it was probably why he hated her. Why he wanted to end her rule.

Khalil had been walking towards her with graceful, predatory intent, but he stopped at her sharp words and raised an eyebrow. 'You complained this morning about being kept in your tent like a prisoner. I thought you would enjoy having company, even if it is mine.' A smile flickered over his face and died. 'Likewise, I thought you might prefer a dress to the admittedly more suitable khakis. I'm sorry if I was wrong.'

Now she felt ridiculous and even a little ashamed, almost

as if she'd hurt his feelings. Khalil waited, his expression ironed out to blandness. 'This is all very civilised,' Elena finally managed.

'It's meant to be civilised, Elena,' he answered. 'I have told you before, I am neither a terrorist nor a thug. Your stay here is, I'm afraid, a necessary—'

'Evil,' she filled in before she could help herself.

'Measure,' Khalil answered. Suddenly and surprisingly, he looked weary. 'If you are going to fight me all evening, perhaps you would prefer to eat in your tent. Or will you try to set fire to this one?'

Elena knew then that she didn't want to fight any more. What was the point? Khalil wasn't going to let her go. And she was wearing a beautiful dress, about to eat a lovely meal with a very attractive man. Maybe she should just enjoy herself. It was a novel concept; so much of her life as queen, and even before she'd ascended the throne, had been about duty. Sacrifice. When had anything been about pleasure?

She gave him a small smile and glanced consideringly at the creamy candles in their bronze holders. 'That would make a big enough signal fire.'

Khalil chuckled softly. 'Don't even think of it, Elena.'

'I wasn't,' she admitted. 'I've come to realise that setting a fire won't do me much good.'

'You have another idea?' he asked and walked forward to take her hand, the slide of his fingers across hers shooting sparks all the way up to her elbow.

'Well, I was thinking of trying to charm you into letting me go,' Elena answered lightly. She did a little twirl in her dress. 'The dress might help.'

Khalil's eyes gleamed. 'You'd tempt a saint, but I'm afraid I'm made of sterner stuff. Flirting won't get you very far.'

She drew back, a blush scorching her cheeks. 'I wasn't *flirting.*'

'No?' Khalil arched his eyebrows as he drew her down to the table. 'Pity.'

Even more disconcerted by his response, Elena fussed with positioning herself on the silken pillows, arranging the folds of her dress around her. Khalil sat opposite her, reclining on one elbow, every inch the relaxed and confident sheikh.

Sheikh. Yes, lying on the pillows, the candlelight glinting on his dark hair, he looked every inch the sheikh.

'Let me serve you,' Khalil said, and lifted the lids on several silver chafing dishes. He ladled some lamb stewed in fragrant spices onto her plate, along with couscous mixed with vegetables.

'It smells delicious,' Elena murmured. 'Thank you.' Khalil raised an eyebrow.

'So polite,' he said with a soft laugh. 'I'm waiting for the sting.'

'I'm hungry,' she answered, which was no answer at all because she didn't know what she was doing. What she felt.

'Then you must eat up,' Khalil said lightly. 'You are too thin, at least by Kadaran standards.'

She *was* thin, mainly because constant stress and anxiety kept her from eating properly. 'And you are familiar with Kadaran standards?' she asked. 'You said something about living in America before, didn't you?'

'I spent my adolescence in the United States,' he answered, his tone rather flat. He handed her a platter of bread, his expression shuttered, and Elena felt a surge of curiosity about this man and his experience.

'Is that why your English is so good?'

A smile flickered across his face, banishing the frown that had settled between his brows when she'd asked about where he had lived. 'Thank you. And, yes, I suppose it is.'

Elena sat back, taking dainty bites of the delicious lamb. 'How long have you been back in Kadar?'

'Six months. Is this an inquisition, Elena?' That smile now deepened, revealing the dimple Elena had seen before. '"Know your enemies and know yourself, and you can win a hundred battles".'

'You are quite familiar with *The Art of War*.'

'As are you,' he observed.

'How come you know it so well?'

'Because my life has been one of preparing for battle.'

'To become Sheikh of Kadar.'

'Yes.'

'But you're already a sheikh, aren't you? Leila told me…'

He shrugged. 'Of a small tribe in the northern desert. My mother's people.'

He was silent and so was she, the only sounds the wind ruffling the sides of the tent, the gentle clink of their dishes. Elena gazed at him, the harsh planes of his face, the sculpted fullness of his lips. Hard and soft, a mass of contradictions, this gentle kidnapper of hers. Her stomach twisted. What was she *doing*? How stupid was she being, to actually consider believing this man, trusting him?

She could tell herself she was here because she needed to know her enemy, needed to make an informed decision about her future, but Elena knew she was fooling herself. She was here because she wanted to be here. And she wanted to trust Khalil because she liked him. As a person. As a man.

'I want to hear the other side of the story,' she said quietly, and Khalil glanced up at her, his expression watchful, even wary.

'Do you,' he said, not a question, and she nodded and swallowed.

'Everyone around you is so sure, Khalil, of your right to the throne. I don't think they're brainwashed or deluded, so…' She spread her hands, tried for a smile. 'There must be some reason why people think you are the rightful sheikh. Tell me what it is.'

* * *

Tell me what it is. A simple request, yet one that felt like peeling back his skin, exposing his heart. Admitting his shame.

Khalil glanced away from Elena, his gaze distant, unfocused. He'd said before he'd tell her his side of the story when she was ready to listen, and here she was—ready.

The trouble was, he wasn't.

'Khalil,' Elena said softly. His name sounded right on her lips in a way that made everything in Khalil both want and rebel.

What was he doing? How had he got to this place, with this woman? It had started, perhaps, from the first moment he'd laid eyes on her. When, in what could be considered courage or folly or both, she'd attempted to escape. When he'd seen both fear and pride in her eyes and known exactly how she'd felt.

When he'd held her in his arms and she'd curled into him, seeking the solace that he'd freely, gladly, given.

And now she wanted more. Now she wanted the truth, which he'd told her he would tell her, except now that she'd actually asked he felt wary, reluctant. *Afraid.*

What if she didn't believe him? *What if she did?*

Finally Khalil spoke. 'My mother,' he said slowly, 'was Sheikh Hashem's first wife.'

Elena's eyes widened, although with disbelief, confusion or simply surprise he couldn't tell. 'What—who was your father?'

He bared his teeth in a smile that was a sign of his pain rather than any humour or happiness. 'Sheikh Hashem, of course.'

A hand flew to her throat. 'You mean you are Aziz's *brother*?'

'Half-brother, to be precise. Older half-brother.'

'But...' She shook her head, and now she definitely seemed disbelieving. Khalil felt something that had started to unfurl inside him begin to wither. *Good.* It was better this way. She wouldn't believe him, and he wouldn't care. It would be easy then. Painful, but easy. 'How can that be?' she asked. 'There's no mention of you anywhere, not even in that book!'

He laughed, the sound hard and bitter, revealing. 'So you read the book?'

'A bit.'

'There wouldn't be a mention of me in it. My father did his best to erase my existence from the world. But the Bedouin tribes, my mother's people, they have not forgotten me.' He hated how defensive he sounded. As if he needed to prove himself, as if he wanted her to believe him.

She didn't matter. Her opinion didn't matter. Why had he even asked her to dinner? Why had he given her that dress?

Because you wanted to please her. Because you wanted to see her again, touch her again...

Fool.

'Why would your father wish to erase your existence, Khalil?'

He gave her a glittering, challenging stare. 'Do you know who Aziz's mother is?'

Elena shrugged. 'Hashem's wife. Her name, I believe, is Hamidyah. She died a few years ago, Aziz told me.'

'Yes, she did. And, before she was my father's second wife, she was his mistress. She bore him a bastard, and my father claimed him as one. Aziz.' He let out a slow breath, one hand clenching involuntarily against his thigh. 'Then my father tired of my mother, his first wife, but Kadaran law has always dictated that the reigning monarch take only one wife.' He gave her the semblance of a smile. 'Not a moral stance, mind you, simply a pragmatic one: fewer contenders for the throne. I suspect it's why Kadar has enjoyed so many years of peace.'

'So you're saying he got rid of his wife? And—and of you? So he could marry Hamidyah?' Elena was gazing at him with an emotion he couldn't decipher. Was it confusion, disbelief or, God help him, pity? Did she think he was deluded?

'You don't believe me,' Khalil stated flatly. His stomach felt like a stone. He wasn't angry with her, he realised with a flash of fury he could only direct at himself; he was hurt.

'It seems incredible,' Elena said slowly. 'Surely someone would have known…?'

'The desert tribes know.'

'Does Aziz?'

'Of course he does.' The words came fast, spiked with bitterness. 'We met, you know, as boys.' Just weeks before he'd been torn from his family. 'Never since, although I've seen his photograph in the gossip magazines.'

Elena shook her head slowly. 'But if he knows you are the rightful heir…'

'Ah, but you see, my father is cleverer than that. He charged my mother with adultery and claimed I was not his son. He banished me from the palace when I was seven years old.'

Elena gaped at him. '*Banished*…'

'My mother as well, to a remote royal residence where she lived in isolation. She died just a few months later, although I didn't know that for many years. From the day my father threw me from the palace, I never saw her again.' He spoke dispassionately, even coldly, because if he didn't he was afraid of how he might sound. What he might reveal. Already he felt a tightness in his throat and he took a sip of wine to ease it.

'But that's terrible,' Elena whispered. She looked stricken, but her response didn't gratify Khalil. He felt too exposed for that.

'It's all ancient history,' he dismissed. 'It hardly matters now.'

'Doesn't it? This is why you're seeking the throne, as—'

'As revenge?' He filled in. 'No, Elena, it's not for revenge. It's because it's my *right*.' His voice throbbed with conviction. 'I am my father's first-born. When he set my mother aside he created deep divisions in a country that has only known peace. If you've wondered why Aziz does not have the support of his whole country, it's because too many people know he is not the rightful heir. He is popular in Siyad because he is cosmopolitan and charming, but the heart of this country is not his. It is mine.' He stared at her, his chest heaving, willing her to believe him. Needing her to.

'How can you be sure,' she whispered, 'that your mother didn't have an affair?'

'Of course I'm sure.' He heard his voice, as sharp as a blade. Disappointment dug deep. No, a feeling worse than disappointment, weaker—this damnable hurt. He took a steadying breath. 'My mother knew the consequences of an affair: banishment, shame, a life cut off from everyone and everything she knew. It would not have been worth the risk.'

'But you would have just been a boy. How could you have known?'

'I knew everyone around her believed her to be innocent. I knew her serving maids cried out at the injustice of it. I knew no man ever stepped forward to claim her or me, and my father couldn't even name the man who'd allegedly sired me. My father's entire basis for banishing both my mother and me was the colour of my eyes.'

Elena stared at him, her own golden-grey eyes filled with not confusion or disbelief but with something that was nearly his undoing: *compassion*.

'Oh, Khalil,' she whispered.

He glanced away, afraid of revealing himself. His jaw worked but he could not form words. Finally he choked out, 'People protested at the time. They said there wasn't enough proof. But then my mother died before he actually married Hamidyah, so it was, in the end, all above board.'

'And what about you?'

He couldn't admit what had happened to him: those years in the desert, the awful shame, even though part of him wanted to, part of him wanted to bare himself to this woman, give her his secrets. To trust another person, and with more than he ever had before, even as a child. He suppressed that foolish impulse and lifted one shoulder in what he hoped passed as an indifferent shrug. 'I was raised by my mother's sister, Dimah, in America. I never saw my father again.'

'And the people accepted it all?' she said quietly, only half a question. 'Aziz as the heir, even though they must have remembered you...'

'My father was a dictator. No one possessed the courage to question his actions while he was alive.'

'Why did Sheikh Hashem make such a strange will?' Elena burst out. 'Commanding Aziz to marry?'

'I think he was torn. Perhaps he realised the mistake he'd made in banishing me, but did not want to admit it. He was a proud man.' Khalil shrugged again. 'Forcing Aziz to marry would make him commit to Kadar and give up his European ways. But calling a national referendum if he didn't...' Khalil smiled grimly. 'My father must have known it was a chance for me to become Sheikh. Maybe that is just wishful thinking on my part, but I'd like to think he regretted, even if just in part, what he did to my mother and me.'

'And do you think people would accept you, if you did become Sheikh?'

'Some might have difficulty but, in time, yes. I believe they would.'

He stared at her then, willing her to tell him she believed him. Wanting, even needing, to hear it.

She looked away. Khalil's insides clenched with a help-less, hopeless anger.

Then she turned back to him, her eyes as wide and clear as twin lakes. 'Then we really are alike,' she said quietly. 'For we are both fighting for our crowns.'

CHAPTER FIVE

KHALIL'S GAZE HAD blazed anger but Elena saw something beneath the fury: *grief.* A grief she understood and felt herself. And, even though she didn't want to, she felt a sympathy for Khalil, a compassion and even an anger on his behalf. He'd been terribly wronged, just as Leila had said.

She thought of him as a boy, being banished from his family and home. She imagined his confusion and fear, the utter heartbreak of losing everything he'd known and held dear.

Just as she had.

She'd been a bit older, but her family had been wrenched from her in a matter of moments, just as Khalil's had. She was fighting to keep her rightful title, just as Khalil was.

With a jolt she realised what this meant: she believed him. She believed he was the rightful heir.

For a second everything in her rebelled. *You believed before. You trusted before. And this man has kidnapped you—how can you be so stupid?*

Yet she'd heard the sincerity in Khalil's voice. She'd felt his pain. She knew him in a way she hadn't known anyone else, because they were so alike.

She believed him.

'How are you fighting for your crown, Elena?' he asked quietly.

She hesitated, because honesty didn't come easily, and letting herself be vulnerable felt akin to pulling out her fingernails one by one. She'd hardened her heart in the last four years. She'd learned to be tough, to need no one.

And yet Khalil had been honest with her. He'd told her his story and she'd seen in his eyes that he'd wanted, even needed, her to believe him.

She took a deep breath. She thought of Andreas Markos and his determination to discredit her—her Council and country's desire for a king, or the closest thing to it. Her own foolish choices. 'It's complicated.'

'Most things are.'

He waited and Elena sifted through all the things she could say. 'My country, and my Council, would like a male ruler.'

'And you wanted that to be Aziz?'

She heard incredulity in his tone and bristled. 'Not like that. We had an agreement—he would attend state functions with me as Prince Consort, act as ruler in name only. It would satisfy the people and, I hoped, my Council. But he wouldn't actually have been involved in any decision making.'

'And you would have been satisfied with that?'

'It was what I wanted.'

'Why not find a man who could truly be your equal, your partner? Who could help you to rule, who could support you?'

Briefly, painfully, she thought of Paulo. 'You speak as though such a thing is simple. Easy.'

'No. Not that. But I wonder why you settle.'

She swallowed past the sudden tightness in her throat. 'What about you, Khalil? Do you want an equal, a partner in marriage as well as in ruling?'

Surprise flashed briefly in his eyes before his expression hardened. 'No.'

'Then why do you think I would want one? Simply because I am a woman?'

'No...' He gazed at her thoughtfully. 'I only asked, because if you needed to marry to please your country it seems wise to pick a man who could be your friend and helpmate, not a stranger.'

'Well, unfortunately for me, I don't have a friend and helpmate waiting in the wings.' She'd meant to sound light and wry but cringed at the self-pity she heard in her voice instead. 'I've been alone for a long time,' she continued when she trusted herself to sound more measured. 'I'm used to it now, and it's more comfortable for me that way.' Even if, since meeting Khalil, she'd started to realise all she'd been missing out on. 'I imagine you might be the same.'

'Yes, I am.'

'Well, then.'

Khalil leaned back in his seat, his gaze sweeping over her in thoughtful assessment. 'So you made this arrangement with Aziz to please your Council?'

'Appease them, more like.' Elena hesitated, not wanting to admit more but knowing she needed to. 'The Head of Council, Andreas Markos, has threatened to call a vote at the next convening.' She took a breath, then forced herself to finish. 'A vote to depose me and abolish the monarchy.'

Khalil was silent for a moment. 'And, let me guess, put himself forward as head of state? Prime Minister, perhaps?'

Amazingly she found herself smiling wryly. 'Something like that.'

'And you think he won't if you are married?'

'I'm gambling that he won't,' Elena admitted. 'It's a calculated risk.'

'I understand about those.'

'Yes, I suppose you do.' They smiled at each other, and as the moment spun out Elena wondered at herself. How could they be joking about her captivity? How could she feel, in that moment, that they were co-conspirators, somehow complicit in all that had happened? Yet she did, and more than that. So much more than that.

'The Thallian people like me, for the most part,' she

continued after a moment. 'And a royal marriage would be very popular. Markos would have a difficult time getting the Council to vote against me if the country approved.'

'I imagine,' Khalil said quietly, 'that your people like you very much indeed, Elena. I think you must be a good queen. You are clearly very loyal to your people.'

Pleasure rippled through her at the sincerity she heard in his voice. It meant so much, more than she'd ever even realised, to have someone believe in her.

'I'm trying to be a good queen,' she said in a low voice. 'I know I've made mistakes—' and she didn't want to talk about those '—but I love Thallia and its people. I want to celebrate its traditions, but also bring it into the twenty-first century.'

Khalil arched an eyebrow. 'And have you had much success so far?'

Elena ducked her head, suddenly shy. She wasn't used to talking about her accomplishments; so often they went unrecognised, by her Council, at any rate. 'A bit. I've introduced some new policies to protect women's rights. I've initiated a review of the national curriculum for primary schools. The education in Thallia has been one of its weaknesses.'

Khalil nodded, encouraging, and shyly Elena continued, 'I also helped to start an annual festival to celebrate the country's music and dance. It's a small thing, but important to our heritage. Thallia is named after the muse of poetry, you know.'

'I didn't know.' His eyes, Elena saw, crinkled when he smiled. She looked away.

'I know it doesn't sound like much.'

'Why belittle yourself or what you've done? There are enough people to do that for you. I've learned that much.'

'We've both persevered,' Elena said quietly. She met his gaze and held it, feeling an overwhelming solidarity with this man who had once been her enemy. They were so alike. He understood her, and she understood him, more than she'd ever expected.

'And this Markos,' Khalil said after a moment. 'He has that power—to call such a vote?'

'Unfortunately he does. Our Constitution states that the monarch cannot enact a law that isn't approved by the majority of the Council, and the Council can't pass one that isn't endorsed by the King or Queen.' Elena gave a rather bleak smile. 'But there's one important caveat: if the Council votes unanimously, the monarch is forced to acquiesce.'

'Even to your own demise?'

'That hasn't happened in a thousand years.' She looked away then, afraid he'd see the fear and shame on her face: the fear that she would be the one to end it. The shame that she wasn't strong enough to keep her crown or the promise she'd made to her father as he'd lain dying.

For Thallia, Elena. You must live for Thallia and the crown.

'You won't be the one to end it, Elena,' Khalil said quietly. The certainty in his voice made her glow inside. 'You're too strong for that.'

'Thank you,' she whispered.

'You have a lot of pressure put on you, for such a young woman,' Khalil continued. Elena just shrugged. 'You are an only child, I presume? The title has always fallen to you?'

'Yes, although for most of my childhood my parents hoped for more children.' Her mouth twisted downwards. 'For a boy.'

'And they were disappointed, I presume?'

'Yes. My mother had many miscarriages, but no more live children.'

'A tragedy.'

'Yes. I suppose it's why they felt a need to keep me so sheltered. Protected.'

'You were doted on?'

'Not exactly.' She thought of how little she'd actually

seen her parents. 'Kept apart, really. I didn't go to formal school until I was thirteen.' When she'd been gawky, over-whelmed and terribly shy. It hadn't been a great introduction to school life.

'And then you became Queen at a young age,' Khalil continued. He reached over to refill her glass with wine. Elena had already finished her first glass; Dutch courage, she supposed, for when she'd been telling him all that truth. She took another sip of wine now as she met his tawny gaze.

'Nineteen,' she said after she had swallowed, felt the liquid slip down her throat and steal seductively through her again.

'I know your parents died in a terrorist bombing,' Khalil said quietly. Elena nodded. She dreaded talking or even thinking about that awful day, hated the memories of the acrid smell of smoke, the stinging pain of broken glass on the palms of her hands, the ringing in her ears—all of it still causing her to wake up in an icy sweat far too many nights.

'I'm sorry,' Khalil continued. 'I know what it is to lose your parents when you are young.'

'Yes, I suppose you do.'

'You must miss them.'

'I do...'

Khalil cocked his head. 'You sound uncertain.'

'No, of course not.' Elena bit her lip. 'It's only that I didn't actually know them all that well. They were away so much... I miss the *idea* of them, if that makes sense. Of what—what I wish we could have been like as a family. That probably sounds strange.'

Khalil shook his head. 'Not strange at all,' he answered quietly, and Elena wondered if he missed the family he could have had too: loving parents, supporting him even now.

Khalil leaned forward, his fingers whispering against her cheek as he tucked a strand of hair behind her ear.

'You look so sad,' he said softly. 'I'm sorry to bring up bad memories.'

'It's okay,' she whispered. Khalil's fingers lingered on her cheek and she wished, suddenly and fiercely, that he wouldn't pull away.

That he would kiss her.

Her lips parted instinctively and her gaze rested on his mouth, making her realise yet again how sculpted and really *perfect* his lips were. She wondered how they would feel. How they would taste. She'd never actually been kissed before, which suddenly seemed ridiculous at the age of twenty-three. But a convent-school education and becoming Queen at just nineteen had kept her from ever pursuing a romantic relationship. First there hadn't been any opportunity, and then she'd been so focused on protecting her crown and serving her country there hadn't been any time. Besides, suitable partners for a reigning queen were not exactly plentiful.

Elena knew she shouldn't be thinking of kissing Khalil now. With effort she dragged her gaze up towards his eyes, saw they were molten gold. His fingers tightened on her cheek, his thumb grazing her jawbone, drawing her inexorably forward. And Elena went, her heart starting to hammer as she braced herself for that wonderful onslaught.

Then Khalil released her, his hand falling away from her face as he sat back in his chair.

Her mind whirled with confusion and disappointment, and her body ached with unfulfilled desire. She scrambled for a way to cover her own obvious longing. 'This is very good,' she said stiltedly, gesturing to her half-eaten meal.

Khalil acknowledged her compliment with a nod. 'Thank you.'

'You have quite an elaborate set-up for a desert camp,' she continued, determined to keep the conversation off dangerous subjects—although every subject felt dangerous now. Everything about Khalil felt dangerous.

Desirable.

'Comfort need not be sacrificed,' he remarked, taking a sip of wine.

'I suppose you feel very secure?' she asked. 'To have such a…permanent arrangement?'

'These are tents, Elena, as luxurious as they may be. My men and I could disassemble this camp in twenty minutes, if need be.'

'How do you know how to do all this if you grew up in America?'

'All this?' Khalil repeated, raising his eyebrows.

'Tents. Horses. Fighting. All this—this rebel stuff.' She realised she sounded rather ridiculous and she shrugged, half in apology, half in defiance. Heaven help her, she'd had two glasses of wine and she was nearly drunk.

'I served in the French Foreign Legion for seven years,' Khalil told her. 'I'm used to this kind of living.'

'You did?'

'It was good preparation.'

Everything in his life, Elena supposed, had been to prepare for being Sheikh, for taking the throne from the half-brother who didn't deserve it.

Aziz… Why could she barely remember his face now? She'd been going to marry him, yet she'd forgotten what he looked like, or how his voice sounded. And with that thought came another fast on its heels.

She wasn't going to marry him any more. Even if he rescued her, or Khalil released her, she wasn't going to marry Aziz.

It was both a revelation and completely unsurprising. Elena sat back, her mind spinning both from her thoughts and the wine she'd drunk. For the first time, she accepted her fate…even if she had no idea what it would actually mean for her title, her crown, her country.

'I'm not going to marry him,' she blurted. 'Aziz. Not even…not even if he found me in time.'

Something flashed in Khalil's eyes and he sat back. 'What made you change your mind?'

'You did,' she said simply, and she knew she meant it in more ways than one. Not just because he was the rightful Sheikh, but because he'd opened up feelings inside her she hadn't known she'd possessed. She couldn't marry Aziz now, couldn't settle for the kind of cold, mercenary arrangement she'd once wanted.

'I'm glad,' Khalil said quietly. They gazed at each other for a long moment, and everything in Elena tensed, yearned...

Then Khalil rose from the table. 'It is late. You should return to your tent.'

He reached for her hand, and Elena let him pull her up. She felt fluid, boneless; the wine must have really gone to her head.

He kept hold of her hand as they stepped outside the tent, the night dark and endless around them. The air was surprisingly cold and crisp, which had a sobering effect on Elena.

By the time they'd crossed the camp to her tent, Khalil's hand still loosely linked with hers, she wasn't feeling tipsy at all, just embarrassed. The evening's emotional intimacies and revelations were enough now to make her cringe.

'Goodnight, Elena.' Khalil stopped in front of her tent, sliding his hand from hers. He touched her chin with his fingers, tipped her head up so she was blinking at him, the night sky spangled with stars high above him.

For a moment as she looked up at him, just as when they'd been in his tent, she thought he might kiss her. Her lips parted and her head spun and her heart started thudding in a mix of alarm, anticipation and a suspended sense of wonder.

Khalil lowered his head, his mouth a whisper away from hers. 'Elena,' he murmured; it sounded like a question. Everything in Elena answered, *yes*.

She reached up to put her hands on his shoulders; her body pressed against his, the feel of his hard chest sending little shocks of sensation through her.

His hands slid up to frame her face, his fingers so gentle on her skin. She felt his desire as well as her own, felt his yearning and surprise, and thought, *We are alike in this too. We both want this, but we're also afraid to want it.*

Although perhaps Khalil didn't want it, after all, for he suddenly dropped his hands from her and stepped back. 'Goodnight,' he said again, and then he started walking back to his tent and was soon swallowed up by the darkness.

CHAPTER SIX

ELENA DIDN'T SEE Khalil at all the next day. She spent hours lying on her bed or sitting outside her tent, watching the men go about the camp and looking for Khalil.

She missed him. She told herself that was absurd, because she barely knew him. She'd only met him two days ago, and hardly in the best of circumstances.

Yet she still found herself reliving the times he'd touched her: the slide of his fingers on her jaw; the press of his chest against her cheek. She replayed their dinner conversation in her mind, thought about his lonely childhood, his determination to be Sheikh. And realised in just three days he would let her go and she would never see him again.

A thought that made a twist of bewildering longing spiral inside her.

Then the next morning Khalil came to her tent. He loomed large in the space and shamelessly she let her gaze rove over him, taking in his broad shoulders, his dark hair, his impossibly hard jaw.

'I need to go visit some of the desert tribes,' he told her without preamble. 'And I'd like you to go with me.'

Shock as well as a wary pleasure rippled through her in a double wave. 'You...would?'

He arched an eyebrow and gave her a small smile. 'Wouldn't you like to see something other than the inside of this tent?'

'Yes, but...why do you want me to go?' A terrible suspicion took hold of her. 'You aren't…you aren't going to show me off as some trophy of war, are you? Show your people how you captured Aziz's bride?' Just the idea made her stomach churn. Why *shouldn't* he do such a thing? He'd captured her, after all. She was his possession, his prize.

Khalil's face darkened, his eyebrows drawing together in a fierce frown. 'No, of course not. In any case, the people I'm visiting wouldn't be impressed by such antics.'

'Wouldn't they?'

'They are loyal to me. And I would never act in such a barbaric fashion.'

'Then why are you taking me?'

Khalil stared at Elena, the question reverberating through him. *Then why are you taking me?*

The simple answer was because he wanted to. Because he'd been thinking about her since they'd had dinner together, since she'd shown how she believed him. Believed *in* him. And having someone's trust, even if it was just a little of it, was as heady and addictive as a drug. He wanted more. He wanted more of Elena and he wanted more of the person he felt he was in her eyes. The man he wanted to be.

The realisation had kept him from her for an entire day, fighting it, fighting the need and the desire, the danger and the weakness of wanting another person. Of opening himself to pain, loss and grief.

By last night he'd convinced himself that taking her to see the desert tribes who supported him was a political move; it would strengthen his position to have Aziz's former bride on his side.

Gazing at her now, her hair tumbled over her shoulders, her heavy-lidded eyes with their perceptive grey-gold gaze trained on him, he knew he'd been fooling himself.

This wasn't some political manoeuvre. This was simply him wanting to be with Elena.

'I'm taking you,' he said, choosing his words slowly,

carefully, 'because I want you to meet the people who support me.'

Her eyes widened. Her lips parted and then curved in a tremulous smile. 'You do?'

Khalil's hands curled into fists. Everything in him resisted this admission, this appalling weakness. Where was his ruthless determination now? All he wanted in this moment was to see Elena's smile deepen. 'I do.'

'All right,' she said, and Khalil felt relief and even joy pour through him. He smiled, a wider smile than he'd ever felt on his face before, and she grinned back.

Something had changed. Something was changing right here between them and, God help him, but he couldn't stop it. He didn't even want to.

'We should leave within the hour. Can you ride?'

'Yes.'

'Then dress for riding. Leila will find you the appropriate clothes.' With a nod, he started to leave, then turned back to face her. 'Thank you, Elena,' he said quietly, meaning it utterly, and the smile she offered him felt like a precious gift.

An hour later Elena met him on the edge of the camp, where he was saddling the horses they would take. Khalil nodded his approval of her sensible clothing, headscarf and boots, a familiar tightness in his chest easing just at the sight of her.

'We should waste no time in departing. It is half a day's ride and I intend for us to arrive before nightfall.'

She glanced, clearly surprised, at the two horses. 'We're going alone?'

'Three men will accompany us, but they will ride separately. We will meet up with the guards before we enter the camp, so all will be appropriate.'

'Appropriate?'

'In the desert, a man and woman generally do not ride alone.'

She nodded slowly, accepting, her gaze darting between the horses and him.

Khalil acknowledged he was breaching protocol in so many ways. 'You'll be safe with me, Elena,' he said and she looked back at him.

'I know that.'

'Do you?' He felt a smile spread across his face. 'Good.'

'I trust you,' she said simply, and for a moment he couldn't speak. He'd kidnapped her, after all. He didn't deserve her trust, yet she gave it. Freely. Wholly.

'Thank you,' he finally said.

She stepped closer to him, so he caught the scent of roses. 'Are we travelling alone because it's safer? I mean, so Aziz won't find us?'

She spoke without any rancour, yet Khalil felt that churning guilt once more, and more acutely this time, because for the first time something felt stronger than his burning need to be Sheikh.

He refused to name just what it was.

'Yes,' he answered. 'Does that...distress you?'

Her clear gaze searched his and she smiled wryly. 'Not as much as it should.'

He acknowledged her point with a small nod. 'Things are changing.'

'They've already changed,' she said quietly, and something in him both swelled and ached.

He shouldn't want things to change. Change meant losing his focus, losing his whole sense of self. What was he, if not the future Sheikh of Kadar? Everything in his life had been for that purpose. He'd had no room for other ideas or ambitions, and certainly none for relationships.

Yet he knew Elena was right. Things had already changed...whether he'd wanted them to or not.

'Let's go,' he said, a bit more gruffly than he intended, and he laced his fingers together to offer Elena a foothold.

She rode just like she walked or stood, with inherent

elegance and pride. Her back was ramrod straight as she controlled the excited prancing of her horse.

'How well can you ride?' he asked and her eyes sparkled at him.

'Well.'

Khalil's mouth curved. 'Let's see about that,' he said, and with a shout he took off at a gallop. He heard Elena's surprised laughter echo behind him as she gave chase.

Elena felt the kind of thrill of exhilaration she hadn't experienced since she'd been a child riding in Thallia as she followed Khalil. It felt wonderful to be on a horse again, the desert flashing by in a blur of rocks and sand. She had had no time for such pursuits since she'd been queen. She hadn't ridden like this in years.

The only sound was her horse's hooves galloping across the sand. She spurred the beast on, eager to catch up with Khalil—or even pass him. Although he hadn't said, she knew it had become a race.

Glancing behind him, Khalil pointed to a towering, needle-like boulder in the distance that Elena knew must be the finish line. She nodded back and crouched low over the horse as the wind whistled past. She was only a length behind him, and in the last dash to the finish line she made up half a length, but Khalil's horse still crossed a beat before hers.

Laughing, she reined the animal in and patted his sweat-soaked neck. 'That was close.'

'Very close,' Khalil agreed. His teeth gleamed white in his bronzed face. He wore a turban to keep out the sun and sand, and somehow it made him look more masculine. More desirable. 'Foolish, perhaps, to race,' he continued. 'There is a small oasis here. We'll let the horses drink before we continue.'

'A small oasis? I'd thought the next one was a day's ride by camel.'

Khalil just shrugged and Elena let out a huff of indignation. 'So you lied to me?'

'I wanted to discourage you from doing something foolish, something that most certainly wouldn't end well.'

'I could have escaped now,' Elena pointed out. 'I was on a horse, with water and food in my saddlebags.'

Khalil gazed at her evenly. 'I know. But you didn't.'

'No.' She hadn't even thought of it, hadn't been remotely tempted. The knowledge should have shamed her, but instead she felt almost ebullient.

They led the horses to the oasis, and as the animals drank Khalil gazed at the horizon with a frown.

'What's wrong?' Elena asked.

'It looks like a storm might rise.'

'A storm?' She gazed up at the endless blue sky, hard and bright, in incredulity. 'How on earth can you tell?'

'Look there.' Khalil pointed to the horizon and Elena squinted. She could see a faint grey smudge, but that was all. If Khalil hadn't pointed it out, she wouldn't have noticed it.

'Surely that's far away.'

'It is now. Storms in the desert can travel all too quickly. We should ride. I want to get to the camp before the storm gets to us. We'll need to meet up with the guards as well.'

They saddled up once more and headed off at a brisk canter. The sun was hot above, the sand shimmering in the midday heat. Elena kept her gaze on the horizon, noticing with each passing hour that the faint smudge was becoming darker and wider. The stiff breeze she'd felt at camp had turned into a relentless wind.

After several hours of tense riding, Khalil guided them to a grouping of boulders. 'We will not be able to outride the storm,' he said. 'We'll have to shelter here for the night and try to meet up with my men in the morning.'

Elena slid off her horse, glancing at the forbidding-looking rocks with some apprehension. 'Where are we, exactly?'

Khalil gave her the glimmer of a smile. 'In the middle of the desert.'

'Yes…' Standing there next to her horse, the desert endless around her, the sky darkening rapidly and the wind kicking up sand, she suddenly felt acutely how strange this all was. How little she knew Khalil, even if her heart protested otherwise.

'Elena.' Khalil stood in front of her and she blinked up at him, nearly swaying on her feet. 'I will keep you safe.'

She believed him, Elena knew. She trusted him, even if it was foolish. When had any other person been concerned for her safety? Paulo had said he had, but he'd been lying. Her father had, but only for the sake of his country, and he'd paid with his life.

Looking up at Khalil, Elena was struck as forcefully as a fist with the knowledge that he would keep her safe because he cared for her as a person, not as a pawn, or even as a queen. Simply because of who she was—and who he was. The knowledge nearly brought tears to her eyes.

'You look as if you are going to collapse,' he said gently. 'Come. I have food and drink.' He took her by the hand, his warm, callused palm comforting as it closed around her own far smaller one, and led her towards the group of immense black boulders.

He was clearly familiar with the territory, for he led her with confidence through the maze of rocks, coming to a stop in front of a large, flat rock sheltered by a huge boulder above it.

He drew her underneath it and she sat down with her back against the boulder, the overhanging rock providing shelter from the rising wind and swirling sand. He removed his turban so she pulled off her headscarf and ran a hand over her dishevelled hair.

'Drink,' he said and handed her a canteen of water.

She unscrewed the top of the canteen and took a much-needed and grateful sip of water.

'And there's food,' Khalil said, handing her a piece of flat bread and some dried meat. She ate both, as did he, both of them silently chewing as the wind picked up and howled around them.

After she'd finished eating Elena drew her knees up to her chest and watched Khalil put the remnants of their meal back in the saddlebags.

He was a beautiful man, she thought, not for the first time; his sculpted mouth and long lashes softened a face of utterly unyielding hardness. As he tidied up she saw several whitened scars on the inside of his wrist and she leaned forward.

'How did you get those?'

Khalil tensed, his mouth thinning. 'Rope burns,' he said shortly, and Elena stared at him in confusion.

'Rope?'

'It was a long time ago.' He turned away, clearly not wanting to say anything further, although Elena wanted to ask. She wanted to know. Rope burns on his wrists… Had he been *tied up*?

She sat back against the rock and watched as he settled himself opposite her. 'Now what?' she asked.

His smile gleamed in the oncoming darkness. 'Well, I'm afraid I didn't bring a chessboard.'

She gave a little laugh. 'Pity. I'm actually quite good at chess.'

'So am I.'

'Is that a challenge?'

His gaze flicked over her. 'Maybe.'

Excitement fizzed through her. Were they actually flirting? About *chess*? 'Perhaps we'll have a match some time,' she said, and realised belatedly how that made it sound— as if they would have some kind of future beyond her time here. Even though she'd accepted she wouldn't marry Aziz, it didn't mean she had any kind of future with Khalil. She'd be deluding herself to think otherwise.

In two days he was going to let her go.

Why did that make her feel so...*bereft*?

'What are you thinking about?' Khalil asked quietly and she turned back to him, wondering if she dared to admit the truth.

'That in two days I might never see you again.' She took a breath, held it, and forced herself to continue. 'I don't like that thought, Khalil.'

She couldn't make out his expression in the darkness. 'Elena,' he said, and it sounded like a warning.

'I know this is going to sound ridiculous,' she continued, *needing* to be honest now, 'but you're the first real friend I've ever had.'

She tensed, waiting for incredulity, perhaps his discomfort or even derision. Instead he looked away and said quietly, 'That's not ridiculous. In many ways, you're the first friend I've had too.'

Her breath caught in her chest. 'Really?'

He turned back to her, the glimmer of a smile just visible in the moonlight. 'Really.'

'Not even at school? In America?'

She felt him tense but then he shook his head. 'Not even then. What about you? No school friends?'

'Not really.' She hugged her knees to her chest, remembering those lonely years in convent school. 'I was terribly shy in school, coming to it so late. And, looking back, I think the fact that I was a princess intimidated the other girls, although at the time I was the one who was intimidated. Everyone else made it look so easy. Having friends, having a laugh. I envied them all. I wanted to be like they were, but I didn't know how. And then later, after school...' She thought for one blinding moment of Paulo and her throat tightened. 'Sometimes it just doesn't seem worth the risk.'

'The risk?'

She swallowed and met his gaze unflinchingly. It was amazing how easy, how *necessary,* honesty felt sometimes. 'Of getting hurt.'

Khalil didn't speak for a long moment. Okay, so honesty wasn't so easy, Elena thought as she shifted where she sat. She had no idea what he felt about what she'd said.

'Have you been hurt, Elena?' he finally asked, and in the darkness his voice seemed like a separate entity, as soft as velvet, caressing the syllables of her name.

'Hasn't everyone, at one time or another?'

'That's not really an answer.'

'Have *you* been hurt, Khalil?'

'That's not an answer either, but yes, I have.' He spoke evenly, but she still felt the ocean of pain underneath. 'My father hurt me when he chose to disown and banish me.'

'Oh, Khalil.' She bit her lip, remorse rushing through her. 'I'm sorry. That was a thoughtless question for me to ask.'

'Not at all. But I want you to answer my question. What were you talking about when you said friendship wasn't worth the risk?'

'I had a friend once,' Elena said slowly. 'And he let me down rather badly. He—betrayed me.' She shook her head. 'That sounds melodramatic, but that's what happened.'

'He,' Khalil said neutrally, and with a dart of surprise she wondered if he was actually jealous.

'Yes, he. But it wasn't romantic, not remotely.' She sighed. 'It was stupid, really. I was stupid to trust him.'

'So this man is why you don't trust people?'

'I've learned my lesson. But I trust you, Khalil.'

She heard his breath come out in a rush. 'Maybe you shouldn't.'

'Why do you say that?'

'Do I need to remind you why you're here in the first place, Elena? I *kidnapped* you.'

She heard genuine remorse in his voice and she reached out and touched his hand, her fingers skimming across his skin. 'I know you did, Khalil, but I also understand why you did it.'

'You're justifying my actions to me?' he asked with a wry laugh, and Elena managed a laugh back.

'I don't know what I'm doing,' she answered honestly. 'And I don't know what I'd do if you let me go right now. I don't know how I'd feel.'

She held her breath, waiting for his reply, needing him to say something—but what?

'I don't know how I'd feel either,' Khalil answered in a low voice, and that was enough. That was more than enough.

Whatever was happening between them, Khalil recognised it as well. Just as he'd said before, *things were changing.*

Things had changed.

'The temperature is dropping,' Khalil said after a moment. 'Here.' He handed her a blanket and Elena wrapped it around herself. The wind howled; the night air was cold and crisp as she huddled against the rock, trying to make herself comfortable.

After a moment she heard Khalil sigh. 'Elena. Come here.'

'Come—where?'

'Here.' He patted his lap. 'You're obviously cold and I know of only one way to warm you right now.'

Her cheeks heated as she thought of other ways he could warm her. Ways she'd never even experienced before. 'But...'

'You've been on my lap before,' he reminded her.

Yes, and she'd enjoyed it far too much. Elena hesitated, torn between the fierce desire to be close to Khalil again and the ever-present need to keep herself safe. What could happen between them, after all? In two days she would return to Thallia, and without a husband. If she had any sense, she'd keep her distance from Khalil.

It seemed she didn't have any sense. She scooted across the rock, hesitating in front of him, not quite sure actually how to get on his lap.

Khalil had no such hesitation. Without ceremony or any awkwardness at all he slid his arms around her waist and hauled her onto him. Once there, she found it amazingly easy to curl into him just as she'd done before, her legs lying across his, her cheek pressed against his chest.

'Now that's better,' Khalil said, and his voice was a comforting rumble she could feel reverberate right through her. He stroked her hair, his fingers smoothing over the dark strands.

'Sleep,' he said, his voice a caress, and obediently she closed her eyes even though she knew she would be less likely to sleep warm and safe on Khalil's lap than when she'd been huddling by herself in the cold.

She was too aware of everything: the solid strength of his chest, the steady rise and fall of his breathing. The warmth of him, his arms snuggled safely around her, and even the scent of him, a woodsy aftershave mingled with the smell of horse and leather.

He continued to stroke her hair, pulling her gently into his chest so she snuggled in even more deeply, her lips barely brushing the warm, bare skin of his throat. Never had anything felt so familiar. So right.

She slept.

And woke in the clutches of a nightmare.

She hadn't had one of her old nightmares in a long time, mainly because she never slept deeply enough to have any dreams at all. Now lulled to sleep in the warmth and safety of Khalil's arms, it came for her.

Smoke. Screams. Blood. Bombs. In her dreams it was always the same: a chaos of terror, bodies strewn over the floor, shattered glass cutting into her palms. And the worst part of all: the heavy weight of her father on her back, his body shielding hers from the explosion, the last words he ever spoke whispered into her ear along with his last breath.

'For Thallia.'

'Elena. *Elena.*'

She came to consciousness with Khalil's hands on her shoulders, shaking her gently, and tears on her face. She drew a shuddering breath and felt panic clutch at her even though she was awake, for the darkness and the howling wind reminded her of that terrible night.

'It was just a dream, Elena.' She felt Khalil's hands slide up to cup her face, his forehead pressing into hers as if he could imbue her with his warmth, his certainty. 'Whatever it was, it was just a dream.'

She closed her eyes, willing her heart rate to slow, the terrible images that flashed through her mind in brutal replay to fade. 'I know,' she whispered after a long moment. 'I know.'

The touch of his palm cradling her cheek felt achingly, painfully sweet. 'What do you dream of, Elena?' he whispered and her throat went tight, too tight to speak. He ran his thumb lightly over her lips. 'What haunts you so?'

'Memories,' she managed, her voice choked, suffocated. She reached up to wipe the remnants of tears from her face. 'Memories of when my parents died.'

Khalil's hands stilled on her face. 'You were there?'

'Yes.'

'Why didn't I know that?'

'It was kept out of the press, out of respect for my family. That's what I wanted. It was hard enough, dealing with what had happened, without everyone gawking at me.'

'Yes.' Khalil slid his arms around her and pulled her closer to him. 'I can imagine it was. Do you want to talk about it?'

Amazingly, she did. Normally she never talked about her parents' deaths to anyone. She didn't even like remem-

bering it. But, safe in Khalil's arms, she felt the need to tell
him her story. Share her pain.

'You know they died in the bombing,' Elena began
slowly. 'And as far as I know, my mother died instantly.
But my father—my father and I were alive after the bomb
went off.'

Khalil didn't say anything, just held her close. After a
moment Elena continued. 'I can't remember much after
the first bomb went off. I was thrown across the room and
I landed on my back. I must have been unconscious for a
little while, because I remember waking up, feeling completely disorientated. And everything...' She drew a shuddering breath. 'Everything was madness. People screaming
and crying. So much blood...' She shook her head, closing her eyes as she pressed her face into the solid warmth
of Khalil's chest.

'I crawled across the floor, looking for my parents.
There was broken glass everywhere but I didn't even feel
it, although later I saw my hands were covered in blood. It
was so strange, so surreal... I felt numb and yet utterly terrified. And then I found my mother...' She stopped then,
because she never let herself think about that moment even
though sometimes she felt as if it never left her thoughts:
her mother's lifeless face, her mouth opened in a soundless scream, her staring eyes.

She'd turned from her mother's body and had seen her
father stumbling towards her, terror etched on every fea-
ture.

'There was a second bomb,' she told Khalil, her voice
muffled against his chest. 'My father knew somehow.
Maybe he guessed, or saw something. But he ran towards
me and threw his body over me as it went off. The last thing
he said...' Another deep, shuddering breath. '"For Thallia",' she quoted softly. 'He said "For Thallia" because he
was saving my life for our country, so I could be queen.'

Khalil was silent for a long moment, his arms snugged

around her. 'And you think that was the only reason he was saving your life,' he surmised quietly. 'For the monarchy, not for you. Not because you were his daughter. Because he loved you.'

His words, so softly and surely spoken, cut her to the heart, because she knew they were true and she was amazed that Khalil had been able to see that. Understand it.

'I never knew what they felt,' she whispered. 'I hardly ever saw them, all through my childhood. They were devoted to Thallia, but they never spent time with me.' She let out a shuddering breath. 'And then they were gone in a single moment, and I didn't know if I missed them because they were dead or because I never actually knew them in the first place.' She closed her eyes. 'Is that awful?'

'No, it's understandable.'

'But it seems so ungrateful. My father gave his life for me.'

'You've a right to your feelings, Elena. They loved you, but how were you to know it if they didn't show it until they'd died?'

She pressed her face even harder against his chest, willing the tears that threatened to recede. She wasn't even sure what she was crying for. Her parents' deaths? The lack of relationship she'd had while they'd been alive? Or simply the swamping sense of loss she felt, as if she'd experienced it for ever?

Until Khalil.

She twisted to look up at him. 'I've never told anyone all that.'

'I'm glad you told me.'

'I'm glad I did too.' She hesitated, because she felt a need to reassure him and, perhaps herself, that she knew this wasn't real—that whatever intimacy had sprung between them was separate from what was going on in their lives. It didn't really count.

Yet she said nothing, because it *felt* like it counted. It

felt like the only thing that counted. Khalil had given her something, or maybe he'd just showed her she already had it: a capacity to share, to trust. To love.

She looked up at him, searching his face, wanting to know what he was feeling, if he felt the same pull of attraction and empathy that she did. But then she met his gaze and saw the fire burning there and her breath caught in her chest as desire, raw, fierce and overwhelming, crashed over her.

His face was so close to hers she could feel his breath fanning against her cheek, see the dark glint of stubble on his chin. His lips were no more than a whisper away from hers and, as she stared up at him and heard his breath hitch, she knew without a doubt she wanted to close that small distance between their mouths.

She wanted him to kiss her.

His head dipped and her heart seemed to stop and then soar. His lips were so close now that if she moved at all they would be touching his. They would be kissing.

Yet she didn't move, transfixed as she was by both wonder and fear, and Khalil didn't move either.

The moment stretched between them, suspended, endless.

His breath came out in a shudder and his hands tightened around her face. She tried to say something but words eluded her; all she could do was feel. Want.

Then with another shuddering breath he closed that small space between their mouths and his lips touched hers in her first and most wonderful kiss.

She let out a tiny sigh both of satisfaction and surrender, her hands coming up to tangle in the surprising softness of his hair. Her lips parted and Khalil deepened the kiss, pulling her closer as his tongue delved into her mouth, and everything in Elena throbbed powerfully to life.

She'd never known you could feel like this, want like this. It was so intense and sweet it almost felt painful. She

pressed against him, acting on an instinct she hadn't realised she possessed. Khalil slid his hand from her face to
cup her breast, and a shocked gasp escaped her mouth as
exquisite sensation darted through her.

Khalil withdrew, dropping his hand and easing back
from her so she felt a rush of loss. He reached up to cover
her hands with his own and draw them down to her own
lap.

'I shouldn't have...' he began then shook his head. Even
in the moonlit darkness she could see the regret and remorse etched on his harsh features.

'I wanted you to,' she blurted and he just shook his
head again.

'You should sleep again, if you can,' he said quietly and
Elena bit her lip, blinking hard. She wondered, with a rush
of humiliation, if she'd actually been the one to kiss him.
In that moment it had been hard to tell, and she'd wanted
it so much...

Had she actually thrown herself at him?

'Sleep, Elena,' he said softly, and he repositioned her on
his lap so her head was once again pillowed by his chest.
He stroked her hair just as he had before and Elena closed
her eyes, even though sleep seemed farther away than ever.

What had just happened? And how could she feel so
unbearably, overwhelmingly disappointed?

CHAPTER SEVEN

DAWN BROKE OVER the dunes, turning the sand pink with pale sunlight. The storm had died down and the desert had reshaped itself into a new landscape of drifts and dunes. Leaving Elena sleeping in their rocky shelter, Khalil went to check on the horses and get his bearings.

And also to figure out just what he was going to say to her when she awoke.

That kiss had been completely unplanned. Incredibly sweet. And it had left Khalil in an extremely uncomfortable state of arousal for the rest of the night.

He hadn't been able to sleep with Elena on his lap, her hair brushing his cheek, her soft body relaxed and pliant against his. His whole body, his whole *self*, had been in a state of unbearable awareness, exquisite agony.

Sleep had been the farthest thing from his mind.

But now, in the cold light of day, reality returned with an almighty thud. He could not act on his attraction to Elena. He could not nurture any softer feelings for her. He had a goal, a plan, and neither included the Queen of Thallia beyond keeping her captive and then letting her go.

Except, somehow he had forgotten that when he'd held her in his lap. When he'd shared dinner with her in his tent, and invited her to accompany him to visit the desert tribes. When he'd encouraged her to share about her life, and had told her a little bit about his. When he'd let her into his mind and even his heart. *When he'd kissed her.*

He'd told her things had changed, and he felt the change in himself. He was losing sight of his priorities and chasing rainbows instead. How could he be such a fool? How could he let his focus slip, even for a second?

It was time to get back on track, Khalil knew. To forget the fanciful feelings he'd been harbouring for Elena. What an idiot he was, to feel something soft even for a moment! To trust her. Care for her. It would only end badly... in so many ways. He knew that from hard experience. He wasn't about to repeat the mistake of trusting someone, loving someone.

Not that he loved her, Khalil told himself quickly. He barely knew her. Things had become intense between them because they were in an intense situation, that was all.

He let out a long, low breath and headed for the horses. The animals had weathered last night's storm well enough and were happy for Khalil to feed and water them. He'd just finished and was turning back to check on Elena when he saw her standing between the towering black rocks, looking tired and pale, yet also tall and straight...and so very beautiful.

His gut tightened. His groin ached. And as he stood and stared at her he was reminded of her nightmare, of the vulnerability she'd shown and the secrets she'd shared. He thought of her witnessing the death of her parents, the utter horror of the terrorist attack, and a howl of need to protect her rose up inside him. In that moment last night he'd almost told her his own terrible memories. Laid bare his own secrets.

Almost.

Now he pushed the memories away and gave her a measured smile. 'Good morning. Are you rested?'

'A bit.' She took a step closer to him and he saw uncertainty in her eyes. Questions loomed there that he didn't want her to ask. Had no intention of answering, not even in the seething silence of his own mind.

'We can eat and then we should ride. The settlement we've been aiming for is only another hour or so from here, and I hope my men will be waiting for us there. We can explain to the tribe how we became separated in the storm.'

She nodded slowly, her gaze sweeping over him like a sorrowful searchlight. Khalil tried not to flinch under it; that guilt was coming back, along with a powerful desire to pull her into his arms and bury his face in her hair, to comfort her—and himself.

What a joke. He was the last person qualified to give or receive comfort. The last person to think of caring or being cared for. He half-regretted taking her on this god-forsaken trip; he wished he'd left her to stew in her tent. But only half, because even now, when he knew better and had told himself so, he was still glad to see her. Was glad she was here with him.

'Come,' he said, and beckoned her back towards their rocky shelter. They ate the remaining flat bread and dried meat in silence, and then Khalil saddled the horses while Elena watched.

A moment later they were riding across the desert, the sky hard and blue above them, the air dry, and becoming hotter by the minute.

He watched her out of the corner of his eye, admired her long, straight back, the proud tilt of her head. She would never be bowed, he thought with a surge of almost posses-sive admiration. She would never allow herself the possi-bility of defeat. Looking at her now reminded him of how it had felt to hold her: the soft press of her breasts against his chest; the way her hair had brushed his cheek; the smell of her, like rosewater and sunshine.

His horse veered suddenly to avoid a rock, startling Khalil, and he swore under his breath. Already he was losing his concentration again, forgetting his focus. All because of Elena.

Not that he could blame her for his own lack of control. No, he blamed himself, and this sudden need that opened up inside him like a great, yawning chasm of emptiness longing to be filled. He wasn't used to feeling such a thing; for thirty years he'd basically been on his own. The only person he'd let close in all that time was Dimah, and that relationship had had its own problems and pitfalls.

No, he wasn't used to this at all. And he didn't like it. At all.

Liar.

Two hours after starting off, they finally rode into a small Bedouin settlement on the edge of an oasis. There had been no sight of his men, and uneasily Khalil wondered how it would look to the Sheikh for him to ride in alone with Elena. He pushed the thought from his mind. There was nothing he could do about it now.

He'd been here once before on one of his tours of duty through the desert, getting to know the people he was meant to rule, rallying support. Much to his amazement, they had welcomed him.

Such a response still surprised him after all these years: that anyone could accept him. Want him.

Yet he still didn't trust it, because he knew all too well how the people you loved, the people you thought loved you back, could turn on you. Utterly.

Several men came up as he swung off the horse, offering their greetings and taking the horses away before leading Khalil to the Sheikh's tent. He glanced back at Elena who was looking pale but composed as several women hustled her off to another tent.

Deciding she could handle herself for the moment, Khalil went to greet the tribe's Sheikh and explain why he was here. It would be better, he knew, to leave Elena alone for a while.

For ever.

* * *

Several clucking women surrounded Elena and she was carried along with them to a tent, bemused by their interest, and more than a little hurt by the stony look she'd seen on Khalil's face as he'd turned away.

So he regretted their kiss last night. Clearly. And she should regret it too; of course she should. Kissing Khalil was a very bad idea. Caring about him was even worse.

The trouble was, she couldn't regret it. She ached with longing for another kiss—and more. For *him*.

She'd come to this desert tribe because she'd wanted to, because she wanted to see the people who cared about Khalil.

As she cared about him.

More, it seemed, than he wanted her to.

Once in the tent, the women fluttered around her like colourful, chattering birds, touching her hair, her cheek, the clothes she wore that were now grimed with dust and dirt. Elena didn't understand anything they said, and it appeared none of them spoke either English or Greek, the two languages in which she was fluent. They all seemed wonderfully friendly, though, and she let herself be carried along by the wave of their enthusiasm as they fetched her fresh clothing and led her down to the oasis where the women of the village bathed.

After a moment's hesitation at the water's edge, she took off her clothes as the other women were doing and immersed herself in the warm, silky water. After a night in the desert and hours of hard riding it felt wonderful to wash the dirt from her body, scrub the sand from her scalp. She enjoyed the camaraderie of the women too, watching as they chattered, laughed and splashed, utterly at ease with one another. She was gratified by their willingness to include her even though she was a stranger who didn't even speak their language.

After she had bathed she slipped on the unfamiliar garments the women gave her: a cotton chemise and then a loose, woven dress with wide sleeves embroidered with red and yellow. She left her hair down to dry in the sun and accompanied the women back up to the camp where a meal had been laid out.

She looked for Khalil, and tried to ignore the flicker of disappointment she felt when she could not find him.

In the camp the women ushered her into their circle and plied her with a delicious stew of lentils, flat bread and cardamom-flavoured coffee similar to what she had drunk with Khalil. As they ate and chatted, they mimed questions which Elena did her best to answer in a similar fashion.

Within an hour or two she felt herself start to fade, the exhaustion from the night spent outside and the endless hours on horseback making her eyelids begin to droop. The women noticed and, laughing, brought her to a make-shift bed piled high with woven blankets. Grateful for their concern, Elena lay down in it, and her last thought before sleep claimed her was of Khalil.

She woke the next morning to bright sunlight filtering through the flaps of the tent that was now empty save for herself. Today, she acknowledged with a heaviness she knew she shouldn't feel, was the last day of her imprisonment. Aziz's six weeks were up. He would have married someone else or forfeited his title. Either way, she wasn't needed, and Khalil could let her go.

A thought that mere days ago would have brought relief and even joy, not this sick plunging in her stomach. She didn't want to leave Khalil, and she didn't want to face her country and Council alone. How would she explain what had happened? She supposed she'd go with what Khalil had originally suggested: 'a necessary detainment'. Perhaps she would tell the Council she'd changed her mind about the marriage when she realised Aziz's claim to the throne wasn't legitimate.

She spared a second's thought then for the man she'd

intended to marry, a moment's regret. He'd been kind to
her. Looking back, she saw how his easy charm had hidden
a deeper part of himself, something dark, perhaps painful. What had his experience of Khalil's banishment, his
sudden arrival at the palace, felt like? How had it affected
him? She supposed she would never know.

Just as she would never truly know Khalil. She'd had
glimpses of a man who was both tender and strong, who
had the ruthless determination to kidnap a monarch but the
gentleness to cradle her and wipe away her tears. A man
she knew she now cared about, whom she might never see
again after today.

Sighing, Elena swung her legs onto the floor and combed
her hands through her tangled hair, wondering where everyone was and just what this day would bring.

When she was as presentable as she could make herself,
she stepped outside the tent, blinking in the bright sunlight.
People bustled around the camp, busy with various tasks
and chores; she could not see Khalil.

A woman from the night before approached her with
a smile and gestured for her to come forward. Elena followed her, stopping suddenly as she caught sight of
Khalil talking with a group of men. The woman followed
Elena's transfixed gaze and giggled, saying something
Elena didn't understand, but she had an uncomfortable
feeling she'd got the gist of.

This was confirmed a few moments later when Khalil
broke apart from the men to join her by a fire where she'd
been eating some bread and tahini for breakfast.

'Good morning.'

She nodded back her own greeting, her mouth full of
bread and her cheeks starting to heat. It was ridiculous, to
have this kind of reaction to him, but it was also undeniable. All she could picture was the look of both tenderness
and hunger on his face right before he'd kissed her. All she

could remember was how wonderful it had felt—and how much more she had wanted.

Still did.

'You slept well?'

She swallowed her mouthful of bread and nodded once more. 'Yes, I was exhausted.'

'Understandable.'

His expression was unreadable, his tawny eyes veiled, and Elena had a terrible feeling he was going to leave it at that. Something that had become almost easy between them now felt stilted and awkward. Which was, she acknowledged, perhaps as it should be, and yet...

She felt the loss.

'What happens now?' she asked, more just to keep the conversation going than any real desire to know, although she should *want* to know, considering this was her future. Her life. She forced herself to say the words that had been throbbing through her since she'd woken that morning. 'The six weeks are up.'

'I know.'

She gazed up at him, tried to read his expression, but he looked utterly impassive. 'Are you going to let me go?'

'I promised I would.'

She nodded jerkily, feeling bereft and unable to keep herself from it.

'We should stay here for another night, if you are amenable. There is a wedding in the tribe and a big celebration is planned this evening.' He hesitated, and it almost looked as if he were blushing. 'We are the guests of honour.'

'We are? I could understand why you might be, but—'

'The members of the tribe are under the impression that we are newly married,' he interjected in a low voice. 'I have not corrected it.'

'What?' Elena bolted upright, gaping at him before she could think to close her mouth. So that was why the woman had looked at Khalil and giggled. 'But why are they under that impression?' she asked, her voice coming out in something close to a squeak. 'And why haven't you corrected it?'

'They are under it because it is the only reason they know of why a man and woman would be travelling alone together. If the storm hadn't arisen, we would have entered the camp with my men—'

'But couldn't you have explained about the storm?'

'That would not have been a good enough reason. The desert tribes are traditional. I didn't explain because to do so would have brought disapproval and shame upon both of us.' His mouth and eyes both hardened. 'Something I should have considered more carefully. I acted foolishly in asking you to accompany me.'

Elena blinked, trying to hide the hurt his recrimination made her feel. He regretted her company, along with that kiss. She drew a breath, forced herself to think about the practicalities. 'And what happens when they discover we're not married?'

'Ideally, they won't. At least, not while we're here.'

'Eventually, though…'

'Eventually, yes. But by that time I will be installed as Sheikh and I will be able to make any apologies or explanations that are necessary. To do so right now would invite even more instability.' He sighed, shifting his weight restlessly. 'I admit, I don't like lying, not even by silence—but this is a critical time, not just for myself, but for Kadar. The less unrest there is, the better.'

'So I am meant to pretend to be your wife?' Elena asked, her voice a hushed and disbelieving whisper.

Khalil's gaze seemed to burn into hers. 'Only for one day and night. Will that be so hard, Elena?'

She felt her body flood with warmth, her face flush. No, it wouldn't be hard at all—that was the problem. She looked away, willing her blush to recede. 'I don't like lying,' she muttered.

'Nor do I. But there is no choice. Although I would have

hoped that such a pretence would not be quite so abhorrent
to you.' His eyes glowed with both knowledge and memory, reminding her of their kiss. It felt as if he were taunt-
ing her that he knew she wanted him, that such a fantasy
would not be unpleasant at all but far, far too desirable.

Elena broke their locked gaze first, looking away from
all the knowledge in Khalil's eyes. 'And after tonight?' she
asked when she trusted her voice to sound as level as his
had been. 'Then you'll let me go?'

'Yes. I'll take you to Siyad myself. Now that Aziz will
be forced to call a referendum, there is no need for me to
remain in the desert.'

She swallowed, her mind spinning with all this new information. 'What will happen to Aziz?'

Khalil shrugged. 'He will return to Europe, I imagine.
He has a house in Paris. He can live the playboy life he
so enjoys.'

'That's not fair,' Elena protested. 'He might be a playboy,
but he has his own business, and he's done a lot of good—'

Khalil flung up a hand. 'Please. Do not defend Aziz to
me.' She fell silent and he gazed at her, his mouth thinning. 'Are you so disappointed,' he asked after a moment,
'not to marry Aziz?'

'Only because of what it means for my country. My
rule.'

'You are a strong woman, Elena. I think you could stand
up to your Council without a husband propping you up.'

She let out a short laugh, not knowing whether to feel
offended or flattered. 'Thank you for that vote of confidence, I suppose.'

'I didn't mean it as a criticism. You've shown me with
your actions how strong and courageous you are. I think
you could face your Council on your own, convince this
Markos not to depose you. The vote has to be unanimous,
doesn't it?'

'Yes.' She eyed him shrewdly even as she fought a lonely

sweep of desolation. 'Are you trying to make me feel better, or ease your own guilt at having wrecked my marriage plans?'

He looked surprised by the question, or perhaps his own answer. 'Both, I suppose. Although a few days ago I wouldn't have given your plans a single thought.' He shook his head wonderingly, and then his expression hardened once more and he rose from her side. 'I will be busy meeting with various leaders of the local tribes today, but I will see you at the wedding festivities tonight.'

She nodded, still smarting from their conversation, and all Khalil hadn't said. That he didn't feel.

She spent the rest of the day with the women, preparing for the wedding that evening. She helped make bread and stew meat, then when the food was finished and the sun was high in the sky the women headed back down to the oasis to prepare themselves for the festivities.

The bride was a lovely young girl with thick, dark hair, liquid eyes and a nervous smile. Elena watched as the women prepared her for her wedding: a dress of bright blue with rich embroidery on the sleeves and hem, hennaed hands and feet and a veil made of dozens of small copper coins.

What would her own wedding have looked like? she wondered as she watched the women laugh and joke with the young bride. A solemn, private ceremony in one of the reception rooms of the Kadaran palace, no doubt, witnessed by a few of Aziz's staff. Nothing fancy, nothing joyful or exciting.

And the wedding night? She shivered suddenly to think how she would have been giving her body to Aziz, a man she barely knew. Would she have felt for him even an ounce of the desire she felt for Khalil?

Inexorably her mind moved onto the man who always seemed to be in her thoughts. The man everyone here thought was her husband. Wouldn't it be wonderful, she thought suddenly, longingly, to pretend just for one day, for one night, that he was? That she was young and giddy with love, just as this pretty bride was?

What was the harm in that—in a single day of pretending?

Tomorrow she would return to reality. Soon she would be back in Thallia, facing a disapproving Council, forced to tell them her marriage plans had been cancelled. Perhaps facing the end of a monarchy that had lasted for nearly a thousand years—all because she hadn't been strong or smart enough to hold onto her crown.

Yes, one day of pretending sounded wonderful.

And so Elena let herself be carried along once more by the women; she didn't protest when they dressed her in a gown of silvery blue, lined her eyes with kohl, placed copper bangles on both arms and a veil of coins over her face. She understood they wanted to celebrate her recent marriage, just as the young bride was celebrating hers, and she didn't resist.

She wanted to celebrate it too.

The sky was deep indigo and studded with millions of stars when the ceremony began. The entire tribe had assembled and Elena watched, enchanted, as the ceremony played out amidst a riot of colour, music and dance. The women and men sat separately, and although she looked for him she could not find Khalil amidst the men gathered under a tent. She wondered if he would even recognise her in the Bedouin dress, headscarf and veil, wondered what he would think of her like this.

After the ceremony people circulated freely to enjoy food, music and dance. Several giggling women pushed Elena towards a group of men and then she saw him standing there, dressed in a traditional white cotton *thobe* richly embroidered with red and gold.

Khalil seemed to stare right through her and Elena knew

he didn't recognise her. Emboldened by the women who had pushed her forward, or perhaps simply by the desires of her own heart, she walked towards him.

'Greetings, husband,' she said softly. She'd meant to sound teasing but her voice came out earnest instead. Khalil glanced down at her, clearly startled, and then heat filled his eyes and his whole body tensed.

'Elena.'

'What do you think?' She twirled around and her dress flared out, the coins covering the lower part of her face jingling as she moved.

'I think you look lovely.' He placed a hand on her shoulder to stop her in mid-twirl, and drew her closer to him. 'Very lovely indeed. Sometimes something hidden is more alluring than something seen.'

Suddenly she was breathless, dazed by the look of undisguised admiration in his eyes. 'Do you really think so?' she whispered.

'Yes. And now I think the people of the tribe are expecting us to dance.'

'Dance?'

'I know the steps. Follow my lead.' And with one hand on her waist, the other clasped with hers, he led her to the circle of dancers.

The next hour passed in a blur of music and dance, every second one of heightened, almost painful awareness. Khalil's hand in hers, his body next to hers, his gaze fastened to hers, everything in her pulsing with longing. She'd never felt so beautiful or desirable, so heady with a kind of power she'd never, ever experienced before.

When she moved, Khalil's gaze followed her. When she spoke, he leaned forward to listen. She felt as if she were, at this moment, the centre of his universe. And it was the most wonderful feeling in the world.

She never wanted it to end.

But of course it did; the bridal couple was seen off and

people began to trail back to their dwellings. Elena turned to Khalil, uncertainty and hope warring within her. He gazed down at her, his expression inscrutable.

'They have arranged for us to share a tent tonight. I hope you don't mind.'

Mind? No, she didn't mind at all. 'That's...that's all right,' she managed.

Smiling faintly, Khalil threaded his fingers through hers and drew her away from the others...towards the tent they would share.

CHAPTER EIGHT

KHALIL KNEW HE was a little drunk. He hadn't had any alcohol to drink; none had been served. Yet he still felt dazed, almost drugged with possibility. With something deeper and stronger than mere lust, even if part of him wanted to give it that name, make it that simple.

He held the tent flap open for Elena and watched as she moved past him, her Bedouin clothing emphasising the sinuous swing of her hips, her graceful gait. Once in the tent she turned to him and he saw the expectation in her eyes, felt it in himself.

Tonight, to all intents and purposes, they were married. Husband and wife.

'Did you have a good time this evening?' he asked and she nodded.

'Yes… I don't know when I've had a better time, actually.' She let out a little laugh, sounding self-conscious, uncertain. 'I haven't gone to many parties before.'

'Not gone to parties? Not even royal or state functions?'

She shook her head, her grey eyes heartbreakingly wide above her veil. 'I've gone to those, but they weren't…they weren't fun. I could never just be myself. I was always Queen Elena and sometimes it felt like an act.'

'A danger of wearing the crown so young, I suppose. But you should be proud of yourself, Elena, and all you have accomplished.'

He took a step towards her, the need to touch her growing with every moment they spent together. His palms itched and he had to keep himself from reaching for her. 'And were you yourself tonight, Elena? Looking as you do, like a Bedouin girl?'

'Strangely, yes.' She let out another laugh, this one breathy. 'I felt more free tonight than I have in a long time.'

'Free—and yet captive.' He didn't know why he felt the need to remind her of the truth of their situation just then, only that he did. Perhaps he was trying to remind himself to hold onto reality when all he really wanted was to slip the veil from her face and the dress from her body.

'I don't feel like a captive any more, Khalil. I want to be here with you. You might have brought me here, but I'm choosing this now.'

He saw a bold purpose in her eyes now. The innocent, it seemed, had become a seductress. A siren. She walked towards him, lowering the veil of coins away from her face, and placed her hands on his chest. He gazed down at her long, slender fingers, felt them tremble against him. 'Tonight I want to forget everything, Khalil. Everything but you.'

Desire pulsed through him, blurred his brain along with his vision. 'Elena—'

'*Please.*'

He covered her hands with his own; he'd meant to remove them but as soon as he touched her he knew he wouldn't. He knew he needed at least this much, because there wouldn't be much more.

There couldn't be.

'Elena,' he said again, and she shook her head, her hair escaping from underneath her veil, tumbling about her shoulders as dark as a desert night.

'Don't, Khalil,' she whispered. 'Don't say no to me now.'

'Do you even know what you're asking?' he demanded, his voice low, raw and ragged with a desire he couldn't deny.

'Yes, I do.' She met his gaze. 'I'm asking you to make love to me. With me.'

Khalil's breath escaped in a hiss. 'Yes, but you don't know what that means.'

Her eyes flashed sudden fire. 'Don't tell me what I know or don't know, Khalil. I'm perfectly aware of what it means. What I'm asking.'

He arched an eyebrow. 'Are you sure about that, Elena? Because, if I'm not very much mistaken, I believe you're a virgin.'

She flushed but didn't lower her challenging gaze. 'Practical experience isn't required to make an informed choice.'

He almost laughed then, both amused by and admiring of her boldness and courage. His hands tightened on hers as he considered the possibility.

One night... One wonderful, amazing, incredible night...

'It's dangerous,' he began, and she shook her head.

'I know there are ways to prevent a pregnancy, if you don't have any protection.'

Her cheeks had turned fiery and he almost laughed. 'Oh, you do? As it happens, I have protection.'

Surprise made her jaw drop. 'You do?'

'Not,' he continued swiftly, 'because I intended to use it.'

She eyed him sceptically. 'Really?'

'I just like to be prepared.'

She looked uncertain then, even vulnerable. 'Have you had many lovers, then?'

'Not as many as you're thinking, and none in the last year. I've been too busy with other things.' *And none like you.* Untouched. Innocent. Amazing. He couldn't believe he was seriously thinking about taking Elena up on her offer. About making love to her.

'When I said it was dangerous, Elena, I didn't mean an unplanned pregnancy. I was talking about the...the emotional risks.'

She flinched and then recovered her composure. 'I'm aware of the risk, Khalil,' she told him. 'And I'm not under the illusion that this would be anything but one night. I'm not asking for more from you.'

'I know that.'

'Then what's the problem?' He just shook his head, both torn and tempted. Her smile turned flirtatious, even sultry. 'I suppose I'll just have to seduce you.'

Surprise flared deep inside him, along with an almost unbearable arousal. 'I don't think that's a good idea,' he managed. He knew she wouldn't have to do much and he would cave completely. He would take her in his arms and lose himself in her kiss, in her body.

He took a defensive step backwards and Elena's mouth curved in the kind of wicked little smile he hadn't known she was capable of.

'Scared, Khalil?'

'Tempted, Elena. And I'd rather not be.'

'Are you sure about that?' Slowly she lifted her arms, the wide sleeves of her dress falling back to reveal her slender wrists, and began to unwind her headscarf. Her kohl-lined eyes were wide and dark as she slowly unwrapped the garment, and Khalil simply watched, entranced by the utterly feminine and sensual act of undressing.

He heard his breath come out in something close to a pant as she dropped the headscarf and then shrugged out of her dress.

Underneath she wore only a thin chemise of bleached cotton, the material nearly transparent. He could see the temptingly round fullness of her breasts, the shadow between her thighs. He stifled a groan.

She moved closer, her eyes full of an ancient feminine power. She knew how she affected him and it made her bold.

It made her irresistible.

Her hands slid up his chest and he knew she could feel

how his heart was racing. His mind had stalled at the sight of her and it now kicked desperately into gear.

'I really don't think this is a good idea, Elena.'

'Too bad, then, that I do.' She stood on her tiptoes and brushed a butterfly kiss across his mouth. 'That's only the second kiss I've ever had,' she whispered against his lips. 'The first was two nights ago, when you held me on your lap.'

He closed his eyes. He was the only man who had ever kissed her? Didn't she realise how much she was giving him, offering him freely? Didn't she know how hurt she might be afterwards? No matter what she said or promised now, she was young. Inexperienced. Innocent.

He forced his eyes open, wrapped his hands around hers and attempted to draw them away from him. 'I don't want to hurt you, Elena.'

'You won't.'

'You don't know that. You *can't* know that, because you've never done this before.'

'And when am I going to get a chance to do it, Khalil?' she asked, her honest gaze clashing with his. 'I was going to give myself to a man I barely knew for the sake of my country. That possibility has been taken away from me now. You've taken it away from me, and I think it's only fair you offer me something in return. You owe me a wedding night.'

He let out a ragged laugh. 'I never thought of it that way.'

'Think of it that way now,' she said, and kissed him again. Her lips were soft, warm and open and her breasts brushed his chest. Khalil's arms came around her without him having made a conscious decision to embrace her, yet suddenly he was. He pulled her closer, fitting her softness against his body, pressing against her, craving the contact. And as her lips parted and she innocently, instinctively deepened the kiss, he knew he was lost.

This was what she wanted. Needed. Elena wound her arms around Khalil's neck as he took over her tentative kiss and made it his own. Made it theirs. His tongue slid into her mouth, exploring its contours and causing shivers of amazed pleasure to ripple through her. She had never known a kiss could be so consuming. So...*much*.

He slid one hand from her shoulder to cup her breast, his palm warm and sure. Elena shuddered under his touch. The intensity of her pleasure was almost painful, and yet achingly exquisite. And, while this was so much more than she'd ever felt or experienced before, it still wasn't enough. She felt an ache deep inside for more and she acted on it.

She pushed the *thobe* from his shoulders, and wordlessly Khalil shrugged out of it; the loose linen shirt and trousers he wore underneath followed. He was completely naked and utterly beautiful, long, lean, lithe and yet incredibly powerful, his body rippling with muscle. Now more than ever he reminded her of a panther, beautiful, awe-inspiring and just a little bit scary.

This was scary. Wonderful, exciting, new—and scary. She took a deep breath and waited for him to make the next move because she wasn't sure what it should be.

He lifted the hem of her chemise and she raised her arms so he could take it off her. She wore nothing underneath and, as his gaze roved over her nakedness, she felt a twinge of embarrassment, extinguished when he ran a gentle hand from her shoulder to thigh.

'You are so beautiful, Elena.'

'You are too,' she whispered and he laughed softly and tugged on her hand, leading her towards the bed.

He lay down on the soft covers and drew her down next to him so they were facing each other. Elena's breath was already coming in short gasps; her senses were on overload simply by lying next to Khalil, his naked body so close to hers. His chest rippled with muscle and his belly was taut and flat. Her gaze dipped lower and then moved up again;

she might have been talking a big game but she was still inexperienced. Still a little nervous.

Khalil took her hand and placed it on his bare chest. 'We can stop,' he said quietly; it amazed her how he always seemed to know what she was thinking, feeling. 'We can always stop.'

'I don't want to stop,' she told him with a shaky laugh. 'That doesn't mean I'm not going to be a little nervous, though.'

'Understandable,' he murmured, and kissed her again, a kiss that was slow and soft and wonderful. A kiss that banished any lingering fears or feelings of nervousness. A kiss that felt like a promise, although of what Elena couldn't say.

He slid his hand down her body, rested it on the flat of her tummy, waited. Everything in Elena quivered with anticipation. She wanted him to touch her…everywhere.

Still kissing her, he moved his hand lower. He waited again for the acceptance that she gave, his fingers brushing between her thighs, everything in her straining and yearning for even more.

And as he touched her with such wonderful, knowing expertise she realised she wanted to touch him too. She felt a new boldness come over her, a certainty to take what she wanted—and give him what he wanted. She smoothed her hands over his chest, slid her fingers across the ridged muscles of his abdomen. She wrapped them around the length of his arousal, causing his breath to come out in a hiss of pleasure which increased her own and made her bolder still.

With each caress the pressure in her built, a desperate need demanding satisfaction. And even she, in her innocence and inexperience, knew how it would finally be satisfied.

She rolled onto her back as he put on the condom and then positioned himself over her, braced on his forearms, his breath coming out in a ragged pant as he waited. 'Are you sure…?'

'Of course I'm sure, Khalil,' she half-laughed, half-sobbed, because by then she was more than sure. She was ready.

And then he entered her, slowly, the sensation so strange and yet so right at the same time. He went deeper, and with an instinct she hadn't known she possessed she arched her hips upwards and wrapped her legs around his waist. Pulled him deeper into herself.

'Okay?' he muttered and she almost laughed.

'Yes. Yes. More than okay.' And she was. She felt powerful in that moment, as well as loved. As if, with Khalil, she could do anything. She could be the person she was meant to be. She'd thought trusting someone, loving someone, made you weak, left you open and vulnerable to hurt. But right now she felt utterly strong. Completely whole.

And then he started to move, and the friction of his body inside hers increased that ache of pleasure deep within her, a sensation that built to such strength she felt as if it would explode from her, as if she would fly from the force of it, soaring high above the little camp, above everything.

And then it happened, everything in her peaking in an explosion of pleasure: she cried out, one long, ragged note, and fell back against the pillows, her body still wrapped around Khalil's, his head buried in the curve of her shoulder.

Neither of them spoke for several long minutes; Elena could feel the thud of Khalil's heart against her own, both of them racing. She stared up at the ceiling of the tent and wondered how she'd gone as long as she had without experiencing such incredible intimacy. Feeling such an amazing sense of rightness and power.

Slowly Khalil moved off her. He lay on his back, staring up at the ceiling, and Elena felt the first pinprick of uncertainty. Suddenly he seemed remote.

'I didn't hurt you,' he said, not quite a question, and she shook her head.

'No.'

'Good.' He rose then, magnificent in his nakedness, and went to dress.

'Khalil…' She rose up onto her elbows. 'Don't.'

'Don't what?'

'You owe me a wedding night, not a wedding hour,' she told him, trying to sound teasing even though nerves leapt in her belly and fluttered in her throat. 'Come back to bed.'

He stared at her for an endless moment, his *thobe* clenched in one hand, and Elena thought he would refuse—walk out of the tent and leave her alone with nothing but memories and regret. Then with a slight shrug he dropped the garment. He returned to the bed, sitting on its edge, away from her. She saw several faded white scars crisscrossing his back, and wondered at them. Now, she knew, was not the time to ask.

'I don't want to hurt you, Elena,' he said quietly. 'And I don't mean physically.'

She swallowed hard. 'I know you don't.'

He gave a slight shake of his head. 'The closer we become, *seem*…'

Seem. Because tonight's intimacy wasn't real, at least not for him. 'I understand, Khalil,' she told him. 'You don't have to warn me again. Tonight is a fantasy. Tomorrow it ends. Trust me, I get that. I accept it.'

He let out a weary sigh and gently she laid a hand on his shoulder, her fingers curling around warm skin, and pulled him back towards her. After a second's resistance, he came, lying next to her, folding her into his arms and then hauling her against his chest.

It felt like the only place she'd ever really belonged.

For tonight.

Neither of them spoke for several long minutes; Khalil stroked her hair and Elena rested one hand on his chest, perfectly content.

Almost.

The knowledge that this was only temporary, only tonight, ate away at her happiness, poked holes in this moment's peace. She tried to banish that knowledge; she wanted to dwell only in the fantasy now.

Closing her eyes, she imagined that they were in fact wed, that the ceremony tonight had been theirs. That they lay here as husband and wife, utterly in love with each other.

As she embroidered each detail onto the cloth of her imagination, she knew she was being foolish. Understood that envisioning such a thing, such a life, even if only as a fantasy, was dangerous.

Khalil didn't want a relationship, a loving relationship, and she didn't either. At least, she shouldn't. She'd never wanted it before. She'd chosen not to look for love, not to trust someone with her heart, her life. She'd done it once before—not romantically, but the betrayal had still wounded her deeply. Had made her doubt not just other people but herself.

How could she have trusted someone who had used her so spectacularly?

And how could she ever risk herself to trust again?

No, she was better off without love or romance. Keeping it as a fantasy, a single night.

And maybe, if she kept telling herself that, she'd believe it.

'What are you thinking about, Elena?' Khalil asked, his voice a quiet rumble in his chest.

'Nothing—'

'Not nothing,' he interjected quietly. 'You've gone all tense.'

And she realised she had; she was lying stiff in his arms, her hand curled against his chest. Gently he reached up and flattened her fist, smoothing her fingers out before resting his hand on top of hers. 'What were you thinking about?' he asked again.

She sighed. 'Just…some memories.'

'The same memories that give you nightmares?'

'No. Different ones.'

'Not good ones, though.'

'No.' She let out a little sigh. 'Not particularly.'

'I'm sorry,' he said after a moment, and somehow that felt like exactly the right thing to say.

'So am I. But I don't want to think about bad memories tonight, Khalil. I want to be happy. Just for tonight.'

He squeezed her hand lightly. 'I won't stop you.'

'I know, but…' She wanted more than his acquiescence; she wanted his participation. 'Can we—can we pretend?' she asked, her voice quavering slightly with nervousness. 'Can we pretend, just for tonight, that we're…that we're in love?' She felt his body tense underneath her hand and she hurried to explain. 'I know we're not. I don't want us to be, not for real. I don't want to love someone like that.' Khalil remained ominously silent, so she continued stiltedly, 'I just want to feel like I do for one night. To forget everything else and just enjoy feelings I can't afford to have in real life.' She sounded ridiculous, Elena realised. What was she really asking? For him to *pretend* to love her?

How absurd. How pathetic.

And Khalil still hadn't said anything.

'Maybe it's a stupid idea,' Elena muttered. Inwardly she cringed at the whole ridiculous proposition she'd put before him. 'I didn't mean… You don't have to worry that I'll suddenly…' Her throat tightened and she was about to force herself to go on, to reassure him that she wouldn't fall in love with him or start expecting emotions and commitments from him simply because they'd had sex, but then Khalil spoke first.

'For one night,' he said slowly. 'I think I can manage that…my darling.'

Surprise gave way to mirth and even joy, and she let out

a bubble of laughter, shaking her head. 'Now, that rolled off the tongue quite nicely,' she teased.

'Did it not, dearest?' He raised his eyebrows, turning to her with an enquiring smile. 'What shall I call you, then, essence of sweetness?'

She turned her head towards the pillow to muffle her laughter. '*Essence of sweetness?* Where do you come up with that stuff?'

'It comes naturally, my dewy petal,' he purred. 'Can't you tell?'

Tears of laughter started in her eyes. Her stomach ached. And she felt the biggest, sloppiest grin spreading over her face. 'Sorry, but I can't tell.'

Khalil rose on his arms above her, a wicked smile curving his mouth and glinting in his eyes. 'What a dilemma,' he answered softly. 'Since I don't seem able to tell you how I love you, then perhaps I should show you.'

And then Elena's laughter stopped abruptly as he did precisely that—showing her with his mouth, his hands and body. And he showed her very well indeed.

CHAPTER NINE

KHALIL AWAKENED TO sunlight streaming into their tent and Elena's hair spread over his chest. He'd slept the whole night with his arms around her, his body entwined with hers, and it had felt good.

Unbearably good.

What on earth had possessed him to participate in her little game? Pretend to be in *love*? And, never mind the danger involved in that all too enjoyable charade, what about the fact that he'd slept with her at all? That he'd taken her virginity? No matter what she'd assured him about understanding the emotional risks, he knew it was dangerous. Dangerous for her, and even dangerous for him, because already he wanted her again—and not just in bed.

In his life.

And there was no place for Queen Elena of Thallia in his life.

The next few days and weeks were crucial to his campaign to retake the throne that was rightfully his. He couldn't waste a moment's energy or thought on anything but his goal, a goal he'd nourished and cherished since he'd been seven years old and had been dropped into the desert like a dog no one wanted. Treated like one too, kicked and beaten and abused.

And, in any case, he didn't do love. He didn't know how. Trusting another person with *anything,* much less his heart—dried-up, useless organ that it was—was next to impossible for him. He wanted to trust people, men like Assad who had sworn their loyalty to him, but he still always felt that prickle of wary suspicion between his shoulder blades. He was still, always, waiting for the sudden slap, the knife in the back. The betrayal.

When you lived your life like that, love had no place in it. Relationships had no place, save for expediency.

And as for Elena? He glanced down at her, her face softened in sleep, her dark, lush lashes feathering her cheeks. Her lips were slightly pursed, one hand flung up by her head. Despite his mental list of reasons to walk away right now, desire stirred insistently. He knew just how he could wake her up...

Swearing under his breath, Khalil extracted himself from Elena's embrace and rolled from the bed. He heard her stir behind him, but he was already yanking on his clothes, his back determinedly to her.

A serving maid entered, blushing, with a pitcher of hot water and inwardly Khalil swore again. The news of their night together would spread throughout the whole tribe. They would know he had consummated a union that he intended to reject shortly.

And his plan to explain later why he'd been travelling alone with Elena would no longer work. He'd acted dishonourably and the tribe would know it. When they found out he and Elena weren't married, they would feel both betrayed and angry, and how could he blame them?

It was a fiasco, and all because he'd wanted her so damn much. How could he have been so weak?

'Khalil...?'

He turned to see her sitting up in bed, her dark hair tumbling wildly about her shoulders, her hooded grey eyes sleepy but with a wariness already stealing into them.

'We need to get moving,' he said brusquely. 'Assad is coming with a vehicle this morning. He'll take us to a new camp and then we'll move onto Siyad. You'll be back in Thallia this time tomorrow, I hope.'

She looked away, hiding her face, but he still felt the hurt he knew he'd caused her. Damn it, he'd *warned* her about this. He couldn't blame Elena, though. He could only blame himself. He'd known she was a virgin, inexperienced and innocent. She was bound to read more into their night together, even if she'd said she wouldn't.

Hell, he'd read more into it. Felt more than he was comfortable with.

And now he had no idea what to do, how to make things right: with Elena; with the tribe; with this country of his that teetered on the brink of civil war, made worse by his own foolish choices.

What an unholy mess.

After Khalil had left the tent Elena rose slowly from the bed and reached for the Bedouin-style dress he'd stripped from her body the night before.

Had it only been the night before? It felt like a lifetime ago. Felt like a different life, one where she'd known pleasure, joy and love.

It was only pretend, you idiot.

Sighing, she slipped on the chemise, only to see her Western clothes lying neatly folded by the pitcher of water. She took off the chemise and washed quickly, scrubbing the scent of Khalil from her body, before putting on the clothes she'd come here in.

Time to return to reality.

By the time she'd eaten breakfast—with the other women, Khalil not in sight—some of her equilibrium had been restored, along with her determination.

She'd had setbacks before, been hurt before. And this time she had no one to blame but herself. Khalil had been honest with her, unlike Paulo had been. He'd told her what she could and couldn't expect, and he'd been true to his word. She could not fault him.

And so she wouldn't. She'd had her night, her fantasy, and she'd treasure it—but she wouldn't let it consume or control her. Life had to go on and, with the end of her captivity looming ever nearer, she needed to think about her return to Thallia.

Just the thought made her feel as if she'd swallowed a stone.

After breakfast Khalil came for her, his *thobe* billowing out behind him, the set of his face exceptionally grim. Even scowling he was handsome, with the dark slashes of his eyebrows and those full, sculpted lips. His eyes seemed to glow fire.

'Are you ready? We should leave as soon as possible.'

Elena rose from where she'd been sitting by the fire and brushed the crumbs from her lap. 'I'm ready now.'

Nodding, Khalil turned away, and wordlessly Elena followed him. Assad was waiting by an SUV with blacked-out windows. Elena slid inside, fighting a weird sense of déjà vu. She'd been driven in a car like this when she'd first been captured. Now she was being driven to a freedom she wasn't sure she wanted.

They rode through the unending desert, Assad driving while Khalil and Elena sat in the back, not speaking, not touching.

Despite the ache Khalil's stony silence caused her, Elena forced herself to think practically. In two days she would, God willing, be back in Thallia. What would Andreas Markos have done in her absence? Would he have heard of her abduction, or would Aziz have managed to keep it secret?

She'd only been in the desert for a handful of days, even if it had felt like a lifetime. Perhaps Markos and the rest of her Council weren't yet aware of what had happened.

'Have you heard any news?' she asked Khalil abruptly,

and he turned, eyebrows raised. 'Has Aziz admitted that I'm missing? Does my Council know?'

'Aziz has admitted nothing. I doubt your Council is aware of events.'

'But how has he explained—?'

'He hasn't. He hired someone to pretend to be you and it seems everyone, including your Council, has believed it.'

Shock left her speechless for a moment. 'He did? But—'

'They appeared on the palace balcony two days ago. From a distance the woman fooled the people, or so it would seem. That's all I know.' He arched an eyebrow. 'Your Council wasn't expecting to hear from you, I presume?'

'Not until I returned.' She'd been meant to be on her honeymoon. 'You should have told me,' Elena said and Khalil eyed her coolly.

'What purpose would it have served?'

'It just would have been good to know.' She stared out of the window, tried to sift through her tangled feelings. She wasn't exactly surprised that Aziz had come up with an alternative plan; she'd suggested as much to Khalil. She wasn't hurt by his actions either. But she felt…something and with a jolt she realised it *was* hurt—not for what Aziz had done, but for what Khalil hadn't. Not telling her had been a tactical move, a way of treating her like a political pawn rather than a—what?

Just what was she to him now?

Nothing, obviously. She closed her eyes and thought of him covering her with kisses last night, both of them laughing. *It was pretend. You knew that.*

But it still hurt now.

'I'll be able to tell you more when we return to camp,' Khalil said. He drummed his fingers against the window, clearly restless. 'What will you do when you return to Thallia?' he asked. Elena opened her eyes.

'Do you really care?'

'I'm asking the question.'

'And the answer is, I don't know. It depends what state my country is in. My government.'

'Your Head of Council won't have had time to call a vote to abolish the monarchy.'

'No, but he will as soon as he can.'

'You could marry someone else in the meantime.'

'Suitable husbands are a little thin on the ground.'

'Are they?' He turned back to the window, frowning deeply. Elena had no idea what he was thinking. 'Just what was your arrangement with Aziz?' he asked, still staring out of the window.

'I told you.'

'I mean in practical terms.'

Bewildered, she almost asked him why he wanted to know. Why he cared. Then, with a mental shrug, she answered, 'It was a matter of convenience for both of us. We'd split our time between Thallia and Kadar, rule independently.'

'And that pleased your Council?'

'My Council was not aware of all the terms of the marriage. They probably assumed I'd be more under Aziz's influence.'

'And they didn't mind a stranger helping to rule their country?'

'He's royal in his own right, and as I explained they're traditional. They want me under a man's influence.'

Khalil nodded slowly, his forehead knitted in thought. 'And what about heirs?'

A blush touched her cheeks. 'Why are we talking about this, exactly?'

'I'm curious.'

'And you want me to satisfy your curiosity?' Her temper flared. 'What for, Khalil? None of it is going to happen anyway, and in any case it has nothing to do with you.'

He turned to her with a granite stare. 'Humour me.'

Her breath came out in a rush. 'We planned for two children, an heir for each of our kingdoms.'

'And where would these children have been raised?'

'Initially they would stay with me, and when they were older they would split their time between the two countries.' She looked away, uncomfortably aware of how cold and clinical it sounded. 'I know it's hardly an ideal solution, but we were both desperate.'

'I realise that.'

'Like I said, it doesn't matter anyway.'

'But you still feel you need a husband.'

She sighed and leaned her head back against the seat, closing her eyes once more. 'I do, but maybe you're right. Maybe I can face my Council on my own, convince them not to call the vote.'

'It's a risk.'

She opened her eyes. 'You don't sound nearly as encouraging as you did before.'

He shrugged. 'You have to choose for yourself.'

'Seeing as there's nothing to choose, as I have no prospective husband, this whole conversation seems pointless.'

'Maybe,' Khalil allowed, and turned back to the window. 'Maybe not.'

He could marry her. The thought made everything in him rear up in shocked panic. Marriage had never been on his agenda. Yet ever since he'd seen that serving girl this morning, and realised the repercussions of his night with Elena, the thought had been rattling around in his brain like a coin in a box.

He could marry her—marry the woman who was intended as the Sheikh of Kadar's wife. It would help strengthen his claim, stabilise his throne, and it would give Elena what she wanted too.

Why not?

Because it's dangerous. Because the emotional risks you warned her about apply to you too.

Because you care about her already.

Elena had spoken of a cold, convenient union, but would it be like that if he was her husband? Would he be able to keep himself from caring for, even loving, her?

Did he even want to?

His mind spun and seethed. He felt the clash of his own desires, the need to protect himself and the urge to be with her—care for her.

And did Elena even care for him? Just what kind of marriage would she want them to have?

Once back at the camp—which to Elena looked like just another huddle of tents, horses, cars and camels amidst the dunes and black rocks—Khalil strode away and Leila met Elena and brought her to her private tent.

'A bath, perhaps,' she murmured and Elena thanked her, nodding wearily. She felt overwhelmed by every aspect of life at the moment: the end of things here, her responsibilities in Thallia, her non-relationship with Khalil.

A quarter of an hour later she watched as two men filled the copper tub with steaming water. Leila scattered it with rose petals and brought a thick towel and some lovely smelling soap, and Elena's throat suddenly went tight with emotion.

'Thank you. This is so kind…'

'It is nothing, Your Highness. You could use a little pampering, I think.'

The older woman's sympathy was almost her undoing. Elena nodded, swallowing past the tightness in her throat as Leila quietly left.

As she soaked in the tub Elena's thoughts returned relentlessly to Thallia and matters of state. She had no husband. She could explain why and, since it looked as if

Khalil would become Sheikh, she thought her Council would accept it.

But in a few weeks' time, if she were still single, Markos would call for the vote to abolish the monarchy. Somehow she had to convince him not to call it, or at least convince her Council not to vote against her.

Could she do it on her own? Did she dare risk her crown in such a way? Khalil believed in her, perhaps more than she believed in herself. Just remembering the warmth of his smile, the confidence she'd seen in his eyes, made her ache.

No, she couldn't risk it. A royal wedding and a devoted husband were what had been going to save her, no matter what Khalil said about her being strong enough to face her Council alone. He didn't know what she was up against. Didn't understand what she'd been through.

Sighing, Elena leaned her head back against the tub. The only way to avoid such a disaster would be to prove Markos wrong—to return with a husband.

Too bad that was impossible.

Unless she married Khalil.

Elena smiled mirthlessly as she imagined Khalil's horrified reaction to such an idea. He would never agree to marry her. He'd been appalled by the possibility that she might harbour any tender feelings for him. He'd sounded contemptuous of her arrangement with Aziz.

Elena sat up suddenly, water sloshing over the sides of the tub. Marrying her could potentially be beneficial for Khalil. She'd seen the approval of the Bedouin they'd been with, how they'd liked seeing him with his bride.

And since he'd already acted as if they were married…

Could it be possible? Did she even dare suggest a thing? The potential rejection and humiliation she faced made her flinch.

Then, in a sudden, painful rush of memory, Elena recalled her father throwing himself over her, saving her life from the explosions and gunfire around them. Sacrificing himself...for Thallia. For the monarchy.

How could she not do whatever it took to ensure her reign?

An hour later she was dressed in another outfit Leila had brought her, a simple dress of rose-coloured cotton. She twisted her hair up in a chignon and wished she had some make-up or jewellery to make her feel more prepared. She was going to talk to Khalil. Beard the lion in his den.

Taking a deep breath, Elena square her shoulders and exited the tent. Two guards immediately moved in front of her, blocking her way.

Fury surged through her, shocking her with its intensity. 'Really?' she asked them. 'After everything, you still think I'm going to run off into the desert?'

They stared back at her blandly. 'Do you want for something, Your Highness?'

A husband. She took another deep breath. 'I would like to speak to Khalil.'

'He is not—'

'Available? Well, make him available. I need to speak to him, and it's important.'

Leila came hurrying over, her face creased with concern. 'Your Highness? Is something wrong?'

'I'd like to speak to Khalil,' Elena stated. Her voice wobbled and, furious with herself, she bit her lip. Hard. 'Do you know where he is, Leila?' she asked, and thankfully this time her voice was steady.

Leila gazed at her, a certain sorrowful knowledge in her eyes, and Elena had the sudden, awful suspicion that Leila knew she and Khalil had slept together.

'Yes, I know where he is,' she said quietly. She spoke in Arabic to the two guards, but her voice was too low for Elena to make anything out. Then she turned back to her and said, 'Come with me.'

Elena went. Leila led her to a tent on the opposite side of the camp, pausing outside the entrance to turn back to her.

'Khalil has been through much, Your Highness,' she said quietly. 'Whatever has happened between the two of you, please remember that.'

So Leila had definitely guessed, then. Elena forced the realisation away and met her gaze squarely. 'I just want to talk to him, Leila.'

'I know.' The older woman smiled sadly. 'But I can tell you are hurting, and I am sorry for it. Khalil is hurting too.'

Khalil hurting? *I don't think so.* But Elena was still considering Leila's words as she stepped into the tent and looked upon Khalil.

He was seated at a folding table, his dark head bent as he scrawled something on a piece of paper. He didn't look up, just lifted one hand, signalling her to wait.

'One moment, Assad, please.'

'It's not Assad.'

Khalil glanced up swiftly then, his gaze narrowing as it rested on Elena. She stared back, levelly, she hoped, but after a taut few seconds she knew she was glaring.

'Elena.'

'*Khalil.*' She mimicked his even tone, slightly sneering it. Oops. Not the way she'd wanted to start this business-like meeting, but then Leila was right. She *was* hurting, even if she didn't want to be.

He sat back, resting his arms lightly on the sides of his chair. 'Is there something you need?'

'You had said you would look at the news,' Elena reminded him. 'Find out if people know what has happened.'

'So I did. I haven't seen anything so far. Aziz is keeping quiet.'

'And how will you return me to Thallia?' she asked coolly. 'Royal jet? Economy class? Or will you roll me up in a carpet like Cleopatra and then unroll me in the throne room of the Thallian palace?'

'An interesting possibility.' His gaze rested on her, assessing, penetrating. 'Why are you so angry, Elena?'

'I'm not angry.'

'You sound angry.'

'I'm frustrated. There's a difference.'

'Very well, then. Why are you frustrated?'

'Because I came to Kadar with a plan to save my throne and I no longer have one.'

'You mean marriage.'

'Yes.'

His gaze narrowed. 'And what would you like me to do about it?'

'I'm glad you asked.' Elena took a deep breath, tried to smile as she met his narrowed gaze. 'I'd like you to marry me.'

CHAPTER TEN

SHE'D BEATEN HIM to it, Khalil thought bemusedly, even as an elemental panic clawed at his insides. He'd been considering marriage to Elena as a solution to both of their problems since this morning. Yet looking at her now, seeing the hope and determination blazing in her eyes, everything in him resisted. There had to be another solution.

Slowly he shook his head. 'That's impossible, Elena.'

'Why is it impossible?' she demanded.

'Because I have no wish or reason to marry you, Elena.' Better to be brutal. Nip it in the bud, if he could. 'You may be desperate, but I am not.'

She flinched, but only slightly. 'Are you sure about that, Khalil?'

'Quite sure. You asked for a wedding night, Elena, not a marriage.'

'Well, now I'm asking for a marriage.'

'And I'm telling you the answer is no.' He rose from his chair, fought the panic that was crashing over him in tidal waves. 'This discussion is over.'

She raised her eyebrows, a small smile playing about her mouth. A mouth he'd kissed. Tasted. He forced his gaze upwards but her eyes just reminded him of how they'd been filled with need and joy when he'd slid inside her. Her hair reminded him of how soft and silky it had felt spread across his chest. Everything about her was dangerous, every memory a minefield of emotion.

'You don't even want to think about it?' she challenged and he folded his arms.

'I do not.'

'You almost sound scared, Khalil,' she taunted, and fury pulsed through him because he knew she was right. Talking about marriage scared the hell out of him, because he was afraid it wouldn't be the cold, convenient arrangement she'd intended to have with Aziz. She'd want more. *He* would.

And that was far, far too dangerous.

'It's simply not an option,' he told her shortly.

'Even though you've already told people we're married?'

He felt his jaw bunch, his teeth grit. 'I didn't tell anyone.'

'Semantics, Khalil. The result was the same. And, no matter what you tell yourself or me, there will still be repercussions for you.'

'I'm perfectly aware of that, Elena.' He heard a patronising note enter his voice and knew it was the lowest form of self-defence. Everything she was saying was true, yet still he fought it. 'As I told you before, by the time people learn the truth I will be established in Siyad as Sheikh.'

'And that's how you want to start your rule? Based on a lie?'

He pressed his lips together, forced the anger back. 'Not particularly, but events dictated it be thus. I will deal with the consequences as best as I can.' All because of his own stupid weakness concerning this woman.

'And what if your people decide you might be lying about other things? What if they assume you lied about your parentage and Aziz is the true heir?'

Just like his father had lied. He would be no better, and the realisation made him sick with both shame and fury. 'Are you trying to argue your way into a marriage the way you argued your way into my bed?' he demanded, and she flinched then, her face crumpling a little before she quickly looked away. Khalil swore softly. 'Elena,' he said quietly, 'I understand you feel you need a husband. But I am not that man.'

He couldn't be.

'It makes sense,' she whispered. She still wouldn't look at him and the fury left him in a weary rush. He wanted to pull her into his arms. Kiss her sadness away.

But he couldn't marry her. He couldn't open himself up to that weakness, that risk, that *pain*.

'I can see how it might make sense to you,' he said carefully. 'You need a convenient husband.'

'And you need a convenient wife.' She swung around to face him with a challenging stare. 'Your people want you to marry. We saw that when we were with them. They think you're married to me already! One day you'll need an heir—'

'One day.' Khalil cut her off swiftly. 'Not yet.'

'I won't ask anything of you that you wouldn't want to give,' Elena continued doggedly. 'I won't fall in love with you, or demand your time or attention. We can come to an arrangement, like I had with Aziz—'

'Don't mention his name,' Khalil said, his voice coming out like the crack of a whip. Elena's eyes widened; she was startled, and so was he.

Where was all this emotion coming from? This anger and…*hurt*? Because the thought of her with Aziz made his blood boil and his stomach churn. He couldn't bear to think of her with anyone else, not even a man he knew she didn't love, barely knew.

They stared at each other, the very air seeming to spark with the electric charge that pulsed between them: anger and attraction. Desire and frustration.

'I won't, then,' Elena said quietly. 'But you could at least think of it, Khalil. You'll have to marry some day. Why not me? Unless…' She paused, nibbling her lip. 'Unless you're holding out for love.'

'I am not.'

'Well, then.'

He just shook his head, unwilling to articulate just why he was rejecting her proposal out of hand. He couldn't admit to her that he was actually *scared*. 'What about you? You're not interested in love?'

She hesitated, and he saw the truth in her eyes. She was. She wouldn't admit it to him, but she was. 'I can't afford to be interested in love.'

'You might decide one day you want someone who loves you,' he pointed out, trying to sound reasonable when in fact he felt incredibly, insanely jealous at the thought of another man loving her. *Touching* her.

'I won't,' she told him. 'I won't let myself.'

'Even if you wanted to?'

'Are you worried I'm going to fall in love with you, Khalil?'

No—he was terrified that he was already in love with her. Khalil spun around. 'Put like that, it sounds arrogant.'

'I'll try to keep myself from it.' She spoke lightly, but he had a feeling she was serious. She didn't want to fall in love with him, and why should she? He would only hurt her. He wouldn't love her back.

Except maybe you already do.

'We've both been hurt before,' Elena said after a moment. 'I know that. Neither of us wants that kind of pain again, which is why an arrangement such as the one I'm suggesting makes so much sense.'

It did. He knew it did. He shouldn't be fighting it. He should be agreeing with her, coolly discussing the arrangements.

Instead he stood there, silent and struggling.

Elena didn't want his love, wouldn't make emotional demands. In that regard, she would make the perfect wife.

And yet looking at her now he saw the welter of hope and sadness in her eyes. Felt it in himself. And he knew that no matter how they spun it, no matter what they agreed on, marriage to Elena would be dangerous. Because, even if some contrary part of him actually longed for the things he said he couldn't do, didn't want—love, intimacy, trust, all of it—the rest of him knew better. Knew that going down that road, allowing himself to feel, yearn and ache, was bad, bad news.

No matter how practical Elena's suggestion might be, he couldn't take it.

'I'm sorry, Elena,' he said. 'But I won't marry you. I can't.'

She stared at him for a moment, her wide, grey eyes dark with sadness, and then turning darker still with acceptance. Slowly she nodded.

'Very well,' she said, and without another word she turned and left the tent.

Khalil stared at the empty space she'd left, his mind spinning, his heart aching, hating that already he felt so bereft.

It had been worth a shot, Elena told herself as she walked back to her tent, escorted by the same men who guarded her. They didn't speak and neither did she, because she knew she wouldn't be able to manage a word. Her throat ached and she was afraid that if she so much as opened her mouth she'd burst into tears.

Back in her tent she sat on her bed, blinking hard to contain all the pain and hurt she felt. Then suddenly, almost angrily, she wondered why she bothered. Why not have a good cry? Let it all out? No one was here to hear her or think her weak or stupid or far too feminine.

She lay down on her bed, drew her knees up to her chest and swallowed hard. Crying—letting herself cry—was so hard. She'd kept everything in for so long because she'd had to. Men like Markos were always looking for chinks in her armour, ways to weaken her authority. Shedding a single tear would have been just handing them ammunition. The only time she ever cried was when she had nightmares.

In Khalil's arms.

She hadn't consciously, deliberately accessed that hidden, vulnerable part of herself for years, and it was hard to reach it now, even when she wanted to. Sort of.

She took a shuddering breath and clutched her knees harder, closed her eyes and felt the pressure build in her chest.

Finally that first tear fell, trickling onto her cheek. She dashed it away instinctively, but another came, and another, and then she really was crying. Her shoulders shaking, the tears streamed as ragged sobs tore from her throat. She pressed her hot face into the pillow and let all the misery out.

It was not just sadness about her wrecked wedding, or Khalil, but about so much more: the needless deaths of her parents and the fact that she hadn't been able to grieve for them as she should have. Her broken relationship with Paulo, her shattered trust. The four lonely years she'd endured as Queen, working hard for the country she loved, suffering Markos's and other councillors' sneers and slights, trying desperately to hold onto the one thing her parents wanted her to keep.

And yes, she realised as she sobbed, she was crying about Khalil. He'd helped her in so many ways, opened her up, allowed her to feel and trust again. She'd miss him more than she wanted to admit even to herself. More than he'd ever want to know.

Khalil turned back to the reports he'd been studying, reports detailing Kadar's response to Aziz, polls that confirmed outside of Siyad he was not a popular choice as Sheikh. It was news that should have encouraged him, but he only felt restless and dissatisfied—and it was all because of Elena. Or, really, all because of him and his reaction to her and her proposal.

He should have said yes. He should have been strong and cold and ruthless enough to agree to a marriage that would stabilise his country, strengthen his claim. Instead he'd let his emotions rule him. His fear had won out, and the realisation filled him with self-fury.

'Your Highness?'

Khalil waved Assad forward, glad to think about something else. 'You have news, Assad?'

Assad nodded, his face as stony and sombre as always. Khalil had met him eight years ago, when he'd joined the French Foreign Legion. They'd fought together, laughed together and saved each other's lives on more than one occasion. And, when the time had been right for Khalil to return to Kadar, Assad had made it possible. He'd gathered support, guarded his back.

None of this would have been possible without Assad, yet Khalil still didn't trust him. But that was his fault, not his friend's.

'Is something the matter?' he asked and Assad gave one terse nod.

'Aziz has married.'

Khalil stilled, everything inside him going cold. He'd always known this was a risk, yet he was still surprised. 'Married? How? Who?'

'We're not sure. Intelligence suggests someone on his staff, a housekeeper or some such.'

'He married his housekeeper?' *Poor Elena.* No matter what she had or hadn't felt for Aziz, it would still be a blow. And with a jolt Khalil realised he shouldn't even be thinking about Elena; he should be thinking about his rule.

Aziz had fulfilled the terms of his father's will. He would be Sheikh.

And Khalil wouldn't.

Abruptly he rose from his chair, stalked to the other

side of the tent. Emotion poured through him in a scalding wave, emotion he would never have let himself feel a week ago. Before Elena.

She'd accessed that hidden part of himself, a part buried so deep he hadn't thought it existed. Clearly it did, because he felt it all now: anger and guilt. Regret and fear. *Hurt.*

'All is not lost, Khalil,' Assad said quietly, dropping the honorific for once. 'Aziz is still not popular. Secretly marrying a servant will make him even less so.'

'Does that even matter?' Khalil bit out. 'He's fulfilled the terms of the will. He is Sheikh.'

'But very few people want him to be.'

'So you're suggesting a civil war,' Khalil stated flatly. 'I didn't think Aziz would go that far.' And he wasn't sure he would either, no matter what he'd thought before. Felt before.

Risking so much for his own crown, endangering his people, was not an option he wanted to consider now.

Things were changing. *They'd already changed.*

He wasn't the cold, ruthless man he'd once been, yet if he wasn't Sheikh…

What was he?

'A civil war is not the only option,' Assad said quietly. 'You could approach Aziz, demand a referendum.'

Khalil let out a mirthless laugh. 'He has everything he wants. Why would he agree?'

'There is something to be said for a fair fight, Your Highness,' Assad answered. 'Aziz might want to put the rumours and unrest behind him. If he wins the vote, his throne is secure.'

And Khalil would have no chance at all. He would have to accept defeat finally, totally—another option he didn't like to consider.

'There are a lot of people in Siyad,' he said with an attempt at wryness, and Assad smiled.

'There are a lot of people in the desert.'

'Aziz might not even agree to see me. We haven't seen each other since we were children.'

'You can try.'

'Yes.' He nodded slowly, accepting.

'You still have the stronger position,' Assad stated steadily. 'You always have. The people are loyal to you, not to Aziz.'

'I know that.' He felt his throat go tight. Did he really deserve such loyalty? And did he dare trust it? He knew how quickly someone could turn on you. Only the day before his father had thrown him out of the palace, he'd sat in on one of Khalil's lessons, had chucked him under the chin when Khalil had said his times tables.

Stupid, childish memories, yet still they hurt. They burned.

'So you will speak to Aziz?'

Khalil ran his fingers through his hair, his eyes gritty with fatigue. A thousand thoughts whirled through his mind, and one found purchase: one way forward, one way to solidify his position and strengthen his claim to the throne.

Now more than ever, he needed to marry Elena.

Aziz's bride. The woman the country had already accepted as the Sheikh's wife-to-be. The woman at least one tribe already thought was his wife.

He'd reacted so forcefully against it because he didn't want to risk his emotions or his heart. So, he wouldn't. Just like her, he couldn't afford to look for love. He'd keep a tight rein on his emotions and have the kind of marriage both he and Elena wanted: one of mutual benefit…and satisfaction.

Just the thought of being with Elena again sent desire arrowing through him.

'The servant is not even Kadaran,' Assad said quietly, and Khalil wondered if his friend and right- hand man had guessed the progression of his thoughts.

'Neither is Elena,' Khalil answered, and Assad smiled faintly. Khalil now knew he had been thinking along the same lines.

'She is a queen, an accepted choice. Marrying her would work in your favour.'

'I know.' Khalil took a deep breath, let it out slowly. 'I know.'

'Then...?'

'I'll go find her.' And by this time tomorrow, perhaps, he would be married.

The camp was quiet and dark all around him as Khalil walked towards Elena's tent. A strange mix of emotions churned within him: resolve, resignation and a little spark of excitement that he tried to suppress.

Yes, he would enjoy Elena's body again. But this would be a marriage of convenience. No more play-acting at love. No more pretending. No more *feeling*.

The guards stepped aside as he came to the tent and drew the curtain back—and stopped short when he saw Elena curled up on her bed, her face pressed into her pillow, sobbing as if her heart would break.

Or had already been broken...by him.

'Elena...Elena!'

Elena felt hard hands on her shoulders drawing her up from her damp pillow and then cradling her against an even harder chest.

Khalil. For a second she let herself enjoy the feel of him. Then she remembered that she'd been bawling her eyes out and twisted out of his embrace.

'You should have knocked,' she snapped, dashing the tears from her cheeks. She probably looked frightful, her face blotchy, her eyes red and swollen...

She sniffed. *And* her nose was running. Perfect.

'Knock?' Khalil repeated, one eyebrow raised in eloquent scepticism. 'On the flap of a tent?'

'You know what I mean,' she retorted. 'You should have made your presence known.'

Khalil regarded her quietly for a moment. 'You're right,' he finally said. 'I should have. I'm sorry.'

'Well.' She sniffed again, trying desperately for dignity. 'Thank you.'

'Why were you crying, Elena?'

She shook her head as if she could deny the overwhelming evidence of her tears. 'It's been a couple of very long days,' she muttered. 'I was... I'm just tired.'

'You weren't crying as if you were just tired.'

'Why do you care?' she demanded. Perhaps going on the offensive was best.

Khalil opened his mouth, then shut it again. 'I don't *care*,' he answered. 'But I want to know.'

'I've got a lot going on in my life that has nothing to do with you, Khalil. Maybe I'm crying about *that*.' She wasn't about to admit that she had been crying about him along with everything else that had gone wrong in her life.

'I wasn't assuming you were crying about me,' he stated quietly. His voice was calm but he sounded as if he was trying not to grit his teeth.

'Weren't you?' Elena retorted. 'Ever since spending the night together you've been completely paranoid that I'm obsessing over you, and I can assure you, I'm not.'

'What a relief.'

'Isn't it?'

They glared at each other. Elena folded her arms and tried to stare him down; Khalil's eyes sparked annoyance and his mouth was compressed.

'Why did you come into my tent, anyway?' she finally asked, their gazes still clashing. 'Have you learned something? Some news?'

'Yes, I have.'

Her stomach rolled and she felt her nails bite into her

palms. 'What have you heard? Has Markos called for a meeting?'

'I haven't heard any news from Thallia, Elena. I think they still believe you are safely with Aziz.' Khalil's mouth was still a hard line but his expression seemed softer somehow, his eyes almost sad. 'It's Aziz,' he said after a pause. 'He's married someone else, just like you said he would.'

'He has?' Her eyes widened as she considered what this meant for Khalil. 'He did it within the six weeks?'

'Yes.'

'Then he fulfilled…?'

'The terms of my father's will.' Khalil nodded. 'Yes, he did. But you…? You're not sad?'

She stared at him in disbelief. 'About Aziz? I gave up on him a while ago, Khalil.'

'Yes, but…still…he chose someone else. Rather quickly.'

'So did I.' She gave him a look filled with dark humour. 'At least Aziz received a positive answer to his proposal.'

'Yes…' He shook his head, almost as if to clear it. 'About that proposal…'

'Trust me, you don't need to remind me how much you don't want to marry me, Khalil. I got that the first time.'

'I'm sorry if I seemed…negative.'

She rolled her eyes. 'That's an understatement.' Better to joke than to cry. In any case, she wasn't sure she had any tears left, just a heavy sense of weariness, a resignation that nothing was going to be easy. That she'd probably lose her crown.

'You surprised me,' he said. 'I wasn't expecting… I've never expected…'

'I know.' She shook her head, exasperated, exhausted and definitely not needing to hash through all this again. 'Why are we even talking about this, Khalil?'

'Because,' he answered evenly, 'I've changed my mind.'

She blinked and then blinked again, the meaning of his words penetrating slowly. 'You've what?'

'I've changed my mind,' he repeated clearly. 'I want to marry you.'

Elena opened her mouth, then closed it again. 'Well,' she finally managed. 'That was a charming proposal.'

'Don't be absurd, Elena. This is about convenience, for both of us.'

'You didn't seem to think so an hour ago.'

'Aziz's marriage has made me realise I need to strengthen my position.'

'But if he's married,' Elena said slowly, 'he's fulfilled the terms of the will. How can you fight that?'

'I can't. I don't want to start a war. The only thing I can do is confront him openly—demand he call the referendum. Perhaps I should have done that before, but it seemed too easy for Aziz to refuse. Perhaps it still is.'

'And marrying me will strengthen your position when it comes to a vote.'

Khalil gazed at her evenly. 'Yes.'

'That's quite a sacrifice for you to make,' she said a bit sharply. 'Just to look good for a vote.'

'I am the rightful Sheikh, Elena,' Khalil said, his voice rising with the force of his conviction. 'That is who I *am*, who I always will be. I've lived my entire life waiting for the day I took the throne. Every choice I've made, every single thing I've done, has been to that end. Not for revenge, but for justice. Because it is right—' He broke off, forced a smile. 'In any case, marrying you is not a sacrifice.'

'No?'

'We are friends, are we not? And we have enjoyed each other's bodies. Neither of us wants anything more.' He smiled, reached out to touch her face. 'It's a match made in heaven.'

'That's an about-face if I've ever seen one,' she huffed.

'I admit, your proposal shocked me. I reacted emotionally rather than sensibly.'

'I didn't think you had emotions.'

'You know I do, Elena.' His gaze seemed to burn into hers. 'I will be honest. This—' he gestured between them '—scares me.'

Elena felt as if a giant fist had taken hold of her heart. 'It scares me too, Khalil.'

'So that is why we will agree to this convenient marriage,' he answered with a small smile. 'Because neither of us wants to be hurt again.'

'Right,' Elena agreed, but to her own ears her voice sounded hollow. They didn't want to be hurt again—but she wondered if she or Khalil would be able to keep themselves from it.

CHAPTER ELEVEN

ELENA GAZED OUT of the window of the royal jet at the perfect azure sky and marvelled at how quickly things had changed. Just forty-eight hours earlier she'd been sobbing into her pillow, stuck in the middle of the desert with no possibilities and no hope.

Now she was flying back to Thallia with Khalil by her side, planning a wedding in just a few days' time, and everything was possible.

Well, almost everything. She snuck a sideways glance at Khalil who sat opposite her, his face looking as if it had been chiselled from marble. A deep frown had settled between his brows and his mouth was its usual hard line. He'd barely spoken to her since he'd reconsidered her marriage proposal, a proposal which Elena had wondered more than once whether she should have accepted.

Yet in the moment before she'd agreed, when he'd been waiting for her answer, she'd seen a look of uncertainty on his face, almost as if he were bracing himself for a blow. As if he expected her to reject him.

That moment of vulnerability had been gone in an instant, but it still lingered in Elena's mind. In her heart. Because it made Khalil a man with softness and secrets, a man she was starting to understand and know better and better.

Which, Elena acknowledged, violated the terms of this very convenient marriage. It was what she had first suggested, after all. If some contrary, feminine part of her wanted something different, something more…well, too bad.

She had other, more important things to think about. Like the fact that she was going to face her Council in just a few hours, and with a different fiancé in tow. She glanced again at Khalil, grateful that he'd agreed to accompany her to Thallia and marry in a private ceremony in the palace. It had made sense, rather than something furtive and hurried in the desert; both of them wanted this marriage to be accepted by the public as quickly as possible.

After she'd presented him to her Council, they'd return to Siyad and Khalil would demand Aziz call the referendum. Khalil had told her Aziz had retreated with his bride to a remote royal palace for his honeymoon. The announcement from the palace had simply said the Sheikh had wed, not the name of his bride. Siyad buzzed with speculation, but no one knew what was really going on. Khalil had said Aziz was just buying time. Things would come to a head when they returned from Thallia and Elena hoped that both of their countries—and thrones—would be secure.

Even then she didn't know what life with Khalil would look like, or even where or how they would live. She and Aziz had discussed all these details, outlined everything in a twenty-page document that had been drawn up by lawyers from both of their countries.

But everything with Khalil was unknown. Looking at his grim expression, she wasn't sure she wanted to discuss it now.

Instead she tried to plan what she would say to her Council. To Markos. No doubt he'd be contemptuous of her sudden change of groom. Perhaps he would claim she was being deceived by Khalil, as she had been by Paulo.

She thought of all the things Markos could say, all the contempt he could pour on her, and in Khalil's presence, and inwardly she cringed.

'What's wrong?' Khalil asked, turning to fix her with a narrowed gaze, and Elena realised her reaction had been visible too.

'Nothing…' she began, only to acknowledge she would have to tell Khalil about her mistakes. Better to hear it from her than Markos.

And actually, she realised, she *wanted* to tell him. She wanted to be honest, to share her burden with someone. To trust him with the truth.

'Elena?' Khalil prompted, and she took a deep breath.

'Khalil…I need to tell you some things.'

His gaze swept over her. 'All right.'

Elena took another deep breath. She wanted to tell Khalil, but it was still hard. 'I was young when I became queen,' she began. 'As you know. My parents had just died and I suppose I was feeling…vulnerable. Lonely.'

'Of course you were, Elena.' His face softened in sympathy. 'You'd had an isolated childhood and then you lost the two people who were closest to you.'

'Even if they weren't all that close.'

'Still, they were your parents. You loved them, and they loved you.'

'Yes.' She nodded, feeling a sudden, surprising peace about what Khalil had so simply and surely stated. Her parents had loved her. No matter how little they might have shown it during their lives, they'd loved her in their own way.

'So what happened when you became queen?' he asked after a moment, his voice gentle, and Elena gave him a rather shaky smile.

'My mother's brother, Paulo, came to stay with me after the funeral. I hadn't known him very well—he spent most of his time in Paris or Monte Carlo. I don't think my father liked him all that much. He'd stayed away, in any case.'

'And after the funeral?'

'He was very kind to me.' She sighed, a weary acceptance and regret coursing through her. 'He was funny and charming and in some ways he felt like the father I'd never had. The one I'd always wanted. Approachable. Genuine. Or so I thought.'

'He wasn't, I presume.' Khalil's frown deepened. 'This is the man who betrayed you.'

'Yes, he did, yet I trusted him. I listened to him, and I came to him for advice. The Council didn't want me to rule—Andreas Markos had tried to appoint himself as Regent.'

'But you're of age.'

'He made the case that I didn't have enough political experience. And he was right, you know. I didn't. I'd gone to a few royal functions, a few balls and events and things. But I didn't have the first clue about laws or policies. About anything real or important.'

'You learned, though. I've read some of the bills you helped draft online, Elena. You're not a pretty princess sitting on her throne, you're an active head of government.'

'Not at first.'

'The Council should have given you time to adjust to your new role.'

'Well, they didn't, not really.'

Khalil shook his head. 'So what happened with Paulo?'

'He advised me on some real-estate deals: government subsidies for tourist developments on our coastal region. I thought he was helping me, but he was just lining his own pockets.'

'How could you have known?'

'It wasn't just that,' she hastened to explain, practically tripping over herself to tell him the whole sordid truth. She needed him to know, craved for him to accept the whole of her and what she'd done. 'Every piece of advice he gave me was to benefit himself. And there were worse things. He forged my signature on cheques. He even stole some of my mother's jewels, which weren't hers to begin with. They were part of the crown jewels and they belonged to the government.'

She closed her eyes, filled with remorse and shame. 'I was completely clueless, pathetically grateful for all his support. Markos uncovered it, and had him sent to prison. Kept the scandal from breaking in the press, thankfully— not for my sake, but for Thallia's.'

'That must have been very hard.'

'Yes.' Her throat was so tight it hurt to speak, but she kept going. 'You know what's really sad? Sometimes I still miss him. He completely betrayed me in every way possible, and I actually miss him.' She shook her head, suddenly near tears, and Khalil reached over and covered her hand with his own.

'He seemed kind to you, and during a time when you craved that kindness. Of course you miss that.'

'Do you miss your father?' she blurted, and Khalil stilled, his hand tensing over hers.

'I've hated my father for so long,' he said slowly. 'And I can't ever forget what he did.' His face contorted for a second, and she knew how difficult this was for him to admit. 'But I do miss his kindness to me. His—his love.'

'Of course you do,' she murmured and Khalil gave her a wry and rather shaky smile.

'I never realised that before. I was too busy being angry.'

'Are you still angry?'

'I don't know what I am,' he said, sounding both surprised and confused, and then he shook his head. 'We weren't talking about me, though. We were talking about you. You shouldn't blame yourself, Elena, for trusting a man who did his best to endear himself to you.'

'I should have known better.'

Khalil shook his head, his hand tightening on hers. 'You were young and vulnerable. It wasn't your fault.'

'The Council thinks it was. Or, at the very least, it completely undermined any confidence they might have had in me. Markos has been working steadily to discredit me ever since.'

Khalil frowned. 'How?'

'Rumours, whispers. Gossip that I'm flighty, forgetful. So far I've managed to keep him from destabilising me completely. I hope—I hope my record speaks for itself.' She turned to him, needing him to believe her just as he had once needed her to believe him. 'I've worked hard since the whole Paulo debacle, Khalil. I've poured my life into my country, just as my father wanted me to. Everything I've done has been for Thallia.'

'I know it has,' Khalil said quietly. He squeezed her hand. 'Your devotion to your country is something I've never questioned.' He gave her a small smile. 'After all, you were willing to marry for it.'

'As were you.'

'Hopefully it was a wise decision on both our parts.' He removed his hand from hers and sat back, his brow furrowed.

Elena suspected he regretted the intimacy of their conversation. She knew that wasn't part of their marriage deal. And yet, watching him covertly, remembering how her body yearned and her heart ached for him, Elena wondered how she could have fooled herself into thinking she'd ever be satisfied with a marriage of convenience.

With Aziz it had been different. He'd been a stranger, and she'd given little thought to their marriage beyond the hard practicalities. Now she wondered how she could have been so blind. So naïve. How could she have coped with such a cold approach to marriage, to motherhood? *How would she now?*

She stared out of the window, realisations trickling despondently through her. She didn't want a loveless arrangement any more. She wanted more from her marriage. More from Khalil.

She glanced back at Khalil; he looked distant and pre-occupied. The things she wanted now seemed more un-likely than ever.

Khalil stared out of the window as the jet descended to-wards the runway, the waters of the Aegean Sea sparkling jewel-bright in the distance. He could see the domes and towers of Thallia's ancient capital, the sky a bright blue above, the sun bathing everything in gold.

He turned to look at Elena and saw how pale she'd gone, her hands clenched together in her lap so tightly her knuck-les shone bony and white. He felt a shaft of sympathy for her, deep and true, in that moment. She'd endured so much, yet had stayed so strong, even if she didn't think she was. Even if she didn't trust herself.

He trusted her. He believed in her, believed in her strength, her courage, her goodness. The knowledge made something in him break open, seek light. He leaned for-ward and reached for her hand. She turned to him, clearly startled, her eyes wide with apprehension.

'You're stronger than they are, Elena,' he said quietly. 'And smarter. They may think you need me, but you don't. You are a legitimate and admirable ruler all on your own.'

Her cheeks went pink and her eyes turned shiny. For a moment Khalil thought she might cry. Then her lips curved in a wobbly smile and she said, 'Thank you, Khalil. But you're wrong—I do need you. I needed you to tell me that.'

They left the plane, blinking in the bright sunlight as they took the stairs down to the waiting motorcade. The paparazzi, thankfully, weren't present; Elena had told him there would be a press briefing from the palace after they met with her Council.

He hadn't liked leaving Kadar, but he understood the necessity of it. A marriage made deep in the desert was essentially no marriage at all. They both needed the positive publicity, the statement their marriage would make not just to Elena's Council but to Aziz.

I took your bride. I'll take your throne. Because both are mine by right.

Khalil felt the old injustice burn, but not as brightly or hotly as it had before. In that moment, looking at her pale face, he was more concerned for Elena than anything that was happening in Kadar. The realisation surprised him, yet he didn't fight it, didn't push the feelings away. He reached for Elena's hand once more and she clung to him, her fingers slender and icy in his.

'Welcome back to Thallia, Your Highness.'

Khalil watched Elena greet the royal staff who had lined up by the fleet of cars. She nodded and spoke to each one by name, smiling graciously, her head held high.

She looked pale but composed, elegant and every inch the queen despite the fear he knew she had to be feeling. Admiration and something deeper swelled inside him. Queen Elena of Thallia was magnificent.

Two hours later they were at the palace, waiting outside the Council Room. Elena had changed into a modest dress in blue silk, feminine yet businesslike, her heavy, dark hair pulled back in a low coil. Khalil wore an elegantly tailored business suit and, as they waited to be admitted to the Council Room, he wondered what this Markos was playing at. Was he keeping Elena waiting on purpose, to unnerve her? A petty show of power? Based on what Elena had already told him, it seemed likely.

He turned to Elena. 'You should go in there.'

'I'm meant to wait until I'm summoned.'

'You are Queen, Elena. You do the summoning.'

'It's not like that, Khalil.'

'It should be. You're the one who can change things, Elena. Remember that. *Believe* it.'

She stared at him uncertainly for a moment and he imagined how hard it must have been for her, all of nineteen

years old, devastated by grief and so utterly alone, trying
to assert herself against the sanctimonious prigs of her
Council. The fact that she was still here, still strong, both
amazed and humbled him.

'You can do it,' he said softly. 'You can do anything you
set your mind to, Elena. I know that. I've seen it.'

She gave him a small, tremulous smile. 'Except maybe
make a fire in the middle of the desert.'

He felt himself grin back at her. 'There were a few
flames going there. If that snake hadn't come along...'

'If you hadn't come along,' she shot back, her smile widening, and then she drew herself up and turned towards the
double gold-panelled doors.

He watched as she threw open the doors, grinned at the
sight of twelve slack-jawed, middle-aged men rising hast-
ily to their feet as Elena walked into the room.

'Good afternoon, gentlemen,' she greeted them regally,
and Khalil had to keep from letting out a cheer.

Elena could feel her heart thudding so hard it hurt and she
could hear the roar of her blood in her ears. She kept her
head high, her smile polite and fixed, as she gazed at each
member of the Council in turn, saving Markos for last. Her
nemesis's eyes were narrowed, the corners of his mouth
turned down, and she felt a flash of relief. If he'd made any
headway with the rest of the Council, he'd have been looking at her in triumph, not irritation. She was safe...so far.

'Queen Elena. We have been wondering where you had
gone.' Marko's gaze flicked to Khalil. 'A honeymoon in
the desert?' he suggested with only the faintest hint of a
sneer, but as always it was enough. He made it sound as if
she'd run off with her bodyguard, heedless of her country
or its demands.

'There has been no honeymoon yet,' Elena answered
crisply. 'But things, as you have surmised, have changed.
I wisely ended my engagement to Aziz al Bakir when I

realised he was not the legitimate claimant to the throne of Kadar. Marriage to an impostor would hardly benefit Thallia, would it…Andreas?'

Markos's eyes flashed annoyance or perhaps even anger. 'And who is this, then?' he asked, his gaze flicking back to Khalil.

'This is Khalil al Bakir, sheikh of a northern desert tribe and Aziz's older brother. He is the rightful heir to the throne of Kadar.' Elena felt the sudden surprise tense Khalil's body, felt it in herself. She'd spoken with a certainty she felt right through her bones.

'I have chosen to marry Khalil instead, in an arrangement similar to the one I had with Aziz.' She looked at each councillor in turn, felt herself practically grow taller. Khalil had been right. She was strong and smart enough, yet she was still achingly glad he was by her side. 'I trust that this will be agreeable to all of you, as it was before?'

'You change husbands at the drop of a hat,' Markos said, his lip curling in contempt. 'And we are meant to take you at your word?'

For a second Elena felt herself falter, everything in her an apology for past sins, but in her moment of damning silence Khalil spoke. 'Yes,' he stated coolly. 'As she is your queen and sovereign, you will most certainly take her at her word. Queen Elena has demonstrated her loyalty to her country again and again. It will not be called into question simply because once long ago she gave her trust and her loyalty to a man who should have, by all measures, been worthy of it.' Elena watched in amazement as Khalil nailed each councillor with a hard, challenging stare. 'We will not speak of this again. Ever.'

She barely heard the answering buzz of murmured assurances and apologies; her mind was spinning from what Khalil had said, how he'd stood up for her, supported her. When had someone last done that?

She'd kept herself apart, refused to trust anyone, because it had felt stronger. Certainly less risky. But in that moment she knew she was actually stronger with Khalil, and the knowledge both thrilled and humbled her.

She turned to her Council with a cool, purposeful smile. 'Now, shall we discuss the meeting with the press?'

CHAPTER TWELVE

ELENA CLOSED THE door quietly behind her and leaned against it, her eyes closed, exhaustion making every muscle and sinew ache. It had been a long, stressful, overwhelming and yet ultimately successful day.

She hadn't had a chance to tell Khalil how grateful she was for his support, from the showdown with the Council to his effortless grace and charm before the press. It had been a tense diplomatic moment, supporting Khalil's claim to Kadar's throne publicly, and one her Council had initially balked at. But Khalil had stood by her and it was her turn to stand by him.

Side by side. That was the kind of marriage she wanted. And today it had felt as if Khalil wanted it too.

Maybe all he needed was time to get used to the idea, to learn to love again...

Because she loved him. It had been utter foolishness to pretend she didn't, or wouldn't. She'd been fooling herself as well as Khalil, but now she wanted to be honest. Wanted to admit her feelings for him, her love, respect and desire.

Yes, desire. She'd felt it all day like an in-coming tide, lapping at her senses, washing over her body. Every aspect of him appealed to her, from his hard-headed pragmatism to his sudden sensitivity, to that sensual blaze of heat in his eyes...

They hadn't spoken privately since the plane, since she'd told him about Paulo—and she'd seen no judgement or condemnation in his eyes, just understanding and a surprising compassion, which just added to her desire. He was, she'd realised, not for the first time but with growing certainty, a *good* man.

After the press conference he'd gone to deal with matters relating to Kadar, and she had met with her personal assistant to review the schedule for the next few days. A team of lawyers had hammered out an agreement concerning the marriage terms that they'd both signed, and then they'd eaten dinner with a handful of dignitaries before parting ways, Khalil to a guest suite in another wing and she to her own suite of rooms.

Already she missed him. She needed to talk to him, she realised; they'd set the wedding for tomorrow and yet had barely discussed the details beyond a clinical meeting with the legal team. In any case, she didn't want to talk business; she just wanted to be with him.

Swiftly she turned around and opened the door, slipped from her room and down several corridors to where she knew Khalil was staying.

She stood in front of his door, her palms slightly damp and her heart beginning to race. She knocked.

'Enter.'

Elena stepped inside and the whole world seemed to fall away as her gaze focused on Khalil. He'd undone the studs of his tuxedo shirt, its tails untucked from his trousers so she could see a bronzed expanse of taut belly, and her breath instinctively hitched.

Khalil's gaze darkened, although with what emotion she couldn't tell. 'I thought you were one of the staff.'

'No.'

A tiny smile twitched at the corner of his mouth. 'I realise.'

Hope ballooned inside her, impossible to control. One smile and she was lost. 'I thought we should talk.'

'About?'

'We're getting married tomorrow, Khalil,' she reminded him with a smile, and his smile deepened.

'I know that, Elena.' He turned to face her fully, his arms folded across that magnificently broad chest. 'Are you having second thoughts? Cold feet?'

Surprise at his question, and the shadow of vulnerability that crossed his face, made her shake her head decisively. 'No.' She took a breath and forced her gaze away from his pectorals. 'Are you?'

'No.'

'Even though you didn't want to marry?'

She shouldn't have pressed, Elena realised. Any levity they'd been flirting with disappeared in an instant. 'You know my feelings on the subject.'

'A necessary evil?'

He inclined his head. 'That might be a bit harsh.'

Elena rolled her eyes, inviting him into the joke, wanting to reclaim the lightness. 'Well, that's a relief.'

He smiled again and Elena felt a giddy rush of joy. She really did love his smile. She loved...

But she wouldn't tell him that now. She knew he wasn't ready to hear it, and she wasn't sure she was ready to say it.

'Why are you here, Elena?' Khalil asked quietly.

'I told you, to talk.'

He took a step towards her, his muscles rippling under his open shirt, his eyes glinting gold with amusement— and knowledge. 'Are you sure about that?'

Suddenly her mouth was dry. Her heart beat harder. 'No,' she whispered.

He took another step towards her and then another, so if she lifted her hand she could touch him. He smiled down at her. 'I didn't think so.'

Of course he didn't think so. Her need for him was obvious, overwhelming and undeniable. And the very force of it made her bold. 'I want you, Khalil.'

Appreciation flared in his eyes. 'I want you too.'

Want. So basic, so huge, yet Elena felt even more than just that. She felt gratitude and admiration, respect and joy, all because of what he'd done, who he was. How he'd helped and strengthened her. She'd never expected to feel that way about someone, to have that person fulfil a need and hope in her she hadn't even known she had.

The need to tell him all that she felt was an ache in her chest, a pressure building inside her, so she opened her mouth to speak, to say even just a fraction of what was in her heart.

But Khalil didn't let her.

He curled his hands around her shoulders and drew her to him, stealing her words away with a kiss. It was better this way, Elena had to acknowledge as she lost herself in the heady sensations. Khalil didn't want her words, her declarations of emotion. He just wanted this.

And so did she.

He drew her to the bed and down upon the silken sheets, stripping the evening gown from her body with one gentle tug of the zip. Neither of them spoke, and the silence felt hushed, reverent. This time tomorrow they would lie in a bed like this one as husband and wife.

But Elena knew she already felt like Khalil's wife in her mind, in her heart. She cared too much for him, she knew, but in this moment, when his hands were touching her with such tenderness and his mouth was on hers, she didn't want to think about *too much*. She didn't want to police herself, or limit her joy. She just wanted to experience all Khalil was offering her…however little that turned out to be.

And, in that moment, it felt like enough.

Afterwards they lay entwined among the sheets, her palm resting over his heart so she could feel its steady thud against her hand. Khalil stroked her arm from shoulder to wrist, almost absently, the touch unthinking and yet incredibly gentle. She felt almost perfectly happy.

If only, she thought, they could stay like this for ever.

It was a foolish wish, nothing more than a dream, yet she was so tired of the scheming and trying, the politics and the uncertainty. She just wanted this. Him. *For ever.*

'When will you speak with Aziz?' she asked softly, because no matter what she wanted reality had to be faced.

'As soon as we return to Kadar I will seek out a meeting. He will hear of our marriage, of course, and I will have to address that.'

'Do you think he'll be angry?'

She felt Khalil tense, and then he shrugged. 'I have no idea. You know him better than I do.'

'I do?' She raised her head, propping herself on one elbow to study his face. 'Did you not know him as a child?'

'I left the palace when I was seven. I only met him once, from memory, when my father wished for his sons to see each other.'

He spoke evenly, but she could still feel the tension in his body, under her hand. She gazed at him, realising afresh how much she didn't know...and how much she wanted to.

'It must have been very hard,' she said softly. 'To have to leave everything you knew.'

'It was strange,' Khalil acknowledged. His expression had become shuttered, his eyes giving nothing away.

She eased away from him so she could look up into his face. 'I know you don't like to talk about it, Khalil, but what happened with your father must have been terrible.' Her gaze fell on the scars that crisscrossed his wrists. 'Why do you have rope burns on your wrists?' she asked softly.

She thought he wouldn't answer. He didn't speak for a long time, and she wondered at the story those scars told, a story she had no idea about but knew she wanted and perhaps even needed to hear.

'I was tied up,' he said finally, his voice flat, emotionless. 'For days. I struggled, and these scars are the result.'

She stared at him in helpless horror. 'Tied up? When—?'

'When I was seven. When my father banished me.'

'But I thought you went to America with your aunt.'

'She found me when I was ten. For three years I lived with a Bedouin tribe in a far corner of Kadar. The sheikh liked to punish me. He'd tie me up like a dog, or beat me in front of everyone. I tried to escape, and I always failed. So, believe me, I understood how you felt as a prisoner, Elena. More than you could possibly know.' He let out a shuddering breath and unthinkingly, just needing to touch him, she wrapped her arms around him, held on tight.

'I'm sorry.'

'It was a long time ago.'

'But something like that stays with you for ever, Khalil!' She remembered now how he'd told her it mattered how she was treated. 'But this man, this sheikh—why did he treat you so terribly?'

Khalil gave a little shrug. 'Because he was a petty, evil man and he could? But, no, the real reason I suppose is because my mother was his cousin and she brought shame to his family with her alleged adultery. In any case, Abdul-Hafiz already had a grudge against her family for leaving the tribe and seeking their fortunes in Siyad.' His arms tightened around her. 'That's why my father banished me to that tribe—he returned me to my mother's people, knowing they would revile me. And so they did, at least at first. The irony, perhaps, is that I rule them now as their sheikh.'

He was trying to speak lightly but she still heard the throb of emotion underneath. Elena couldn't even imagine all he wasn't saying: the abuse, the torture and utter unkindness. To tie up a seven-year-old boy for *days*? To beat him so his back was covered with scars? Fury warred with deep sorrow, and she pressed her cheek against his back, her body snug against his.

'I'm so glad you escaped.'

'So am I.'

Yet could anyone really escape such a terrible past? Elena knew Khalil bore as many scars on his heart as he did on his wrists and back. No wonder he didn't trust any-one. No wonder he had no use or understanding of loving relationships.

Could she be the one to change him? Save him?

She shied away from such questions, knowing how dan-gerous they were, yet already the answers were rushing through her.

Yes. Yes, she could. She wanted to try, she needed to try, because she loved him and couldn't imagine a life without him. Without him loving her.

And she began in that moment, rolling onto her stom-ach and pressing her lips to his wrist, kissing the places where he'd been hurt the most. Underneath her, she felt Khalil shudder.

'Elena…'

She kissed her way across his body, touching every scar, taking her time with her tongue and her lips, savouring him, showing her love for him with her body because she couldn't with her words. Not yet.

And Khalil accepted her touch, his hands coming up to clutch her shoulders as she moved over him and then gently, wonderfully, sank onto him, taking him into her body, filling them both up to the brim with wonder and joy and pleasure.

His eyes closed and his breath came out in a shudder as she began to move, pouring out everything in her heart in that ultimate act of love—and praying Khalil understood what she was saying with her body.

Sleep was a long time coming that night. Khalil stared up at the canopied bed, his arms around Elena as her breath-ing evened out, and he wondered why on earth he'd told her so much, had said things he hadn't admitted to any-one, not even Dimah or Assad. He hated to think of anyone knowing the truth of his utter humiliation as a child, yet he'd willingly told Elena. In that moment he'd wanted to, had wanted someone to understand and accept him totally.

And her response had nearly undone him. The sweet selflessness of her touch, the giving of her body... He still wasn't sure he knew what love was, but he imagined it might feel like that. And, if it did, he wanted more. He wanted to love someone and know he was loved back.

Foolish, foolish, foolish. Insanity. This was a marriage of cold convenience, not love or trust or intimacy. He'd told Elena he wanted none of that, and he'd meant it.

How had he changed?

Yet he knew he had. He'd been changing since the moment he'd met her, since he'd seen a reflection of himself in her. She'd begun changing him even then, softening him, opening up his emotions, unlocking his heart.

How could he go back to the cold, barren life he'd once known?

How could he not?

He'd learned to trust her with so many things—with his feelings. With the truth. Could he trust her with his heart?

Their wedding took place in the palace chapel, with only the Council members and their wives, as well as a few ambassadors and diplomats, in attendance.

Elena wore a cream silk sheath dress and a matching fascinator, no veil or bouquet, or really anything bridal at all. She'd picked the outfit with the help of her stylist when she'd arrived in Thallia, thinking only of what image she wanted to present to her public. She'd wanted to seem like a woman in control of her country and her destiny, perfectly prepared to begin this businesslike marriage.

She hadn't wanted to look like a woman in love, yet she knew now that was what she was. And as she turned to Khalil to say her vows she wished, absurdly, perhaps, for a meringue of a dress and a great, big bouquet, a lovely lace veil and a father to give her away.

Never mind, she told herself. *It's the marriage that matters, not the wedding.* Yet what kind of marriage would she have with Khalil?

Last night had been so tender, so wonderful and intimate in every way, physically and emotionally. Yet this morning he seemed his usual, inscrutable self, stony-faced and silent, dressed in traditional Kadaran formal wear, a richly embroidered *thobe* and loose trousers. He looked magnificent—and a little frightening, because Elena had no idea what he was thinking or feeling.

The ceremony passed in a blur. Vows were spoken, words read, then Khalil drew her to him and pressed his mouth against hers in a cool kiss.

She still had no idea what was going on behind those veiled eyes.

Elena circulated through the guests at a small reception after the ceremony, her gaze tracking Khalil's movements around the room, even as she chatted with councillors who oozed satisfaction now that she was wed and taken care of.

She felt as if everything had changed for her—but had it for him? Should she even hope it had? It might be better—wiser, safer—not to let things change for herself. Not to open herself up to all of the pain and possibility that loving someone meant.

It was too late for that, she knew. She couldn't stop what she felt for Khalil, just as she couldn't keep the waves from crashing into the sea or the moon from rising that night. Her love for him simply *was*.

After the reception they retired to a suite of rooms in its own private wing, as much of a bridal chamber as the palace had.

Elena took in the champagne chilling by the canopied bed, the fire crackling in the fireplace, the frothy nightgown some accommodating member of staff had laid out for her.

'It's all a bit much, isn't it?' she said with an attempt at wryness. She felt, bizarrely, as if they were pretending, as if they were going through the motions of marriage and love when last night she'd felt they'd known the real thing.

'It's thoughtful,' Khalil answered with a shrug. He hesitated, his gaze pinned to hers even though Elena had no idea what he felt or what he intended to say. 'You looked beautiful today. You still do.'

A thrill of surprised pleasure rippled through her. 'Thank you.'

'I couldn't take my eyes off you.'

'I couldn't take my eyes off you, either,' she admitted with a shy smile.

His answering smile was assured. 'I know.'

'Oh—you!' Elena gasped with a shocked laugh. 'You sound unbearably arrogant, you know.'

'But it's true.'

'It would be more gentlemanly for you not to remark on it.'

'Why?' he asked as he reached for her. 'When the feeling is mutual?'

She stared up at him, suddenly breathless. *Just how much was mutual?*

He feathered a few kisses along her jaw. 'And this is what I've been wanting to do all day long.'

'Why didn't you, then?' Elena managed as she tilted her head back to give him greater access.

Khalil pressed a kiss to the tender hollow of her throat. 'What do you think your stuffy councillors would have thought if I'd dragged you out of that ballroom and returned you with messed hair, swollen lips and a very big smile on your face?'

Elena let out a choked laugh, her mind blurring as Khalil's mouth moved lower. 'I think they would have been pleased. I'd have been put in my place as a dutiful wife.'

'I like the sound of those duties,' Khalil answered as he

tugged at the zip of her dress. 'I think you need more instruction on just how to carry them out.'

Her dress slithered down her body, leaving her in nothing but her bra and pants, her whole body on fire from the heat of Khalil's gaze. 'I think I do,' she agreed...then they didn't speak for quite a while after that.

Later they lay in bed just as they had last night, hands linked and limbs entwined. Sleepily, utterly sated, Elena thought how this did feel like for ever. Maybe they could be this happy...for ever.

'I need to go to Paris,' Khalil said. His fingers tightened briefly on hers as he stared up at the bed's canopy. 'To see my Aunt Dimah. She moved there a few years ago. She should hear of our marriage from me. And I'd like you to meet her.'

'Of course,' Elena said simply. She was glad to share in any part of Khalil's life that he wanted her to.

'And after that,' he continued, 'we will return to Kadar. I received a message from Aziz today, just before the wedding. He has agreed to meet with me.'

'That's good news, isn't it?'

'I hope it is. I hope I will be able to convince him to call the referendum.'

'And if he refuses?'

Khalil stared up at the ceiling. 'I don't know,' he said quietly. 'I don't—I don't want war. But I can't imagine giving up my claim to the throne, either. It's everything to me.' He turned to her then, a new, raw vulnerability shadowing his eyes. 'Not everything,' he amended. 'Not any more. But it's important, Elena.'

'I know it is.'

'Everything I've been, everything I've done, has been for Kadar. For my title.'

'I know,' she said softly. She leaned over and kissed him. 'I know how important this is, Khalil, and I believe in you just as you've believed in me. You'll succeed. You'll convince Aziz and win the vote.'

He smiled and squeezed her fingers. 'I pray so.'

'I know it.'

'I'd like you to be with me when the referendum is called,' Khalil said after a moment. 'It's important for the people to see you support me. But it shouldn't take long, and afterwards you can return to Thallia. Those were the terms of our agreement.'

Elena thought of the soulless piece of paper they'd both signed just yesterday, outlining the nature of their marriage: so cold, so clinical. She felt his fingers threaded through hers, his legs tangled with hers, and she mentally consigned that piece of paper and all of its legalese to the rubbish heap. 'I'll need to return to Thallia, of course,' she said. 'But do you want me to stay longer?' She twisted to face him, and was gratified to see a light blaze in Khalil's eyes.

'Yes,' he said simply, and she squeezed his hand, never feeling more certain of anything in her life. She loved this man and she would go anywhere with him.

'Then I'll stay,' she said simply, and Khalil closed the space between them and kissed her.

CHAPTER THIRTEEN

THE NEXT MORNING they boarded the royal jet to Paris. Since last night Elena had felt closer to Khalil than ever before, even though neither of them had put a name to what they felt. Perhaps it was too early to put such fragile feelings into words; in any case, Elena was simply glad to be sharing Khalil's life, and that he wanted her to.

'You must be very close to your aunt,' she said as the plane took off and they settled into their seats. A royal steward brought a tray of coffee and pastries into the main cabin.

Khalil poured milk into both of their coffees, his mouth twisting in something like a grimace. 'I am, but it is a complicated relationship.'

'How so?'

'When Dimah found me, I'd been in the desert for three years. I was…' He paused, his gaze on the bright blue sky visible from the plane's windows. 'Difficult. No, that is putting a polite spin on it—feral is a better description.'

Feral. Elena swallowed and blinked back sudden tears. Emotions, ones she'd suppressed and denied for so long, were always so close to the surface now; Khalil had made her feel, want and love again. 'I hate to think of what you endured, Khalil.'

'It was a long time ago,' he answered. 'But I admit, it affected me badly. I'd been treated like an animal for three years, so even after Dimah found me I acted like one. I didn't trust anyone. I barely spoke.' He shook his head, his features tightening. 'She was very patient. She took me to New York to live with her and her husband. She brought me to learning specialists and therapists, people who helped me adjust to this strange new life.'

'And you did adjust?'

Khalil grimaced. 'Some. But I haven't ever felt truly at home in America. No one understood me, or knew what I experienced. Not even really Dimah.'

'Did you tell her?'

'A little. I don't think she really wanted to know. She wanted me to forget Kadar completely, but returning to claim my birthright has always been what has motivated me. Dimah has never understood that.'

Surprise flashed through her. 'Why not?'

'The memories are too painful for her, I suppose. She grew up in Siyad, but she always longed to leave. When my mother died, she was heartbroken. She left to marry an American businessman and never wanted to return.'

'But she knows it is your right.'

'What she knows is that she provided a good life for me in America. She sent me to boarding school and university, helped me start my own consulting business before I joined the French Foreign Legion. She thought all those things would help me to forget Kadar, but I always saw them as stepping stones to returning. I don't think she has ever understood how much it has meant to me.'

'And yet the two of you are close,' Elena said quietly. 'Aren't you?'

'Yes, we are close. She saved me, quite literally.' The smile he gave her was bleak. 'I owe her a debt I can never repay, and I hope that one day she understands that I am attempting to redress it by claiming my birthright and becoming Sheikh.'

'Even though she doesn't want you to.'

'Yes.' He paused, his gaze moving once more to the

sky. 'Claiming my rightful inheritance will expunge any stain from my mother's memory. It's not just for my sake that I am pursuing this path. It's to right old wrongs, to repair the very fabric of my country that was torn when my father decided to pursue his own selfish whims instead of justice. Putting aside my mother with no real reason rent the country in two. I want to repair it.'

'And I want to help you, Khalil,' Elena said. She reached over and took his hand, and he squeezed her fingers in response. Encouraged by this show of affection, she took a deep breath and said some of what was in her heart. 'I know we agreed to live virtually separate lives in that document we signed, but I don't want to live that way any more.' She gazed into Khalil's clear, amber eyes, unable to tell what he thought about what she'd just said. 'You once asked me whether I wanted a loving, equal partner for a husband, someone who could support me. I said I didn't because I'd never even imagined someone like that existed.'

'Neither did I,' Khalil answered quietly and her hopes soared.

'Then you feel differently now too?'

'I don't know what I feel, Elena. I never expected or wanted any of this.' He sighed restlessly, but didn't let go of her hand. 'I feel like I've experienced something with you that I never thought I would. I want more of it. More of you. More of *us*.'

'I want that too,' she whispered.

'But this is all new to me. And frankly it's frightening.' He gave her a wry smile, but she still saw bleakness in his eyes. 'I haven't trusted anyone like this since I was seven years old with a child's simple heart. Since my father told me I wasn't his son.'

'I know, Khalil. And I want to be worthy of your trust and—and even of your love.' She held her breath, waiting for his reaction, wanting him to say it back: *I love you*. She hadn't said it quite as clearly as that, but still she thought he must know how she felt.

'I want to trust you,' Khalil answered after a long moment. He took a deep breath, squeezing her fingers once more. 'I want to love you.'

And in that moment it seemed so wonderfully simple, the way forward so very clear. They both wanted a loving relationship, a proper marriage. Why shouldn't they have it? Why shouldn't it be possible?

As they left the airport for Dimah's townhouse near the Ile de la Cité Khalil marvelled at the change in himself. He felt like some shell-less creature, pink, raw and exposed, everything out there for another person's examination. It was a strange and uncomfortable feeling, but it wasn't necessarily *bad*.

He'd been glad to tell Elena about his childhood, his aunt, his own fears and weaknesses. He'd never talked that way to another soul, yet he craved that kind of honesty with Elena.

He just didn't know what to do next. How it all would actually *work*. Take one step at a time, he supposed. For now he needed to think about Dimah.

He'd phoned her from Thallia, so she was waiting as their limo drew up to her townhouse and their security detail quickly got out to check the surrounding area.

Dimah came out to the front steps, her face wreathed in a tremulous smile, her wispy white hair blowing in the breeze. She looked so much older, Khalil thought with a pang, and he'd last seen her less than a year ago when he'd stopped in Paris on the way to Kadar.

'Dimah.' He put his arms around her, feeling her fragility. 'This is my wife, Queen Elena of Thallia.'

'Your Highness,' Dimah murmured and curtseyed. No matter how frail she looked or felt, she was still every inch the lady.

'I'm so pleased to meet you,' Elena said, and took Dimah's thin hand in both of her own.

Once inside, Dimah arranged for refreshments to be brought to the main salon, chattering with Elena about women's things while Khalil's mind roved over his arranged meeting with Aziz next week.

He'd been amazed that his half-brother had agreed to meet with him; it had given him hope. Perhaps Aziz really would see sense. Perhaps he would call the referendum.

And what about his wife?

Perhaps a quick and quiet annulment would get the nameless woman Aziz had married out of the way. Yet the fact that Aziz had been willing to marry so quickly made Khalil uneasy. It made him wonder if his half-brother wished to be Sheikh more than he'd thought he did.

'Khalil, you are not even paying attention,' Dimah chided. Her eyes were bright, her cheeks flushed. 'But I don't blame you. Anyone can tell you are in love!'

He felt Elena start next to him, saw her glance apprehensively at him. Was she worried for his sake or her own? He smiled and reached for her hand. It felt amazingly easy. 'You're right, Dimah,' he said. 'My mind is elsewhere.'

Elena beamed.

'I'm afraid I must excuse myself,' he said a few minutes later as he rose from his chair. 'I have business to attend to. But we will dine with you tonight, Dimah, if that is acceptable?'

She waved a hand in easy dismissal. 'Of course, of course. Go ahead. I want to get to know Elena properly.'

Suppressing a wry smile, Khalil gave his bride a look of sympathy before striding from the room.

'I can't tell you how pleased I am Khalil has found you,' Dimah said once she was alone with Elena. 'Anyone can tell how in love you are.'

Elena smiled, felt that tremulous joy buoy her soul.

'Do you think so?' she murmured, craving the confirmation of Khalil's feelings. 'I want to love you' was, she
acknowledged, a little different from 'I love you'.

'I know it,' Dimah declared. 'I've waited so long for
Khalil to find someone to love, and to love him back. I pray
now he'll forget all this foolishness with Kadar.'

Elena tensed, unsure how to address such a volatile subject. 'The sheikhdom of Kadar is his legacy, Dimah,' she
said gently. 'It's his birthright. He will not forget it.'

'He should,' Dimah said, her voice rising fretfully. 'He
should. I keep telling him. There is nothing good for him
there.' She bit her lip, her eyes filling with tears, and Elena
frowned.

'Why do you want him to forget it?' she asked. 'Wouldn't
you like to see him restored to his rightful place, and your
sister's memory—'

'No.' Dimah cut her off swiftly. 'No. We mustn't talk
about that.' She shook her head, seeming to come to herself. 'I want to hear more about you and your wedding.
Tell me about happy things. Tell me about when you first
realised Khalil loved you.' She smiled eagerly, like a child
waiting for a story, sounding so certain of something Elena
still wondered about.

Yet in that moment she knew she wanted to be like
Dimah and believe. She wanted to hear and speak of happy
things, to be certain that, no matter what happened with
kingdoms or countries or thrones, she could be sure of her
love for Khalil…and his love for her.

Gazing at Dimah's expectant face, Elena felt her own
doubts begin to melt away. If Dimah could already see
how Khalil loved her, then surely he did? Elena saw it in
his eyes, felt it in his touch.

Maybe Khalil wasn't sure what love looked or felt like,

but Elena believed he loved her. She loved him. Nothing else mattered.

Nothing could change that.

Leaning forward, she began to tell Dimah all about how she and Khalil had fallen in love.

CHAPTER FOURTEEN

THE NEXT MORNING Elena came downstairs with Khalil to find Dimah standing in the centre of the salon. 'I need to talk to you,' she said, looking pale and resolute, and Khalil frowned.

'Dimah, what is it?'

'I need to tell you something.' Dimah closed the doors to the salon and turned to them, her fingers knotted anxiously together. 'I should have told you before, Khalil, a long time before. I never wanted to, but…' She trailed away, clearly nervous, and Khalil shook his head.

'I don't understand.'

Elena felt a sudden, terrible thrill of foreboding. She had a mad impulse to tell Dimah not to say anything. Not to change anything. Last night they'd all chatted and laughed over dinner, and then Khalil had taken Elena upstairs and made sweet love to her for half the night. She'd fallen asleep in his arms, perfectly content. Utterly secure in his feelings for her, and hers for him.

Yet now, standing there, looking at Dimah's anxious face, remembering her fretful pleas yesterday about Khalil forgetting Kadar, Elena's stomach knotted. Without even thinking about what she was doing, she flung out one hand.

'Don't.'

Khalil turned to stare at her incredulously. 'Do you know what she's going to say, Elena?'

'No, but…' What could she say? That she had some sort of premonition?

'But what? What do you know, Elena?' Khalil rounded on her and Elena blinked up, stunned at how quickly he had become suspicious, even angry. Dimah hadn't said anything, Elena didn't even know what she was going to say, yet here was Khalil, glaring at her accusingly.

'Khalil,' she whispered and he turned back to Dimah.

'What do you need to tell me, Dimah?'

'I should have told you a long time ago, Khalil.' For once Dimah's voice was low, certain, which made Elena all the more anxious. What was she going to say? 'Perhaps even when you were a boy, but I was afraid. Afraid first for you, and how you would take it, and then afraid for me. How you would feel about me keeping such a secret.'

Khalil stared at her, his expression shuttered. 'You are speaking in riddles.'

'Only because I am still afraid to tell you the truth,' Dimah admitted quietly. 'But I can see you have changed, Khalil. I know you love Elena—'

'Don't tell me what I feel.' Khalil cut her off brusquely and everything in Elena cringed and shrank. What was happening, and how had it all gone so wrong, so quickly?

Because it hadn't been strong enough to begin with.

'Khalil.' Dimah faced him directly, bravely, as if she were facing a firing squad—a death sentence. 'Hashem is not your father.'

His expression, amazingly, did not change. It did not so much as flicker. He didn't even blink.

'Say something,' Dimah said softly and a muscle in his jaw bunched.

'Nonsense.'

'You don't believe me?' Dimah blinked, incredulous.

'Why are you telling me this now, Dimah, after so many years?' He nodded towards Elena. 'Is it because of Elena? Because you think I've changed?'

Elena flinched; he sounded so contemptuous.

'Partly. You have more to live for now, Khalil, than being Sheikh.'

He clenched his hands into fists. 'But you're lying. Hashem is my father.'

Dimah cocked her head and in that moment Elena imagined the older woman was looking at Khalil as she had when he'd first come to her, wild and angry and so very terrified. 'Why would I lie, Khalil?'

He shrugged, the movement abrupt, aggressive. 'You never wanted me to return to Kadar. Maybe my marriage to Elena has given you the opportunity—'

'What opportunity? To deny you your birthright?'

'It *is* my birthright.'

'No,' Dimah said with heavy finality. 'It is not.'

Khalil shook his head. He held himself rigid, his gaze unblinking. '*No.*'

Everything in Elena ached as she realised what he was facing: the loss of his life's purpose, his very self. No wonder he wanted to deny it.

'I know it is a terrible thing for you to accept—'

'How can I accept it?' he demanded, and for a moment it seemed as if he almost wanted an answer to the question. 'Why would you not tell me for twenty-five years?'

'I told you, I was afraid!' Dimah's voice rang out, harsh and desperate. 'The more time passed, the more difficult it became. I did not want you to think badly of me, or your mother. Her memory seemed like the only thing that sustained you.'

'And you are tainting her memory now!' Elena saw the agony in his eyes. 'She was always so gentle with me. How could you do such a thing, Dimah? How could you accuse her of such a crime?'

'Oh, Khalil.' Dimah's voice broke. 'I'm a pitiful old woman, I know. I should have said something before. Long before. I closed my eyes to your ambition because I thought you would let go of it, in time. When Aziz became Sheikh, at least. I hoped that, in telling you now, I might finally set you free from this fruitless hope you've clung to for so long. That you'd be happy with the life you are making with Elena.'

'Why would my father make his will so open-ended, if I was not his son?' Khalil demanded.

'Maybe because Aziz has never seemed interested in Kadar,' Dimah offered helplessly. 'I don't know why, Khalil. But I do know what is true, and I'm sorry I didn't tell you sooner.'

Elena stepped forward and reached out one trembling hand. 'Khalil,' she began, but he jerked away from her.

'This suits you, doesn't it?' he said in a snarl. 'Now you'll have just what you wanted—a puppet prince at your beck and call.'

She blinked, stung. 'That's not fair. And that's not what I want at all.'

'It's certainly not what I want,' Khalil snapped. 'I'll never forget Kadar and my birthright and everything that has ever been important to me. Everything I've ever *been*.' His voice broke on the last word and he turned away from her, his head bowed.

'I'm sorry,' Dimah said quietly. 'I should have spoken before. I knew I had to speak now, since you were intending on returning to Kadar.'

'How would you even know such a thing as this? My mother—'

'Told me. She wrote me a letter, admitting everything. She even had a photograph of him, Khalil. Of your father.'

'*No.*' The one word was a cry of anguish and it broke Elena right open. Without even thinking of what she was doing or how Khalil might react, she went to him.

'Khalil.' She put her arms around his rigid body. 'Khalil.'

Tears started in her eyes. What could she say to him? How could she make this better?

'It can't be true,' Khalil said, and she heard then the agonised acceptance in his voice. He believed. He didn't want to believe, but he did.

'I can show you the letter, if you like,' Dimah said quietly. 'The photograph.'

Khalil gave a little shake of his head, then shrugged out of Elena's embrace, his back to them both. 'Who was he?' he asked, his voice barely audible.

'One of the palace guards,' Dimah answered in a whisper. 'You have his eyes.'

Khalil let out a sound that was almost a moan. Then he shook his head. 'I can't—' He stopped, stared blankly for a moment. 'I need to be alone,' he said, and walked out of the room without looking at either of them again.

It couldn't be true. *It couldn't, it couldn't, it couldn't.*

He sounded like a little boy, Khalil thought with a surge of fury. Like a terrified little boy, begging for mercy.

Don't hit me. Please don't hit me. Where is my mother? My father? Please...

The tears had run down his dirty face and Abdul-Hafiz had just laughed.

Now Khalil swore aloud and slammed his fist against the wall, causing a dent, bruising his hand and bloodying his knuckles.

It *couldn't* be true.

Yet he knew it was. And with that awful truth came the even more terrible realisation that everything he'd built his life on had been for nothing.

Every choice he'd made, every hope he'd had, had been for clearing his mother's name and claiming his legacy. His birthright. It had been who he was, and now that it had been taken away he was left spinning, empty, exposed. He had nothing. He *was* nothing.

He would not, would never, be Sheikh of Kadar.

Neither, he acknowledged with leaden certainty, would he be Elena's husband.

Elena paced the salon of Dimah's townhouse, her mind spinning, her heart aching. Khalil had left that morning, right after that awful confrontation, and although it was nearing midnight he had still not returned.

Dimah had gone to bed, after reassuring her that Khalil would return soon and things would look better in the morning. Elena had felt like shaking her. Things wouldn't look any better in the morning, not for Khalil. She knew what kind of man he was, how strong and proud. How he'd built everything on the foundation that the throne of Kadar was his by right. To have it taken away would devastate him...and he would be too proud to admit it.

And how would he be feeling, knowing that the man he'd thought was his father wasn't? That the truths he'd insisted on believing for so long, that had been sustaining him, were actually lies?

She longed to see him, to put her arms around him and comfort him. To tell him it didn't matter to her whether he was Sheikh or not. She didn't care who his parents were, or if he had a title. She wanted to tell him she loved him properly, not just hint at it. She wanted that love to make a difference.

And yet, deep down inside, she was afraid it wouldn't.

She heard the front door open and the slow, deliberate tread of a person who seemed utterly weary, even defeated. Elena hurried to the door, her heart thumping in her chest.

'Khalil.'

He turned to face her, the lines of his face haggard and yet his expression strangely, terribly blank.

'Elena. I didn't think you would still be awake.'

'Of course I'm awake!' she cried. 'I've been worried about you, Khalil, wondering how you are, how you're coping—'

'Coping?' He spoke the single word with contempt. 'Don't worry about me, Elena.'

'Of course I worry about you.' She bit her lip then took a deep breath. 'I love you, Khalil.'

He let out a hard laugh and Elena flinched. 'A little late for that, Elena.'

'Late? Why?'

'Because there is no reason for us to be married any more.'

'What?' Shock reverberated through her so her body practically vibrated with it. She stared at him in disbelief. 'No reason? Why is that, Khalil?'

He stared at her evenly, unmoved. 'You know why.'

'I know you no longer have a claim to the throne of Kadar. I know you've suffered a great disappointment. But I am still your wife. We're still *married*.'

'We'll get an annulment.'

'An annulment? How? We've made love, Khalil.'

'It can be done.'

She shook her head slowly, shock warring with hurt. Then both were replaced by a deep, hard anger. 'You coward,' she said, and her voice was cold. 'You selfish, thoughtless *coward*. You think because you have no need of me and our convenient marriage you can just forget your vows? Forget me?'

'How is this marriage convenient for you, Elena? I have no title, no claim. *I'm* the pretender. Do you think your Council will approve your marriage to me? Or will Markos just use it as a reason to depose you, consider it another foolish choice you've made?'

She blinked back tears. 'I don't care.'

'You should.'

'Forget my Council!' Elena cried. 'Forget our countries

or convenience. You told me you wanted to love me, Khalil. What happened to that? Did you decide you didn't want to any more? Or were you lying?' Her voice and body both shook as she demanded, 'Do you have no honour at all?'

'This isn't about honour,' Khalil retorted. 'I'm setting you free, Elena.'

'Setting me free? You haven't even asked if I want that kind of freedom. Don't hide behind excuses, Khalil. You're a better man than that.'

'Am I?' he demanded, his voice ringing in the sudden silence. 'Am I really, Elena? I don't even know what I am any more, if I am not my father's son. If I am not—' He drew a ragged breath. 'I've built my life on something that is a lie. Everything I've done, everything I've been…it's gone. So what am I now?'

'You are,' Elena said quietly, 'the man I love. I didn't fall in love with the Sheikh of Kadar, Khalil. I fell in love with the man who kissed my tears and held me in his arms. Who protected and encouraged and believed in me. I fell in love with that man.'

'And that man no longer exists.'

'He does.'

Khalil shook his head then stared at her openly, emptily. 'What am I going to do now, Elena? What purpose can I serve? Who can I even be?'

A tear trickled down Elena's cheek. 'You can be my husband, Khalil. You can be the Prince Consort of Thallia. You can be the father to our children.' He didn't answer, so she continued, her voice rising with determination. 'You can be the man you've always been, Khalil. A man with pride and strength and tenderness. A man who commands people's loyalty and who works hard for it. Why limit yourself? Why be defined by who sired you, or a title? There is so much more to you than that. So much more to *us*.'

She took a step towards him, her hands outstretched. 'Kadar is in your blood, Khalil. It's still your country, and you are still Sheikh of your own tribe. You told me you wanted to repair your country, and you still can. Aziz will need you to help him. Kadar needs you. People will look to you for the way forward, for peace.'

Khalil didn't talk for a long moment. Elena held her breath, hardly daring to hope, to believe…

To trust.

Now, more than ever, she needed to trust him. 'Khalil,' she said softly, his name a caress, a promise.

'Don't you even care?' he asked after an endless moment. 'Doesn't it matter to you that I'm no one now? I'm just some nameless bastard.'

And then she realised he needed to trust her as much as she needed to trust him. To trust her to love him, even now. Especially now. 'I told you, you're my husband, and I am your wife. It doesn't matter, Khalil. It doesn't matter at all.'

She saw a flicker of hope in his eyes, like the first light of dawn, then he shook his head. 'Your Council—'

'You told me I didn't need a husband to stand up to my Council, and I don't. I'm stronger now, Khalil. You've made me strong.' Another step, and she was touching him, her hand curling around his arm. 'But I need a husband to be my helpmate and equal. Someone I can love and support, who will love and support me. Standing side by side with me.'

Khalil closed his eyes briefly. 'I feel as if everything I've ever known, everything I've counted on, has been ripped away from me. Destroyed.'

'I haven't,' Elena said softly. 'I'm still here.'

He reached for her hand. 'After so many years of anger, I don't know what to feel now. My father had a right to banish me.'

'Did he? He could have treated you far more kindly than he did.'

'And my mother…'

'You don't know what her situation was, Khalil. How unhappy she was, or what drove her to it.'

He nodded slowly. Elena knew it would take a long time for him to find peace with these revelations,, but she wanted to help him

He turned to her, his eyes wide and bleak, his voice raw. 'I love you, Elena. I didn't think I even knew what love was, but you've showed me in so many ways. You've believed in me, trusted me even when I didn't deserve to have that trust. I still don't know if I do. I don't know what the future can look like,' he told her, a confession. 'I don't know how to *be*.'

'We'll figure it out together.' She stood in front of him, letting all her hope and love shine in her eyes. 'I love you, Khalil. And you love me. That's all that matters.'

His face crumpled for a second and then he pulled her into his arms. 'Oh, Elena,' he said, and he buried his face in her hair. 'Elena. I love you so much. I'm sorry for being a fool. For being afraid.'

'You think this doesn't scare me?' Elena answered with a wobbly laugh, and she felt Khalil's smile against her hair.

'Then maybe we'll be scared together.'

'That sounds good to me.'

Khalil's arms tightened around her. 'I don't deserve you.'

'I could say the same thing.'

He kissed her then, softly, and it was a kiss that held so much tenderness and love that her heart swelled. 'I still don't know what will happen. What—what the future looks like. I'll have to talk to Aziz, renounce my claim...'

'I know.'

'You're right. I can still help Kadar. I want to.'

'They need you, Khalil. I need you.'

He pressed his forehead against hers, his hands framing her face. 'I love you.'

She smiled against his palm. 'You told me that before, but I don't think I'll ever get tired of hearing it.'

'Me neither.'

'I love you, Khalil.'

He closed his eyes. 'I never thought I'd ever hear any-one say that to me.'

'I'll say it. I'll keep saying it.'

He kissed her again, pulling her even closer to him. 'Don't ever stop saying it, Elena. And I won't either. No matter what happens.'

'No matter what happens,' she promised.

Neither of them knew just what the future held. Khalil would need to grieve; they both needed to grow. And their love, Elena knew, would keep them strong.

* * * * *

If you enjoyed this book,
look out for Aziz's story in
COMMANDED BY THE SHEIKH
by Kate Hewitt.
Coming next month.

MILLS & BOON®

Why shop at millsandboon.co.uk?

Each year, thousands of romance readers
find their perfect read at millsandboon.co.uk.
That's because we're passionate about
bringing you the very best romantic fiction.
Here are some of the advantages of
shopping at www.millsandboon.co.uk:

* **Get new books first**—you'll be able to buy
  your favourite books one month before they
  hit the shops

* **Get exclusive discounts**—you'll also be
  able to buy our specially created monthly
  collections, with up to 50% off the RRP

* **Find your favourite authors**—latest news,
  interviews and new releases for all your
  favourite authors and series on our website,
  plus ideas for what to try next

* **Join in**—once you've bought your favourite
  books, don't forget to register with us to rate,
  review and join in the discussions

Visit **www.millsandboon.co.uk**
for all this and more today!